FRESH STARTS

TALES FROM THE PIKES PEAK WRITERS

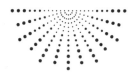

MORGEN LEIGH   TERRY ODELL   MICHAEL CHANDOS

MARILYN K. MOODY   HARPER BARROW

GWYNNE STANKER   LILY LAPIN   T. R. KERBY

BILL MAY   LAURA MAHAL   C. S. SIMPSON

BOWEN GILLINGS   KENDRA GRIFFIN   NIKIA HUNT

TUSHAR JAIN   JOSH CLARK   C. E. BARNES

SARAH REILLY PANCOAST   LIZZ BOGAARD

DENISE HANSEN   TAMI VELDURA   KATIE DAY

STEPHANIE AMADEO   SHELLEY KITCHURA NELSON

KAREN ALBRIGHT LIN   DAVID STIER   IAN NELIGH

MEGAN E. FREEMAN   JERE ELLISON

DEBBIE MAXWELL ALLEN

EDITED BY

LOU J BERGER, JAMIE FERGUSON, KATHIE
SCRIMGEOUR, AND JENNY KATE

COPYRIGHT

CONTENTS

INTRODUCTION

Pikes Peak Writers has never before published an anthology. When I first volunteered to take up the task of bringing this project to life, I had no idea what I was doing. This, too, is my first anthology. What I didn't know was the huge task that lay before me, but I found luck to be on my side with the astounding team that came together: Jamie Ferguson—Editor, Jenny Kate—Marketing Director, Lou J Berger—Editor, and myself—Lead Coordinator. A special thank you to DeAnna Knippling for her early work on the anthology and the contribution of the theme on the back cover.

Getting this first anthology from conception to publication has been challenging. With two hundred and fifty-five submissions, it was a monumental task to pare it down to only thirty. There were many authors who deserved to be a part of this anthology, but we had to make tough choices based on the book as a whole. We thank each author who submitted work and look forward to reading more!

When we began this project, nearly three years ago, we did not dream of how much this anthology would be needed today. *Fresh Starts* was a concept born out of the frustration and rash of bad news and depressing stories in the headlines of 2017. Our concept was to bring a light into the darkness that was creeping into our day-to-day lives. Today, that light is needed more than ever as we all work to regain a new normal following the COVID-19 pandemic. The stories, memories, and poems in this anthology tell of personal challenges, whether real or imagined, of ordinary people who have their worlds crumble around them, only to find a way through and rise above the maelstrom of despair.

We hope you enjoy this collection of works by the members of Pikes Peak Writers.

—Kathie Scrimgeour

THE PLAN

MORGEN LEIGH

July 4, 1998

I stood at the open sliding glass door in the kitchen, the hot air inside and outside like a stagnant cloud. I was sweating. Tense. Waiting. The feverish 2-year-old on my hip rested his head on my shoulder. I looked at the stove clock. 9:48 pm. Past his bedtime. Past time in general. I kissed the top of his damp head and adjusted the strap of the canvas bag slung diagonally across my chest. The weight if it, of him, of it all, anchored me. I swayed back and forth to soothe him and keep the tenseness in my body from rendering me frozen.

I'd slung the strap across my chest in this way because that position would make the bag harder to wrest away from me. Part of *The Plan.* In the bag was an empty wallet and a book to add weight. An empty bag would tip him off. My driver's license and the $300 in cash I had managed to scrape together over the past eight months were under the front seat of the car, not in the glovebox. Too obvious. I'd spent the last hour packing the '82 Tercel with a single large suitcase, mostly filled with the kids' clothes and favorite stuffed animals and books. I'd collected the things most precious to me, as well—the word processor my dad had bought me, floppy disks, the notebooks I wrote my stories in, and a few clothing items.

I just needed my daughter.

I ran through the steps in my head. *Stay calm, don't let him upset you. If he gets your bag away from you, don't panic, it's a decoy anyway. If he thinks he's got your keys and money, it will feel like a victory and he'll let his guard down. Eyes forward. Just keep moving.*

Just. As if it was *that* easy.

I squeezed the car key in my left hand. My house and mailbox keys were under the front passenger seat of the Tercel. *Remember, there are two more keys in magnetized boxes in each front wheel well of the car. It's unlocked. Car seat is in place. Eyes forward, don't worry about what James is doing. Just keep moving.*

Just. I *just* needed Libby.

The counselor at TESSA had told me I could leave without my children. I thought she was joking. The sleeping boy hooked into my arm felt heavy, but I didn't put him down. I would never put him down. Noisemakers and fireworks popped and fizzed in the townhome parking lot. I suddenly didn't feel so alone.

It had been four consecutive days of verbal, emotional, and physical battering. For nearly 96 hours James had stayed at my shoulder, mere inches from my body, occasionally grabbing my breasts and between my legs. He followed me as I did laundry, scrubbed the bathrooms, and prepared meals for the kids and for him. He made awful accusations and threats, whispered horrible things into my ear all day, all night. He made sure I inserted a contraceptive sponge before climbing on top of me. He never hit me. That would leave a mark, and he had a reputation to protect. An upstanding and inventive member of society. A go-getter. An American success story, waiting to happen. Kicking, choking, shoving, shaking, spitting, restraining, punching holes in the walls, breaking personal possessions, threatening to kill the kids, kill me, kill himself—none of that constituted abuse in his eyes. To this day, he will tell you he never abused me.

James collected people like some people collect stamps or rocks. But, once they were no longer of use to him, he would toss them away, deem them unworthy, and set his crosshairs on the next target. Many times, over the past twelve-and-a-half years, I had wished he would toss me away. That would have made things easier. If he made the choice, he could control the narrative. Controlling the narrative fed his overinflated ego, reinforced the notions he held about himself as a superhero, someone you not only *wanted* to know, but *needed* to know. "They'll write books about me," he'd say. "I'll be on Letterman." Some people, like me, swallowed his lies whole, where they sat like a tumorous mass of hope in our bellies, eventually metastasizing into fear, guilt, and shame—the holy trifecta in a malignant narcissist's dangerous arsenal. If one person can exhaust another to the point where they can barely stand on their own two feet, or make a decision without fear of the consequences, the work is done, the cycle established.

Funny, how hope and desperation dance together. Internalization is powerful.

9:58 pm. Standing in the heat, holding my sick son, I replayed the moment that had broken me open months prior. It had been a very bad day. I'd gone to the public library so Liam could see the bunnies, and play with the toys, and I could have some peace away from the house-prison I had been relegated to, except for banking and groceries. James had implemented a "no leisure reading" rule. Amway material only, nothing else. And no television. Recently, he'd gotten it into his head that *Free Willy*, one of Libby's favorite movies, was demonic because there was a Native American character in it, and Native Americans didn't believe in Jesus Christ. As I clandestinely strolled the library stacks, breathing in the comforting musk of ink and paper, a book with a purple cover found me. Within a few paragraphs I saw the sentence that would light a terrifying fire in my belly.

He can't abuse you if you're not there.

I found a seat in the play area. In the book, the author referred to "crazymaking," a process whereby the abuser systematically gaslights his victim into believing she's nuts, slowly chipping away at her core self and leaving a self-doubting, empty husk in its place. How many times had James told me, with condescending compassion, that I needed psychological help? How many times had he done or said something, and then told me I had misunderstood because I was igno-rant and stupid? I began to cry and didn't really stop until *The Plan* began to formulate, weeks later, with the help of counselors at TESSA, where I had secretly started taking empowerment classes.

James noticed I was different. More agreeable, less willing to engage in his circular arguments. Part of *The Plan*. It unsettled him that he wasn't able to get the desired response out of me anymore. So, he dug in, his latest efforts fueled by the insecurity he felt when his upline mentor told him there was no reason I shouldn't be able to take a creative writing class at the community college, as long as I fulfilled my domestic duties at home. Unable to tolerate this slackening of my leash, and utterly convinced I'd had an affair with one of the men in the class, James launched his worst attack yet. But I stayed calm, smiling as I prepared his food, folded his underwear, spread my legs. I told him I could never cheat on the best man I'd ever met. The proverbial light at the end of the tunnel was growing brighter, but by then I had also resolved myself to dying. If James killed me and my children during my escape attempt, then at least I would have died on my feet, protecting my children.

10:10 pm. James would want to leave the park before the fireworks finale to avoid the crowds of people trying to get to their cars. That always frustrated him. When I saw his car pull in, my heart jackhammered into my throat. I adjusted the strap of my bag, tightened my grip on the key, held my son closer. *Stay calm. Eyes forward. Keep moving.*

I had opened the sliding screen door so there wouldn't be an additional barrier between me and my daughter, us and the car. Libby approached first, a big smile on her 9-year-old face, already starting to tell me about the fireworks. When she was within reach, I realized I didn't have a free hand to take hers. I quickly transferred the car key into my other hand, inadvertently jostling Liam awake, who grinned and leaned toward Libby, throwing me off balance. I pulled him back, took her hand, and began walking, eyes forward, down the patio steps toward the sidewalk, toward the Tercel.

"Where are we going?" Libby asked.

My lack of answer seemed to signal James about what was happening. He immediately blocked my path on the steps. I veered onto the grassy mound that the kids liked to roll down. He reached for my bag, grabbed the strap, and yanked hard. I stumbled, tightening my hold on Liam and Libby's hand, and recovered my balance as James reached again. I turned and said, calmly and clearly, "You touch me, I scream *fire.*" Part of *The Plan.* He glanced at the people in the parking lot and stepped back, then stepped forward again, hands clasped loosely just above his navel, a stance I had come to know well. It meant, *I'm about to say something and you'd better listen good, and do what I say, or you will pay.* The muscles of his jaw tightened, released, tightened again. He said, just as calmly and clearly, "Take my kids back inside right now, you stupid cunt."

I turned, pulling Libby with me, and felt a sudden sting at the back of my right shoulder just inches below where Liam's head was. Deviating from my rule of *eyes forward*, I glanced over my shoulder as we rounded the passenger side of the Tercel, and saw James reaching into the rock bed for another stone. He pitched it at me, missing this time. Sweat streamed from my armpits. I let go of Libby's hand and opened the car door, another stone hitting the windshield. I popped the passenger seat forward and secured Liam in his car seat, terrified that James would seize the moment to seize Libby. But he was too preoccupied with selecting rocks to throw. I told Libby to get in and lock the door. Thankfully, my usually questioning daughter did as she was told, her eyes wide, seeing everything.

Another *thwack*. James was now scooping handfuls of stones from the rock bed and hurling them in rapid succession. But he was also walking backward, away from us, toward the parking lot entrance that I would hopefully soon be driving out of. My heart thumped so loud I couldn't hear the noisemakers or fizzy pops of the fireworks in the parking lot anymore. My hands shook. *Keep moving.* I rounded the back of the car, opened the driver's side door, got in, locked it, pressed the clutch, turned the key and backed up. James stood at the entrance, watching. I had a vision of him jumping in front of the car, making me run him over. Or, jumping on top of the hood, something he had boasted about doing to a previous girlfriend he suspected of cheating. I rounded the corner. James lifted his arms and flung a cantaloupe-sized river rock at the car, hitting the trunk with a thunderous crash. Libby whipped around in her seat, tears filling her wide eyes. I turned onto Dublin Avenue, then again onto Academy Boulevard. I was aiming toward my mother's house, but that's not where we were going. I wanted James to see that. Part of *The Plan*. It was then that I heard my own voice, the words overpowering my thrumming heartbeat —*itsokayitsokayitsokay...*

"Where are we going?" Libby asked again, her voice like a sweet little bell ringing me home.

I'd forgotten to turn on my headlights. I'd forgotten to fasten my seatbelt. I looked at my daughter's freckled, tear-streaked face and tried for what I hope to this day was a reassuring smile. I accelerated the Tercel, our tiny, trusty get-away car.

"It's okay, Libby. We're on an adventure."

ABOUT THE AUTHOR

A voracious reader as a youngster, Morgan Leigh spent entirely too much time with her nose stuck in a book and scaring the hell out of friends and family with her unsettling, dark tales. Her fiction and creative non-fiction have appeared in numerous magazines and e-zines over the years and her first novel, *bloodbrothers*, was published in 2020. When not writing, she can be found teaching at the University of Colorado and leading weekly adaptive chair yoga classes. She is currently finishing a second novel and writing a memoir. Morgen writes and breathes in Colorado but threatens to move to Tucson every winter.

MY NAME IS MARJORIE

TERRY ODELL

Marjorie struggled to heft her Louis Vuitton luggage up the steep wooden steps of the Colorado mountain cabin. On a cruise—her kind of vacation—stewards would have already delivered her bags to her stateroom. As she reached the porch, the cosmetic case slipped from her grasp. "Oops."

Caroline grabbed for the falling case. "Got it, Margie."

Inwardly, Marjorie cringed at the nickname but managed a smile for her coworker. Petite, scrub-faced, with a blonde ponytail, Caroline looked more like a teenager than a fourth-grade teacher. "Thanks. Maybe I over-packed a little."

Beside her, Suzanne plopped down her compact duffle bag. "Don't sweat it. Just beware. We might come a-borrowing." She fished around in the depths of her nylon daypack. With a flourish, she extracted a key. "Ta Da." Suzanne unlocked the door and kicked her duffel inside. "Come on in, ladies. Eagle Lake awaits."

As Marjorie explored the cabin, she breathed a sigh of relief. Fresh air perfumed the space once the windows were open. Worn but comfortable furnishings filled the living room. The two bedrooms contained real beds, with clean sheets and towels in the linen closet. A generator provided electricity, and there was a gas stove in the kitchen. And, thank goodness, a bathroom with a real flush toilet.

"What did you expect, Margie?" Suzanne asked as they made their beds. "Outhouses?"

"Well … maybe. And, please, call me Marjorie."

"Right. Well, Marjorie, this may be the sticks, but we've got a few luxuries just like the folks in New York City." Suzanne's smile took the sting out of her words. "Loosen up."

"I *am* loose."

"Honey, you're tighter than one of Cher's gowns. It's the first week of summer vacation, and we've got a whole week to ourselves. No unruly kids, no homework to grade, or parents to appease. Or men. This week is ladies only. It's an annual ritual for us."

"I still don't understand why you wanted to include me," Marjorie said.

Or why she had given in to Suzanne's repeated invitations and come along at all.

Marjorie felt like Suzanne's pet project. Maybe Suzanne was filling the hole left when her youngest son went away to college.

Had she agreed because, deep down, Marjorie knew she needed to sever ties to her old life, and, like it or not, her colleagues had invited her to join their tightly-knit circle.

Did she want to be part of it?

Or, was she here because she couldn't come up with an excuse *not* to join them? Not one that would let her face them when school was back in session.

"Because ever since you moved to Live Oaks, you've been a recluse," Suzanne said. "All you do is teach—which you do very well —and then go hide in your little bungalow."

At least there, nothing reminded her of New York or Frank. "I like my little bungalow. And I'm not a recluse."

"Not this week, you aren't." Suzanne moved to Marjorie's side and gazed into her eyes. "I know you don't want to talk about it, but it's obvious your divorce tore you apart. You need to remake your life. Let us be part of it. You might be surprised to find we're not all that different from your big-city friends." Suzanne gave Marjorie a gentle pat on the shoulder. "I'm going to make sure Karen's got the generator going."

Marjorie finished making her bed and unpacked her gear. She looked at the hiking boots, floppy-brimmed hat, daypack, backpack, and everything else Suzanne had told her to buy. By the time she factored in all the new equipment and clothes, a cruise might have been cheaper.

She would donate everything to charity after this week was over. The trip shouldn't be a total loss—someone might actually get good use of the stuff, and she'd get the tax write-off.

She tested the facilities and freshened her makeup before joining her colleagues in the living room.

"So, you done any hiking?" Caroline asked.

"Not unless the cabbies were on strike," Marjorie said.

"Guess that goes for fishing and canoeing, too." Karen wiped her hands on her jeans and pushed her glasses up on her nose. Without her usual makeup, Karen's freckles stood out like freshly-spattered paint against her fair skin.

If these women thought she was going to appear anywhere *au naturel*, they had another think coming. Didn't they know the sun was a death sentence? "Sorry. I tried to tell Suzanne this wasn't the right trip for me, but she wouldn't take no for an answer. I hope I'm not too much of a burden."

"Don't be silly," Suzanne said. "You'll have fun. We're sure of it."

Marjorie noticed the glances the women exchanged. They were definitely *not* sure of it. She sucked in a breath. She'd agreed to come. She'd brought the gear. She'd made the commitment, and if there was one thing Marjorie believed in, it was honoring commitments.

Over the next few days, Marjorie managed not to capsize the canoe or poke out anyone's eyes with a fishhook, and she didn't think she slowed the pace too much on their hikes. Evenings were another matter altogether. Although the women tried to include her, too often their conversation drifted into shorthand.

"Remember when Fred had that—"

"Oh, my God, yes. That was hysterical! And what about the time—"

"You mean Jane. Yes. But then when Jim lost his—"

"That was too bad, wasn't it?"

Eventually they'd look at her, change the subject, and she could tell the women were forcing themselves to include her in the conversation. She tried to join in, but all it did was make her uncomfortable. After two nights of Scrabble and jigsaw puzzles, Marjorie stopped trying to be a part of the group and sat by the fireplace with a book. Even as she read, she heard the occasional lulls in conversation, the subdued voices, and she knew she was the topic at hand. Probably telling stories about her being the stuck-up, big-city girl who couldn't bait a hook. She'd wonder again why she had left New York City for a small town in Colorado.

Granted, the views of the Rockies were magnificent and the fresh air a delight, but had moving to Live Oaks been the smart thing to do? The forty-seventh floor condo in New York was part of her divorce settlement. She could have stayed.

No, she couldn't. Not after the way Frank had humiliated her.

He'd generated most of the income. Had all the right connections. They went to the best restaurants, Broadway shows, all the top social events. And, dammit, so what if she enjoyed it? She loved Frank. She would have loved him even if they didn't have money. But she loved her teaching job, too, low-paying or not. And the kids. With none of her own, the kids filled the only void in her marriage.

"Give it time," friends said after the split. Their friends were really his friends, she'd realized when they stopped calling. So, she ran.

She'd sold the condo and grabbed the first teaching job as far away from Frank as she could get. She'd swallowed her pride and grief, and now here she was, forty-two, stuck in another universe where people called her Margie. Where Friday night meant bowling, pizza and beer, or the movie theater with two screens. Not dinner and a Broadway show. Not wine and cheese at a gallery opening.

With four days to go before she could return to Live Oaks, which now appeared to be the epicenter of civilization, Marjorie begged off the afternoon fishing expedition with a feigned headache.

After two hours, Marjorie closed her book. The solitude wasn't as comforting as she had thought it would be. She applied lipstick and sunscreen, grabbed her floppy hat and fishing pole, and tromped out of the cabin, unable to believe she felt guilty about not going fishing. She winced as her brand-new hiking boots rubbed on her just-as-new blisters. The other women actually enjoyed turning slimy wriggling creatures into a meal. Didn't they know that making dinner meant taking food out of Styrofoam takeout containers and putting it on plates? For parties, you put it on serving platters.

She followed the trail toward the lake, scratching her mosquito bites. At the water's edge, she realized her companions were nowhere to be seen. Probably visiting the 'ladies' trees. Marjorie hadn't been able to get used to communing that closely with nature, not with the cabin a mere ten-minute walk from the lake. Marjorie stutter-stepped around the missing boards on the weathered dock and made her way to the far end. She lowered herself to the wooden platform, careful to avoid the menacing splinters, hugged her knees to her chest and stared out over the water, a blue-gray reflection of today's overcast skies. The blue-gray that so closely matched the color of Frank's eyes.

Damn Frank, anyway. Hot tears stung. Seventeen years, she'd given him. She'd never noticed things slipping away. Had she been that blind? She'd driven herself crazy looking back, trying to see the signals. And she still couldn't. He hadn't put up a fuss when she filed for divorce. Went off with his twenty-something sexpot, happy as a schoolboy.

The sun had dropped to the tops of the mountains surrounding the lake. Purple shadows stretched across the dock.

"Margie!" came a shout from above.

She wiped her eyes. "I'm down here! Be right up." She hoisted herself to her feet and headed to the cabin to face dinner. And, so help her God, if it looked back at her, she didn't know what she'd do.

"Hi, girls," she said with a forced smile as she climbed the steps to the porch. "How was the fishing?"

"Great!" Suzanne said. "We must have just missed you. We took the back trail. Hope you don't mind that we've already cleaned the fish."

"Oh, shucks," Marjorie said. "Here I was looking forward to playing Davy Crockett, and you've taken all the fun out of it."

Suzanne pulled Marjorie aside. "Listen. You're more than a teacher. We all are. Let us meet the other side of you. Maybe you'll find out you like us, too. And," she said in a voice meant for the whole group, "in the spirit of friendship, we'll all pitch in with dinner, even though it's your night to cook."

Marjorie heard a dull popping sound. She turned to see Caroline extending a glass of white wine. "Thanks." She took a sip and found it crisp and refreshing. Much better than the beer and boxed wine they'd been drinking on previous nights. "This is good. What is it?"

Caroline displayed the bottle. "An Oregon Pinot Gris. We've been saving it for a special occasion, and I think tonight's it."

Now was not the time to mention Frank's tastes had run to French wines and she'd gotten several cases as part of the divorce settlement. "I'm not familiar with this one."

"We've got plenty more," Caroline said. "So, what's your favorite fish recipe?"

Marjorie thought a moment. "That would be the Dover sole at L'Orangerie." She couldn't help but join in the ensuing laughter.

"All right," Karen said. "Let's see what we can do to help." She pulled a cast-iron skillet from a cabinet and added a copious amount of butter. She smiled at Marjorie. "Don't look at me that way. There are no calories or cholesterol in anything cooked in the woods."

"How about working on a salad?" Suzanne asked. "You can tear lettuce, right?"

"I think I can manage," Marjorie replied. She reached for the large wooden bowl. As she tore the Romaine, she found herself thinking of the Caesar salad at L'Orangerie. Frank's favorite. If anyone noticed the vehemence with which she ripped apart the leaves, nobody mentioned it, although Caroline kept Marjorie's wine glass filled.

Caroline snapped green beans and set them in a pot on the stove. Suzanne rubbed garlic onto slices of French bread, spread them with more butter, and popped them in the oven. Karen breaded and pan-fried the fish. Marjorie managed to get into the spirit of things—okay, the third glass of wine did help—and reached for the skillet to transfer the cooked fillets to a platter.

"Damn!" She yanked her hand back from the handle and tears sprang to her eyes. Her palm was already bright red. She clamped it under her arm.

"Let me look at that," Karen said. She pulled Marjorie to the sink and ran cool water over the burn. "That's gotta hurt. Suzanne, I've got some bandages in the first aid kit in the bathroom."

Suzanne dashed from the room and returned with a roll of gauze and handed it to Karen.

"Sorry. Not much good around the kitchen, am I?" Marjorie said. "In New York, I dusted my stove."

"Don't you worry about a thing," Karen said. "It's not a serious burn, and it'll probably be fine in the morning. Hurt like hell for a while, is all. But I think you have something else hurting you a lot more, Margie."

"I'm over it," Marjorie snapped. "And if you call me Margie one more time, I swear—"

The unfinished threat hung awkwardly in the air. Karen held the roll of gauze and took Marjorie's hand. Marjorie yanked away, sending a fresh wave of fire through her palm. Tears trickled down her face, and she felt herself being led to a chair.

"It doesn't hurt that badly." Marjorie sniffed. "I don't know why I'm crying." And suddenly, the bitterness poured out.

"I came home early. Power outage at school. He ... Frank ... they —God, what a cliché. Right out of the soaps. Wife comes home, finds husband in bed with bimbo. A bimbo he's been boinking for almost a year. A surgically enhanced bimbo at that." She gulped. "And he's still with her, and he's happy, and she's ... she's pregnant! He never wanted kids with me." The sobs began full force.

"Finally." Suzanne sighed and put her arm around Marjorie. "You go ahead and cry."

Marjorie, encircled by the three women, made no effort to stanch the tears. When they ran dry, Marjorie looked into the faces of her colleagues. She saw not pity, but genuine friendship.

"New York doesn't have a monopoly on sleaze-bags, you know," Karen said. "We're not living perfect lives ourselves. We try to be there for each other. We'll be there for you, if you'll let us."

"How about we move this bonding session to the table?" Suzanne said. "Our dinner's getting cold."

Caroline opened another bottle of wine, and the women shared the gossip of Live Oaks as they enjoyed their meal. New Yorkers didn't have a monopoly on dysfunctional relationships, Marjorie discovered, they just talked about them more.

As they ate—and drank—her colleagues confessed their own problems, with the understanding that what happened at Eagle Lake stayed at Eagle Lake.

Caroline's mother had just been moved into a nursing home, and

Caroline was going to have to fit a second job into her schedule to pay the bills, since her husband's attitude was "She's *your* mother, you deal with it."

Karen's son had come out of the closet, and his father was having serious acceptance issues, to the point of kicking him out of a lot more than the closet, and he'd been hiding his perceived shame behind far too much bourbon.

And Marjorie's guess that Suzanne had been dealing with empty-nest syndrome had been only half-right. She suspected her husband had been cheating on her, and had felt an underlying kinship with Marjorie.

"So, Marjorie," Suzanne said after they'd washed the dishes. "You don't seem to care for Scrabble or jigsaw puzzles. Anything you'd like to do tonight?"

"You play bridge?"

Three negatives. Suzanne headed toward the cabinet that housed the games. "There's got to be something we can all enjoy. Monopoly? Parcheesi? Trivial Pursuit?"

"Wait," Marjorie said and dashed to her bedroom. She reappeared carrying her cosmetic case. "I hereby declare this the Eagle Lake Spa. Facials, anyone?"

"I knew this trip would be good for you, Marjorie," Suzanne said a half-hour later, her face covered in an avocado-cucumber masque.

"I think you're right." Marjorie smiled at her green-faced friends. "And, why don't you call me Margie?"

ABOUT THE AUTHOR

Although Terry Odell had no aspirations of becoming a writer until long after receiving her AARP card, she's now the author of over thirty novels, novellas, and short stories. She writes mysteries and romantic suspense, but calls them all "Mysteries With Relationships." Her awards include the Silver Falchion, the International Digital Awards, and the HOLT Medallion. A Los Angeles native, she moved to Florida where she spent thirty years in the heat and humidity. She now enjoys life with her husband and rescue dog in the cooler, dryer climate of the Colorado Rockies, where she watches wildlife from her windows.

BUTTERFLY

MICHAEL CHANDOS

Billie fidgeted on the secluded dock as she waited to make her latest midnight delivery. Transporting rum from Cuban sailing ships out in the Gulf was risky business, but it was a promising way to make big money. Her best friend, Della, stayed aboard the Painted Lady, Billie's Gulf fishing boat, named after her favorite Mississippi Delta butterfly.

A 1928 Lincoln town car, resplendently out of place with its polished maroon paint and sparkling white canvas top, burst from the darkness onto the dock. Two transporters, disguised as small lumber trucks, and a scout car with armed guards followed.

The Lincoln rolled to a stop next to Billie's boat. The driver got out but stayed close to the front of the car, his Tommy gun held ready as he covered his very important passenger. The brawny gangster slid from the right seat of the Lincoln and towered over the five-foot-one-inch Billie.

"Have you been cheating me, Butterfly?" he said. He brushed the dust off his dark suit and centered his black-banded Stetson boater. His starched white shirt shone in the partial moonlight. He had a .44 Special holstered under his arm.

"This is an unexpected pleasure, Mr. Puglisi. And, no sir," said Billie, "I never done that and I never will." She stood straight in front of the gangster boss. Billie carried a .32 Colt revolver under her belt, but it remained where it was. Della pointed her long double-barreled shotgun straight at Puglisi's Italian silk tie.

"You girls break me up," he said. He inspected each case of rum, and his man marked the inventory sheet, before the transport crew hustled the cases into the fake lumber trucks. Transferring the cases took mere minutes, so Billie kept the Lady's engine at idle. One truck drove away and the second was quickly filled. Both were headed up the Mississippi to St. Louis.

"Someone sent me bad booze last month. It was in real rum bottles, with real Cuban labels, and it was real poison. Killed a couple guys in Kansas City, in fact. Burned 'em all up inside. Mister Nitto expects me to correct that problem. Immediately." He pulled his coat back to make certain she saw the .44.

"Listen, Mr. Puglisi. I'm a tiny black woman with two little kids, one friend, no husband and a three-room shack off Bayou L'Ours. I started transportin' rum with a leaky fishin' boat and now I own a proper Gulf fishin' boat, with a snug cabin and a reliable engine. My kids wear new shoes and clean clothes. No way I'm gonna kill that golden goose by stupid cheatin'. This is great money. Hell, we all love Prohibition down here." Billie smiled.

Puglisi didn't smile back. "Some soon-to-be-dead bastards are picking up cases from the rumrunners, switching out high-quality Cuban rum with rotgut moonshine, and selling the good stuff to local saloons. Making money on both ends. Taking money from me. I will make that stop."

"It's gotta be somebody with access to stills and a way to bottle the stuff," said Billie. "Only a few local rumrunners own a big enough operation for that."

Puglisi loomed over her. "I like you—you understand this business —but if our goods are stolen again, Butterfly, we will kill whoever's doing it and then move further down the coast to where the crooks stay honest, and you'll be out of the good money, forever." He leaned in. "You'll be back to selling bugs and blowjobs on Bourbon Street again. White men love creamy skin like yours."

"I never done that!" said Billie. Her hand went to her .32. Puglisi's driver and Della both raised their guns to their shoulders. "You best watch your words." She looked Puglisi in the eye. He smiled and motioned to his driver to lower his machine gun. Della didn't move her shotgun.

"You have twenty-four hours to find out who's doing it, with proof, or we're leaving."

"Now, wait… I got some ideas on who your thief might be. And I think I know where I can get you proof."

"I figured you would. Don't fail me, Butterfly."

Artists in the French Quarter called Billie *Butterfly* because she earned money capturing colorful butterflies on the Delta to sell to tourists. Only close friends knew her as Billie Moore, and that her main source of income came from rum-running for the Chicago Outfit.

Puglisi gave her a cold smile and tipped his hat. He and his driver climbed back into the Lincoln. "Loading's done. Beat it." The last lumber truck left in a cloud of gray exhaust smoke, followed by the Lincoln and the scout car.

Billie threw the hawser to Della, jumped aboard the Painted Lady, and hit the throttle. Everyone disappeared into their own share of the darkness.

The waterway back to Billie's homestead was a messed-up mix of low islands, more like floating vine paddies interconnected with puddles. Straight, dredged canals and narrow, indistinct passages led everywhere. To make navigation even harder, everything looked different when the tide came in, and big boats and hurricanes stirred it up and changed what went where. Piloting your boat away from the main dredged canal was risky during the day—and impossible at night —unless you were from here and knew the markers and mileposts.

Della was her guard dog. She always called Billie "Ma'am," even though Billie was over ten years younger. Della had wandered into the bayous a year ago, maybe to escape the sheriff's bloodhounds. Billie found her across Barataria Bay, clinging to a tree, muddy, desperate, and half-crazy. She nursed Della back to health and Della stayed with her. Della was coal-dark, with taut muscles and tendons showing through her thin skin. She had hard eyes and razor cheekbones. She seldom spoke. She'd been hurt bad by her abusive husband and was all locked up inside. Billie thought that, maybe, she'd killed him.

Billie set her long Gulf boat down a narrow, curving branch off the East Fork of Bayou L'Ours, her home. "I'm glad we aren't in the old boat with this rain."

Billie liked to talk to Della, but Della seldom answered. "I bet you sleep with that shotgun, Della, assuming you sleep at all."

Della sat impassively on a bench seat on the opposite side of the cabin. She stared ahead, her eyes always searching for something, the long, double-barreled shotgun clutched in one hand. She had looped a homemade bag filled with more shotgun shells around her neck. Both women wore denim bib overalls, pale blue shirts, and black boots, all wet and soiled from the day's work.

"The only locals with a big enough operation are either Adrien Comeaux or that damn Captain Brankie of the Slippery Jim." Billie slowed the Lady as they approached her tin-roofed shack, three rooms with a screened-in porch and a dock, all hers. Della jumped onto the small dock with the hawser to tie off the boat. "Adrien's an honest shrimper, and he's always been kind to me. I wouldn't play cards with that damn Brankie unless I left my coin purse at home and carried my pistol with me. I think we'll slip across the Bay in the old boat before dawn and see what Brankie's up to. I know he keeps a buildin' up Bayou Dulac big enough for a warehouse."

"OK. Jus' wake me, Ma'am." The most Della had said all day.

S tained black by long use on the warm bayou waters, the old boat was almost invisible at night. It resembled a long lifeboat with no cabin and it ran low in the water. Billie and Della sat hunched over on the bottom of the boat, just undefined lumps in their dark clothing. The small gas motor ran at mid-throttle. They glided across Barataria Bay, barely disturbing the oily smooth surface.

"That low moon is just enough to run by," said Billie. "You haven't met Brankie yet, Della. A son of a bitch. I always try to get to the rumrunner sloop before he does to get my share, because he hogs all the rum when he can. We must be really quiet. These guys might shoot."

Billie closed the throttle to idle as they coasted past Brankie's commercial dock. The centerpiece of Brankie's camp was a square, two-story hardboard house, with a bunkhouse behind and outbuildings in between. The big dock looked freshly painted; the house didn't. A fifty-foot fishing boat was tied up on the left with two smaller long-boats docked on the right on a shorter jetty. Fishing nets hung from the larger ship's king post to dry.

"There's the Slippery Jim, a Gulf boat like mine, but newer and bigger. All those boys are surely sleepin' still, but keep your eye out for a watchman. The warehouse is up around there."

Billie steered the old boat up a narrow channel. The trees and flowering bushes threatened to close off the inlet, and vine paddies floated off the shore and spread across the water. The warehouse was just a dark blob through the trees. A simple dock jutted out nearby.

Billie stopped the motor and held the boat in the darkness under some bushes opposite the dock to wait and watch.

Della pointed.

"Yeah, I see his cigarette. Probably just the one watchman." Billie parted the bushes a little. "I think we can paddle along those vines and hide the boat under the old dock over there, and then creep up to the warehouse to the right. See his candle lantern? Keep an eye on that. It's murky and dark under the cypress and pines, and he won't go anywhere without it."

"OK, Ma'am."

They skimmed along the shore, using short paddles, and then crossed the murky inlet by gliding through a mass of vines. The low-riding old boat was silent and almost invisible in the leaves. Skeeters buzzed and circled in the heavy air.

As they approached the bushes next to the warehouse dock, Della slithered over the side into the green bayou water and tied the old boat to a pole underneath. Billie tied the stern off so that the hull was hidden under the decking. Billie slipped into the waist-deep water and waded to shore. Both women crept up the small hill to the side of the warehouse away from the watchman. Billie held her pistol and Della, of course, carried her shotgun. Billie pointed at the black rectangle of an open window.

"I don't hear nuthin'," said Billie as she crouched under the opening. She stood up at the window to check out the room. "Don't see no guard or no lights on inside. Try that door. Stop if it squeals."

Della turned the doorknob and pushed on the door. It scraped open about ten inches on its rusty hinges and then stopped. Enough of a gap for two small women. Della peeked in and then leaned into Billie.

"Quiet and dark, Ma'am," she said. The women wormed their way in and closed the door behind them.

Light from the partial moon filtered through the trees. Some of the moonlight made it through the dirty front window into the interior of the warehouse. Straw and trash littered the floor, and dust and tiny bugs floated in the air.

"The air in here smells like sweat and spittoons," said Billie.

Three large worktables dominated the center of the room. A wide main door opened on the far wall. No other lights were on, but the work done here was obvious.

"Damn, look at that," said Billie. "Bottles, cases, five-gallon tins of shine and worktables. Don't bump nuthin', Della. And don't hit no bottles."

Billie could see the candle lantern through a window across the open room. The watchman rolled another cigarette.

"Della, find some real hooch in phony bottles while I look for a Cuban bottle of rum refilled with shine. Even if resealed with pitch, those Cuban bottles will smell like diesel."

Billie found a group of bottles standing like bowling pins next to an interior door. "There's a bit of sticky pitch around the tops, but they're empty," she whispered. "These bottles are waiting to be filled with shine."

"There." Billie picked up a tall cylindrical bottle of clear brown glass with a long narrow neck topped by a pitch-sealed cork. "Look at that label: *Ron Anejo de Cuba*. That's the same brand of aged rum we hauled to Puglisi last night. This junk is pale yellow and looks oily," she said, "and it smells like my boat engine. This is shine from some backwater still."

Della held up a similar bottle, cylindrical and tall, but there the resemblance ended. The dark golden rum sloshed as she held it up.

"That's the real stuff. Beautiful," said Billie.

"Look here, Della, there's fake labels stacked on the worktable. Funnels over there. This is a regular rum piracy factory."

The candle lantern moved. The women dropped to the floor and ducked under one of the tables.

The watchman came in the main door, carrying his candle lantern and a rifle. He toured the warehouse workroom and stopped at the door Billie and Della had used to sneak in. He put down the lantern and tugged, and the door opened a little, then he slammed it closed. He picked up the lantern and, with one last look, left by the main door.

"We found what we came for," said Billie, breathing again. "Time to fade away."

They crawled to the rusty door, but it wouldn't open. The watchman had swung a bar across the door and it wouldn't budge.

"Here, Ma'am." Della handed her bottle to Billie and scrambled out the window with her shotgun. Billie passed both bottles to her and then slipped out herself.

Della untied the old boat. The eastern horizon showed the beginnings of dawn and robber flies sang to greet the new day. "We gotta get going, it's gettin' light," said Billie. They paddled to the opposite side of the bayou and then hugged the shore further away before starting the motor.

Someone shouted and Billie looked back. The watchman with the lantern and another man ran to the end of Brankie's commercial dock. "Gotcha, Brankie," said Billie with a sneer. The engine idled along until they were out in Barataria Bay before Billie opened the throttle. She took a winding route through floating islands. No one gave chase.

"We'll meet Puglisi in Leeville around one this afternoon. I want to stop at the shack to see if the girls are up and dressed, then we'll leave them at Mabel's until this is over."

"Yes, Ma'am." Della cracked a rare smile.

At the secluded Leeville landing, Della tied off the Lady as Billie spread out a basket lunch on the hatch cover. The four long wooden piers were made for large fishing boats. The shore behind had been cleared to the road, and storage buildings headed each pier. Fishing gear and assorted nautical garbage cluttered the docks.

"You seldom see this wharf all empty," said Billie. "The fishin' boats must be out in the Gulf. I'd rather a few of them were still here. We stand out too much, and some people will wonder why we ain't out fishin', too."

"Should I get the guns, Ma'am?"

"No, that'd be too obvious. Jus' be certain you can get 'em if we need 'em."

While waiting for Puglisi, Billie strolled around the wharf. She stretched her arms over her head. "Oh, this warm sun feels good. And that rain looks like it's gone for a while."

Two men in a farm wagon drawn by draft horses stopped about a hundred yards away, but they didn't speak or get down. They watched Billie pace on the wharf. Della signaled to her.

"Ma'am, two white men are on that wagon down there, and they are checkin' us out," said Della. She stared at the men like a sheep eyeing a stalking wolf.

"Yeah, I saw 'em. Is your shotgun handy?"

Della pointed at her bag. Besides the shotgun shells, she carried Billie's small .32 revolver.

"Della, put a slip knot on the hawser in case we gotta get outa here fast. Start the engine and keep it idlin'. And gimme my gun."

Della handed it over and Billie hid it in the front of her bib overalls.

Puglisi's Lincoln sped onto the wharf and pulled up to Billie. The scout car stayed up near the road as Puglisi and his driver got out. The driver stayed close to his door, his Thompson by his side. One of the guards in the scout car swung his Tommy gun in the direction of the men on the wagon and they drove off.

Della handed the two bottles up to Billie, who then presented them to Puglisi. "That what you was lookin' for?"

Puglisi held up the bottles in the sun. "Yeah. This is one of the brands of Cuban rum we handle. And, dammit, it's filled with shine. What horse piss," he said. "Looks more like fuel oil than rum. Ha, a fake bottle filled with our rum, I'll bet. Where'd you get it, Butterfly?"

"This came from a nasty ship captain named Brankie. You're sure to know him. Owns several ships, but most often runs rum with the Slippery Jim? He's on Bayou Dulac across Barataria Bay. His warehouse is full of your stolen rum, big tins of shine, and phony bottles and labels." Billie smiled. "It'll burn like hell, I imagine."

"I imagine it will. Good job, Butterfly. I know who you're talking about. A cheap goon. I'll talk to the sheriff about motivating the Coast Guard to grab that piker." He started to get back into the Lincoln, but stopped. "There's a rendezvous with a Cuban sloop off Grand Terre at dawn tomorrow. I want you to go back to Brankie's place and guarantee he meets that sloop. Then lay back and watch the fun. These boys will burn good."

"You know, if the Coasties grab the sloop, it's gonna cost you some hooch," said Billie.

"Getting the government to solve my business problems saves me time and money. Some other friends will attend to their warehouse. It's just normal bootlegging business."

"When you see the sheriff, tell him Butterfly needs a favor. It'll help." Billie jumped aboard the Painted Lady and pulled on the mooring rope. She slammed the throttle forward and her Gulf boat surged ahead. Della took up a firing position out the cabin window.

Billie disappeared into the swamps of Bay Desespere as Puglisi sped off toward the sheriff's office in Galliano.

"Della, when we get to the shack, we'll hang fishing nets on the Lady's small crane and place traps and other fishing equipment on the deck. When we get up in the morning, we'll dress the part with rubber boots and stuff. Then we'll cruise into the Bay just before the sun rises and shout insults at the Slippery Jim to get 'em to race us to the sloop. We'll let 'em win. Before the Coast Guard shows up, we'll slide away and blend in with the fishing fleet off Mendicant Island. We'll see the sloop from there, and maybe we can watch the Coast Guard capture Brankie and his crew."

"They'll fight," said Della.

"Then maybe the Coasties will sink Brankie and solve all our problems." She swung the Lady up to her dock. "Tie off the hawser, Della."

Della put down her shotgun and went forward. She grabbed the hawser, jumped onto the dock and tied it off. "I'll run around to the old boat and check it's tied off good too, Ma'am." Della disappeared around the corner to the chicken coops behind the shack.

Billie picked up the food basket and entered her shack. A light flashed and she slapped down on her back, halfway in the door and half out on the dock. She felt pain on her jaw and she couldn't focus her eyes.

"I knew that was you this morning, Butterfly, you and that witchy friend of yours. What did you steal, bitch? Huh?" asked a male voice. "If the Captain finds out you was stealin', he's bound to kill you, and fire me and Jackie. So talk."

"Maybe she couldn't hear you, Caleb. Hit 'er agin," said another male.

Caleb picked up Billie by the collar. Billie tried to pull her pistol from the front of her overalls. Caleb smashed her in the face and the pistol flew into the murky bayou water off the dock. Billie flailed her arms, trying to ward off the next blow.

"Where's that witch? And where's your little girls? I looked forward to meetin' them," said Caleb.

"You'll never find 'em." Billie tried to scoot away.

"I bet I could. Jackie, check around back for that skinny black bitch friend of hers."

Jackie started to jump from the dock to the shore when Della flew by him and into the Lady. She grabbed her shotgun, fired both barrels and blew Jackie in half.

Caleb hit Billie, dropped her to the dock, and jumped into the Gulf boat. Before Della could reload, Caleb hit her in the face. Della went down to her knees and Caleb kicked her in the jaw. She hit the wall of the cabin hard and lay slumped, unconscious.

Billie rolled off the dock and slid into the warm bayou waters. She felt her way into the cypress roots and vines that jutted off the side of her property. She couldn't see well from her right eye and gasped for air through a broken nose and a bloody mouth. As she hid, she could hear Caleb trashing her shack, smashing dishes and breaking furniture. When he finished, he came out to the dock.

"Did you drown, Butterfly? I'm takin' your boat and your friend. I may kill her for what she did to Jackie. I won't burn your place this time 'cause even your ugly kids need a place to live. Sorry, it ain't too livable at the moment." Caleb whipped off the hawser and jumped into the Painted Lady. "You stay away from us. You'll die next time, you hear me?" He started the engine and sailed away.

———————

It took an hour for Billie to climb up the bank and to cross her garden yard to her shack. Her nose throbbed and her right eye was swollen shut. Her jaw wasn't broken, but it hurt like hell, and her lips were split. The back of her head bled from when the first punch had knocked her flat. She had trouble maintaining balance, so she used a short spade as a cane.

It looked like Caleb had smashed everything in the shack. Shattered dishes and crumpled clothing littered the floor. He had dumped all her food on the ground. Her daughter's watercolors and family photos were torn to shreds. Years of building her homestead, gone. Billie fell to the floor.

"No cryin' now, Billie." She pulled herself across the floor to her bedroom. "You know what to do. Cry later, girl."

Billie kept her patent medicines and folk remedies in a cabinet on top of the wash basin. Now, the bottles and jars were tossed around the room. Billie retrieved three jars and used the bedstead to stand up. She shuffled to the wash basin and poured what was left of the clear water into the basin and began to clean her injuries. She applied an herbal poultice from a square container to the back of her head and wrapped a long towel around to keep it in place. A salve from another jar dressed her bleeding lips and eyebrow. She collapsed onto her ripped mattress.

"I'll get you, Caleb. I'll get you good." She closed her eyes, but only for a moment.

———————

The eastern sky glowed faintly yellow when Billie cast off in her old boat, a rusty hatchet her only weapon. Venus shone above the bayou in the direction of Brankie's dock, maybe for good luck. The bleeding on her brow and scalp had stopped. Her right eye felt as hot as a smoldering cinder. Billie made no effort to be quiet this time.

The Painted Lady was tied off to the left of the Slippery Jim. Captain Brankie sat in the Jim's cabin and looked ready to leave. Caleb stood on the end of the dock, preparing to make the hawser free. He saw Billie in her little boat and grinned.

"Captain Brankie, you bastard," she yelled. "Gimme back my boat."

Brankie waved her off as he backed from his dock. "I'm gonna run you over, Billie."

The old boat was nimble; Brankie aimed for her, but Billie circled out of the Slippery Jim's path. Then she saw Della. Ropes tied her to the anchor capstan on the bow of the Slippery Jim. If they dropped anchor anywhere in the Gulf, she would go over the side.

Billie screamed. "Della!" Della raised her head. She looked bloody and weak, awful. She probably had spit at Brankie and they had punished her, for fun.

Brankie opened his throttle and left Billie and her old boat behind. She broke off the chase to return to Brankie's dock for the Lady. Caleb waited on the end of the dock as if he knew she'd be back. He gripped a long club in his hands.

Billie slowed next to one of the smaller docks and leapt from the old boat, hatchet in hand. She ran as best she could to the large dock and charged the smiling Caleb. Billie raised the hatchet above her head and screamed her battle cry. Caleb flipped the long club to horizontal and lunged, striking Billie in the chest before she reached him. She fell on her back with Caleb towering over her. He raised the club for a killing blow. Billie twisted in a desperate move and swung the hatchet with both hands, striking him just above the left knee. He screamed, folded against the fractured leg like a toppled stilt-man and fell into the bay.

Caleb took some time to come up. Perhaps, like many bayou boat-men, he couldn't swim well. Certainly, his massively bleeding, nearly severed leg made swimming almost impossible. Billie kneeled on the deck and offered no help. It took less than a minute for Caleb's splashing to stop. He floated, shoulders up and face down, with water up to his ears, his heavy clothes and boots sure to keep him that way.

"Say amen," whispered Billie. She struggled up, and boarded the Lady. She steadied herself by holding the deck railing as she went forward. She used the hatchet to cut the lines to the dock, started the engine and headed out at full throttle after Brankie and the Slippery Jim.

The mast and sails of the Cuban rumrunner resolved from the early morning mist, cruising just beyond the twelve-mile limit, in international waters. The Slippery Jim ran out of the Bay toward the sloop well ahead of Billie and tied up alongside. Billie intended to merge with the fishing fleet, but first she had to rescue Della.

The Cuban crew, dressed in khaki pants, white shirts and soft straw hats, formed a line and started to hand cases of rum over the side. Brankie's crew stacked the wood cases on the Jim's broad weather deck.

A thin column of smoke rose above the horizon to the east. The two bootlegging crews saw it, too. They knew that sign: a Coast Guard picket boat was racing toward the sloop and the Slippery Jim. The seventy-five-foot interceptor ran much faster than the rumrunner fleet, and it hosted a one-pound deck gun and two mounted .30 caliber machine guns. The rumrunners scattered.

Brankie swung away from the sloop at full throttle as the Cuban crew raised sails. The sloop set sail toward sanctuary, further out in the international waters of the Gulf. Safety for the Slippery Jim lay in the shallow waters of Barataria Bay.

Everyone in the fishing fleet stopped to watch the drama. Brankie steered into the inlet between the Grand Terre Islands. The speedy

Coast Guard picket boat closed and sounded its klaxon. The deck gun roared. The shell splashed forward of the Jim, a warning shot, but Brankie didn't slow. The next shell was very close. The third hit on the weather deck, just behind Della, puncturing the hull below the water line and catching the rum on fire. The Jim lost speed as it tilted badly to port.

Billie saw her opportunity and slammed the throttle forward. The Lady hit the Slippery Jim just forward of the cabin, forcing it to dip into the water, and slid up onto the bow. Billie struggled forward, tumbled over the railing and crashed to the Jim's deck. Brankie fired his pistol through his cabin windows, but his attention was split between Billie and the on-coming picket boat, and his aim was poor. She clawed her way up the slanting deck to the capstan and hacked the anchor ropes with the hatchet. A solid whack split the ropes that held Della.

"Get up, Della," Billie shouted above the sounds of the battle. Careful not to injure her further, Billie pushed Della over the railing onto the deck of the Painted Lady, then climbed over herself. Della moaned from her injuries, but still managed to hold on to the short tail of the Gulf boat's hawser. Billie staggered to the cabin and threw the engine into reverse. The Lady didn't move off Brankie's burning boat. The ropes hanging from the Slippery Jim's king post had snagged her.

With the weight of Billie's Gulf boat and the hole in the hull, the Slippery Jim was sinking. Billie stumbled out with the hatchet and cut the snagging ropes as best she could. As the Jim's bow dipped into the water, the Lady floated free and Billie backed it away. She steered to the west and went forward into the fishing fleet.

Brankie's crew aimed rifles and pistols at the approaching picket boat, but a fourth close cannon shell convinced them it was better to surrender. Captain Brankie continued to shoot from his cabin, drawing gun fire from the Coasties. The cabin splintered from the machine guns and Brankie's gunfire ceased. The picket boat came alongside the Slippery Jim as the burning rum set the entire boat on fire. The Coasties took on the remaining crew, then cast off to a safe distance as the Jim burned to the waterline and sank. Brankie never left his cabin.

Billie steered the Lady toward Barataria Bay. Once on course, she went forward to pull Della into the shelter of the cabin, laid her on the bench seat, and covered her with a dry blanket.

"Thanks again, Ma'am."

"We're both an ugly sight, ain't we?"

"Yes, Ma'am, but we'll mend up."

"Brankie went down with his ship."

"Good. And the warehouse?"

"I see a lot of black smoke on that side of the Bay. Must be the sheriff, with a little help from Mr. Puglisi," said Billie.

"And us."

"Yeah, and us. We'll get to Mabel's. It'll frighten my girls to see us lookin' like we do, but we need her help now."

"Mr. Puglisi should be happy."

"He damn well better be."

ABOUT THE AUTHOR

In the real world, Michael Chandos is the pseudonym for a retired rocket scientist, a licensed Private Investigator and author. He has published mystery and SF in the US and the UK. His story "West Texas Barbecue" was nominated for the Macavity award and was published in the Anthony-nominated anthology *The Eyes of Texas*. His story, "The Happy Ending," in the online *The Dark City Crime & Mystery Magazine*, is a noir mystery with a happy ending. Really. He lives in Black Forest, Colorado with two dogs, a wife and a vintage race car that doesn't work.

BLUE TURF CREATION MYTH

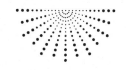

MARILYN K. MOODY

And to our land of potatoes came a wise
and brave Athletic Director, called Bleymaier.
It was a time of little money and a time
of lousy and losing football teams.
Fans were discouraged and lost
hope of ever creating a football dynasty.
Then the great Bleymaier, clad
only in Bronco gear, proclaimed:

Let there be blue turf.
Let our football field be like no other in college football.
Let ESPN marvel at the brightness of the blue.
Let our rivals curse the blue and perish on top of the
        blue.
Let it be true "Ducks do Crash on the Blue."
Let our blue uniforms and turf camouflage and confuse.
Let no one else build a blue football field.
Let us trademark the blue turf.

GO BRONCOS!!

Some wanted to fire Bleymaier and his President,
but they prevailed and became praised as geniuses and
        prophets.
The Bronco Nation grew strong and the kingdom of
        Boise
became known for its football warriors and
        people made
pilgrimages to view the blue turf and walk on the sacred
        field
and buy many many blue T-shirts.

And so the blue turf was born, and the blue turf will
forever for all eternity remain.

Amen.

ABOUT THE AUTHOR

Marilyn K. Moody grew up on the pancake-flat prairie of Central Illinois—and still prefers open spaces and distant horizons. Two of her recent poems are included in a 2020 Colorado Book Award winner, *Rise: An Anthology of Change.* She has also published poems in *Progenitor Art & Literary Journal* and *The Great Isolation: Colorado Creativity in the Time of the Pandemic.* While living in Boise, she walked often on the hallowed blue turf and accumulated enough orange and blue T-shirts to last a lifetime. She now lives near Denver.

LAST BEST HOPE

HARPER BARROW

The Children's Hospital parking garage is silent and dark at six-thirty in the morning. The engine off, I sit quietly and listen to Corbin's breathing, slow and rhythmic. He's asleep in his car seat. As well he should be, since I woke him up early to put him in the van, still in his pajamas.

I sip at my coffee, close my eyes, and try to soak in the peace and quiet, let the stillness of the garage somehow settle my churning insides.

It still doesn't feel real, even after all the appointments, and consultations, and agonizing, and tears. My son—two years old, just a baby—will have half his brain surgically removed in just a few hours.

He whines softly, and my eyes fly to the rearview mirror, certain he's having another seizure. No, his face is relaxed, his eyes are still closed. He is simply dreaming. But the thought shakes me into action.

My heart is thumping now, the peaceful moment has passed.

With a deep breath, I unbuckle my seat belt.

We check in, confirm our insurance carrier, tape on our wristbands, and find our way to the pre-operative waiting area. I avoid looking at the other parents, sure I'll see my hopelessness mirrored in their eyes. I avoid looking at the other children, as well, sure I'll see one sicker than my son. Or healthier. I'm not sure which is worse.

The truth is, I don't want to connect with anyone else, even for the few seconds it takes to make eye contact. It makes this all too real. No, I want to forget. I want it to be over with. I want to start fresh, with a healthy, perfect baby.

We don't get to pick what we *want*.

My son, Corbin, is a wonderful child. Sweet and affectionate, quick with a wave or a high five, even for strangers. He is magnetic, with bright blue eyes and chubby, squeezable cheeks. Aside from the weakness on his right side, which keeps him in a wheelchair when he should be up and running around like the toddler he is, no one can tell he's damaged.

And that's what he is: brain-damaged.

Seizures, sometimes a dozen in a day, interrupt his life and the private, happy moments of our family.

Out to dinner with our other kids and—SMACK—Corbin's forehead would fly into the table. My heart would break with pride and sadness to see my daughter rush to his side, to hold him through the spasms, to keep her baby brother safe, and to stop him from hurting himself further. Seconds later, he'd come out of it, only to cry and grab at his forehead, welted from the table.

In the grocery store, Corbin would sit in the cart, leg swinging, grabbing at boxes of pasta like a normal child until—BANG—he'd lurch forward, nearly throwing himself from his seat. Last time he did this, his big brother caught him in mid-air and held him to his chest, glaring at shoppers who had stopped to stare.

We started keeping a helmet on him. It protected his head, but advertised his disability like a great, big, neon sign. The curious stares from strangers were nearly as bad as the injuries he gave himself.

Worse, still, was watching him slowly melt away. His awareness, his response time, his intelligence grew less and less with every spasm. The doctors told us that Corbin would lose all cognitive function and, eventually, die if the seizures were allowed to continue. It was a well-documented outcome for his particular type of seizures. Less than five percent of children like Corbin lived past five years old.

For months, we tried every type of medication available. Hormones. Anticonvulsants. Steroids. Twice-daily injections into his tiny thigh muscles, holding his arms down while he screamed and thrashed. Still, his spasms became stronger, more frequent. The spark that was Corbin—his personality, his future—grew dimmer and dimmer every day. As did our hope.

Finally, there was one solution left. Surgically remove the part of his brain causing the seizures.

The entire left hemisphere.

"Corbin?"

I jump at hearing his name, then smile at the assistant and hold up my hand. "Right here." I kiss Corbin on the cheek, then pull his backpack to my shoulder and follow the woman through the double doors.

The aide—she says her name is MacKenzie—records his weight and vital signs, then flirts with him for a few minutes. "He's adorable," she says as she leads us through to a new hallway.

I nod. It's true. He *is* adorable. And innocent. Trusting. Beautiful. All the good things that are possible in the world. I have to preserve what I can of him.

She leads us to a room with a chair and a stretcher. The front wall is glass. A nurse's station is directly across. Blond and brunette heads hunker below the counter, typing and charting. MacKenzie hands me a small hospital gown—purple with koalas in space suits—and a tiny pair of thick orange socks.

"Please put these on him." She smiles warmly. "Corbin's nurse, then the doctors, will come in soon. Do you need anything else?"

I shake my head, still avoiding her eyes, and the door slides closed with a hiss.

Before, in the van, when I had thought it was our last moment of peace and quiet, I had been wrong. It is even more silent now, in the room where we wait. Only, this time, my pulse thumps behind my ears, making them ring.

Pushing the thick air from my lungs, I force a smile and unbuckle Corbin's belt. "Hey, baby," I whisper. "Let's put on this pretty nightgown, okay?"

In response, Corbin grins and reaches for my glasses. I pull back out of his reach and heft him up to my waist. "Stinker." I smile, despite myself. It releases the grip inside my chest a bit. Then I lay him on the stretcher, pull off his footie pajamas, change his diaper and try to tie the gown on properly. They never fit, always too small or too big, with the knots right behind his neck. Finished dressing, he sits happily, trying to pull the sock from his left foot. I keep one hand on him, a move long since perfected to keep him from flying into the hard ground when he has a seizure.

There is a short parade of doctors and nurses, each with a list of medications to confirm and a paper to sign. Corbin's neurosurgeon comes in last.

"Hey, buddy," he says as he slides the glass door shut behind him. "Ready for your big day?"

Corbin gives him a high five and a lopsided, toothy grin. Will he be able to do that when he wakes up? Will he *wake up*? My gut clenches.

"Are you ready?" Dr. Olsen says, looking at me this time. He frowns, and his eyebrows push together. "Are *you* ready for this?"

"Yes." I nod, then shake my head. "I mean, no, I'm not. But, I know we have to do this." I swallow hard. "Just scared, I guess."

His lips pinch together, in a move I know he means to be comforting but nearly comes across as condescending, and it occurs to me that he likely has this conversation all the time. He wakes up every day, takes a shower, eats a bowl of raisin bran and goes in to work to cut open brains. The brains of children. What kind of person does this? In what kind of awful world is this even a career option?

I don't want to be rude. I try to smile, but I'm sure it looks strained. It's not Dr. Olsen's fault. He's the only one who can save my baby now, if it's even possible.

Dr. Olsen pulls up a chair and sits across from me. "Do you have any other questions?"

We've been through it a million times. I don't have a question. I want him to promise me that Corbin will be better after today. That his seizures will stop. He'll be a nearly normal kid. Live a long happy, pain-free life. Hell, today, I'll settle for assurance he'll wake up at all.

"No," I whisper. "I'm ready. We're ready."

"Okay, then. His nurse will be in soon to get him." Dr. Olsen smiles at me once more, gives Corbin a last high five and says, "See you in there, buddy."

I hear the door slide open and closed, but I don't watch him go. Instead, I stand and pull Corbin from the stretcher. I hug him in my lap, for the last few minutes I have with him, and silently hope he won't have a seizure right then. I want my baby—warm and normal in my lap —for a few more minutes.

While we wait—Corbin's fist tight around my thumb—I try not to think of what comes next. The nurse will return, all smiles and bright scrubs. She'll hold her arms out to him, and he'll go to her because he trusts everyone. And I'll *let* him go, because I *have* to. Then, she'll carry him to a freezing-cold operating room, with bright lights and equipment, machines that watch his heart rate and blood pressure. They'll lay him down again, and by now he may be aware something different and scary is happening, because all the people have masks on and they're strangers and moving fast. They'll put a mask over his face, scented with mango lip balm, and he'll go to sleep. They'll insert a big tube into his airway, and many small tubes into his arms and legs, to give him various fluids and pain medications, probably antibiotics. Maybe they'll miss the veins, and he'll have bruises.

Then, after he's arranged on the table, and all members of the medical team have called out their names, someone will clean his head. I don't know what she'll use exactly, but in my mind's eye its brown, or maybe blue, and she'll saturate his hair with it, wipe in circles and wipe it off again. They aren't shaving his head. I had asked them about it, earlier, and Dr. Olsen said they don't do that anymore because it allows "microabrasions" and can complicate recovery. I remember nodding, but now I can't quite picture how they'll do it.

Will they just part his hair to the side? They must.

Dr. Olsen will ask for a scalpel, and a technician will hand him one. He will run the blade along my son's skin, from his forehead around back behind his ear. It will bleed as they pull his skin back, exposing the shiny white bone of his skull—at this point, I squeeze my eyes shut and tears start to come. I can't picture it any more. I don't know how they cut through his skull. A saw? I shudder and my mind flings itself away from the thought. I hold Corbin closer to me. He squirms, uncomfortable with the attention, but I hold tight. My tears drop into his hair.

The door slides open and I pull him tighter.

"Corbin?" The nurse's voice is too perky, but I'm thankful for the slight hint of empathy I can hear. "Are you ready?"

I nod, without looking at her, my face deep in his hair. I give myself a moment, let a few more tears leak out, then take a deep breath. When I make eye contact with her, she looks concerned, but not surprised.

"Ready?" She asks, again.

I'm nowhere near ready. But I stand, pulling Corbin up with me. "Corbin, you're gonna go with this lady, okay, and take a big nap." I kiss him on the cheek and he pushes away and smiles. "I'll be there when you wake up."

Predictably, he turns to her and holds his arm out. She takes him, props him against her hip. "Wow. What a big boy!"

I feel light and cold and dead with him apart from me, but I don't want him to be scared. So I lean over and kiss him again. I want to snatch him back, but I don't. "I love you, buddy." I whisper to him.

"We'll see you soon," the nurse says as she steps out of the room.

Not sure I heard what she said, I nod again, the only movement I'm capable of. Corbin's blue eyes are trained on mine. He's still not quite sure what's happening, but seems happy to have the attention.

As she walks away, I step out into the bright hall to watch them go. Corbin's eyes follow me over her shoulder.

He's gone. I try not to think about what comes next.

***

For eight hours, I wait. My husband and our other children join me, mid-morning, in the private room they reserve for the families who have to wait the longest or are most likely to hear bad news. We are both, I'm sure of it.

Each hour, a nurse calls, giving us updates. They are usually vague, but we wait for them, hovering over the waiting-room land-line like we are drowning in the ocean, and each update is our scuba tank. Finally, Dr. Olsen himself shows up, surprising us. I blink at him, like my sad mind can't quite place where I've seen him before. Then I snap to standing, my magazine falling to the floor. "Is Corbin okay?"

He pauses. And smiles, though I sense he's holding back. "It went well."

"Can we see him?" My husband asks. Yes, I think, that's what I wanted to know, thankful at least someone is functioning.

"He's in recovery, but he'll be up in intensive care in about an hour. You can see him there."

"Thank you, Doctor," my husband says, and shakes his hand. I go through the motions too, shaking and thanking, but I'm already gathering up Corbin's bag.

The last hour is the longest of all.

———————

The PICU is quiet and dark, but not like the parking garage. The lights are off, with curtains pulled across the glass doors of all the rooms to provide privacy, but there is a hushed urgency about the department. The alarms are on low, people are whispering, like they know it's bedtime for the sick children in their care, but important things are happening. I practically sprint to the room number they gave us. Corbin's name is written on a card beside the door.

I know he's alive because the monitors are moving with jagged lines and numbers, but his body is motionless in the dim room. Nurses rush around, tucking, adjusting, but they step back when they see that Corbin has visitors.

My baby looks small in the bed, the white covers tucked up to his chin, revealing only his head. I recognize his cheeks, still chubby and pink, but his mouth is obscured with a thick oxygen mask, his hair is all wet and pasted to his head, an angry line of blue stitches running from forehead to ear. And his left eye, the side they operated on, is puffed closed and red, like he got punched.

I hope he will forgive me for letting this happen to him.

I hope that, someday, I can explain to him why they took half his brain, and that he'll understand. That he'll be smart enough to understand.

That there might actually *be* a someday.

For a moment, I pause, gathering my strength. He moves, a simple lifting of the blankets. I rush to him and without thinking, reach beneath the sheet for his hand. My fingers touch tape and tubing and I slow down, not wanting to disrupt the IV. Still, I stand on my tippy toes and lean over to look into his face.

"Corbin?" I whisper. "Corbin? Mommy's here."

His eye—the one not swollen—opens, and trains on me. He struggles briefly, then settles again.

I squeeze his fingers and hold my breath. Is he in there? Does he know me?

They squeeze back.

ABOUT THE AUTHOR

Eternal optimist Harper Barrow is a veterinarian and mother by day, writer and roller derby player by night. Her non-fiction articles have been featured in numerous local publications and she also writes regularly about her trials of being the mother of a disabled child on her blog, which has been featured on scarymommy.com. Her fiction won third place in the NYC Midnight Short Story Contest, second place in the Rocky Mountain Fiction Writers Colorado Gold Contest and was published most recently in *Krampus Tales: A Killer Anthology*. She received her undergraduate and graduate degrees at Colorado State University and currently lives, works, and plays near Denver, Colorado.

WHITE FOX AND THE WATER WOMAN

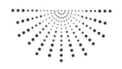

GWYNNE STANKER

Ozarks, Pitcher Mountain, ca. 1890

The early March sun streamed in through the church windows, flooding the altar with sunlight. Hobart looked away from his bride and at Ida Jane only once during the ceremony. She felt his eyes, imploring, upon her face. She refused to look back, to give him the satisfaction. She stayed only as long as was proper, listening to the traitor say his "I do's."

As he kissed the heart-shaped lips of the woman he didn't love, Ida Jane got a shock—the woman was pregnant. Ida Jane knew, she could see the signs. She wasn't in training with Maddy to become a midwife for nothing. All the signs were there, for one who knew how to look. Hobart had sown his seed between the thighs of another, while Ida Jane, fool that she was, had been saving herself for him.

Hobart made a handsome groom: tall, straight-backed, with dark, deep-set eyes, a head of lush, black hair, and the beginnings of an equally lush beard. Ida Jane felt as if the Devil's hands were squeezing her heart. How she had loved him… But now all she felt was a dark chasm the size of Goresham Gulch open in her heart. How could her fool of a heart go on beating, split in two as it now was? She wished it would stop beating altogether, so the pain would go away.

As well-wishers surrounded the happy couple, Ida Jane left, circling around to the back of the little white clapboard church. Ripping off her Sunday-best shoes, (though it was a Saturday) she slung them into the bushes. She hated the shoes. She hated Hobart. She hated herself, so easily played the fool. At first, as she climbed, the calluses on the soles of her usually bare feet welcomed the rough stones, the twisted roots, and, finally, the thick carpet of pine needles. Out of habit, she pinched into a bubble of pine sap oozing down the nearest trunk, and rubbed the aromatic goo into her hair before realizing it was what she always did before meeting up with Hobart. She flushed, snatched her hand back, but it was too late, the scent would cling to her for hours, maybe even days, almost waterproof yet invisible, like a terrible shame she could not shed.

She should go home, change out of her good dress, but, instead, she stepped up her pace, heedless of the branches that grabbed at her clothing and long, dark hair. She stumbled, at last, onto the footpath that wound up to the lake—best fishing in Suther County. The path was well-trodden, and would make for easier going. No one would be there today. They would all be partaking of the wedding breakfast. She would not be missed. Upon this thought, she began to run, each bare footfall thudding out a word only she could hear: *Fool! Fool!*

When she could run uphill no longer, she walked until she recovered, and then ran again, pushing herself. It was mid-day when she came to the small lake. As she had expected, no one was there. She stopped at the water's edge and bent over, her hand against a tree trunk, huffing in great breaths. The mountain air was crystalline, almost bubbly in her lungs, but she did not notice this. In a few minutes, her breathing steadied, her heartbeat slowed. She experienced thirst, but did not drink. Her hair was in disarray, sweaty and itchy. Her beautiful Sunday-best dress, *White! It's white, you fool!* was ripped and stained. She tore it off her body, ripping it to shreds, until it lay in a ragged heap around her feet, which were now bleeding from the small cuts and bruises of her long, uphill run.

She stared, not moving, into the still, dark surface of the water. By some trick of the noonday light, she could not see her own reflection, and she felt as insubstantial as a ghost, as if she were not there at all. She shed her underclothes and walked into the water. It was shockingly cold, reminding her that she was not a ghost at all, just a stupid, jilted woman. She walked deeper into the water until just her head was above the glassy surface, her toes barely touching the muddy bottom. She breathed upon the surface of the water, breathing out all the dead hopes and dreams of the life she had thought she would have, breathed out the man she had thought loved her, the home they would have had together, the children whose faces, even now, she could clearly see; breathed out and out until her mind was blank and her lungs were empty.

Then she lifted her knees and let herself slip under. She could feel her hair spreading out above her on the surface of the water. One of her last thoughts was that everyone knew of her shame. Broken heart? Or broken pride? The two felt like the same thing to her. She sucked in a lungful of water. It tasted icy, brackish. Let her die, then. She released herself to the darkness and sank.

Her body betrayed her. It kicked violently, struggled toward the light, the air. She resisted, sank again. Then she felt a strong hand under her armpit, another gripping her hair. It hurt. Her head broke the surface, she coughed, gagged in a mouthful of air and water. Her hair was released. Someone dog-paddled beside her, pulling her toward the shore, but she fought instinctively. *Let me go. I hate you, I hate you, I want to die.* Then she was face down on the stony shore, someone pushing against her shoulder blades, the water gushing out of her mouth, her nose, the water streaming away from her eyes. She began to shiver, violent spasms that shook her body. Hands lifted her—strong hands, these were a man's hands—and carried her up the sloping embankment, sat her on a bed of dead pine needles, wrapped a shirt, his shirt? around her, held her shoulders until the gagging and shudders subsided.

She was naked. She didn't care. Her eyes cleared and, she looked up into a man's dark face. He had kind eyes, eyes that pretended not to notice her nakedness. He was a young man, but not as young as she. She glanced around. Discarded upon the stones lay a fishing pole and, close by, a single boot, followed by another dropped closer to the water's edge. She looked back at him again. The man had dark hair, hair as long as hers—wet now from the water—braided down his back. She thought about the fishing pole. He had assumed no one would be here, had somehow known about the wedding celebration. No Pahocsie would come here if the whites might be here, since the ownership of the pond was disputed.

She realized she knew this man, Stephen Duran, and had, in fact, been in his cabin some six months ago. Word had come across the mountain from the town of Pahocsie that an Indian man was asking for help, his wife was ill, about to give birth, he expected difficulty. The Pitcher Holler midwife, Maddy, Ida Jane's mentor, had refused to go. "I don't birth no Injuns," she'd stated flatly. Ida Jane had looked at the woman in astonishment. What difference did that make? So, Ida Jane, a midwife in training, had gone herself. It had been a sad day. Ida Jane had seen right away the wife would not survive the birth, her eyes already dulling before the babe was even out. Ida Jane had tried as hard as she could to save the child, a boy, but it had been stillborn.

The man's grief had been terrible. She had left him to it, untying Momma's mule from the front porch post and riding it bareback, down around the mountain and up the other side again, to Pitcher Holler. Distraught that she hadn't been able to save even the child, she had refused to accept any payment—these were her first deaths. The man told her that his wife had "the sickness that eats from the inside." Much later, Ida Jane had found out that Stephen Duran was a much-respected medicine man by both the other Pahocsie and the whites of that town, no small feat, widespread prejudice against the Indians being what it was. Stephen Duran must have tried everything he knew, and then had swallowed his pride and asked the whites for help. How he must have loved them, his poor lost wife and their doomed, baby son.

Though Ida Jane knew that, had Maddy been there, she could have done no more than Ida Jane had done, and though she still continued to help Maddy and learn from her, Ida Jane had never looked up to Maddy again in the same way as before.

And now, her own dress torn to shreds, Ida Jane was wearing Stephen Duran's plaid shirt. The faint scent of his body rose about her. He had walked a few feet away from her and now sat on the shoreline, putting on his boots. They were thick-soled logging boots like her father had worn.

"You must go home," he said. He stood up, walked back to her, looked around. "Where are your shoes?" He spoke perfect, unaccented English. How had she not noticed this when they had met before? This man had spent time in the white man's schools.

She shook her head, refusing to get up. "I have no shoes. I have no home."

His wet dungarees made a rustling sound as he squatted down beside her, his brown chest catching the sunlight as it filtered through the trees.

Stephen Duran studied her face. "You have suffered a loss," he said at last. She did not respond, but, ashamed, could not meet his eyes. "But, you are young," he continued, "there will be other loves for you, children, even. You must go home, now."

She shook her head, "Not so much younger than you," she rallied, and then, "I shall not marry."

"Young," he repeated. "White man's childhood lasts forever. It is different for us." As he rose to leave, he pulled her to her feet.

This time she looked into his eyes. "How did you do it? Go on living, I mean, after … ?"

He was silent. "There are others, those I can still help." He turned to go.

"Please," she said.

He kept on walking, "You are not one of them. Go home where you belong."

"Please don't go."

He did not turn around. "You don't mean that. You will hate yourself tomorrow and be ashamed that you spoke to me in such a way."

"Please," she said again. "I will take no husband. I want to know what it is like."

He kept walking, "I am not the one for you. You know this."

"I could not save them, your wife and son, but I tried, you know I tried." She paused, "You owe me."

His shoulders tensed. He stopped walking, turned toward her, "I have saved your life."

"I didn't ask for that," she said.

"I do not ask for this," he replied.

"Take your shirt, then," she said, shucking the shirt over her head. Naked and carrying his shirt, she closed the distance between them. Gone were the violent shivers that had seized her from before. Her body flushed with heat. She stepped in so close to him that he could not help but feel the heat, smell the pine sap still clinging to her wet hair. He allowed himself to notice her nakedness. She saw the hunger spark in his eyes.

"They will shoot me," he said.

She dropped his shirt to the ground, "They will never know."

"You desire this?"

She nodded.

"You must say it." His voice was guttural.

"I desire it," she said, and he pushed her roughly against a tree trunk. She felt the bark abrade the skin on her back, but in her passion, she did not care.

———

Something happened to White Fox when he placed his hands on her waist, something he did not expect. His two hands seemed to melt into her flesh, and he experienced a connection between his groin and his heart that he had not felt before, not even with poor, lost Little Basket, for, until this moment, he had felt desire for no woman since Little Basket's death. That this feeling should come now—with this strange white woman with her sad eyes and broken heart—astonished him. As he moved within her, the melting heat between them persisted, building to a crescendo when their two cries exploded into the still air, causing a flock of birds to spring from the treetops above with a loud flapping of wings.

He pulled away from her, and without a word, the woman walked away from him, down the stony shore and into the dark water until it came up past her waist. He had no fear for her, for this time she went to bathe. She whirled around three times, her arms upraised, her hair whipping behind her in a circle, water droplets flying into the air and catching the sunlight, then disappearing back into the pool. For one instant, as he watched her, time stood still for White Fox, and he had the deep realization that all we ever really have is the moment we are in—and that certain moments choose us, altering the cells of our hearts, and living on there in our heart's memory for as long as we draw breath.

He watched, immobile, as the woman emerged from the pool, the water sheeting off her too-white breasts and too-white thighs. She turned and walked away from him and up the stony shoreline to where the shreds of a white garment lay. She used the rags to dry herself, then walked back to him, smiled, and took up his discarded shirt and put it on, buttoning it down below her thighs. She and he were as easy with one another as if they had known each other for years. It was then that he confessed to her that when he had first come upon her in the center of the pond, her dark hair floating above her in the water, her pale limbs flashing below, he had been afraid, thinking she was a water spirit surfacing to lure him to his death. And, together, they laughed about this. In some way that he still could not understand, this woman had freed him, and he found himself wishing to give her something in return.

"I wish you to live, Su nis` ki wa," he said. "There will be many people for you to help. You will find your right path. You know my English name. Now, I will give you my secret, Indian name, so that you will know that you are a person of importance and that your life matters."

"Why are you calling me this 'Su nis` ki wa?'" she asked, her tongue stumbling over the unfamiliar syllables. Of course, he would have known her real name from before.

"It means Water Woman." He thought it unlikely that they would ever meet again. As he walked away from her into the trees, he said over his shoulder, "I am called White Fox. Tell no one."

The mule was harnessed to the wagon and Momma stood in front of it, peering up at Ida Jane, who held the reins. Momma had on her dark traveling dress, her gray hair sticking out from the sides of her bonnet, a carpetbag in her hand. She had a stubborn expression on her face. All Ida Jane could think was that Momma looked so tiny and frail Ida Jane could blow her over with a good sneeze.

"You can't come, Momma, you're not well, and I got to take care of Aunt Meldie, she's dying."

"So am I. And would you leave your own dear momma to die alone?"

Ida Jane fidgeted on the buckboard seat while the mule stamped a foot, then lowered its head. It could stand there forever while they argued. "I think you got a few good years left in you, Momma." Ida Jane tossed her long, dark hair, "And I got to go," she said flatly.

"Me and Meldie never got on, but she's my sister, Ida Jane, and you can't birth that young'un alone."

There was a moment of shocked silence. "How'd you know, Momma?"

"You think I don't know my own daughter? And besides, I'm the one does the laundry. Think I don't know when certain things ain't happening? What'd you do, Ida Jane? What'd you do?" Under her breath she muttered, "Always was headstrong, always was."

Ida Jane said nothing, her chin in the air, but Momma knew when she had won. She stepped around the mule and came forward to the side of the buckboard, threw her carpetbag into the wagon and climbed up beside Ida Jane. It took her a moment, and she kept on talking, "Why, time was, Hobart Smith would have shot anybody laid a hand on you."

"Those times are done, Momma. He's married to Edie Barrows now."

Momma snorted. "Fool of a man. Edie's a weak little milksop, can't hold a candle to my Ida Jane."

Ida Jane smiled, "I'm glad you're coming, Momma. This ain't any of it going to be easy."

"We'll figure it out, Babycakes," Momma said, patting Ida Jane's knee.

"Giddy up." Ida Jane snapped the reins, and the mule woke up and started forward.

T hat Ida Jane and White Fox would meet each other on the street was inevitable. But it didn't happen in Pahocsie as Ida Jane had feared. It happened one day after Aunt Meldie died, and Ida Jane was just too sad to stay in the cabin alone. Momma had to go down to

Barney's Four Corners, so Ida Jane went with her. They went on a Sunday, just before sunset, when they knew no Pitcher Holler folk were likely to be there. Barney wasn't religious. He kept his store open seven days a week. Momma was still in the store when Ida Jane stepped off the low, wooden boardwalk that fronted Barney's, and, her arms full of groceries, she stumbled and nearly fell. White Fox appeared out of nowhere to catch her arm and steady her.

White Fox was surprised, too. He didn't plan it exactly, but one day he'd seen her in Pahocsie, and, being curious, he made it a point from then on to know where she was. He'd gone down to Barney's to trade half his winter's cache of smoked venison for ammunition for his rifle, though he still preferred hunting the old way with bow and arrow— why announce your kill to the world?—when she stumbled and he caught her. Their eyes met. They did not speak or acknowledge one another in any way. Such acknowledgment would have endangered her and the child, of whom he could not have helped being aware, for she was heavily pregnant.

When Ida Jane looked up at White Fox, she had the sensation that, since she'd come to Pahocsie, he had never been far away, though when she looked outside her aunt's cabin into the woods or around the only street Pahocsie had, she never saw anyone. "I'm so sorry," she said out of habit. He merely nodded. A chance encounter, she thought, looking around. They were alone on the boardwalk. No one was there to see. Their eyes met again for a split second, and then they walked past each other.

Ida Jane had still made no decisions about what to do with the child, but not long after her visit to Barney's, Momma helped Ida Jane birth the babe. It was more difficult than Ida Jane would have thought, but they managed. When she saw the child, all decisions were made for her. He was a healthy boy, dark-skinned, dark-haired, dark-eyed—he looked Indian. She could see no part of herself in him. She did not name him.

"Ida Jane, you're not going to give away my only grandchild!" Momma wailed.

"He ain't ours to keep, Momma. He belongs with his people."

"We're his people, too."

"Besides, he ain't your only. MayReatha's got a bunch."

"She keeps them hid away in Cameron country where I don't hardly ever see them."

"And Bobby Jo's got five."

"They're down to Fort Suther. Don't get to see them, neither."

"Momma, they're likely to shoot him and me, both. Is that what you want?"

———

W hen she had recovered from the birth and was strong enough, she took the babe, which she suckled herself, and walked up the mountain until she reached the small, dark fishing pond where he had been conceived. She found the pond as still and beautiful as before. She would go each day at noon, wait for an hour, and then begin the long walk back down to Pahocsie. If she encountered fishermen, which happened occasionally, she would turn back, but this happened less and less often. It was late fall, and snowy in the upper reaches. Even as her own shadow would hit the crust of ice on the water, the fish, sluggish and dark, would sink away to the muddy bottom. She shivered, thinking that, were it not for White Fox, she would be sleeping down there among them.

Ida Jane always sat on the Pitcher Holler side of the pond, letting her mind go still, listening to the sounds of the water rippling on the shore, the pine needles rustling in the wind. He came on her fifth visit, fishing pole in hand, as he had the first time, from the Pahocsie side of the pond. He stopped when he saw her. His face was expressionless.

"White Fox," she said.

"Water Woman."

"Would you like to see your son?" She held the infant out to him.

"My wife died of the sickness that eats from the inside," he said. "My son died with her. I have no sons."

She said nothing for a moment, then, "I would think, by now,

White Fox would have other loves, other children, even," repeating his words to her from the first time they had met.

"All of that died with Little Basket," he said. There was a note of finality in his voice.

She nodded, understanding, only too well, how he felt. Some losses could not be filled.

He came around the pond, leaned his fishing pole against a nearby tree trunk, and stood in front of her.

Ida Jane was not a small woman, was even considered tall by the standards of her village, but he dwarfed her, with massive shoulders and strong arms and hands, hands that had once pulled her from the water. She had to look up to see his face, yet, as before, she was not afraid.

Her arms were starting to tremble, for, as they had talked, she had continued to hold the infant out to him. He did not take it, but peered curiously at its face. "Looks Indian," he said, without a trace of irony in his voice. "What's his name?"

She said nothing at first, uncertain of his intention, but pulled the child in close to her. Then, "He waits for both of his names, his English one and his Indian one."

"He is half-white," White Fox said.

"He doesn't look it," she answered, "and he will have no kind of life in Pitcher Holler. You know how they treat Indians." She hesitated, "And those who consort with them."

He said nothing to this, only continued to peer at the child who had large dark eyes that appeared to look solemnly into his own. The infant had not made a sound since the woman had arrived.

"Do you desire this child?" Ida Jane said at last, again echoing his words from before and pushing the infant against White Fox's chest. She would have sworn he wore the same plaid shirt he had worn the day she met him, except that she had worn that one home, to curious looks from the villagers in Pitcher Holler. There had been talk—rumors—but she had refused to speak of that day to anyone, till now. She had not cared what they had thought. Now, she must care, for the sake of the child.

At last, White Fox nodded and held out his arms.

"You must say it," she said, and now her voice trembled.

He lifted his eyes from the infant and studied her face. She was unable to conceal her feelings, yet was determined to look into his eyes. He had seen her heart break once before. He was seeing it, again. To draw this out would only hurt her further. "I desire him," he said and took the child from her.

She dropped her eyes and moved a step back from him, not looking at the babe.

"How do you wish him to be named?" he asked her.

She thought for a moment. "John," she said. It had been her father's name. "How will you explain him to your people?"

"I will not explain. They will not dare to question the great medicine man White Fox. I might turn them into a turtle."

He smiled at her, and she thought again how much she liked this man, but she was unable to return his smile. There were no smiles in her on this day.

His face grew serious. "You cannot change your mind, Ida Jane Wallace, and come back for him." It was the first time he had ever used her real name, and he said the next harsh words almost without inflection, "It will be as if he is dead to you."

"Yes, White Fox," she said, addressing him by his Indian name, "it will be as if he is dead to me, and that is what I will tell Maddy, the only one, besides Momma, who knows of him, yet I will know he is where he belongs." She watched as White Fox, cradling the child in one arm, bent and retrieved his fishing pole and then walked around the far side of the pond and entered the woods.

As before, at the last instant he looked back at her. "His true name shall be Little Fish," he said, "until he can choose one for himself." He disappeared into the trees.

She waited until she could no longer hear the sounds of his passage, until the sounds of the forest resumed, bird calls, pine branches moving in the icy breeze. And then, from the depths of the woods, she heard the infant cry. It pierced her heart, causing her insides to contract and the milk to spring from her breasts to wet the front of her long-sleeved, high-necked blouse. She fell to the ground, rolled onto her side, both arms around her belly, and rocked back and forth, causing brown leaves to adhere to her woolen jacket, her mouth open in a silent "O" of pain. She curled inward, her long skirt hiding her boots. Her dark hair, which had been drawn into a bun at the base of her neck, came free in her struggle and tangled about her face and shoulders. She lay there for a long time, as the light left the sky, the wind dropped, the trees grew quiet and the frozen pond went black behind her. Finally, when there was no more light and no more sound, she got to her hands and knees and stayed there for a few moments, staring down at the dark earth. Then she got to her feet, cleaned her face and hands in the cold water, gathered her hair back into a bun and, finding the well-worn path by instinct, started down the mountain toward Pitcher Holler. Only after she had been walking for some time, for she had to go slowly in the dark, did she become aware of the limp in her gait, as if she had not recovered from a recent injury. And try as she might, she could not seem to lose it.

Many years later, in the late autumn when all the trees that had leaves were bare of them, and when Ida Jane and White Fox were both old and no one cared if they spoke to each other or what they said, she saw him sitting on the edge of the wooden boardwalk that fronted the general store and trading post known as Barney's Four Corners. Ida Jane was white-headed and bent over her cane, so that she walked with two thumps from her boots followed almost simultaneously by the tap of her cane. Thump, thump, tap. Thump, thump, tap.

He sat on the edge of the boardwalk, clutching a blanket about him for warmth, his long gray braid hanging down his back. Ida Jane, in her granny dress and bonnet and grasping her shawl about her shoulders, thumped over and, with some difficulty, lowered herself down right next to him, the sole of her boot just inches from the sole of his boot.

He did not turn toward her. "I see you, Water Woman," he said.

"You can't see me, White Fox, you're blind."

He sniffed. "I know you by your scent. You still smell like new-cut pine."

"More like dead pine needles," she said, with some asperity. "And you smell skunky."

He laughed outright, and his face came alive. "You did not think I smelled skunky on that day."

She cackled in glee, then sobered, "How is John, our Little Fish, did he thrive?" Over the long years, she had heard stories, had glimpsed the boy several times from a distance, but, true to her word, had not sought him out. She would have been nothing more than a strange white woman to him.

He said nothing for so long she feared he might not answer, but then, "He did, and he married a white woman and had two children, Nicholas and Ava. But our blood is strong. They both look Indian—though it seems we Pahocsie are trying our damndest to breed ourselves into extinction. There are almost no pure-bloods left."

So, she had grandchildren. Ida Jane was ridiculously happy to know this, but before she could ask after them, he interrupted her. "I must tell you that John died in a logging accident not long after his white woman left us and went down mountain."

Ida Jane did not expect this, and it hit her hard, first, like a blow to the heart, then to her insides—but it was not the man, John, she grieved, for she had never known him—it was the lost infant. She had never expected she would feel such pain again, had not, in fact, known her body still harbored it. In one second, seventy years collapsed away from her as she felt again what her body had never forgotten, her insides constricting, her aged breasts stinging as if with the milk the infant would never suckle, and the feeling, for the third time in her life, that she wanted to die, *Please let me die, I want to die.* He heard her deep inhalation and her cane striking the edge of the wooden porch as she released it, one hand flying to her mouth, the other to her heart. As before, she made no sound but bent over and suffered in silence. He did not resume talking until her breathing returned to normal. It took a while.

Finally, she spoke as if nothing at all had just happened, although her voice was hoarse, "You still speak English so perfect, better than I do."

"White man's awful school. They took me away from my parents —I cried for many nights—and they cut off all my hair, but I have grown it long again. Ava has attended the little school in Pitcher Holler, you have, perhaps, seen her. And Nicholas attended the college in Fort Suther. His mother is an anthropology professor there. It is a different world, now, than the one we knew."

How much, how very much she liked this man, "In today's world, we might have had a life together, White Fox."

He chuckled, a deep sound he made in his throat, "But we did have a life together, Water Woman. You whites, you think time is measured in minutes and hours, months and years. It is not. Time is measured in the heart."

"In the heart," she repeated, and he felt, then, the faintest touch of the edge of her boot on the edge of his boot.

He did not draw his foot away, but inclined his head toward her, "Have you had a good life?"

"I've been respected," she said, "I ain't sure I've been loved."

"It is good to be respected. And you have been loved, Water Woman."

He heard the sharp intake of her breath and then felt the wood give and then rise a little as she stood, felt the small wind of her skirts as she turned, and heard the thump of her cane as she stepped back up onto the wooden porch. He thought he heard her murmur something as she thumped away from him. It sounded like, "In the heart...in the heart."

As it happened, though Ida Jane was the younger, White Fox would outlive her. Mourners at her newly dug grave were mystified to discover, laid carefully upon the dark mound, a twig, its ends bound into the shape of a heart; and from this heart-shaped twig dangled a single turquoise carved into the shape of a little fish.

ABOUT THE AUTHOR

From the jungles and savannahs of Africa to the backwoods of the Ozarks, Gwynne Stanker's characters find themselves smack on the border of that no-man's-land where races and cultures intersect—often violently—but where, sometimes, just sometimes, they find their common humanity. She writes in the mainstream and historical genres, but always with an element of fantasy, because she finds the real world to be a magical place. She has taken top honors in her genre in a major writing contest.

FRESH STARTS

LILY LAPIN

vom·i·to·ri·um
/ˌvämə'tôrēəm/

Noun
1.
Each of a series of entrance or exit passages in an ancient Roman
amphitheater or theater.
2.
A place in which, according to popular misconception, the ancient
Romans are supposed to have vomited during feasts to make room for
more food.

Lexico Powered by Oxford

This essay concerns itself with the word vomitorium as it has been
misconstrued.

In 1971, when I had graduated from high school in a small town
eleven miles south of Philadelphia, I distinctly did not move to
New York City. Rather, I planned to loop around it, taking a temporary
detour. Averting my eyes to shield them from the city's blinding glare,
I considered New England instead. It simply seemed less daunting.

Growing up, I'd had a few flings with New York, like a girl playing
at house or baking in an Easy-Bake oven, mimicking motherhood.
When I was thirteen, my mother took my brother and me there for a
week. We stayed at the Plaza, like the character in the *Eloise* story. My
mother later said she spent the money she'd brought to last for the
entire trip on the first day. We went downtown to the Village, where I
bought a pair of railroad-striped, hip-hugger, bellbottom jeans. In my
new jeans, I walked ahead of my mother and brother—I was a cool
local girl—only to turn to find they'd disappeared around a corner,

engaged in debate about going to the then-landmark FAO Schwartz toy store. Cool girl, not so much. I had no idea where I was.

When I was fourteen, I met a bunch of New York and North Jersey Jewish kids at summer camp. Al-the-Waiter—from Flushing, he was a camp waiter, hence the name—developed a crush on me. He'd offer me extra potato latkes and tuck socialist literature into my sleeping bag on the bottom bunk. I hung with the MaLarky sisters: one, a counselor-in-training, was a year older; one, a camper like me, was a year younger; me, sandwiched in the middle. When I visited Al in ninth grade, we all met up in the city and sneaked into a Simon and Garfunkel concert at Lincoln Center. Climbing the steps to the very back of the concert hall as the duo started to sing *The Sound of Silence,* we were so far away their heads appeared dime-sized. It didn't matter. They were magnificent.

New York.

But, moving there on my own?

No way.

Still, I didn't want to get stuck too close to home. I wanted something new and challenging, just not *too.* My godmother—a free spirit—offered me a ride to Boston. I piled my stuff into her white, black-topped, convertible mustang and we were off. It broke my mother's heart.

Boston.

Boston turned into a twelve-year detour, I waitressed at multiple muffin shops—I grew increasingly blasé about muffins—while dragging myself through a fine arts degree, realizing it had been a waste, then returning to school to study commercial art, which was more practical.

This was pre-computer. Our tools were X-Acto knives and wax.

I fell in love, failed at love, slept around, fell in love again, and emerged at twenty-six as a married woman, with a moderately successful commercial art career and a low-level cocaine habit.

By the time my then-husband dragged me out of Boston—confessing years later, only after our divorce was finalized, that he'd initially moved to escape the addiction—I was cresting thirty.

We deposited ourselves in an annoyingly suburban Connecticut town *seven-tenths* of a mile—I clocked it—from my in-laws, who despised me. As the feeling assumed mutuality, I came out of the closet as a full-blown agoraphobic.

Still, I was that much closer to New York City. The city was slowly reeling me in, clarifying its intention to become my destiny. A formidable force, New York has a way of doing that. You can only deny it for so long.

If I could just get myself out the front door…

After much in-front-of-the-mirror self-persuasion, repeated before each outing—I gained not a shred of reliable confidence—I'd set out for the city. Drive to the downtown Connecticut train station, timidly park obscurely in remote parking, and, shaking the whole way, walk to catch the train into Grand Central on 42nd Street. Once there, the further I walked away from the station—I could not work up the nerve to descend below to the subway platform—the more I shed the skin of Suburban Commuter and embraced the guise of Native New Yorker.

I was set on trying to get a show. All these years after art school, where I'd barely hung on, my work had come into its own, in the forms of 3-D collages and dioramas. Trudging around the city, I'd take my slides from gallery to gallery.

They laughed at me or I was snubbed.

I wasn't sure which was worse.

After fruitless encounters, I'd flee east on 42nd street—before I turned back into a country pumpkin—to Grand Central, back to Podunk, Connecticut. Once there, like a crab, I'd scuttle to my car, soon to be hitting the garage door opener and entering the cave-like sanctuary of my boring, suburban home. There I'd routinely hyperventilate in the dark before emerging from the car and barricading myself inside the house.

One trip back, I'll never forget. It was a turning point. Summer. Hot. I was walking east on 42nd, toward the station, behind a tall stiletto-heeled woman. White mini suit, Tina Turner hair, hip-swinging, long-legged runway stride—I can never wear white. Stains are magnetically drawn to me as to a blank canvas, and white doesn't flatter the dull shade of my teeth.

Abruptly, she stopped. I did too, hesitant to pass her. Expertly, she turned her head to the right and vomited, daintily wiping her mouth with a hanky she deftly pulled from her bag.

I'd never seen a person vomit so artfully. It was like a cartoon vomit scene. The vomit arced from her mouth, cleared her ensemble, and, in one mass, landed softly on the sidewalk, like a baby being tucked in.

And I'd never seen vomit so pristine: white, or maybe ivory, shaped like fluffy cumulus clouds. When *I* throw up, there is always the sad visual of my latest meals mixed together in a fashion that is just wrong. What had this woman been eating? Nectar of the gods, a slice of Heaven?

Perfect vomit, spit up in perfect form, by a Native New Yorker.

"Are you okay?" I called out as I ran toward her.

She did not turn or answer, as if I had opened my mouth but no sound had escaped. She'd barely paused and, now, she was in full strut again, not rushing, just heading east. And I was left, alone, beside her expertly placed white pile of vomit.

That's when I got it. The moment she stepped away, it was no longer she who'd puked. As for me, as long as I stood there, I was assuming the responsibility of *her* vomit.

It took me a few minutes to let it sink in. It was so surreal, I wondered if it had even happened.

Then I started walking east. Soon, it was as if I'd never even been there.

———

When the train arrived back in Connecticut, I started out to the remote parking lot where I'd stashed my car. The heat beat down. There was no sound, no one around. Probably, folks were sheltered inside, hiding from the oppressive summer day. As I passed the first dusty, unpaved parking lot, the interior of a parked car spontaneously burst into flame.

Odd.

Pre-cell phone, as I walked, I looked about. No pay phone in sight. Nobody yelling "Fire!"

I could scream and no one would hear me.

I did not break my stride. I did not look back.

The further away I got, the less connected I became to the event.

I never did hear the car explode.

That day I knew. Next trip in, like a Native New Yorker, I'd make the descent into the bowels of the New York City subway system.

After three years of suffering insufferable in-laws—we'd lived *seven-tenths* of a mile away. Remember, *I'd clocked it.* Even my own parents had finally refused to socialize with them—we left Connecticut. I can still remember the rush I felt as I swung onto the Fort Lee Hudson Terrace exit after crossing the George Washington Bridge, my four cats and two rabbits tucked into my car.

Hoboken, New Jersey.

Just like I pictured it. I've never felt prouder than when I attached my Jersey plates.

And at this point, New York City and me, well we were neighbors.

My marriage didn't last long after that. But moving to New Jersey was the beginning of the rest of my life.

ABOUT THE AUTHOR

Lily Lapin is a visual artist and writer. During a commercial art career in the NYC fashion hosiery business, she discovered the art of train writing on her long commutes under the Hudson River. Her work addresses the strange, sad, complex, and funny. She makes intricate collages and dioramas that often include altered toys. To free herself from the limitations of space that art objects occupy, she also writes fantastical stories and odd personal essays. She currently lives in Colorado where fantasy inspires, as well as Zooming with her North Jersey Write Group cohorts to fine-tune her craft.

NO SERVICE

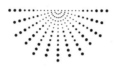

T. R. KERBY

S weat ran down Craig's ribs, and his muscles tightened into cables as he hung beneath the overhang by his fingertips. One more massive effort and he'd be over. He flinched as his phone jangled in his pocket, splitting the epic silence. Now was *not* the time to take a call. The only thing between him and a very unpleasant fall was a precarious grip barely wide enough for three fingers. It beeped once, telling him a voicemail would be waiting when he summited the face.

He heaved upward and hooked an arm over the ledge. Jagged granite claimed some flesh as he dragged himself up. He lay on his back, panting, staring into a flawless sky, blue as a lake. One of his life's goals achieved. Climbing the most difficult face of the most coveted peak in the Rocky Mountain chain. And he did it solo. The grin made his cheeks hurt. He certainly didn't *feel* like a dying man.

He stood up and unhooked the ropes and harness, letting them fall to the ground. His small backpack joined them at his feet. The view stretched for hundreds of miles in every direction. Snow lurked in the shadowy crevices and melted into rivulets that trickled among the boulders. Green and yellow lichen clung desperately to the rocks.

He turned in a slow circle, taking in the expanse of peaks surrounding him. The ridge beckoned, so he followed it to the north, jumping from boulder to boulder. No evidence of any other humans existed. He could be the last man on earth.

The air warmed as he dipped into a low depression, out of reach of the wind. Sunshine warmed his shoulders and insects buzzed around him. Crystal water bounced among the rocks and disappeared toward the edge. This must be the source of the misty fall visible from his camp last night. The water led him west toward the lowering sun.

The canyon narrowed and the walls climbed over his head until it finally spit him out onto a flattened granite slab the size of a bus. He peered over the edge. One more step, and it could all be over. He could spare his wife and daughter the misery of the coming months.

"Must be bad for you to think about jumping."

The voice jolted him, and he scrambled to keep his footing, lurching away from the precipice. "Jesus!"

"No, but I'm flattered." The mountaineer chewed the end of his pipe and squinted into the brilliant sky. "Was Jesus a climber, I wonder? He did have that sermon on the mount." A black beard framed his round face, and a mustache underlined a crooked nose. A moth-eaten cap perched at an angle on his head.

"You scared me to death!"

The mountaineer shrugged. "Seems that's where you're headed, anyway."

"Who are you?"

"Beaumont." He held out a massive hand. They shook.

"I didn't see you there."

Beaumont perched on a rock and leaned against the cliff face. His brown woolen shirt tucked neatly into pants that ended just below his knees. Heavy socks bridged the gap between calf and hobnailed boots. Coils of rope and an ice axe lay next to the rock beside a simple bedroll. He twirled and untwirled the chain of an open pocket watch around his fingers. "Been here the whole time." He patted the rock.

Craig sat next to him. "How'd you get here?"

"Climbed. Same as you."

"With that gear?" Craig snorted. "Man, I haven't seen gear like that except in old photos."

"There have definitely been some upgrades, but this worked well enough."

Craig glanced at the watch face. Delicate hands lay on a white field ringed with thin Roman numerals. It read two o'clock. A jagged crack stretched across the glass. "Your watch is broken."

"What makes a young man like you want to jump to his death?"

"What makes you think I want to?"

"I've seen the look before. So what is it?"

Adenocarcinoma. Ugly word for an ugly condition. "Cancer."

"Ah." The watch chain whirled. "How long did they say?"

"A year at most."

"So you thought you'd take a short cut."

"I don't want to die, but I also don't want my wife and daughter to watch me waste away."

"How old is your daughter?"

"Five." The sunlight struck the fall foliage in the valleys below and the colors blazed to life, orange, red, yellow, gold. "I'd give anything to stay right here, forever. Breathe this air. Look at those trees. Count clouds."

"Wouldn't you miss your family?" Beaumont turned the watch in his hand. A dove in flight was engraved on the back. It appeared there had been other things once, but the lines were worn away. "You should go to them. They'll want this time with you."

"I can't put them through this. My insurance will take care of them. They'll be okay."

"Is it them you're really worried about, or yourself?"

"I won't lie. It's scary as hell. How could this happen? I take care of my body. Exercise. Eat right. Pisses me off." He scrubbed his palms across his face. "If I was alone, I could face it. No one else would suffer."

Beaumont stared into the distance. "There are less messy ways than throwing yourself into the rocks. What if you *could* spend the rest of your days here, as you say you'd like?"

"What do you mean?"

"I've been on this ledge since 1905."

Craig laughed. "Good one."

Beaumont wasn't laughing.

"Holy crap. You're serious? You need some psych therapy."

Beaumont held up the watch. "I found this right here on this rock. A folded note was stuck under it, but I couldn't make out many of the words. Only *danger*, *open*, and *birds*. Made no sense to me at the time. The watch was beautiful, so I picked it up and opened it. Read two o'clock, same as it does now. Closed it to put in my pocket and this happened." He snapped the gold cover shut.

The screeching sounded like the brakes of a freight train bearing down on them. The whooshing of wings like the wind, pushed before speeding engines. Dust kicked up in mini tornados and stung against his face. "What is that?" Craig shielded his eyes from the debris.

Beaumont took hold of his wrist. "When they come, don't run.

They're attracted to movement. They can scream in your face, but they can't touch you."

The mountaineer was a nut case. Beaumont held fast as Craig tried to tug his arm free. "Let go, you lunatic!"

Beaumont tipped his head toward the precipice. "Take a look."

A flock of impossible creatures hovered at the lip of stone. Craig scuttled closer to the cliff at his back.

"Steady, now," Beaumont said.

The largest of the beasts shrieked, baring a mouthful of pointed teeth. Her gaze locked on the mountaineer with quick little jerks of her head. The facial features were almost human, but not quite. Muscular arms supported a massive fan of black feathers, the sky showing through where a few were missing. Her fingers ended in obsidian claws that would put a grizzly's to shame. Ribs laddered the torso and pendulous breasts swung in defeat with every wing stroke. Her legs dangled, talons replacing toes.

Craig found himself clinging to Beaumont's bicep.

"Those, my dear man," Beaumont said, "are harpies."

"It's a hallucination. They aren't real."

"They are quite real, I assure you. And very angry at me for sitting here so long without letting them eat me." He held up the watch. "It keeps them at bay. As long as I hold it, they can't harm me." He flipped the cover open and the harpies screeched, then flew away in a flurry of feathers and wind.

Craig inhaled. "Good god."

"The watch has kept me immortal and comfortable on this ledge. I don't get cold, hot, or hungry, although I miss the experience of food. The view is unbeatable, and the solitude beyond compare. Don't ask me how it works. I don't know."

"Why not take it with you and climb down?"

Beaumont smiled. "There's the rub, you see. You can't. Once you open it, you're bound by its magic. You cannot leave the mountain. Cannot descend below timberline. Cannot jump to your death. You simply exist here, in limbo."

"What happens when you try?"

"There are barriers. Invisible walls. Impenetrable. I've tried."

"And if you toss the watch?"

Beaumont gestured into the abyss. "A date with those lovely ladies would be my guess. I've not cared to test the theory."

"You've really been here over a hundred years?"

The mountaineer nodded. "It's beautiful, but I'm tired. I don't know what's next, but it's time to find out." He looked across the expanse of mountain ranges. "If you want immortality and freedom from your disease without splattering yourself all over, I'll give you the watch."

Craig stared at the timepiece in the mountaineer's outstretched hand. Sunlight rimmed the edges with fiery gold and made the white face glow. The Roman numerals whispered. Encouraging him to stop time, stop the progression of his own mortality, end the fear and confusion. All he had to do was take it.

"If you don't open it," Beaumont said, "you can still walk away. Go home to your family and face your demons together. Keep that in mind." He snapped the cover closed. Shrieks and wind filled the air as he put the watch on the stone between them and walked away with a deliberation born of over a century of introspection.

Hammering wings blocked the sun and beat around Craig's shoulders. He rolled into a fetal position and covered his head. The stench of rotten flesh filled the air, and then everything stopped. Silence wrapped around him. He peered through the lashes of one eye. No monsters in sight. He lowered his arms and uncurled his body.

Beaumont was gone. One torn boot stood alone in the middle of the ledge, like a monument.

Craig walked to the precipice and peered over. A single black feather drifted down, rocked by a gentle breeze. He turned to the watch waiting on the boulder. It was warm in his hand, inviting. The dove on the surface peaceful in flight. It conjured memories of his daughter chasing pigeons in the park, squealing with delight as they flew around her, feathers falling like snowflakes. She wouldn't remember much about her dad, only the pictures and stories her mother shared. That was better than hours spent in hospitals with pinging devices and the antiseptic silence that no child should have to endure.

His wife was beautiful and smart. She would have another love, another father for their child. His insurance would ensure she didn't have financial worries.

And he wouldn't have to die. Waste away to a shrunken shadow of his former self. Live his last days in agony hooked to a tangle of tubes and wires.

The watch was a win-win solution. He flipped open the face. Pristine, crack-free glass covered the delicate hands and Roman numerals. Two o'clock. He wrapped the chain around his fingers and leaned against the warm rock as a molten sunset lit the peaks.

He remembered the voice mail left as he'd hung a body length below the summit. He dug the device from his pocket. *No Service* scrolled across the top of the screen. Didn't matter now. The time for calls was past. He punched opened the voicemail and held the phone to his ear. His wife's musical voice filled his head.

Craig, honey. Oh my god! You have to call me right away. The lab mixed up your results. The tumor is benign. Come home so we can celebrate. We love you so much!

His gaze fell to the watch in his hand. The harpy engraved on the back was laughing.

ABOUT THE AUTHOR

T. R. Kerby has led a life of high adventure and travel to exotic places… Ok, not so much, but she has worn a lot of hats. She has been a fry cook, a trail guide, a horse trainer, and a veterinary technician as well as other less interesting things. Her weaknesses include chocolate and rescuing lost souls, mostly animals, but sometimes people. She currently lives in the Rocky Mountains with some of her rescues including her husband, two dogs, and a herd of horses. She brings her varied life experiences to the table in her books and short stories.

DEATH FOUND YOU

BILL MAY

Death found you.
A squirrel in the road,
A pet, even a plant,
Some friend or kin.

Endings were everywhere.
You felt empty.
Naught. Nil. Never.
A void: Nothing.

But Something persists.
It's all around you.
Perhaps it's hidden now,
But you can find it.

Look—a downed tree nursing new life:
Moss and mushrooms and saplings.
New growth in the sunlight
Freed by the fallen giant.

Look around—
Birds, ants, buzzing things,
Ferns and flowers and fruits.
They're allies.

Look everywhere.
Movement beneath the water.
Beauty and bounty in the garden.
All connected.

Look inside. See who you are.
Your body, an inheritance.
Your mind, responding, growing.
Who you are becomes your legacy.

Bound together.
Created and creating.
Transformations, not endings.
Life and Death and Life.

Death does not stand alone.
Neither do you.

ABOUT THE AUTHOR

Bill May lives in Oregon with his wife, Nan, and their two poodles. He enjoys wine, horseback riding, playing online poker with his grandsons, and exchanging political humor with his three daughters. Before retiring, Bill got paid to have fun teaching literature and creative writing. Unfortunately, his teaching career left him with a relentless inner critic. Occasionally he's able to shut it up long enough to complete short stories and poems. "Death Found You" is his first published work of poetry.

SCARS

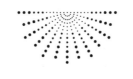

LAURA MAHAL

M iriam Montague had not ceased talking as she drove from Seville toward Cadiz. Señor Mata insisted they stop in El Puerto de Santa María for tapas and drinks. El Puerto was the very place for sherry and bullfights, oracles, and narrow escapes. It just so happened to have a bar that was Romero Mata's querencia. His sanctuary of retreat.

"Do you eat the Seville oranges? I imagine they must be as sour as they are small."

Old man Romero Mata remained silent, alternately stuffing his mouth with bread layered with tomatoes and olive oil and thin-sliced mojama—salt-cured tuna with Marcona almonds.

Miriam picked up a square of marzipan, then set it down, eyeing it with distaste. She wiped her fingers on a napkin as whitewashed as the houses they'd passed in the Spanish countryside. She spat words as if he'd forced her to touch the slick sweet. "Why don't you give up your hobbies, Señor Mata?"

Mata was entertained by Miriam's vicious rubbing. "Na. I'm too young for that."

The evening light cast an orange glow to everything in the room... dust on lampshades and bottles of vintage Spanish wine. Photos in tarnished silver frames behind the bar. One of the photos was of Romero as a much younger man, impossible to recognize without a great deal of brandy and a squinty-eyed evaluation. He raised his tumbler of fresh-squeezed juice in a salute. It would be easier to see through a whiskey and soda than this glass of juice, orange-tinged like the dust that hid forty or more years of memory and history. Sweet juice, when what was needed was something strong and bitter. A man's drink.

He finished the juice and pushed the glass toward the bartender, who gave a slight shake of his head. The reporter must have paid well. The newspaper she worked for told her to get the story. Deny Señor Mata his drinks, if necessary.

Romero's voice was fiercer than he'd intended, grumpy even. "Damn if I am going to sit around on the front porch."

She'd driven her fancy Renault from the Right Bank of Paris to the southern tip of Spain, and knew not a single thing about the attractions of Seville orange trees and their fruits. Mme. Montague had not done her research. The Moorish poets had understood ever so much more than she. But, likely, they hadn't been quite so beautiful, either. Youth and beauty covered a multitude of sins—as did the lilac and verbena scent of her French perfume.

Miriam paused, unsure. She started to explain. "I didn't—"

Romero Mata wasn't in the mood to listen. "Hell, I can always find something to do. Why should I tip-toe around life?"

He prodded and she retreated, lifting her blouse to let in the breeze. Miriam wore yellow—the color of Seville. Her waist was small, yet she lacked the grace of a flamenco dancer. She was a reporter, there to do a job. Not a woman at all, but a pen and a pencil in a short skirt.

The old man's voice became commanding. It penetrated the café—his café, some might say—and slid up her blouse. "Brandy." She blanched and nodded, beckoning to the bartender. This time, the bartender scurried to fetch Romero's brandy. He was both a regular and a legend. Some customers left pesetas on the bar, for the sole purpose of buying the old matador a drink. For luck, they might say. Or in honor of Mata's father, who was a legend in his own way.

The drink lingered at Romero's chest, where he held it. Miriam kept her eyes fixed on the slender stem between his fingers.

"Do you remember your father?"

When Romero spoke, his voice was husky, and his eyes distant. If the reporter was worth her salt, she would recognize when a man had the look of a veteran about him, one who had been to war or who had lived through it. In which case, she should know that one brandy would not be enough to buy that memory.

"My father worked for a furniture maker before he went into the mortuary trade. Father provided for us. My mother chopped liver fine and mixed it with cornmeal mush. She poured it in pans and let it harden, then sliced and fried it."

The reporter, who had peppered him with questions all day, now reached for a different choice of sweet, a local favorite called turrón blando, every bit as popular as las tejas del Puerto but stickier. Finding it no more to her taste than the marzipan, she mutely wiped honey residue from her hands, weaving the cloth napkin in and out of her fingers like a peace flag.

Her slippery fingers made him remember war. Cleaning rifles with rags that had never been as white as the cloth napkins of the café. Rags that might be used to sop up blood as readily as they polished a bolt-action Mauser. "The place was beautiful until the mortars redecorated."

This girl was too young to understand, sitting with her head cocked like a dove.

"I cannot hear from this ear." He pointed.

Old man Mata stared out the window. The orange-red ball of sunset was gone. The air was pungent with the smell of bergamot. He sat, like a walled churchyard, and ordered another drink from the boy who swept beneath the tables.

Two dogs entered the café. A stout bulldog and a curly, black Portuguese puppy. The bartender shooed the dogs out with the boy's broom and a string of colorful curses. The puppy wet the floor. The bulldog paused to sniff the door frame and then lay down by the entrance.

Miriam demanded, as petulantly as a child, "Show me your scars. You will, won't you?"

Romero was spared answering when the bartender brought yet another brandy. The old man decided that he would not lower his trousers for her. This journalist could arouse a young toreador and get her way. He was not so impressionable.

After some time, he said, "Yes. I will show you." His voice hinted at seduction, if there was such a thing left in his ancient body. "I will show you."

She hurriedly paid for their drinks. In Euros, noted Romero. He dropped a handful of pesetas on the floor for the cleaning boy to sweep up. Then, he felt badly for making extra work. Romero slipped the boy a cigar and patted him on the head affectionately. The boy had once beaten the old man quite badly in a game of checkers. Romero remembered such things.

They stepped over the dogs, which lay just outside the open door of the café. Tanned boys ran by, shouting and waving sticks, and the puppy leapt up to join the youthful parade. The bulldog remained motionless. It glanced at the old man. Romero tapped his leg, and the dog followed, close at his heels.

Miriam's voice was a little breathless.

"Do you keep a place here? I thought you stayed in Seville. Someone told me you once lived in Key West, and spent a year in Las Vegas. That you had an American lover."

The bulldog darted in front of her and Miriam had to sidestep, nearly colliding with a woman who carried a stack of Bisque tiles. Romero watched while the women argued, retrieving the keys to his apartment from deep in his trousers' pocket. The dog said nothing.

Once she had recovered the civility of her tongue, Miriam caught up to him. "Did you live here as a boy? Did the American woman ever stay with you? What was her name and how did the two of you meet?"

He led her through a carved door, not far from an elderly woman who made the sign of the devil in their direction. Whether this was intended for the reporter from Montmartre, or him, was of no concern to Romero. He passed through a curtain of wooden beads that advertised the name of a drink he had once favored. He ducked as if to avoid her questions. The French girl didn't care about his scars. They were old news. *What had he promised to show her?* Something.

"Come in," he said in the general direction of her Seville yellow blouse, before disappearing into another room.

The reporter followed him, the bulldog not far behind. She sat on the edge of a small divan, ankles crossed. The bulldog glared at her, strands of saliva dripping from his jowls.

Romero came back quickly to find that Miriam had tucked her legs underneath her. As he handed her a thick book, he said, "You may look. My father is in there." White corners showed where the leather had worn away. She sat upright to take it from him, turning her head to sneeze as she opened it.

"That is him?"

"Yes."

"And your mother?"

"Yes."

"And you?"

"No." He paused. "That was my brother."

"What happened to him?"

"War."

Romero reached across her lap without sitting and turned the page. The dog took that as an invitation, it seemed, and hopped up to circle three times, then lay sprawled upon the divan.

"My father, with his tools." An unsmiling man stood next to a lathe. He was perhaps unaware of the camera, or uninterested.

"What is he making?"

"A flute. For my cousin, Isabella. She still plays. My father was very good. There was no need for her to buy another."

"And this, your mother?"

"Yes. As I said, Mother made the corn mush. My cousin Isabella makes it, too. Isabella is an exceptional cook. She has outlived three husbands and, even now, someone asks to marry her."

Miriam was ready to turn the page. She was looking for scars, not woodwind instruments. Romero had forgotten why she had come.

He sat, and the bulldog shifted position. The dog allowed just enough space for them to hold the edges of the album; Romero on one side, Miriam on the other. Dog and memories in-between.

"What happened to them?"

"Mother died in childbirth. The baby was turned inside her. My baby sister, Adoncia, was saved but then died of influenza before entering school."

"That was a waste."

Romero snapped the book closed. The bulldog, startled, growled at Miriam.

"I'm sorry, Señor Mata. I shouldn't have said that."

He stood and left the room.

From the kitchen, he could hear her pacing, restless. Maybe even rubbing her hands, planning something devious, leaving the bulldog in a state of suspicion.

Romero came back, wine glass in hand. "For you, Mademoiselle Montague."

She took the glass, but remained standing. Miriam met his eyes. "I'm sorry. I didn't mean to be disrespectful of your mother or your sister."

Old man Mata did not answer, but stooped to stroke the dog. Muscles at the back of the matador's neck flexed. Despite his age, he had the strong shoulders of a younger man, and though it had been some decades since a woman had looked at him this way, he could feel her eyes upon him. One never forgot what it was to be thirty-five or even forty. And she, not more than twenty-five, if that. She, who knew hardly anything of life as yet.

Romero took his time to stand. Not because anything ached. Her awkwardness amused him. She stood rigid as a soldier.

Miriam Montague spoke in a rush, eager for forgiveness. "What about your father? Shall we talk about him?"

He went back to the kitchen without replying, returning with a gin and tonic for himself. Possibly, she preferred gin to Spanish wine but, if so, she did not say this. He sat once more on the divan and patted the dog, which nestled against him. The spot where Romero sat was warm. He liked to think Miriam had accomplished this with her curvaceous backside.

Romero answered her, as if nothing had gone amiss between them. "He made coffins during the war."

She made a small sound, like "Oh" with her mouth in a tight ring. She looked remarkably like a fish, despite her small waist and large breasts. For a moment, the old man thought of his bed in the next room. Until he remembered the photo album he'd put on the nightstand.

The only sound was that of the fan that cooled the room.

Miriam excused herself and found her way to the toilet. When she returned, her lipstick newly pink like a city schoolgirl's, she found a gin and tonic in place of her untouched wine.

"I'm sorry," she said. Romero looked at her—really looked at her —for the first time.

The dog snorted in its sleep. Romero pushed it off the divan. She sat in its place. Their shoulders would touch if she leaned in, and she did. She held her gin and tonic and asked, "What happened to him?"

"He made coffins during the War."

"I remember. You told me. Was there something more?"

Romero remembered that she had come a long way. He should ask her if she wanted to lie down, but not now. Miriam was drinking the gin much too quickly.

He was an old man, yet he felt her shoulder through the blouse. The material was coarse, quite thick for the season. This surprised him. She was French. He thought she would wear something finer.

"Yes, there was something more, though that was enough. Wouldn't you agree?"

Miriam nodded, her chin tipping down so that he noticed the part in her hair. He didn't remember what they had eaten earlier in the day, but she clearly had had mustard with her meal. Romero could smell it on her fingers, and a dab was there, where she had pressed down on her part. It matched her yellow blouse.

He took her under the chin and kissed her, watching her eyes bulge in disbelief. "Yes, definitely a fish," Romero said out loud, before he kissed her again. Miriam fluttered her arms in protest, as Señor Mata, a national hero of Spain, stood without any sign of a stoop. Straight and tall, Romero unbuckled his belt and dropped his trousers to the floor.

Anyone could see where he had been gored, repeatedly.

Her keenness to touch his gashes was unrestrained. Miriam seemed to have forgotten he was an old man she was here to interview. Romero Mata stood still while she worked his scars with hands that smelled of mustard, soft from the marzipan and the turrón blando.

The fledgling reporter was too young for lapses of memory, yet she had forgotten about his father. His mother, his sister. His brother who died in the war. Mortars that changed the landscape; he'd called it redecorating. Later, she might recall that, but for now Miriam was caught in something more powerful than she could resist—the lust of those who follow bullfighting. She wasn't the first woman who had fallen prey to Romero's scars. She began to unbutton her blouse.

The old man stood as still as if he'd died in that spot.

He watched her hands, fingers busy with tiny blue buttons. He watched Miriam remove the blouse entirely.

He wanted to ask if she knew she was wearing the colors of Seville. *Al Bero*, also the name of the bullfighting ring. But she wouldn't know. Just as she didn't know of the bitter oranges of Andalusia.

The very young and attractive Miriam Montague removed her skirt, her bra, her panties. She dropped them on the floor next to the bulldog. She then took the man she called Señor Mata by the hand and led him to his own bed, where she lay draped across the afghan like a poster boys passed around the battlefield. She pouted a little as he hesitated, her full lips splayed like a fish. He remembered she'd come all the way from Montmartre, and must be tired.

Romero picked up the album from the nightstand, cradling it in his hands near to his chest where, earlier, he had held his brandy. He bowed extravagantly as he exited the room.

"Bonsoir, Mademoiselle."

The old man paused by the bulldog, corkscrew-tail motionless, its eyes following Romero's movements. The dog sniffed the woman's underthings without interest and then rolled over, tummy to the ceiling. The matador's thoughts were elsewhere.

He remembered a girl who had worked at a bar in Key West. Winona. Winona Simone. Her name was beautiful, though she was not. It was reputed that Winona was the only one to turn down the offer to sleep with Ernest Hemingway, who had favored the bar on Duval Street.

Romero had met him, once. Hemingway. They had talked about Spain. Spoken about bullfighting, of course. Ironically, the famous American writer had gone back to Spain at exactly the time that Romero Mata had moved to Key West to take care of his elderly father, Amando.

Romero had liked Winona enough to stop drinking when she asked him to. Not with words, but with a glance, a slight lift of her clefted chin. Winona was flat-chested and feisty. Sometimes she was a blonde. Sometimes a brunette. She lived by her own music.

When he finally asked her to come home with him, Winona had hesitated.

"Is there anything I need to know about you, first, Señor Romero?"

"What do you mean?" he had asked. "Please, call me Romero. Otherwise, you make me feel as if I am years and years older than you. I don't think the age between us is so great, is it?"

Winona had ignored his suave mannerisms and cut to the chase. "Do you live with anyone?"

He was surprised he remembered this so clearly, when at least forty or more years had passed since he had last stepped into Sloppy Joe's. The photo album was still clutched to his chest. Romero set it on the divan, then leaned down to stroke the bulldog's spotted belly. Memories surrounded the old man, and the dog leaned contentedly into Romero's hand.

"Yes." Romero had told her, his voice soft. "I live with my father. He is Señor Mata, and I, only Romero. But you won't see him. He doesn't speak anymore. My father is too far gone."

Winona had taken Romero by the hand and they had left the bar together, walking down Duval Street like any other couple out on a Saturday night. They'd gone to his house. Winona had pointed at the draped Spanish moss by a discreet motel, but he'd shaken his head, clutching her hand tightly. Their hands were damp from the humidity.

She, he could ask questions of.

"Did you know the Indians used the moss to make loincloths?"

Winona shook her head, quiet as they approached his front door. Perhaps she was younger than he had first thought.

His father looked out the window. Winona waved before Romero could stop her. Señor Amando Mata waved back, then disappeared.

When they unlocked the door, Romero's father stood in the foyer, his dressing gown open, the ties hanging loose at his sides. Garish flamenco dancers encircled his shoulders, the French flannel faded from numerous washings. Señor Mata was old and prone to soil himself. Yet he reached for Winona, and she went without a moment's hesitation.

She went straight to his father's arms, and Romero's cheeks worked in silent misery. Winona would never come back to his house, and he could no longer go to Sloppy Joe's to drink. It was an ending that smelled of old man and lost time. Spanish moss draped over a tree to kill it, as surely as his old man would kill what Romero had hoped to start with this bar girl.

Except, Winona was made of stiffer stuff. She had surprised Romero, taking his father by the crook of one arm, reaching to pull him close by her other side. She drew them both into his house as if she knew her way. She found the kitchen and promptly buttered some toast. Expertly spreading jam to reach each corner. Winona's precision was that of Romero's mother. Señor Amando Mata sat upright at the table, a handkerchief across his lap, awaiting the midnight snack.

"Can I get you something else?" she asked Señor Mata, who declined his head genteelly.

Romero spoke to her as he helped his father to stand. "Wait for me. We will get him settled, and then we will go upstairs." But Señor Mata shook his head theatrically, indicating he wished to stay. In fact, he pointed at his son and said, quite clearly, "¡Siéntate!" Romero had stumbled around the heavy table to take his seat.

Winona had turned to the sink, full of dishes. Some of the food had dried for several days. Yet, she hadn't chastised Romero. She didn't speak to him as she tidied the place, engaging his father in conversation. Señor Amando Mata mumbled long answers, some almost intelligible.

Romero's heart thumped, and he leaned against the back of his chair, eyes closed. He could smell the clean smell of dish soap and the sweet odor of boysenberry jam. Winona's bright light had reached dark places in the room, and his father was sitting straight, noticing. Romero could feel the warmth of Winona and Amando's interaction. It was the longest, best hour of Romero's life when Winona and Señor Mata laughed together.

Together, Romero and the bar girl, oh, that lovely girl with the

musical laugh, put Señor Mata to bed. The old man went, meekly, so
very tired. Not just from eating bread and jam. Romero was aware that
he and his father's dark corners had gone undusted for too long.

After Señor Mata was tucked in, with a kiss on his forehead from
both Romero and Winona, Winona followed Romero down the hall. He
pulled her and she tugged back, laughing like a child who wants ten
more minutes at the park. Winona came to Romero in his bed. He
clutched her, tears overflowing the banks he had long ago dismantled.

"My father was a tremendous man," Romero told her. She lay on
her side, propped on an elbow. Winona kept her hands to herself while
he let the tears flow. Neither wiped them away.

"He built coffins during the Great War."

She rolled toward him, onto her stomach, her lovely fair skin like a
beach that beckoned. Romero reached to stroke her spine and she
rolled again, onto her back. He lightly touched her small, perfect
breasts until she fixed his fluttering hands into place.

"How did he manage that?" Winona asked, her voice as soft as her
skin. "How did he keep his sanity?"

Romero inhaled her scent of boysenberry and the bar, which
lingered like a stiff drink. Not an oversweet margarita. He pressed his
lips to her skin and they refrained from talking for several minutes.
When he spoke, Romero's words were muffled.

"He didn't. Amando buried my mother, Belén, my sister, Adoncia,
and made coffins for the soldiers that never came home. My father
built coffins for everyone else's sons. He made each one as beautiful as
if it would house Philippe. They never found my brother Philippe's
body and my father slowly went mad."

Winona twirled a curl idly around her finger while she rested her
head on Romero's chest. "But you stayed with him. You are a good
son. He is happy, now." The bar girl sounded convincing. Romero
wanted Winona to keep talking. To never, ever stop.

"You made your choices and you kept on living, didn't you?
Whether you took your chances in the bullring or on the battlefield,
you chose to live. That's what your family would have wanted, your
mother, your brother, your sister. Your father must have understood

why you lived on the edge. I thought the stories were exaggerated. I didn't know much about you."

Winona would have kept twirling her finger except he had to hold her, tighter. Romero reached her hand to his thigh. Eventually, every girl was scared away. He didn't want to wait.

"I've told everyone I was gored. You must have heard that?"

She nodded, not moving her hand.

"Do you believe me?"

Winona kept her hand in place on his thigh but reached the other to Romero's lips. "Tell me in your own words, then I'll tell you if I believe you."

"I was in my twenties. The bull caught me and I went down into the dust. The Toro kept coming back. The crowd was cheering for him, you know. They were rooting for El Toro to win." Winona said nothing, her arms stretched wide, four fingers on his scar, four fingers on his lips. Her breasts were open to him, open like the sea. As inviting as the sea. Romero didn't want to make up stories anymore. He wanted to swim in her. To let her waves cascade over his body.

"Do you believe me?" He wasn't going to say he'd been bayonetted in street fights, an angry young man who wasn't agile enough to earn his name as a proper bullfighter.

She rolled onto her back before she answered.

"I believe it would be tough to take care of a broken parent when you were only a boy. You earned your scars, Romero, and it doesn't matter how you got them. You may tell whatever stories you wish. I see your father is well-cared for. Though you need someone to come in and do your dishes and help with the laundry. I could come on my nights off. I'd be happy to spend time with Señor Mata. You don't have to be here with us. He and I get along just fine."

Romero lay there for a moment before he asked if she wanted to go for a midnight swim.

In the morning, when he went to make Winona a cup of coffee, Romero found his father in the hallway. The old man was slumped over, an album in his hands. The picture of Amando's younger self posed, next to a lathe, opposite the photo of his wife, Belén, preparing a pan of corn mush. Winona came from the bedroom and found them both. Son crying. Father frozen in time.

She brought a tea towel in which to wrap the album.

"You won't want to look at it anytime soon, but you must promise me you will save it, for the day you want to open it again."

She brought a washbasin and a towel from the linen closet and gently bathed the old man. Romero watched Winona do everything. He couldn't speak.

She went into Señor Mata's bedroom and returned with a pressed suit and a pair of pajamas with matadors on them. "Which one?" she asked Romero.

He pointed. She dressed his father in the faded pajamas, very lovingly, as if Señor Mata were her father, too.

When everything was done, Winona touched Romero's arm.

"You know where to find me. I'm going to come back on Wednesday and clean the house. Leave a key under the mat if you will be out. I'll make a meal and leave it on the table."

She hesitated for a moment.

"I believe you have been gored."

Romero looked up at her, confused. She was too bright; she could not be thus mistaken. His reputation extended only as far as the bars, where elderly men drank, and legends were born, and lies were served along with toast and marzipan.

"There is no wound greater than love lost," Winona said.

"Spare no expense on his coffin, Romero. But if you want your scars to go away, you'd best build it by hand. Build it for Philippe, for Adoncia, Belén and Amando. Build it for yourself, and bury each and every one of your regrets."

Romero, who the world now remembered as Señor Mata, an accomplished matador, looked back into his bedroom and saw the French girl, who had come from Montmartre to ask him about his wounds. Miriam was young, drunk, and softly snoring.

The old man quietly closed the bedroom door. No one would ever see his scars again.

ABOUT THE AUTHOR

Laura Mahal hopes that the ghost of Ernest Hemingway will forgive her for traipsing into his hallowed territory. She often writes literary fiction, attempts comedy on occasion, and routinely slips in speculative themes. Her work appears in a wide range of publications, from *Fish in Ireland* to *Veterans' Voices*, *Still Coming Home*, *The Blue Mountain Review*, *OyeDrum*, *Across the Margin*, *Chiaroscuro*, *Encore*, and *DoveTales*. Laura recently won a national essay contest for Women on Writing, is currently editing a novel for Lighthouse Writers Book Project, and is generally trying to stay out of trouble, except for "good trouble," of course.

MEMORIES

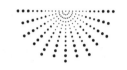

C. S. SIMPSON

It's early morning in the high New Mexican desert. The cool, crisp air burns my lungs as I run southward along the wide, paved path, listening only to the pounding of my feet on the pavement and my rapid breathing. I don't enjoy running most of the time; I prefer to walk briskly instead. But today, running is just what I need to get a grip on myself. The sun hasn't yet crested over the Sandia Mountains, making for an ideal winter morning workout. I still have twenty minutes before I should be back home to get ready for the coming day. Plenty of time.

These daybreak getaways feel like the only time I get to myself anymore, apart from quiet car rides brought to me by the technological miracle of smartphones. The commuter traffic on Tramway Boulevard is picking up, and several other runners and cyclists have joined me on the path. The northeast corner of Albuquerque was mostly undeveloped when I was a kid, and now it's full of homes and businesses. The city has changed a lot in the last forty years.

I guess everything does.

I'm a desert rat. I was raised that way by my dad, who could never get enough of this desolate-looking place. I know people who've moved here for work and have nothing but contempt for the frequent dust storms that sandblast their houses and windshields. I have a colleague from tree-lined Pennsylvania who calls this place "The Face of the Moon." It may not be a bad physical comparison to the naked eye, yet I wholly disagree. The moon is a gray, lifeless, stagnant rock, whereas the New Mexican desert is full of various flowering cacti, piñon pines, roadrunners, lizards, rabbits, bobcats, coyotes, and the ever-moving salmon-tinged land I call home.

Reaching Academy Road, I turn around and run back toward home. According to my Fitbit, it's 7:36 a.m. The light of dawn reaches through the high canyons made by the sheer rock walls of the Sandias, bathing portions of the shaded western slope in striped shafts of brilliant sunlight. The steel cables of the hanging Sandia Peak Tramway glint in the early morning sunlight, looking like thick strands of spider silk. Snow still nestled deep in the cracks and crevices of the mountain reminds me of the growing spider veins on my legs.

Middle age has been kind to me thus far, but I know it won't always be so. Some disease or sickness will find me someday too.

My precious father, the man who helped me fall in love with the desert, died five days ago from early onset Parkinson's. His decline was slow at first, the simple tremors more bothersome than troublesome. The doctors gave him drugs and dietary suggestions, and he followed their directions to the letter. Then, his medication just stopped working. The experts don't know why. The muscle tremors grew until his body shook violently, making the strong man I'd known my entire life weep bitterly his last few months.

It changed him before it took him.

He's only been gone for a few days, but I already know I'll miss him like crazy for the rest of my life. My mother's been strong so far. She panicked for a while, back when he was first diagnosed, so by the time he could no longer swallow and was hallucinating, she'd already resigned herself to being a widow.

I've not yet made that kind of emotional journey. I'm still working on it. Who am I, if not my daddy's little girl? Yes, I'm an adult, a wife, a mother, and a bank officer, but I was daddy's girl first. This defined me all through elementary school, got me teased in middle school, and won me the jealous stink eye throughout high school. My peers just couldn't understand my close connection to my father.

I'm not sure I do either. It's as if he and I were twins, born a generation apart. Strange, I know, yet that's how I've always felt.

Now that he's gone, I feel the need to dive deeper into myself, to see who I really am without his constant love and support to hold me up. My experience with being an only child wasn't the suffocating presence I'd heard other kids talk about in school. Maybe I needed that extra parental attention—I don't know. Maybe the twinned feeling thing with my dad was so powerful that no amount of parental attention and control could faze me.

Reaching my neighborhood entrance, I turn and slow to a fast walk, wheezing like an asthmatic. I'm getting old, for sure. I need to cool down this last half mile to my house so I don't wake my boys with loud panting. Besides, it's all uphill from here into the foothills of my neighborhood and I'm already tired.

My father's funeral is set for five-thirty this evening, after school and many work hours, so most people can make it. I've agreed to stand up and share something, though I'm still not sure what that will be. How do you sum up a person's entire life with a few words? Hopes, dreams, accomplishments—they all seem so small and useless in the light of death.

Maybe I can talk about how close we were and how I'll miss him. But those are *normal* mourning words, right? My dad was better than normal. He was amazing. How can I possibly convey the depth of this new, massive black hole in my soul to friends and family?

As I reach my street, I see Mrs. Kirkpatrick wave as she exits her courtyard. Her ten-month-old cockapoo puppy coughs and strains at the end of a bright pink leash.

"Sorry to hear about your father, Cheryl," she calls out.

"Thank you. Me too." *How else should I answer?*

"Do you have time to chat?" The puppy yanks so hard in my direction that it sounds like it's choking. Mrs. Kirkpatrick doesn't seem to notice as she walks slowly toward me.

"No, sorry. I need to get the boys up and ready, then get over to my mom's. Another time?"

"Okay." Her face visibly droops, a sadness taking over her aged features. "See you later, then." She heads the other way with the manic puppy.

I continue walking around the curve of the street and wonder what she wants to talk to me about. We don't know each other very well, but she does go to church with my parents. Maybe she wants to ask me something about the funeral, or what kind of food my mom likes. Except, Mom's already buried in "sorry your husband died" casseroles.

There are no sidewalks in my neighborhood, and I suddenly snag my leg on an overlong spike from a Christmas cactus that's stretching into the narrow road.

"Damn ..." I mutter as I reach for the two-inch spine sticking out of my purple jogging pants. I hiss at the pain as it detaches from my flesh and fling it back at the offending plant. *That's what I get for not paying attention.* Apparently my thoughts are too absorbing this morning. "Stupid, stupid, stupid," I whisper to myself.

Back in the house, I head straight to the master bathroom. I can get my sons out of bed *after* a hot shower. I strip the sweaty clothes off of my still-cold body and slip into the steamy water. The penetrating warmth loosens my shoulders. I didn't realize that I've been so tense until now. But, of course I'm tense. My dad is dead.

I don't want him to be dead yet.

My sons haven't reached high school, and I know my father would've been a great help to both of them with their coming adolescent angst. He was a family therapist, and a damn good one. I never felt as if he were "analyzing" me or using his gift of reverse psychology to manipulate me. If he *did* practice those skills on me, I was wholly unaware. Like I said—he was a damn good therapist.

Was.

My tears fall fast, surprising me, and add the taste of salt to the shower water streaming down my face. I feel my facial features twist as I sink to the tile floor in a wet, naked heap of soapy pitifulness.

My father is a "was."

I won't ever be able to text him a funny meme, a close-up picture of a cactus flower, or call him just to hear his deep, smooth baritone. His voice has been a balm to my soul my entire life.

Never again.

I force myself to stand, finish my shower, and get dressed. I need to get the boys ready to go to Grandma's house. I told her we'd be there by ten o'clock, and we still haven't picked out our clothes for the funeral.

Damn funeral.

My youngest son, twelve-year-old Joshua, is already awake when I peek into his room. He blinks at me from under the covers.

"Hey, kid. Why don't you think about what you're going to wear tonight while you're getting dressed? You can lay it out on your bed before breakfast and I'll see if it's appropriate."

"Sure, Mom. Dad said goodbye earlier and woke me up." Josh rubs at his eyes, an unconscious pout forming around his mouth.

"Yeah, love is rough," I reply without any sympathy. I grin at him and Josh smiles back. "I'm gonna get your brother up too."

I leave his door jamb, head across the hall to my nearly fourteen-year-old's room, and knock before pushing open the door to his dark man-cave. "Blake? Blake, honey, it's time to get up."

A moan emanates from the far corner.

"Come on, son, you can do it. We told Grandma we'd be at her house in less than two hours."

Blake moans again, but sits up in bed anyway, his shadow of a body barely registering on my retinas.

"Can I turn on the light?"

"Sure," he mumbles.

I flip the switch and catch his squinting eyes. "I need you to pick out what you're going to wear tonight while you're getting dressed. Lay it out on your bed before breakfast and I'll see if it's a good choice."

Blake nods as he rubs his eyes too.

"Thank you." My dad was always polite to me, and I've kept the tradition with my kids. I'm stern when I need to be, but for the most part, these boys respond to good ol' positive reinforcement—which includes politeness.

Clothes for tonight. I haven't picked out my outfit yet, either. I wander back into my closet and stare. My clothes are organized according to color, and the black section is surprisingly large for someone living in the desert. What can I say? Black goes with everything.

As I thumb through the dark clothes, looking for inspiration, my mind turns to a hot day at Cliff's Amusement Park when I was in third grade. My mom was sick with a sinus infection, and Dad had wanted to get out of the house with me. Daddy Dates were treasured days, and when he asked what I wanted to do, Cliff's came to mind immediately. The day had warmed up into the high nineties, taking my dad by surprise. We were both hot, tired, and cranky after only an hour or two, and I was starting to lose it in line for the Galaxy roller coaster. I remember the look on his face as my tired, heat-addled mind reverted to stomping toddler antics. He was disappointed, yes, though the look was full of more pity than anger, somehow. I wonder what he was thinking?

I'll never get a chance to ask.

The sound of young men arguing in the kitchen behind me brings my mind back to the present with a jerk. *How long have I been standing here?*

I head to the kitchen to break up the argument, but by the time I round the corner, it's over. Boy tempers can flare and cool so quickly. I grab a granola bar from the pantry and fiddle with the packaging while I stare at my children. They're growing too fast. Where will *I* be when *they're* forty years old?

"Can we eat leftover pizza for breakfast?" Blake asks.

"Ooooo...me too," Josh calls out as he lunges for the open fridge door.

"Hey!" Blake reaches for the pizza box at the same time, throwing an elbow out at the last second to catch his little brother in the ribs.

"Owwwww! Mommmmm!"

"You can *both* have pizza, no need to bruise your brother."

"I didn't mean to," Blake mumbles.

"Of course you did," I say before he has a chance to argue. "Say you're sorry and let him pick the pieces he wants first."

"Sorry." Blake doesn't look or sound sorry, but I don't have the mental energy to make him say it again.

"Don't kill each other over pizza, boys." As soon as it comes out of my mouth, I regret it. I shouldn't be joking about death with my father's ashes only just cooling from the incinerator. They both shoot me a weird look—kind of like pain mixed with regret, fear, and even humor.

"Sorry," I mumble, then stuff the granola bar into my mouth.

We finish our respective breakfasts before I head back to their rooms to see the outfits they've laid out for the funeral. They've both chosen black slacks and shoes paired with different button-up long sleeve shirts; one is blue and the other is a dark gray. Perfect. Much better than their current basketball shorts and old T-shirts.

"Good job, guys. Please lay them carefully in the hang-up bag on my bed, then you can goof off. I still need to pick out my dress."

Back in my closet, I pick the shoes first. Being that it's January, I don't want to wear anything open-toed. I grab a pair of simple flats, and decide on a black pant suit instead of a dress. At the last minute, I choose a dark green blouse for a pop of color, and lay my choices on top of my boys' clothes in the garment bag. My husband, Max, will meet us at the church after work.

All packed for a depressing night.

I sigh, then zip up the bag and take it to the Ford Explorer parked in the garage, adding it next to the craft supplies I packed last night. Ten minutes to go. Good timing. "Come on, boys. Let's head to Grandma's," I call into the house from the cold garage entry.

The drive down Paseo Del Norte is silent as they stare down at their phones. Maybe they're making future plans with friends, or checking in with their latest game apps. Who knows? I usually prefer to see their faces in the rearview mirror instead of the tops of their sandy-colored heads. But, this morning, I don't really mind.

My thoughts are a raging river of random memories threatening to drown me from the inside.

My father is gone. I'll never again see his face, hear his deep baritone, or hike the foothills with him again. Every time I see my mother, I'll be reminded of the missing piece in our lives.

My chest is aching, pulsing in time with my heartbeat.

I remember riding the aerial tram to the top of the Sandias when the boys were little. All six of us stood on the south side of the nearly empty tram, looking out the long glass windows at the sandy desert ground rising to meet the rocky mountainside. Max was holding a three-year-old thumb-sucking Joshua in his arms, while five-year-old Blake clung to my leg. Blake wanted to act like a big boy and not show his fear, however my dad could sense the tension too. As I stroked my eldest's hair, my father sat cross-legged on the floor next to us. He didn't try to tell Blake that things were going to be alright, that the cables were strong and the tram was safe. He just sat there, looking out, waiting for Blake to take the bait. It wasn't a full minute before my son was sitting inside my father's folded legs, a perfect bucket seat for my little man. I watched them sit together. From their low perch, they were forced to look straight out, not down at the landscape fast dropping away from the rising tram. Blake was calm and content for the rest of the ride. My father knew what my son needed, and how to give it to him, without pointing it out for the rest of the passengers to scoff at.

So many wonderful memories.

What are we, but the memories we leave behind?

That's good. I should use that tonight.

My mental fog clears just in time to make the turn into my parents' neighborhood—I mean, my *mother's* neighborhood. *Damn.* This will take a long time, I fear.

I ring the doorbell, just in case she needs a moment to compose herself. I'm here to help her go pick up her husband's ashes from the funeral home, after all. What else would her mind be focused on today?

She opens the door wide with a sad-sounding admonition, "Oh honey, you don't have to ring the bell."

My mom steps out onto the porch to hug each of the boys tightly, silently, before turning to me. Her eyes are bloodshot. I should've insisted she stay the night with us after dinner yesterday. I know *I* wouldn't have wanted to be alone the night before a funeral. Still, she had insisted on being in her own bed for some reason. To each her own, I guess.

"Come on in, everybody. Someone brought me brownies, and I bet my grand-boys would each love a piece as a mid-morning snack."

Blake and Josh *whoop* and make a beeline for the kitchen while I smile at my sweet mother. "You're awesome, Mom."

"I know," she smiles wanly back, her eyes still sad.

We join the boys in the kitchen just as they're taking their first brownie bites. They smile at each other as they chew.

I sit on a barstool by the counter and decide to get to the point. "We're here to help. What can we do?"

My boys nod as they shovel the last of their brownie squares in their mouths.

"Well," she starts slowly, "the funeral home called first thing this morning and said the ashes are ready, so we don't have to wait until this afternoon to go pick them up."

I nod, hoping my silence will entice more information regarding how we can help her.

"And...I—I have those photos you asked for. I couldn't sleep last night, I just kept—kept thinking."

I know she doesn't want to break into sobs in front of the boys, so I stand up and ask, "Where are the pictures? I'll help you pick some out. We brought the poster board with us, and some craft supplies. The kids can make the memorial board for Grandpa while we're gone."

"Thank you, honey. I don't know what I'd do ..." She can't finish the sentence.

I follow her into Dad's office, where a few dozen photos of my father are scattered on the brown leather couch. Mom sniffs, and I turn just in time to open my arms for another hug. We stand there, both of us crying quietly now, arms wrapped tightly around each other.

Time passes. Our tears subside. Who knows how long we stand in that tight embrace?

She finally pulls back and sinks into the desk chair behind her, wiping at her face. "Good thing I haven't put any makeup on yet."

"Yeah." We each grab a tissue. I turn back to the photos spread out on the couch and reach out to touch the edge of an old, faded picture with all three of us in it.

I'm a toddler in a swimsuit, held high up on my father's bare chest so that our eyes are level, my mom close beside him. We're in my Aunt Betty's backyard, a shimmering swimming pool full of kids behind us. It was one of the dozens of weekend get-togethers with aunts, uncles, and cousins at Betty's when I was growing up. How my father adored those rowdy family Saturdays.

I turn my attention to another image, one of my parent's wedding day. So much joy and love seems to seep from the photo. My mother's bridal bouquet is drooping from the crook of her elbow, forgotten, her sole attention focused on my dad's grinning face looking down at hers.

I was a blessed child to have parents like these.

Another photo catches my attention. It was taken after my college graduation. Dad's standing tall in the middle of the photo, with my black-gowned self on one side and my same-clad future husband on the other. Dad is gripping us so tightly to his sides that we're bowing into him from the pressure. We're all smiling open-mouthed, probably laughing, as Mom snapped the shutter. They knew before I did that Max and I would be married within two years of that very day.

Once again, such joy.

There are snapshots of me, Max, Blake and Joshua, my father as a child, as a teen, and the most recent one of him playing basketball with my boys. Images of some of the happiest days in my father's life.

"These photos are perfect, Mom," I whisper. I turn back to her and sit on the floor, my back leaning against the couch scattered with memories. I sniffle before adding, "They show his love of life and other people. Such a great man."

My mother's face twists again, and she swallows a sob. Her chest heaves silently twice before she takes a shaky breath. Then her face clears, showing a calm I know she doesn't feel.

She's so strong.

"Let's go and get him now, hon. No need to make him wait for us any longer."

So macabre-sounding. I inhale deeply, hoping to capture some of her strength for myself, then stand and offer my hand. We walk back to the kitchen still clutching each other, and inform the boys that we're leaving soon.

"Will you both please empty the car before we leave, then hang up your clothes for tonight? Then you can get started on the board for Grandpa." I hand my key to Blake. "Grandma and I are going to freshen up before we go. And don't eat all the brownies, guys."

They give me ornery grins before mumbling, "Okay," at the same time as they head to the car to unload.

The drive to the funeral home is silent, the air thick with a strange dread. We're both thinking of what's about to happen. We're headed to retrieve a pewter urn filled with the ashes of a man we both loved desperately, but would never have the chance to see, touch, or hear again.

We arrive and I hop out of the driver's seat quickly to walk around the car, open my mother's door and offer my arm. She accepts my support quickly. The cold breath of early morning is gone, though there's still a chill in the light breeze.

We walk slowly into the funeral home together.

After giving our names and purpose, we sit on a flowered couch to wait, clutching hands. This is so hard to believe, even after months of watching my dad wither away in front of my eyes. He is really, truly gone.

A dark-skinned man in a blue-suit enters the lobby, carrying a dull silver urn respectfully in his hands. "Mrs. Moore?"

I'm frozen on the couch. My father is in there, what's left of him, anyway. I stare at the urn as it gets closer, not even seeing the man's face. There are three black lines recessed into the vessel, with my father's full name, birthday, and deathday engraved below them. Deathday? Is that a word? My mind is suddenly fuzzy.

This is it. This is final. This pretty little jar holds all that remains of my larger-than-life father.

My mom stands to accept the cremains, quietly saying, "Thank you."

I snap out of my mild horror and stand too. I look purposefully into the man's dark eyes, intentionally ignoring the silver container now. "Yes, thank you," I add.

My mother extends her arms for the offered urn, her hands steady. Mine? Not so much. I'm glad I'll be driving instead of holding him. Mom pulls the jar to her chest reverently and holds onto it as if it were a newborn babe. Silent tears pour down her cheeks as her emotions spill over again. She doesn't sob or scream—it's just tears.

"Thank you," I say to the man again, and reach out to shake his hand.

He takes my small hand in his two large paws and shakes them once. "I'm sorry for your loss."

Yes. He's sorry. Everyone's sorry.

So am I.

Mom and I head quietly back to her house, and I find I'm driving as if one of my boys were asleep in the backseat. I don't want to disturb the ashes, for some reason. I slow down more than usual for the turns and try not to make any sudden corrections. I wonder how my father-the-therapist would counsel us in this moment.

Grief is strange.

Back at Mom's place, we find the boys have indeed not eaten the entire plate of brownies. There are still two left. Again, I find I don't have the energy to point out the fact that they ate too many, since they followed my instructions to the letter. I wasn't clear enough. And I don't really want to get on to them today, of all days.

My mother disappears to her bedroom with Dad's ashes, and I check in on the memorial board progress on the living room coffee table. My sons have neatly fit all but three of the photos on the poster board, with the entire family represented.

"Whaddaya think, Mom?" Josh asks while I'm still leaning over their shoulders.

"I love it," I answer softly. My heart seizes a little, then continues on.

Blake points to a long blank spot in the center, saying, "We're gonna write his name here in big letters. What was his favorite color?"

"Believe it or not, he loved the color orange."

"Cool. I'll write it in orange, then." Blake picks out a dark orange marker from the box and proceeds to write carefully in big block letters, JOHN WILLIAM MOORE.

I sniff back another wave of emotion, and pat my boys lightly on the head. "Thanks, guys. Grandma really appreciates you putting this together for her, and I do too."

Josh spins on the carpet and grabs my hand. "Mom?"

"Yes?" I raise my eyebrows.

"Grandpa's really in that container Grandma was carrying?"

How to explain? I sink to the carpet and sit cross-legged between my boys.

"Well, the answer is both yes and no. Like I told you before, Grandpa's body was too tired to keep going. The part of him that was physical, flesh and blood, is gone. That's what's left in the pewter urn she was carrying. But the part of Grandpa that was *really* him, like his sense of humor, and the way he loved basketball, and loved all of us—that's never really gone. As long as we each have our memories of him, he'll always be with us."

They frown, but nod their heads anyway. I open my arms like wings, and my sons lean into me, each nestling their head on an opposite shoulder.

"I miss him so much already, Mom," Blake whispers into my chest.

"Me too," says Joshua.

"Me three, my babies. Me three."

We sit curled together on the floor until Blake's phone barks like a dog—his text sound. He slides it off the table then says, "That's Kyle. He said he wants to come tonight, but he needs a ride. Can we please pick him up on the way?"

What a good friend Kyle's been this past week. "Of course, bud. We have to be at the church early, though. Ask him if he'll be ready by three-forty-five."

Blake's fingers fly over the phone and it barks again a moment later. "Yeah, he'll be ready."

"Awesome. You guys can finish this board while I make lunch."

They work quietly while I assemble four sandwiches, slice a couple of apples, and grab a bag of chips before calling everyone to the table. Hopefully Mom's had enough time alone with her husband's ashes that she'll feel like eating something today.

In truth, we all pick at the food. We sit around the table, chewing slowly and avoiding too much eye contact. Conversations are short and to the point.

The witching hour is getting closer, and a strange dread is sinking into my bones. Something about saying such a final goodbye in a few hours is making my head ache terribly. And, I'm still not sure what to say tonight.

I'm done eating, even with a third of my sandwich still staring back at me from the plate. A glance at the other plates shows a similar pattern. Sighing, I push back and pick up the ignored leftovers. "Okay, we have to change and leave to pick up Kyle in about two hours."

Everyone nods.

"Can we go to the park, Mom?" Josh gives me his best puppy dog eyes, hoping I'll cave.

"No, I don't want you guys to lose track of time or get dirty out there. Just hang out in the house or on the patio, okay?"

"Okay," they say in unison.

They leave the table to retrieve their phones from the living room and head outside to the back porch table. They aren't there long before they return to sit at the kitchen counter.

"It's too cold in the shade," Blake offers for an explanation.

Mom helps me clean up. We dance smoothly around each other, putting away food and loading the dishwasher.

I get a movie-like image in my mind of my parents dancing in the kitchen of the house I grew up in. They bounce and spin, laugh and hug. Another beautiful, unbidden memory.

"Thanks for lunch, honey," she says, breaking the spell.

"Huh? Oh, my pleasure, Mom." I smile and give her a quick hug. "Have you seen what the boys did with the pictures?"

"No, I missed it. Is it in the living room?"

I lead her to the now-complete poster board still resting on her coffee table. Along with the photos and my dad's name, the boys have drawn a basketball hovering over a hoop, a movie reel, a guitar, and a couple of cacti in the in-between spaces.

"Aw...it's perfect, boys, thank you so much." She wipes a tear from her cheek and goes for hugs from both of them. "I—I'm gonna go lie down for a bit before we leave."

She wipes her nose and heads back to the master bedroom without waiting for an answer. Her shoulders are bowed forward, as if she's carrying a bag of rocks. Poor Mom.

I flop on the couch, my boys taking positions on either side of me. All three of us pull out our phones.

"Okay, kids. We should leave to go get Kyle in a couple of hours. Meanwhile, let's just vegetate. Want to watch Cartoon Network?"

As expected, I receive two enthusiastic yes's and flip on the TV. We all half-listen, half-watch reruns of 'Teen Titans' while fiddling with various gaming apps. I choose a coloring app and let any conscious thoughts fade away—a mental nap of sorts.

Eleven or twelve colored images later, I check the time and see we still have fifty minutes. I set a timer on my phone for twenty minutes, and return to coloring.

I remember a day in high school when I was sent home for puking in the trashcan during Geometry class. Mom was away on vacation with her two sisters, so Dad had to cancel the rest of his appointments for the day. I felt horrible for making him leave his therapy clients when I believed I could take care of myself if he would just get me home. It's a good thing he stuck around, though. It wasn't a simple stomach bug—it was appendicitis. When dad figured it out, he rushed me to the emergency room, and the medical staff told me he'd saved my life. I was already prepped and on the surgical table when the thing had burst, causing me to scream up at the bright lights. There was no customary "count backward from ten" warning. They had slapped a mask over my face and the world had gone instantly dark. When I awoke, my father was sleeping in the chair next to my hospital bed, a rumpled mess of hair and clothes. I'd never doubted his love for me, though, on that day, I knew beyond a shadow of a doubt that he had saved my life as well as given it to me.

The phone timer startles me out of my reverie. I suck in a sharp breath as my torso jolts, and the boys both giggle at me.

I laugh too, embarrassed. "Sorry! I was really into this coloring thing."

"Is it time to get ready?" Blake locks his phone and stands.

"Yes, please. You guys get changed in the guest room, and I'll check on Grandma."

I click off the TV, then creep into the darkened master bedroom. My mother is curled up on Dad's side of the bed, facing the pewter urn sitting on the side table. She isn't sleeping, though, she's sniffling amidst a pile of scattered tissues.

"Mom?"

She mutters a response, but I can't make it out.

I walk toward her and ask her to repeat herself.

"The bed still smells like him," she whispers.

I don't know how to answer, so I just sit on the edge of the bed next to her and wait.

"How? How will I go on?" Her voice sounds so small that my heart breaks a little more.

My poor mother. I've been lost in my own grief because she's seemed so strong. I'd assumed she had made peace with his death before he actually died. But I've been wrong. *Of course* her heart is broken. *Of course* she feels alone. Did she sleep at all last night? I should have made her stay overnight with us, after all.

I rub her back like I used to rub my sons' when they were too tired to sleep, or not feeling well. "I'm sorry, Mom," I whisper. "We need to leave in about thirty minutes. I should've given you more time to get ready."

She pushes off the bed and swings her legs to the floor. "It's all right. I'm not supposed to look stunning at a funeral, anyway."

I smile wanly. "True. I'm gonna get dressed, then check on the boys."

We're all ready just in time. Josh grabs the poster board, Mom clutches the urn, and we all head over to Kyle's house. Blake's friend is waiting in his driveway for us, dressed in a black suit, white shirt and pale yellow tie. He climbs into the back of the Explorer. As I head toward the church, a chill creeps into my bones. My father's ashes are in my mother's lap and we're about to say goodbye—forever.

I remember driving Dad to a Neurology appointment near Presbyterian Hospital last year. It was before his meds had stopped working, and he was in a good mood that day. He asked if we could walk to the 66 Diner for a malted milkshake afterward. How could I say no to an offer like that? The appointment was a difficult one, though. The doctor wasn't sure the current treatments would be helpful long-term, and was considering more drastic measures that seemed to scare him. Sitting in the diner an hour later, my dad showed his first signs of anger at his diagnosis. The rage on his face as he spoke took me by surprise, and I suddenly wondered what my mother had been dealing with at home. I asked her about it when I dropped him back at home, but her non-answers left me feeling unsettled for a few days.

Mom has shouldered a lot the last few months, yet her love for him is still strong, evidenced by the way she still clutches his cremains.

The Sandia Mountains to my left are lit by the lingering winter light of the early evening. I allow myself a long glance at the foothills as I drive down the street. I see the tramway cables glint once before they disappear into the deep shadow of a valley. This morning, those cables reminded me of my aging body, though, in this moment, I have a feeling they're more like the invisible cords that bind me to my now-deceased father. I'm certain memories of him will continue to briefly flare to the forefront of my mind, then fade into the background once more.

I pull into the nearly empty church parking lot and choose a space right by the front door. The kids pile out of the backseat and head into the building, but Mom and I remain in our seats. We're in no hurry to get out.

I take a deep breath and sigh heavily.

It's time. People will start arriving soon, so I walk around the car to retrieve my mother for the second time today. She's pale and shaky. I need to be strong for her.

All three boys are hanging out in seats at the back wall of the church, laughing quietly over some meme or video, no doubt. Mom and I head to the front of the sanctuary and stop before the table set up with the poster and an eight-by-eleven framed professional photograph of Dad. My mother places the dull silver urn to the side of the picture frame, then touches the image of his cheek before turning to have a seat in the first row.

As we sit holding hands, people arrive and walk to the front, bringing flowers as gifts of remembrance. They place them on the little table until there's no more room, and the bouquets begin to fill up the floor all around it. This visible offering of love for my father creates a combined floral perfume that fills the front of the church. My eyes sting with tears, and I'm suddenly grateful I thought to grab a tissue box.

Max has arrived. I hear his voice rumble behind us, just before he slides into the empty seat next to me. He takes my other hand in his and squeezes. The boys quietly join us too. I drop my head to Max's shoulder and breathe in his familiar musky scent. Something inside me, something I didn't even know was tense, relaxes.

The service opens with my dad's favorite hymn, "Be Thou My Vision," then the pastor gets up and reads my father's obituary. How can so few words convey the real man? Born of...married to...his only daughter...legacy—these words burn in my mind.

When it's my turn to speak, I want to say more, convey more. Yet, I know I can't hold these people hostage all night and into tomorrow morning, sharing every amazing memory I can think of. I want to, but I won't.

Memories. That's all we really have to hold on to.

I'm jolted back to the church setting when I hear my name spoken by the pastor. It's time. I climb up onto the stage, stand behind the lectern, and stare down at the table with the little pewter vessel.

Start with the facts, I tell myself. I look into my husband's eyes and let the strength of his presence flow into me.

"Hello. My name is Cheryl Montgomery, and I'm the only daughter of John and Linda Moore. Thank you for coming to say goodbye to the finest man I've ever known.

"I remember my father—his smile, his infectious laugh, his gentle way with me. He really loved people, that's why he became a therapist. He was a helper at heart. He's probably helped all of us get through something, at least once."

I feel compelled to pause my rushing thoughts, because half of the room is either smiling sadly, laughing shyly, or wiping at tears. These people truly loved him too.

"But, now he's in a mysterious place—a Great Unknown. He's unreachable, and it hurts."

I force down a sob and wipe at a hot tear trickling its way down my cheek.

"It hurts a lot," I croak out. Pausing, I look down at the table with his ashes and try to steady my breathing so I can continue. It works.

"I—I realize now that, in the end, we are nothing but the sum of our memories. And we live on in the memories of those we leave behind. We're destined to fade away, one way or another, yet, for a time, those we were closest to are our repositories of living."

I stand up straighter as this new conviction overtakes me, heart and soul.

"I *will* remember my father. I will tell his stories to my boys and they'll remember him better for it. Someday, they'll tell his stories to their children, and those kids will know my father even though they never met him.

"And, I will make new memories with those I still have with me. You should too. Make them *good* memories, as many as you can, because that's everyone's only reference to you once you're gone. Try to live every day as if it might be your last on this side of the Great Unknown."

I look back down at the pewter urn. "I couldn't have asked for a better father."

My words are gone. No more comes to mind.

I exit the stage and return to my seat, hold Mom's hand and lay my head on Max's shoulder once more. I somehow make it through the end of the whole thing, and the inevitable "sorry-for-your-loss" and "he-will-be-missed" comments. My husband and I gather my mother, the three boys, the ashes, the poster, the framed picture, and the flowers into our two vehicles. The night air is cold and strangely humid, making us shiver. I'd forgotten that it might snow a little tonight. Everyone but Max forgot to bring coats to the funeral.

I should feel empty, yet I don't. There's a strange fullness in my soul. It's as if the service, and all the annoying little conversations afterward, really helped me after all. I didn't expect that. I expected to be left emotionally ravaged and exhausted. Well, I *am* exhausted.

Max volunteers to take Kyle and our boys home, so I can drive back to Mom's with her and Dad's ashes. That's right—Dad's ashes, not Dad the man.

When we arrive, I refuse to drop her off to spend the night alone, insisting instead that she pack a few things and stay with us. "At least for tonight, Mom," I tell her in my own mom-voice. "I won't make you stay forever, but you're welcome to stay as long as you'd like."

She sighs, knowing I won't back down, and leaves the pewter vase with me as she heads into her master closet to pack.

I sit at the kitchen counter, my hands wrapped gently around the urn. Finally alone with the ashes, I whisper, "Hey, Dad. I hope things are good, wherever you are. We miss you. I'm glad you're not suffering anymore."

I smile, suddenly remembering something he told me when I was little and had fallen off my bike: "It's okay, love. Yeah, you fell down, but as long as you're able to get back up again, you'll find your way. I believe in you, kiddo."

I look out the kitchen window, at the glittering lights of the city beyond the Rio Grande and say, "I believe in you too, Daddy."

ABOUT THE AUTHOR

CS Simpson is a multi-genre author of several short stories, a novel, and even a little poetry. She self-published a fable (digital-only), and one of her short stories has appeared in *Shoreline of Infinity 19*.

In addition to reading and writing, CS loves music, movies, and spending time outdoors with her husband and dog under the Colorado skies she calls home.

DAWN TROUBLE

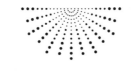

BOWEN GILLINGS

"It never bodes well to face death before breakfast," said Drood, rubbing warmth back into his arms and stepping over a patch of prickly pear. "That's what my pappy always said."

Rom trudged beside him, big and stalwart and pale under the desert moon. "I thought your pappy always said, 'Church is no place for a man.'"

"He did say that," replied Drood.

Rom steered around some spiny redthorn scrub. "And, 'A penny saved won't buy much.'"

"Yep. Sounds like him." Drood plopped onto a flat boulder, leaning his bow beside him. "I think he also said something about 'A wise man knows when it's time to hang up his spurs and move to a warm beach.'"

Rom stopped, scanning the night around them. He thumbed the pommel of his sheathed sword. "Well, seeing as how neither of us ever earned his spurs—"

"You know what I mean," said Drood, rummaging through one of his many pouches.

"I do," said Rom, sitting down beside his friend. "We'll get there. I promise. Right now..."

"We've got a job to do, I know." The smaller man's shoulders slumped, hand still deep in a pouch. "But...the Florisky Coast... Gentle waves. Drinks in coconut shells. You, with your tavern. Me, making little seashell oil lamps..."

The big swordsman chuckled.

"Hey," said Drood. "People love those."

Rom gave a well-creased grin and looked off into the night.

Drood found what he was looking for in the pouch and pulled it out. "You have to admit, though. Pappy's words do seem to fit our current predicament."

"Yeah, well, do me a favor and keep your pappy to yourself 'til we're done with this," said Rom, getting up and brushing off the seat of his trousers. "You're not the only one who's hungry. Besides, the way little Shully told it, it shouldn't be much further." He saw what his companion held and shook his head. "What are you doing?"

"What?" The bowman made a weak attempt to conceal his hand's contents.

"It won't work, you know," said Rom.

Drood uncovered the object and examined it: an ornately gilded box, so small it could hold only a dozen coins or a few thumbnail gemstones. The moonlight cast an eerie shine to its filigree. "It might. I mean, there's no one out here but us. I figure we toss it down a snake hole and be done with it."

"Nope. Forget it," said Rom, starting off again. "You've tried, and tried, and every time that cursed thing finds its way back to us."

His smaller companion stuffed the box back in a pouch and hurried to catch up. "Doesn't mean we should stop trying," he mumbled.

They followed the stars due west toward the canyon lands, where little Shully had spied something horrible enough to get two tired campaigners out in the dark after it. A breeze kicked up, scattering sand across the men's boots and bringing with it a smell different than the dry dust they'd been breathing these past few hours. Both knew that smell. As many battlefields as they'd trodden, it was a smell they could not forget.

Rom wrinkled his nose. "We're close."

"There," said Drood, peering into the gritty wind.

The swordsman looked where his sharp-eyed friend pointed. "I see it."

Low down toward the western horizon, a glow. From here, it appeared small, just a weak red smudge in the darkness. But, even at this distance, it sent Drood's spine tingling and tightened Rom's throat.

"That's no campfire," whispered Drood as the breeze died.

"Never thought it would be," said Rom. "Little Shully wouldn't have been death-white in her ranting if she'd only stumbled on herdsmen cooking dinner."

There was a creak of flexing wood as Drood strung his bow. "What then, flame serpent?"

"Nah," said Rom, "we're too far south."

The archer studied the distant glow again. "You don't think... Not a dragon?"

Rom rubbed his stubbled chin. "Shouldn't be. Not way out here. There's no mine in these parts. No castle. Nothing worth burning or stealing for a hundred leagues."

The fetid breeze picked up once more. Something small and fluttery sprang from a twisted tree to disappear into the night. Somewhere in the cold dark a fox cried at the moon. In the east, a faint line of palest gray showed dawn's approach—a pleasant reflection of its foreboding red counterpart in the west.

Rom thumbed his sword's pommel some more, eyes fixed on the red smudge. "Whatever it is, it doesn't smell friendly."

"No, it does not." Drood took the cap off his quiver, adjusted his pouches, then hefted his bow. "Well..." he added, "we've come this far."

"Too late to turn back," said Rom.

The archer clicked his tongue. "I didn't say that."

"Come on," snorted the big man.

They marched toward the glow, slipping into an easy, accustomed gait that let the slighter bowman keep pace with the tall warrior. A familiar energy spread through them, like the anticipation of reuniting with an old friend.

A fight was coming.

Rumors, bar songs, and tavern tales had it that taking care of terrifying things for simple village folk was what Rom and Drood did best. It was a reputation that always got to places before they did. And one that their best efforts failed to eliminate.

The warriors kept on beneath the sparkling sky, the stink of death growing stronger with each passing minute.

"Still," said Drood, "I could do with a bite to eat."

———

When they reached the canyon, the light in the east had grown, though true dawn was a long way off. The moon still shone bright in a clear sky, and the western horizon still loomed dark. The wind became more insistent, urging them to turn around and go back the way they'd came. But the glow and its reek drew them on.

And now there was noise.

A horrible grinding, wrenching, and sucking rumbled up from the canyon. They first took it for a river, its rushing echo distorted by distance. But, as they peered over the cliff's edge, that theory evaporated along with their energized, old-friend-reunion feeling.

"Definitely *not* a flame serpent," Drood said in an awed whisper, "and definitely not a dragon."

"Nope," said Rom, lying on his belly beside his friend, peering over the edge.

The ground was cold, but not as cold as the chill sweat tickling their spines. Hundreds of feet down, at the base of a sheer rock escarpment, flowed an undulating, throbbing, shapeless red mass. A glob of spilt crimson molasses, big as the village they'd just left, cast a light making the surrounding desert a distorted hellscape. As the men watched, it consumed everything in its path—grass, scrub, cactus, even broad stands of iron-hard acacia were engulfed by it. They didn't burst into flame or wither at its approach. They simply disappeared into the incessant, creeping tide. A streak of lifeless black followed in its wake.

"Still hungry?" asked Rom with a humorless grin.

"Explains the girl's fright," said Drood, edging back from the precipice. "Don't know what that is, but it sure feels…"

"Evil," Rom said. He followed his friend to shelter beneath a stand of gnarled junipers. "Ideas?"

Drood shook his head, staring down the length of the canyon.

Rom rolled his tongue around his mouth, thumbed his sword pommel, and scratched the ground with a juniper twig.

The creature's grinding rumble hummed in the air. All the other desert sounds of their night's trek were gone.

Drood watched his friend with that stick and suddenly stood. "I've got a plan," he said, eyes twinkling.

Rom cocked an eyebrow.

"Really," said Drood. "I do."

Drood had Rom hack off a twisted branch thick as his arm. Then he led them, trotting along the canyon edge. They didn't stop until well ahead of the flowing doom and the bowman found a spot he considered satisfactory.

"The desert got me thinking about that campaign we were on back in Pamarran," Drood said, grunting as he hefted a rock into place. "Remember?"

Rom propped himself against his thick branch. "When we hired on as scouts for that bloated colonel?"

"No," said Drood, wiping his hands on his trousers. "After that, when we switched sides."

"You mean, when you played hero to that doe-eyed farm girl," said Rom.

They stood above a section of canyon where the walls pressed close to form a narrow channel. It was perfect for what Drood had in mind.

"Yeah, well, she seemed worth it at the time. Anyway, you recall how we trapped the colonel's brigade against the river?" Drood's eyebrows raised expectantly.

Rom considered, looked at the branch in his hand, the rocks before them, the scree below, and an appreciative smile stretched his leathery cheeks. "That just might work."

The archer helped his friend wedge the branch beneath a boulder as big as the swordsman and twice as broad. He adjusted the rock he'd moved until it sat in the best possible position for a fulcrum.

The crimson juggernaut flowed into view around a bend.

"Now, when the doomblob's squirmed itself into that slot down there, we heave," said Drood, readying himself on his side of the branch.

Rom took up position opposite and gripped the rough bark. "Doomblob?"

"Fitting name, don't you think?" asked a smug Drood.

His friend sighed.

"Here it comes."

The blob ground and rumbled to the narrowing channel, then slowed. The front of it stretched to a point and then stretched further. It split into a pair of thick, bulbous, probing arms that groped the leading edges of the rocky slot.

"What's it doing?" asked Rom.

"It's…it's searching," whispered Drood, as if afraid his voice might spook their quarry. "I guess it wants to make sure the way is safe?"

"Hmm." Rom shook his head. "Well, if it is checking things out, maybe it's worried about getting hurt. If it's worried about getting hurt…"

"We can kill it," said Drood.

Below them, a hawk screamed. The dark silhouetted speck of it swooped across the creature's red glow then was lost in the gloom. One of the fluid arms stretched tentatively after it, then withdrew back into the flowing bulk.

"It's moving again," said Drood.

Rom grunted and pressed on the branch.

"Not yet," Drood hissed. "Wait until all of it is wedged in."

The big man froze, bracing himself for Drood's signal.

The noise of the creature shifted in pitch as it slid into the tight channel.

"Now."

Both men heaved on the branch. The juniper bent, trembled, and groaned, but didn't break. They gasped and cursed. The boulder didn't move.

"Move," Drood commanded the rock, jaw clamped tight with strain.

Rom threw himself on the branch. "Put your weight on it!"

Both men pressed with everything they had. The branch popped and crackled, but held. The boulder gave a tiny shiver.

"It's…nearly…out of…the narrows," grunted Drood between heaves.

Rom growled. The deep rumble of it mixing with the noise below.

He swung beneath the branch, hanging on it like one of the tree apes they'd seen in the Burnesian jungles. "Come. On."

Drood crawled nimbly atop their lever, balancing and jumping on it in time to the bigger man's yanks. "Work, damnit, work!"

The boulder wasn't moving. Below them the doomblob was about to get away, flowing out into the wider canyon beyond.

The archer jumped hard on the straining branch, but he misjudged his landing. His boot heel crunched onto Rom's clutching fingers.

"Ah!" cried the big man, letting go on reflex.

Drood cried out, too as the branch sprang up with a crunching smack, flinging him through the air like a shot from a catapult, arms wheeling, legs kicking. Rom thrust out a desperate hand for his friend, but too late.

Drood slammed into the boulder with a dull, dry, gasping thud.

And the rock moved.

The dazed archer didn't know what happened, only that he'd stopped flying, his head hurt, and he was tumbling over backward.

"Rom? Rom, help!"

Drood scrambled to get up, to roll off the boulder, to somehow escape before his plan actually *did* work, dragging him down to be smashed among the rocks along with that glowing monster. His fingers clawed. His feet slipped. Air rushed past his head.

"No-no-no!"

He jerked to a stop, a mountainside of rock thundering away below him. A brawny hand clutched Drood's arm. Rom had him.

The big warrior dragged Drood over the cliff's edge, pulling until they were both several feet clear of the scary part, and plopped down. Their huffing and panting were lost in the deafening roar of the avalanche smashing over the doomblob (or whatever that thing was really called).

By the time they'd caught their breath, the click, clack, and pop of the last few rocks coming to rest was all that echoed from below. Across the canyon, far hilltops grew distinct against the purpling sky. Night was losing the fight against day's approach.

Drood chuckled. Rom rubbed his sore arm.

"You've gained weight," said Rom.

"You've gotten old," retorted the bowman, sitting up. He put a hand down to steady himself. "Oooh. My head." With the tips of his fingers he probed his scalp. "Am I bleeding?"

The big warrior gave a cursory look. "I don't think so. Hard to see in this light." He got up, slapping the dust and dried juniper needles from his trousers and jerkin. "Besides, it would take more than a desert rock to crack your thick head."

"Ha. Ha," grumbled Drood. "Very funny…" His voice trailed off as he cocked his head. His eyes narrowed.

Rom propped a hand on his sword pommel. "Well, I think we should be—"

"Shhh!" Drood lifted a warning finger. He looked sidelong at his friend. "You hear that?"

The big warrior heard nothing save for the swirling breeze. He smirked dismissively, but Drood wasn't shining him on. The look on his companion's face was one of serious, eye-widening concern. Then he did hear something, and he smelled it, too.

Drood dismissed his sore head and joined Rom to look down into the canyon.

"Aw, hell."

They stared at the effects of their handiwork. The narrow slot part of the canyon was gone, and the doomblob had gone with it, both buried beneath uncountable tons of rock. Now their spines got sweaty again as, at the base of the scarred escarpment, pulsing, glowing, stinking red patches swelled through gaps in the debris. The noise the thing had made renewed, and grew louder.

"That," said Drood, voice tight as he retrieved his bow and quiver. "Is not good."

Rom, sword drawn and rugged face gone a whiter shade of pale replied, "No, it is not." He furrowed his brow. "Is that thing … ?"

"Eating the rocks?" Drood chuckled in frightened disbelief. "Yes. Yes, it is."

It wasn't so much eating their avalanche, as the avalanche was disappearing into it at a rate much faster than the men had seen the thing move across the canyon floor. The disparate patches of glowing red flowed together. In the time it took the men's mouths to go as dry as the surrounding desert, the thing reformed. Only, now, it was bigger. Much, much bigger.

And it was flowing up the canyon wall.

Toward them.

Both warriors stumbled back from the precipice.

Rom's sword slipped from his fingers, the metallic clang snapping him from his stupefied trance. He snatched up the weapon, then wiped his damp palm on a dirty linen sleeve.

"Your pappy got any wise words that might fit our current predicament?" he asked.

Drood shook his head, dumbfounded.

"Well then," Rom said in a thin voice, "any bright ideas?"

Drood thrust a jerky hand at the cliff edge. "That *was* my bright idea." He cradled his bow like an infant. "Somehow, I don't think arrows are a viable course of action."

"Nor swords." Rom swallowed hard and sheathed his blade. He tried drying his palms again with little success.

The raging red glow grew brighter, rising up before them, a rank, horrible sunrise of doom.

"What, then?" asked Drood, staring transfixed at the cliff's edge. "Tuck tail and flee?"

Rom's lip trembled. He took a deep, steadying breath. "We can't."

"Yes, we can," squeaked Drood, gesturing behind them. "We just turn around and run *that* way." He gave a weak, pleading smile. "The Florisky Coast, remember?"

"That village is counting on us," said Rom.

"Some village is *always* counting on us," countered Drood.

Rom licked his dry lips. "Seems that way."

They took a few more steps back as the evil light brightened and the rumble became the thunder of an approaching storm. Jagged shadows from the surrounding scrub clutched at them across the hardpan.

Drood ran a hand through his hair, then made repeated, short nods. "Fine. So... we fight." His words hung in the air, held there by the knowledge that they'd likely be dead in a few moments, but if they didn't try to stop this thing here and now, a town full of innocent lives would be lost. "What do we fight with?"

Rom looked to his friend, eyes wet, lips pressed tight, holding his fear in check. "We have *one* option," he said above the noise.

Drood met his friend's gaze. The big warrior said nothing. He didn't have to. His winsome, apologetic look spoke for him. A fear greater than that of facing death by an avalanche-eating doomblob twisted Drood's gut.

"No," he said. "Absolutely not."

Rom gently pressed his intent. "The horn."

"You promised," Drood yelled, tears now coming to his eyes. "We made a vow. After last time, never again."

Rom stepped closer, both men now orange in the demonic glow. He set a desperate hand on the shoulder of his longtime companion. "We have to use the horn."

Though the ground trembled with death's approach, the smaller man stood firm. He puckered his lips and waved a dismissive hand at Rom and the world. "Uh-uh. Nope. Not going to happen."

The air-buzzing rumble crescendoed as the blob crested the cliff edge like a vile sun. No warmth came with it, only undulating, stinking, incarnate doom, and a sanguine light that made the world beyond them all the darker. The blob flowed over the lip of the cliff. It amassed steadily, stacking on itself in heavy waves until it towered above the warriors.

Drood staggered back, mouth open. A thin, warm trickle ran down the inside of his leather trousers.

"The horn!" Rom ditched the soft approach and shook his friend like a toy.

Drood whimpered, "But—"

"You got some *other* miracle in those pouches?" Rom shouted.

Drood blinked. He only had the one, and they both knew it.

Rom shook him again, screaming, "Blow the damn horn!"

"Okay, okay," Drood snapped, yanking free. He thrust his bow into Rom's hand then dug into a pouch. He pulled out the little gilded box, the one he'd tried to lose. The one he tried to lose on purpose, time and again, since they'd been cursed with it. With a whimper, he popped it open and took out a silver trumpet no bigger than a church key. It shone with a clear, starbright light all its own.

The roiling mass ebbed closer, and closer still, the men now red in its radiance.

"I'm saying this now and, if we live, I'll say it again." Drood shouted, snatching back his bow. "We're gonna regret this."

Rom nodded. "We always do."

Then Drood put the tiny horn to his lips.

And blew.

At first no sound came—the creature's noise was overwhelming—then, like a child crying on a distant hill, a high, true note sang out.

The doomblob paused in its rippling advance.

Drood stopped blowing.

The world took a beat.

Lightning flashed down from the clear sky. Thunder blasted the night.

Both men were blown from their feet, tumbling and cursing across the hard desert floor. Drood skidded to a stop, upside down against a jutting fin of rock, bow and horn still clutched in his hands. Rom wound up face down on a prickly pear.

The swordsman spat, rolling away and tugging spines from his cheeks.

The blob shuddered under the blast—thrum weakening, glow guttering.

A pure, blinding-white beam tore down from on high, to engulf the amorphous evil.

Rom and Drood shielded their eyes, peering between trembling fingers.

Descending within the light came a womanly figure, robed in silver, feathered wings sprouting from her back. Her skin was ebony. Her eyes like a summer stream. She had no weapon, only a smile.

"There she is," said Drood. "May we live through today…"

"To regret tomorrow," finished Rom.

The winged woman caught sight of the men on the ground and waved as she drifted down. "Hey guys! How ya been? So awesome you called. I was afraid maybe you'd forgotten ab—*ulp!*"

The blob cut her off, shooting out a hateful, wriggling arm that coiled about the heavenly being like a miffed python grabbing a piglet.

She gave a "hmmph!" as the creature yanked her from the sky to engulf her in its gelatinous bulk. Her white light blinked out. The doomblob's glow dimmed. Its rumble quieted.

The world took another beat.

Then crimson flared and the rumble rumbled strong as ever.

Rom and Drood could only stare in shock. Now it was the swordsman's turn to pee a little.

Two writhing arms stretched forth from the creature. Stretched toward *them.*

They yipped and ducked behind Drood's rock.

"What the hell just happened?" piped Drood.

Rom gawped like a landed bass. "I, uh…I don't…she's never…"

"I thought that she was," Drood stuttered, "you know. Invincible."

Rom shrugged, eyes wide in his pale face. He looked at the tiny silver artifact clutched in his friend's hand. "M-maybe if you blow it again?"

"What? We've never done that before." Drood's cheeks quivered.

"We've never needed to before," said Rom. "It's worth a shot, isn't it?"

Drood hesitated.

Rom peered above the boulder's edge. The throbbing tip of a scarlet tentacle pulsed inches from his face.

"Ah!" he screamed and fell back.

"Okay, okay!" Drood raised a panicked hand, puffed out his cheeks, and blew.

The ropey arm froze mid-strike.

Thunder and lightning answered as before. A beam shone down as before. But no angel slid from the sky.

"Crap," whispered Drood.

And yet, the probing arm stayed put. It quavered in the air as if uncertain. It no longer throbbed and pulsed, but shriveled, like a waterskin with a leak.

Rom scrambled to his feet, shielding his eyes from the bright white light. He drew his sword.

Drood skittered over to join him.

The horrible, heaving mass looked, somehow, smaller. Less...horrible. The throbbing and trembling of it didn't speak so much of menace and death as it did of something gone terribly wrong. On the inside. Its rumble softened to the gurgle of an angry creek. Dark blotches formed on it, blotches like pebbly, mottled toad's flesh. And its stink got worse.

"What the—? Is it sick?" asked Drood, pressing his nose into his shirtsleeve.

"Hell if I know," said Rom. He thumbed his sword's crosspiece.

Drood held up the horn. "Should I blow again?"

"No," said Rom. "Let's not push our luck. Try shooting it."

Drood lifted his head. "Are you kidding?"

"See what happens," insisted Rom, brows furrowed, nose wrinkled.

The archer tucked the horn and its box back into a pouch. He nocked an arrow, drew, and loosed. His shaft pierced a patch of toad flesh. Inky black oozed from the wound.

The blob shuddered.

"Well, I'll be..." Rom gripped his blade. "Shoot it again." He grinned a wide, hopeful grin.

Drood did.

More ink. Another shudder.

Thin, probing tentacles reached out, though these were more the wretched, wrinkled arms of an old hag than the thick, smooth, constricting forms of before.

Rom laughed. "Keep shooting!" He left the boulder and charged, swinging at a tentacle with the glee of a child stomping ants.

The arm broke with a snap, splattering into a puddle as it hit the ground.

The blob shrunk; glow dimming, thrum wavering, stink growing.

Rom cheered and hacked away. Drood loosed and loosed, over and over. The white light from the sky disappeared, but every time the men struck, the wounds didn't ooze blackness. Instead, a silvery light sprang forth.

Drood paused in his shooting. "Uh…Rom?" he called.

The swordsman did not respond. He was lost in battle joy, swinging, hacking, and plunging. He shouted curses and insults at the once-great red, terrifying thing that was now more like a shuddering hill of turds gone maroon.

"Rom," called Drood, again. His friend apparently didn't see the bright fissures spreading across the creature, nor feel the deep tremors pulsing through the air.

Drood yelled as loud as he could. "Rom!"

"What!" The warrior snapped, turning on his friend with a savage, can't-you-see-I'm-busy snarl.

Drood pointed with an arrow.

Rom snorted and looked. "I don't know wha— Oh. Damn."

The fissures stretched and wavered. The creature was a cracked and leathery bubble ready to burst.

Rom swore again and ran. He dove for cover beside Drood, knocking his friend off his feet, bow and sword flying.

As a boy, Rom had once heard a temple organist get frustrated at a difficult hymn and slam on all the low keys at once. Everyone gathered had gasped and covered their ears, the sound was so awful. That cacophony was a mere crow's caw compared to the terrible, desperate din that erupted atop that desert cliff. If all the fear, hate, and vile intent of the world were expressed in a single blast, in a single place, this was it.

Horrifying as that sound was, the slime shower was worse.

Both men—and rocks and sand and cactus and scrub for acres

around—were awash with it. Every shade of red streaked with every shade of black (with chunky bits of color somewhere in between) dripped and dribbled and clung…everywhere.

"God, it stinks," coughed Drood, a plum-sized dollop plopping from his chin.

Rom nodded, arms lifted from his sides as if afraid to touch anything. A particularly turd-ish chunk hung from his nose. "That, it does."

A throaty, gleeful laugh danced across the gooey landscape from the other side of the men's rock.

"Is that…?" Drood asked, though he knew the answer.

Rom swept gunk from his eyes with his one clean finger. "Yep."

"Hey!" came the call from behind them. "Hey, you guys!"

With a mutual groan, the gooped warriors stood. Before them danced the winged being Drood's trumpet call had summoned, silver robes glittering in the dawn. She did a little jig at the blasted-clean epicenter of what, just moments ago, had been a mountain of insatiate evil.

"Rom! Drood! It's *so* good to see you." She spread her arms as if to hug them from fifty feet away.

In unison, they gave a dismal reply, "Hello, Anxa."

Rom flicked snot from his hands. Drood turned aside and blew his nose.

The angel strode toward them, slime hissing and evaporating before her, creating a clear path as she advanced.

"Anxa the Magnificent has returned," said Drood so only his friend could hear.

"That she has," replied Rom, failing to clear goo from his scabbard.

"Remember when she insulted that entire gang of bandits, then abandoned you in their tavern to use the privy?" Drood asked.

"Remember when she had you wearing a dress and singing sea chanteys to your ladyfriend's father?" Rom retorted.

"Been trying to forget," said Drood.

"Boys, boys, *boys!*" chuckled the angelic woman as she drew near, broad smile revealing opaline teeth. She lifted one sculpted eyebrow. "You look terrible. Here, let Anxa clean you up."

Both men raised warding hands. "No-no-no. That's alright. We—"

Anxa cut their protests short, sucking in a breath loud as wind at a cave mouth, and blew.

The warriors staggered and tipped, but remained standing. Eyes closed. Mouths closed. Sphincters tight.

Anxa's wind cut off as quickly as the blast had hit them.

They staggered and tipped again. But remained standing.

"There. All better."

Rom blinked. Drood, too. Both were clean of slime, as was the desert for yard upon yard behind them. Rom said nothing about his friend's new, reach-for-the-sky hairstyle. Nor did Drood mention the fly of his companion's pants blown open. Both muttered their thanks to Anxa.

"Forget about it. Well…" She turned and surveyed the surroundings, gesturing to the cliff edge. "Some fun, huh? Damned doomblob caught me by surprise."

Drood elbowed his friend. "Doomblob."

Rom shook his head. "Shut up."

Anxa carried on, "But, I dare say it bit off more than it could chew. Nasty thing messed with the wrong trio, eh?" She pinched Rom's cactus-pricked cheek and thumped Drood on the shoulder.

"Yeah," said the archer, knowing he'd have a new bruise by mid-morning.

"So it would seem," said Rom, with a sore smile.

She scanned their surroundings, checked her robes, and clicked her tongue in disapproval. "Now then, this won't do at all. You two never give me time to prepare for these little visits. Hmm, deserts get hot, so…Oh, I know! What about this?"

With an audible pop like a camel spitting, her robes and wings vanished. Anxa cocked her shapely hips to flaunt a two-piece outfit made with less cloth than a barmaid's washrag.

Rom blushed and averted his eyes.

Drood coughed and puffed out his lips. "Well, uh, it certainly is...airy."

"Right?" grinned Anxa, oblivious to her effect on the men.

Drood nodded. "Yes, but perhaps something a bit more on the conservative side? I mean, look at Rom and me."

Anxa looked at the pair in their jerkins and boots and dirty leather. She cocked her hips the other way as she pondered, causing key parts to jiggle and Rom's face to reach doomblob crimson.

"Hmm. I guess... But I learned my lesson last time about leather pants. So—"

A camel spit pop and she wore billowing pantaloons and a gauzy white shirt that exposed her svelte midriff.

Rom's blush subsided one small degree.

"That's better, I guess," said Drood.

"Great," beamed Anxa. She bent and handed Drood his bow. "There you go. So, what'll we do first?"

"Huh?" asked Rom.

"You called. I'm here. There's no more monster to explode, so where to?" Anxa clapped her hands together. "Ooo, I know. How about we hit that mountain town festival with the music and the dancing and the really good parsnip pies? That place still there?" She looked to each man's blank face.

Neither responded. They'd been run out of that town after Anxa thought it would be fun to see how high she could stack the folks' sheep.

"Or, what about that castle wedding with the grumpy guy in charge? He was a bore and the folks were all stiffs, but the ale was fantastic. Ale's still a thing, right? No ale where I'm from." She jerked a thumb at the blue-tinged sky.

Drood gave a slow nod and regretted it immediately.

"Great! Ale it is." She put her hands on the men's arms. "Now, I can get us there quick as a wink."

Rom stopped her. "N-no need. We can walk. Town is just a day or so that way." He pointed the direction they'd come. Last time they'd "winked" someplace, Rom had redecorated a manor house floor with heave after heave of his previous meal.

"Really?" Anxa gave a sly grin. "Is there ale?"

Rom nodded. He, too, regretted it immediately. Anxa was trouble enough. But a drunk Anxa?

Scars and bruises. It always meant scars and bruises.

Anxa shrugged. "Suit yourselves. Let's go." She strode away, laughing over her shoulder, "I've got forty days and forty nights before you-know-who calls me back upstairs and I aim to make the most of it."

"She always does," Drood said, unstringing his bow. "We *have* to go with her, don't we?"

Both knew ditching her was impossible. They'd tried before. Twice. Just like they'd tried ditching the little horn in its little box. Each attempt failed and the consequences were never…dignified.

"That we do," the big man grumbled. He struggled to close his fly, struggled again, then gave up with a sigh.

Both trudged into the desert after her.

The sun rose. The day grew hot.

Anxa strode on, oblivious and indefatigable. She whistled and skipped and danced and hugged the men while goading them to join her in songs neither knew, songs she belted out off-key.

About an hour later, the pair were keeping a few yards back, mopping sweat from their brows, watching her bend over a coiled, buzzing rattlesnake.

Drood whispered. "Guess we wait a bit longer on those drinks in coconuts and seashell lamps?"

A spitty pop at Anxa's feet and the venomous snake was now a fuzzy kitten. It hissed and tried to scamper away, but she snatched it up, ignored the flailing claws, and rubbed its head, talking to it in baby babble.

"Well," said Rom, "We *did* save the town."

"True," agreed Drood with zero enthusiasm.

Anxa lost interest in the cat and tried matching the call of a desert bird. The noise she made was closer to a hundred rusty hinges grating open at once.

"But, was it *worth* it?" asked Drood.

Rom shrugged. "Is it ever?"

The two warriors trudged on, shading their eyes against the morning sun, knowing full well the next forty days would be hell.

ABOUT THE AUTHOR

Bowen Gillings is an award-winning author whose quirky tales range from superhero suspense to divine family squabbles. He is a devout travel enthusiast, committed martial arts dabbler, and closeted RPG nerd. He enjoys cooking, the outdoors, good whiskey, and good friends. Born in Wisconsin, he grew up in South Dakota's Black Hills, matriculated in Minnesota, and then bounced around Europe with the Army. He's lived on both coasts, danced on the Great Wall of China, and driven a Volvo from Alaska to Louisiana before settling in Colorado with his wife and daughter.

FIVE BLOSSOMS FOR MEDITATION

KENDRA GRIFFIN

robins gather sticks—
monks hold steaming mugs
between open palms

husks fall
on master scrubbing pots—
monkey feasts on fruit

moon skinny-dips
if pond asks nicely
between raindrops

green hands
let stones skip across lilies
and catch fire

barefoot ants march
across cold temple floorboards
chants rise in the mist

ABOUT THE AUTHOR

Kendra Griffin has a passion for writing about underdogs, family relationships, social inequality, diverse ensemble casts, and teenage characters who develop strong identities despite all societal pressure to the contrary. She recently published *The Pox Ward*, the first in her dystopian, post-plague YA series. The sequel, *Apocalypse Thoughts*, arrives in February. Kendra is also a singer-songwriter and occasional poet who loves to encourage others in their creative process. Kendra teaches writing for Aims Community College, frequently hosts creative writing workshops in her community, and was the winner of the 2020 N0CO Jerry Eckert Scholarship.

AGONY IN AGES

NIKIA HUNT

With each swing of the garden hose, each snap of the belt against my back, my butt, or my stomach, I retreated within myself a little more. Each scream thrown against my psyche built more scars upon scars until there were no more feelings, just as there was no more pain. I stopped crying when my stepdad swung. I reasoned that it was better me than my mother. I stopped caring about the bite of his words, or their bark.

One day, I was beautiful and smart and the best daughter ever. The next, I was not even his daughter. I was a stupid thing, a thing that needed punished. Both days couldn't be truth, so neither were. I was neither smart nor stupid, deserving of love nor hate; instead, I was nothing and I sought to disappear, instead.

For the next decade, I lived within a glass palace of nothingness. I was away from reality, leaving a robotic voice recording in my place. An "away" message on the answering machine became my only voice.

I did not feel.

I did not exist.

All that was, or ever would be, was just the glass of the world I'd created within my own mind, ever reflecting the smallest spark of light, amplifying it, and making it into something more than I would ever be.

"Are you paying attention?"

No. I was not.

"Yes, Mrs. Reichenberg."

"Okay, just make sure you are."

She used her *sweet voice* at me. Her *gentle voice*.

She frowned because she knew. The whole world knew, now.

I had run away too many times, only to be carried back in the front seat of a police car, testy at the inconvenience of being returned again.

There was nothing in my eyes; the windows to my soul were hollow.

The school had "suspicions of abuse," and it marked me in the same red letters that marked some paper in my school file, causing the teachers to all look at me with sad eyes. By now, all my "peers" knew they weren't my peers at all. They could see the empty space where things were supposed to be that, for me, no longer existed.

They stayed away unless they needed an outlet for their own angst. It didn't bother me to catch all their pain... Their high school break-ups, their friendships lost, their moments of sorrow...all were thrown at me as snide remarks, giggles in the lunchroom while they pointed, and name-calling.

I never dated. I never had friends. I never felt sorrow. I was an empty vessel into which to throw all their unwanted emotions, knowing they would cease to exist in the same way my own feelings did.

A s I grew older, though, I grew more into myself.
It started when they finally listened to the teachers "suspicions." They suddenly saw the bruises, and my dirty clothes, and noticed the head lice infesting my unkempt, unwashed hair. They suddenly noticed that my mother never came to conferences, or plays, or anywhere that wasn't her bedroom anymore. I was always hungry, always dirty, always empty, and "odd."

They gave me a teddy bear when I went into foster care. It was dressed up like an angel and had plush wings and a wire halo. I still have it. It marks a point.

In foster care, I flinched sometimes when they yelled at football on the television. I hid food in my room and they understood why. They bought me second-hand clothes that *fit,* and washed them when they were dirty. I was required to bathe every other evening.

In group homes, I flinched sometimes because the older kids liked to emulate their parents... but I never told on them because they didn't hit as hard as he did. I still hid food in my room, but they weren't as understanding. They gave us all the same gray sweatpants and white tee-shirts, and made us wash them ourselves. They didn't care if I bathed or not.

Gradually, I found pieces of emotions in the debris that he had left in me, emotions that I used to know.

The important and knowledgeable people experienced with "troubled children" saw the empty stare, and they put me in therapy where I'd be asked three times a day, for an hour, how I felt about everything.

I lied.

A lot.

I don't know if the therapist could tell or not, but I never got put on medication. I never obtained a new "label," despite wondering if I deserved one. Everyone else seemed to have one: bipolar, agoraphobic, or anxious. I almost felt left out, but mostly I felt lucky.

Over time, I found a spark that I knew I could fan into a flame, one day.

They eventually "reunited" me with my family. It was part of some goal they'd written for all of us. A check box they needed to check for state financing, maybe.

He saw the ember inside me and he hated it. He tried to extinguish it in any way he could, but I held on to that emotional deadness and that ability to laugh when he hit me, and it drove him absolutely batshit crazy. I knew he felt powerless when it came to me, because he couldn't hurt me and it grew my power.

He hit me, anyway.

There came a day when it became *my* choice. I was trouble, always, and my probation officer got tired of seeing my "wasted potential." An unknown beneficiary contacted my probation officer and offered to pay for my bus ticket to wherever made sense.

Stay, or go.

I was selfish and I went, leaving my mother to take his wrath so that I might save myself. I was fifteen, and six hundred miles away from him, finally. It only lasted a month.

They came to where I was and made their own home there. I was already independent, and I would never go back. I re-enrolled myself in high school. I fell in love. I felt. I even felt *deeply*.

One day, I realized I was grown. It was an astonishment because it had happened in small pieces, then apparently all at once, in a way I didn't see coming.

He could no longer touch me. I knew how to throw a punch, and I knew how to take one, too. When he reached for my fear, he found my fire, instead. I was no longer interesting to his sickness.

He turned to my mother to feed his lust for creating pain.

She called me once, crying. He had taken her clothes away from her and wouldn't give them back or tell her where they were. He made her less than human, and kept her from leaving by keeping her pants. What a guy.

I broke down her door, baseball bat in hand, and told him. I dared him. *Hit me again.* I'm no small child, hiding welts from people who would have helped me. You're no stronger, bigger, more powerful bull moose. You're older, feeble.

A graying half specimen of an animal, diseased and dying slowly.

You grow frailer every day.

I am young, and strong…

…*and I have a fucking baseball bat.*

Give her back her goddammed pants.

You JERK.

You COWARD.

Pick on someone your own size now that *I* am closer to your own size.

You won't.

Touch her again, once, ever, and I will kill you.

I. will. kill. you.

I let it fill me with the fire I'd fanned and built for years, created out of that very small ember.

I made sure he saw it.

Saw ME.

He didn't touch her after that.

One day, he decided to leave. It wasn't the first time, but it was the last. He took my mother's car, packed all his stuff, and left while she was at work. I don't even remember what they were fighting about. It's funny, now.

He made it permanent when he came back to town several weeks later, in her car, with a new woman. They drove around and he flaunted her. My mother finally broke, disgusted. She finally saw him for what he had always been. Trash.

I saw him when he came back. He drove by my house. My daughter was outside and he waved to her, while driving, holding a beer in his hand.

TRASH.

He had always told my mom that if she ever got a tattoo, he'd never want her again.

It was another way of controlling her, because she'd once told me she would get one if I did. He couldn't let her be her own person, so he made the ultimatum to keep her from herself, and from me.

One day, after she was finally free, I took her to my tattoo artist and we got matching tattoos.

Elephants, for luck.

Hers has the initials of her kids.

Mine says "Mom."

ABOUT THE AUTHOR

Nikia Hunt is a native Nebraskan who once wandered too far from home and ended up in Colorado. Her muse fell in love with the mountainscape and the nature within it and she has been writing and teaching "with a view" ever since.

Heavily influenced by everything gothic and twisted, Nikia's work is generally centered in finding literary beauty in everyday life, especially in the more macabre and sometimes traumatizing parts. Along with reality-based memoir, she focuses largely on fantasy fiction, young adult fantasy, and darkly expressive poetry.

ON ILLNESS

TUSHAR JAIN

It started with us. That's what hurts the most. It started with us.

We had been living in Bhubaneswar for some time, then. Haruk's latest project had brought us there. Bhubaneswar, with its endless ancient temples, was a historian's delight. I had never seen Haruk so happy, almost child-like in his excitement, at times. I knew that moving away from the humdrum teaching life had thrilled his simple academician heart. Haruk had insisted that this was nothing more than a sabbatical, an "experiment" in careers. But I knew that, if things worked out, this was the life he would choose. I'd known my Haruk for over a decade by then. And I knew that he was a wanderer. Like me. Because that's how we had found each other. But that, I think, is a different story, for another time.

For me, Bhubaneswar proved tough to crack. As a poet, I'd always had my fair share of challenges when it came to finances. Back in Hyderabad, I was able to cope well enough. I had my patrons, my regulars, who always turned up at readings of my new work. Twice a week, they paid to sit there and listen to me recite from memory, backed by a musician friend on his synthesizer, notching my verses with jazz. I don't mean to brag, but I did okay. Enough to not need a day job. Well, I guess I do mean to brag; even the barest of survival is no mean feat for a full-time poet. Bhubaneswar, however, turned out to be very different. At first, no matter how hard I tried, I could not locate an art scene in the city. It was all far too scattered to be a 'scene' at all. But, over time, word spread about my being here on Facebook, Twitter and all those things that I still struggle to understand. And, in a couple of weeks, I suddenly had a gig at a book launch. After that, though things got rocky at times, I always had enough work to keep me busy.

Despite the fact that we were well into July, there had been no signs of rainfall. I should mention here that I *love* the rain. Perhaps it is clichéd to be a poet and love the rain, but it's true. The gurgling skies, the smells that take you back, and that feeling on your skin, as if you would never grow old. What's not to love? Since a scorching May, I had been waiting for the monsoon to strike this city with all its fervor. But June turned out to be a dud. And it was not until late July, when I was returning home from a gig at a cultural center, that the clouds crackled and clamored. And rapidly, as if from a wound, darkness bled into the evening, coloring everything.

I remember letting out a squeal, I felt so happy. I stopped midway and stood for a moment, waiting for the rain to break. But it struck me that I had a performance that weekend. Ending up sick was not an option. I couldn't take the few jobs I got lightly; at that early stage, they were nothing short of miracles. So, as soon as I found a rickshaw trundling my way, I hailed it, got in, and guided it home. Throughout the ride, I kept my eye on the churning, growling sky. It started to rain just when I reached my apartment building.

By the time I reached the door to my apartment, I was drenched. It was around six, and I knew Haruk would be inside, working his way through his tumbling heaps and piles of notes. Not wanting to bother him, I didn't ring the bell. With a dripping hand, I dug out my key and opened the door, trying not to make too much noise.

I found Haruk in our bedroom. He hadn't bathed. He was still in his light blue pajamas from the previous night. His glasses were askew, his hair unkempt. His notebooks, over a dozen of them, were strewn all over the bed. Drawn up to him, on a foldable wooden stool, a laptop sat, lighting up his face. Haruk was fast asleep, with his head resting lightly against the headboard.

"Haruk!" I called from the door. He didn't stir. I needed him to wake up and hand me a change of clothes from the cupboard. I'd already brought the rain into our apartment, leaving a trail of wet foot-prints in my wake. I didn't want to make a mess of the bedroom as well. "Haruk!" I yelled. But, once again, Haruk didn't stir.

A little annoyed, hugging myself, I hurried to the cupboard, making an effort not to slip. With a shiver, I brought out a change of clothes and a towel. In a minute, I felt tremendously better in my dry pajamas. I had been mumbling angrily throughout as I changed. I was miffed at Haruk. The man was dozing away so blissfully in the daytime!

Dodging the wet puddles I'd left on the floor, I marched over to Haruk and began shaking him by the shoulder. "Haru! Do you know what time it is? Didn't you say you had a ton of work to get done today? Also, it's raining! Finally, it's r—"

Haruk woke up. And, in that breath of a moment, because I've known my Haruk forever, I knew something was wrong.

He blinked a couple of times, as if adjusting to the light. Then, he gazed around the room. For some reason, he was looking around wonderingly. When he turned to me, he seemed almost startled by my presence there.

"Hey, are you feeling o—"

Haruk flinched as I reached out to feel his forehead with the back of my hand. He kicked away from me, as if frightened, scrambling back on the bed. "Who are you?" he yelled. "Where—" he said, looking wildly about our bedroom, "Where am I?"

I would have thought he was joking if he didn't sound so earnestly jarred. Haruk is a self-made, hard-nosed academician and, thus, the deeply practical one of us. He is the one to stand patiently still in any queue, the one to be polite to a complete stranger, the one to check the locks before we go to bed. Nothing I knew of him suggested him capable of pulling such absurd antics.

Before I could respond, or say anything at all, he was off again.

"What" he said, frantic as before, "what is this p-p-*puh*—"

And as abruptly as that, Haruk started choking.

"Haru!" I exclaimed and ran around the bed to him. He was clutching his throat, trying to make sounds, but suddenly seemed incapable of doing so. He looked at me, bug-eyed.

"What is it, Haru? What is it?" I cried, starting to panic now, trying to pull his hand away from his throat as if that would help.

Haruk moved his lips. He made no sound. A terrified look came over him. He tried to talk again but, like before, nothing happened.

Fifteen minutes later, I was dragging Haruk through the parking lot. Haruk, silent, in the grip of a much larger fear, wasn't as frightened of me as earlier, though he still appeared quite bewildered by me. He was soundlessly mouthing *Who are you?* and *What's happening to me?* over and over. I'd had to forcefully get him out of the house. I'd rushed to our kindly old Sindhi neighbor across the hall, who often let me and Haru use his rusty Maruti Alto. Before he handed us the keys, he glanced at Haruk worriedly and offered to come along. I declined in a rush, forgetting my manners. I didn't think I could've afforded anyone slowing us down at the time.

Had the hospital not been close by, the rain would've certainly delayed us. We didn't live in the best part of the city, and I knew traffic jams would be budding on roads everywhere, like flowers on a vine. I honked my way through a cluster of cars at a red light and brought us to the hospital in an unbelievable thirteen minutes. Throughout, Haruk kept clutching his throat, as if to squeeze out sound, and gazing at the city in utter bafflement, as if he and it were total strangers.

I didn't waste time at the hospital. I parked the car haphazardly and, ignoring the shouts of the parking attendant, pulled Haruk into the Emergency ward. We rushed down a long corridor and barged into one of the bigger rooms. It was full of chattering doctors, a gaggle of nurses, and bed-ridden patients with needles and tubes sticking out of their arms and wrists. Some glanced up at us. A nurse came over.

"First, you need to go to the reception, madam, you—"

"There's something wrong with him!" I cried, hysterical. "He was perfectly fine this morning. I returned home and... and... something— something's wrong with him!" I wished I could phrase things better then, to convey what was exactly the problem with Haru. But, at the time, this was all I could manage. Nothing else came to mind. I looked at Haru, who continued to mouth words mutely.

"Please relax, madam. We'll take care of the patient," the nurse said calmly, taking hold of Haruk's arm. "Go to reception. Give them your names, both patient and attendant. They'll give you a slip. Bring that back here. Everything's going to be fine, madam."

Fretfully, I looked at Haruk. But the nurse had a firm grip on his arm. "The doctors will see to him at once," she assured me. My mind had settled enough to notice the Malayali accent, the crop of rich black hair in a long braid.

After watching the nurse escort Haruk to one of the beds, I turned and sped toward reception. Something in me, something instinctive, didn't want to leave Haruk's side for even a second. But the misfortune that had come with the rain continued to thwart me at every turn that day. When I reached the reception, I found a long, buzzing queue in front of it.

I knew I couldn't wait. I walked past the others and headed straight for the round, squat man at the counter.

"Excuse me, I—"

"Please get in the queue," the man responded mechanically.

"This is urgent," I insisted. "My husband's in the Emergency ward. I need—"

"My daughter's in the Emergency ward, too! Can I come up front as well?" someone called from behind.

I turned to catch sight of the man in the very back of the queue. There were patches, discoloration spotting one whole side of his face. He was carrying a thick file, full of medical tests I guessed, under one arm and holding a Bisleri bottle in the other. I turned back to the portly man at the reception. He had a look on his face. *You see*, it said. "Get in the queue, Miss," he repeated in his bored voice, "The staff in the Emergency ward will take care of your husband. This won't take time."

I was forced to retreat from the front desk and join the queue at the very end. I tried explaining that my Haru had bizarrely lost his voice, all of a sudden. That he wouldn't be able to explain to a doctor what was wrong with him. But the jeers and cries from the people in the queue drowned me out. As a performance artist, a crowd has always held power over me. It can boost me up or break me. My nerves failed me in the end. I moved away from reception, still anxious. These days, at times, I wonder if things would be different if I had stayed at the counter. If I had gotten the little yellow slip of paper and hurried back to Haruk. Actually, let me be honest here: I wonder about it *all* the time.

Minutes passed. They felt like weeks. Uneasy, I had fallen into my old habit of biting off and spitting out my fingernails. I did it plenty as a child; as an adult, I hadn't done it in decades. But now, unable to stand still, and not wanting to leave my spot in the slow-moving queue, I gnawed away. Only three people had received their slips and moved on since my interaction with the man at the counter. I moved past annoyed and shifted to restlessness, and I was steadily inching towards agitated.

In order to take my mind off the stalled queue, I glanced away. And that's when I saw her wandering aimlessly outside the Emergency ward.

It was the nurse I had left Haruk with.

She looked…distraught. She looked everywhere, and at everything, with a strange unfamiliarity. A bald, bespectacled doctor heading for the emergency ward passed her and nodded at her absently. The nurse looked baffled, as if she didn't know the man from Adam.

I felt furious. I'd left Haruk with this irresponsible person and she was here, clearly daydreaming, when she was supposed to be tending to my sick husband! I no longer cared for my place in the queue. Abandoning my spot, I strode over to her.

"Hey!"

She veered towards me in a daze.

"Why are you here?" I fumed, "You just left Haruk in there by himself, didn't you?"

She looked blankly at me, as if she didn't recognize me at all.

"Didn't you hear what I said?" I asked, angrily.

"I—I—d-do I know you?" the woman fumbled.

My ears grew hot, as they do when I'm angry. The nerve of this woman! Back in the Emergency ward, she had seemed so self-assured. And now she was acting like a complete oddball.

I would have given her a piece of my mind when, all of a sudden, startling me, her eyes bugged out. Her mouth dropped open and she clutched her throat with both hands.

I was too struck to reach out and help her. She was doing something I'd witnessed very recently. I had seen Haru undergo something very similar right before—

That's when she looked up at me and started moving her lips. However, unlike a second before, she created no sound. She was trying to talk, but was unable to pull even a syllable out of her throat.

As the woman moved her lips soundlessly in a panic, I didn't know what to do. And then, it hit me. I was, after all, in a hospital of all places.

"Help!" I cried, turning to the bustling reception area. "I need help! This woman—this woman here needs help!"

The people in the queue and those waiting on the benches gave me puzzled looks. A woman picked up her purse from next to her and set it on her lap, as if I was a madwoman about to rush over and snatch it. Craning their necks, some of them tried looking around me. Then, one of them, a swarthy, bearded man in a white kurta and a skull cap spoke up.

"*What* woman?" he asked roughly.

"Are you blind?" I said heatedly. "*This* woman! This nurse right h—"

When I turned around to point out the nurse, I found no one there. She was gone.

"She was—she was right—" I started. I would have carried on too, letting my disbelief unsettle me. The nurse had disappeared in the space of a second! But something else tugged hard at my heart. It's difficult to say what it was—intuition or instinct or something that goes deeper than those things. Right then, I needed to find my Haru. I needed to find him that very instant.

Forgetting about the slip I was meant to take, or about the queue I was supposed to stand waiting in, I ran. I ran straight for the Emergency ward and, on emerging into the narrow hall, I made a beeline for the room near its end, where I'd taken Haruk. Flinging the doors open, when I burst inside, my chest tightened instantly. Haru wasn't in the bed I had left him in.

"Haruk!" I called, looking about, drawing stares from the staff and the other patients. "Haru!" I cried, again. I swiveled at the spot and glanced everywhere. I searched the many faces around me for a familiar one. But I found no sign of him.

A doctor, clad in a typical white coat, hastened to me.

"Please keep your voice down," he snapped. "This is a hospital, for God's sa—"

He was interrupted when an IV bottle hanging next to Haruk's empty bed fell to the ground, making a loud clatter. The oddness of this drew everyone's attention.

"Haru?" I heard myself say for some reason.

After a moment of silence, the doctor next to me was pushed back as if shoved. We were at the entrance, blocking it. Momentarily, the doors of the room opened wide by themselves and closed, with a squeak, on their own. I stood there, along with the others, frightened and utterly bewildered, rooted to the very spot.

That was the last time I saw Haruk.

A year has passed since that day. A whole year. So much has happened. I'm not sure I know where to start, or how to make it all sound coherent. We've lived through so much and, even then, there's so little we know.

Haruk was the first person to be infected with the I-3 virus. Why I-3? Because of the three stages of the disease, stages that follow one another like clockwork. The I-3 does not kill a person. Perhaps that wouldn't have been too bad. Perhaps that would have been, in a way, merciful. In the first stage, the infected lose their memories; they enter a state of total amnesia. The second stage follows soon after that. Here, the virus attacks the vocal cords; the infected end up losing their voice entirely. Then, soon after, the final stage arrives, too swift to counter. And the person, though they live and breathe and exist, are rendered invisible.

I've struggled enough with the science of it to know that I don't grasp even a grain's worth of it. The words, bullish and technical, confuse me. 'Cells' and 'pathogens' and 'immunosuppressant' aren't a poet's words. But, after all this time, reading every scrap of news and forcing down the ton of research published on the subject, I've gathered something of an understanding. And it feels like somewhat enough for my purpose.

The I-3 is extremely contagious in nature, and passes easily from person to person. If the virus happens to make it into someone's body, there's no stopping it. The stages unfold in rapid succession, too quick to control. So far, there is no cure or vaccination. What *is* known for certain is that it doesn't affect everyone. Some, like me, are naturally immune to the I-3. Some, like Haruk, are extremely vulnerable to it.

I'm still in Bhubaneswar. Even if I wanted to, I cannot leave. Once the virus started gaining ground and people's children, grandparents, spouses started vanishing before their eyes, it didn't take long for the government to lock us down. They promptly sealed the city borders and instituted a full quarantine from the rest of the world. So far, luckily, though Bhubaneswar has over ten thousand cases, the virus seems contained, content to live here with us.

On another note, I've recently realized that, in some corners of the internet, I'm famous. I was the first one to start making noise. After Haruk disappeared, I did a lot of running around, banged on numberless doors, and nearly harassed a hospital attendant. It didn't amount to anything. However, when the rogue virus started its devastating spree, I was one of the first people the authorities contacted. When I landed a gig recently, I had an unusual number of people turn up to just numbly goggle at me from their seats. In an instant, I knew that these weren't my regulars. In fact, now that I'm 'famous,' my regulars hardly show up for my readings. I'm no longer the elusive pleasure I was a year ago. And those who do show up... I wonder if they even listen to a word I say.

You cannot walk down the street without running into one or more of the Wraiths. That's what the people of this ancient city, suffocated by superstition, decided to call the infected. The Wraiths roam the streets aimlessly. They have no memories and no way to communicate. And you can never sense them until you take a seat and find something preventing you from doing so; or, if you're eating a pizza and you watch a slice float up and disappear in small bites into thin air. The people here are too terrified, either of the infection itself or of all the religious end-of-days mumbo-jumbo surrounding the phenomenon, to mess with the Wraiths. The Wraiths go on, lumbering about their business, with their slack, empty minds. And we, the uninfected, pretty much do the same, too.

But all that is not the important part. What is important is that, on an ordinary morning, long after that dark day in July, when my wounds were still not quite healed, I ran into *him*.

It had been yet another day without Haruk. By now, numbness had taken shape in my life. That day, I got up, cleaned the apartment and, as it happened all too often, accidentally made breakfast for two. Even after months of searching, I hadn't the faintest clue about his where-abouts. It was obviously impossible to find an invisible man in a big, crowded city. Especially one with no memory of me or even his own name. I could have run down street after street shrieking for Haruk and it wouldn't have made a jot of difference. That Sunday, I was trying to urge myself to go outside, get some chores done, fill up my nearly emptied cupboards with food. It took some convincing, but, in the end, my lowly grumbling belly won out. Unbathed, I pulled on a pair of unwashed jeans and a top and almost forgot to close the apartment door behind me.

By eleven o' clock, I was walking to the nearby *sabzi bazaar* with a jute bag dangling from my left hand for groceries. With my earphones in, I listened to the recording of my last performance. Of late, I had begun worrying that whatever I felt inside would eventually find its way into my work. So, these days, I reviewed my performances obses-sively, ensuring there weren't too melancholy. Poetry was all I had left. I wouldn't be able to bear losing it, too.

Distracted by my thoughts and the recording, I collided with some-one. Stumbling back with a cry, I glanced up to find no one there. Of course, something exactly like this had happened before, quite a few times. I'd accidentally run into a Wraith.

Then, in that instant, something clicked. Something indescribable. It is inconceivable for me, a person who has made words her liveli-hood, to find the right ones, even a handful of them, to describe that feeling. I had nothing, no concrete proof to make any assumptions. And yet I knew it with every fiber of my being.

"Haruk!" I cried.

I waved my hands in front of me and grabbed hold of an invisible arm. Tears sprang to my eyes. "Haruk! It's me!" I said, reaching around the Wraith and grabbing it in a hug. Strangely, I couldn't wrap my arms around Haruk like always. My Haruk, I decided, had gained weight in all his time away. "Haruk!" I cried. "Haruk!" I said. "Haruk!" I repeated over and over.

A Wraith will go wherever you lead it. A Wraith will eat whatever you give it. A Wraith might wander off, as they're prone to, but not if you are careful about keeping the door shut or, better, latched and bolted.

I took Haruk back to our apartment that day. And, from then on, I've taken care of him. Fed him, bathed him and talked to him incessantly. As if we were invincibly young, in the summer of our lives, and not a thing had changed.

Today, it's been a whole week since Haru returned home. Sitting cross-legged on the kitchen counter, finishing a pear, I happened to be reading H.G. Wells' *The Invisible Man* since last night. Ironic, I know. For a lingering moment, I looked at the couch where I'd left Haruk, where now a banana was peeling itself slowly in mid air, and I began to wonder. If I just wrapped him up in bandages from head to toe, like in the book... then, I would know for sure. I would recognize him by his body, the shape of his arms, head, face.

The thought stayed with me for a while. Soon after, I got down, went into our bedroom and stuffed *The Invisible Man* into the dustbin there. Tomorrow, the garbage collectors would rid me of it permanently.

I consider the idea of covering Haruk in bandages to find out if he really *was* my husband, or some total stranger I'd dragged back home in one of the silliest notions to have ever popped into my head. After tossing away the book, I went and sat next to the Wraith. I watched him pick up an orange from the coffee table and begin peeling it slowly. Haru had never liked oranges before. But, then, so much has changed, about him and about me. Quietly, I rested my head against his warm body, closed my eyes, and slept.

ABOUT THE AUTHOR

Tushar Jain is an Indian poet and writer. He is the winner of the Srinivas Rayaprol Poetry Prize, the Raed Leaf India Poetry Award, the Poetry with Prakriti Prize, the DWL Short Story Prize, the Toto Funds the Arts Award for Creative Writing and has been nominated twice for the Pushcart Prize. His first play "Reading Kafka in Verona," was long-listed for the Hindu Metroplus Playwright Award. His work has appeared in various literary magazines and journals such as *Aaduna, Papercuts, The Madras Mag, Vayavya,* and others. His debut collection of poetry, *Shakespeare in the Parka*, was published in 2018.

NOLAN'S BUCKET LIST:
SNOW EDITION

JOSH CLARK

Nolan's Snow Day List

- Sled off THE HILL with the LEGIT snow tube
- Get hot chocolate at Brink's Coffee House
- Mess around with the guys on the frozen lake
- Snuggle with Mika
- Start a fire and watch a movie - also with Mika
- Avoid homework as much as possible
- Build a snowman
- Snowball fight with siblings or the boys
- Beg Mom to make cookies so the house smells good

All local schools are CLOSED - Districts 31 and 49, Gary Charter, and McClelland.

Rolling over in a sleepy coma, I waited for Dave from the Morning Show to repeat himself to confirm I wasn't dreaming.

After moving from Texas a year and a half ago, I couldn't wait for a snow day. It of course snowed here in Colorado last winter, but they hadn't cancelled school.

A snow day changed everything. Coated the town with possibility. Opportunity.

Dave repeated the same information, transforming dreams to reality.

I threw my covers aside, leaving the warm pocket of my blankets, and raced over to my window. A blanket of white lay on the ground. Powdered sugar fell from the sky, falling in lumps. Flakes streaked by our neighbor's streetlight at the end of their driveway.

Last night, the potential for a snow day was as out of reach as graduation. At the time, there was only a dusting. I flushed ice cubes down the toilet and did a snow dance. Neglected to turn my pjs inside out and it worked just the same!

I ran out of my room, bolting down the hall to an illuminated kitchen.

"Mom, Mom," I said, skidding in front of the counter.

She wasn't there. Only her coffee pot, percolating.

"She's taking a shower, Nolie."

I hated that nickname *so* much. Mom called me Nolie-Poly. Cute when you were five. Krista and Trevor weaponized it and used the name as ammunition.

"Why are you up?" I asked, walking to the couch Krista lay flopped over.

"Cause my alarm went off, and they hadn't cancelled school yet, Dingus."

She pushed up from the couch, disgust on her face. "Go put some clothes on. No one wants to see you in your undies."

Consumed by the snow day excitement, I hadn't realized I'd run out in only my boxers.

"Hi, hun," Mom said, wearing a sky blue bathrobe, her hair wet. She frowned at me. "Aren't you cold?"

My brain registered that I was practically naked, and goosebumps had popped up everywhere on my body.

A pillow hit me. "Who cares if he's cold? It's nasty."

I leaned toward Krista. "Oh, shut up."

She grabbed another pillow and, while still laying down, swung it at my head. I evaded it.

"It's too early for this, kids. Go put some clothes on, Nolie-Poly."

Krista snorted and pushed off the couch. "Yeah, *Nolie.*"

I flipped my middle finger at her.

"Mooommmm," Krista wailed.

She's a year older than me, but such a rat.

"I don't want to hear it," Mom said, pouring coffee.

I returned to my room and yanked on a pair of jeans. As I slipped into a thermal shirt, I shoved my desk chair aside and tore *The List* off my cork board.

I've had my snow day list ready for a *long* time.

I folded it a couple times, and shoved the piece of paper into my back pocket as I headed out of my room.

Krista had migrated to one of the bar stools in front of the island. I took a seat next to her.

"Since it's a snow day," Mom said. "How about chocolate chip pancakes?"

I didn't have a smashing breakfast on my list, but this was an awesome way to start off the day.

"Thanks, Mom."

"Sound good to you, Krista?" Mom asked, setting her coffee mug down on the counter.

"Eh, maybe I'll make a smoothie."

"You sure?"

"Yes." She slumped onto the island, her hair flopping over her face.

"College classes cancelled too, Mom?" I asked.

She beamed. "Yup. I get to spend it with my kids."

"Ugh," Krista said. "I was thinking a couch day and Netflix."

"Maybe do something about that face," I said.

"Shut it, Nolie."

Mixing batter, Mom asked, "Both of you have your homework done for tomorrow?"

Krista and I exchanged glances. Pro of having a block schedule usually, but that meant on a free day like this I wasn't finished with the next day's assignments.

"That's a 'no'," Mom said.

Krista and I responded, "I didn't say anything."

"Exactly."

I slammed my hand down on the counter, raising Mom's eyebrows. "It's a snow day, Mom. I have things to do."

Krista snorted. "What do you *have* to do?"

I was silent for a moment. Wisely, I hadn't said a word about my list to my family. Mom probably would find it cute. My siblings would terrorize me.

"Stuff," I said, rolling my shoulder.

"Stuff? Fantasizing about holding hands with your girlfriend?"

"We've held hands."

Krista laughed. "Is that all?"

I blushed. That was none of her effing business.

"Be nice," Mom said.

"At least I'm not sending my girlfriend dick pics."

"Nolan," Mom said.

Steam practically roiled out of Krista's ears. "I told you to stay out of my phone, roach."

Wish I hadn't found those. Certain things you couldn't unsee. There weren't enough layers of clothes on her *boy* to deter my imagination.

"I want you to get some of your homework done before you go anywhere," Mom said.

"Mom."

She glanced at the clock. "It's still early and I'm sure your friends aren't up yet."

Yeah, she was right about Ryker and Dawson, but they weren't the only ones I had plans with today. Mika factored into a lot of the items on my list.

If I wanted a chance to accomplish anything, I needed to get moving.

Chocolate chip pancakes were a good start, though.

I ate and knocked out my Math homework. I still had some English and Social Studies, but they would hold until tonight.

As promised, Krista was bundled up on the couch, the gas fireplace going, rewatching the same show for the millionth time.

I pulled a beanie on and made sure my list was tucked into my back pocket. Thankfully, Mom wasn't around to chew me out for walking out the door wearing nothing more than a hoodie.

The chill struck immediately. My bike was cold to the touch. Sheltered from the overhang, it, at least, wasn't covered in snow.

I sat down on the seat, but shot right back up when my butt made contact. Yeah, I'd ride standing up.

Snow continued to fall, accumulating on my hoodie. The roads appeared to have been plowed. The sidewalks were hit or miss.

I slowed my pace for my already fifteen-minute ride to Mika's after slipping on the ice a few times.

The outside of Mika's house was easy to mistake for a Christmas card. Snow on the rooftop, a lit tree on display inside the main bay window, flashes of red and green lining the roof, and bows tied under the garage lights.

I threw my bike into the snowy yard and raced up to the door, almost eating cement as my shoes slipped on a patch of ice.

I rang the doorbell and quickly thrust my numb hands into my hoodie pocket.

Mrs. Richardson opened the door, rubbing her arms as the cold air struck her.

"Where is your coat, young man? Get in here," she gestured me into the entryway.

My body shook the moment I stepped in. The temperature difference was staggering.

"Your mother lets you outside, in this weather, dressed like that?"

I wasn't about to answer that question, and trusted she wouldn't mention it to my Mom.

"Need something warm to drink? Hot Chocolate? Cider?"

"Cider."

I didn't want to ruin my appetite for hot chocolate at Brink's.

My hoodie grew damp as the snow melted into the fabric, beads of water trickling through my hair as the flakes liquified.

Following Mrs. Richardson into the kitchen, I tracked wet footprints into the house.

"Nolan," Mika's sister said, jumping from her chair. Playdough containers occupied half the table. She ran over and wrapped her arms around my legs, peering up at me. "I got a snow day today. You, too?"

"Yeah, me too."

Lucy wore pink pajamas, with a large snowman on her shirt and smaller ones on the legs.

"Did you come over to play with playdough?

"Uhh…"

Mrs. Richardson poured a jug of cider into a large pot she placed on the stove.

"Where's your sister? I asked. Likely still sleeping…

"Mika's fighting quite a nasty cold," Mrs. Richardson said.

I frowned, wanting to pull out my list. There'd be a lot to rework if Mika couldn't do anything.

"Can I see her?"

"When the cider is ready, you can take her a mug."

I carried them up the stairs, stopping at Mika's closed door.

Juggling the mugs, I managed a small knock before edging my way in.

"Lucy, I already told you once this morning to stay out."

"Nice to see you, too."

Mika looked over from her bed, surrounded by tissues, more over-filling the can beside her nightstand.

"What are you doing here?" She sniffled, batting at her hair.

"I wanted to see you."

"Something wrong with texting?"

I set both the mugs down on her nightstand and rolled the desk chair over after removing a pile of clothes.

"Really, Nolan, I'm a hot mess."

"Yeah, you're sick." I reached for her hand under the blanket and squeezed it. "I think you're still adorable."

She grabbed a tissue and blew her red nose. "Trevor hit you over the head too hard, cause you're insane."

"You hear it's a snow day?"

"My sister kindly informed me this morning. I wasn't going to school anyway, and wish she was."

I pulled the list from my pocket. She was the only one I'd consider sharing it with.

"Think you'll have some energy to do some things today?" I asked, holding my list between my fingertips.

Mika stared at me. Thinking I was some mental case. "No, Nolan. I don't."

"Not even if I make a fire later and we watch a movie?"

She threw her head back on her pillow and looked up at the ceiling. "Text me later. Maybe if I get some sleep."

I let go of completing the list with Mika, but wasn't giving up on it entirely.

———

The sun attempted to peek through the clouds. We were still socked in, but sunlight bounced off the untouched drifts, making them sparkle.

My breath kept drifting back into my face on my ride home. I thought pedaling would warm me up, but I was still freezing.

Where my bike was usually parked sat Dawson and Ryker's sled discs. They zipped pretty good, got some air. You had no control, though. They paled in comparison to the snow tube I had gotten for my birthday.

I was likely the only kid who got a snow tube in June.

Dawson and Ryker were in the living room with Krista. Both of them were on their phones and still bundled in snow jackets.

"There you are," Dawson said, throwing his hands up. "Answer your texts much?"

I blew into my hands, attempting to warm them. It felt like my fingers were going to fall off.

Pulling out my phone, I realized that I had messages from both of them. "Whoops."

"Whoops is right," Ryker said, standing and tugging up his sweatpants.

The twins walked over to greet me. They were the same height, and had identical facial features, except for the birthmark on Ryker's cheek. They also tried to differentiate themselves through hair styles.

Dawson's hair was long and blond, while Ryker's was floppy and dyed black, though his blond roots showed.

"We sledding?" They both asked.

"Heck yeah, let me grab my tube."

I went out into the cold garage. With Dad's car gone, I found our sleds with ease, but I couldn't find my new snow tube, only a couple crappy plastic ones and the toboggan.

I bolted back through the garage door and ran into the twins.

"Easy, there," Dawson said, grabbing my shoulders.

"I can't find my tube."

"Maybe it got sick of you and rolled off to a new owner," Ryker said.

"Shut up," I said, shoving by him.

"Mooommm," I yelled. "Where's my tube?"

Returning into the kitchen, I repeated myself when there was no answer.

"Stop yelling," Krista said. "She's over at the Morrisons."

"What happened to my tube?"

"I didn't do anything with your stupid tube. Trevor probably took it."

I ran down the hall and saw his door was cracked open. "What do you mean he 'took it'?"

Krista sighed. "He met up with his friends while you were at *Mika's*. They mentioned something about sledding."

I clenched my fists. Leave it to my brother to take my stuff.

"Are we going?" Dawson asked.

"Trevor took my tube."

"So?"

"Uh, hello. It's *mine*. And it's the only decent sled I've got."

"Use one of those plastic ones, or the toboggan," Ryker said.

"No, I'm getting it back." I broke my wrist on that stupid toboggan last year, and wasn't doing *that* again.

Dawson laughed. "Your brother isn't giving that back until he's good and done with it. He's more likely to strap you to a toboggan and send you plummeting down the sledding hill."

He wasn't wrong, but I was determined on getting it, somehow. Especially when it hadn't touched snow yet. A pool didn't count.

"Would you three shut it," Krista said. "I'm trying to watch this."

"Be gone soon, Your Majesty," Dawson said.

"I swear," Krista said.

Dawson nudged me. "What'd you do to get your sister's panties in a knot already?"

"She's always like that."

A pillow hit my face.

"If you'd like to see out of both of your eyes come tomorrow," Krista said. "Scram."

"OOOOHHHHH," Dawson and Ryker said, in chorus, slamming against each other like they were in a mosh pit.

I shook my head, then grabbed Dawson's hoodie and dragged him toward the door.

It was almost noon, and I hadn't accomplished a single thing on my list.

Since we had to drag our sleds along, that required walking to the sledding hill. There were a couple solid ones in town, but the elementary school that was only a few miles from my house was the best. Everyone knew it, too.

"Are you sure you don't want to go get a sled?" Ryker asked.

"Yes, I'm sure. Silly to do that when I'll have mine back soon."

"You're delusional," Dawson said. "Since when's Trevor been the giving type?"

"Oh, I know," Ryker said. "He gives Nolan plenty of bruises. Noogies. Wet willies. Pink bellies."

"Don't forget the love taps to the balls," Dawson said, grinning at me.

I punched his arm.

"Easy there, killer," Dawson said. "Just messing."

"Well, stop," I said, pushing him.

Leaping in front of me, Ryker started walking backward, grinning in my face. "Aw, did Nolie-Poly get his feelings hurt?" He rubbed at his eyes, mimicking crying.

I shoved him. Ryker's feet struck a patch of ice, upended his legs, and he landed on his back.

Dawson and I bent down to him. "Are you okay?"

Ryker's eyes popped wide. He sucked in a huge breath. Eyes blinked rapidly.

"Dude?" Dawson asked.

"I'm good," he said, grimacing. "Let me catch my breath."

A few moments later, we each gave him an arm to pull up on. Once back on his feet, Ryker flipped me off.

His brother mashed snow between his bare hands and lobbed it at Ryker's face.

Gasping, he stumbled backward as the snow exploded, Dawson having scored a direct hit.

Ryker made a quick swipe at his eyes and produced his own snowball. It went wide left and thunked against a wooden fence.

The war was on.

All of us hunched over to make our weapons. We continued down the route to the sledding hill, making snowballs as we went, darting into yards, sliding behind trees for cover, hoping for a strike on the others. Faces and butts were our most popular targets.

I was glad to mark one item off my list.

The hill was packed. At no other time would you willingly get so many kids at a school. Especially from tykes to teens.

It took mere seconds to find Trevor. He and his crew shoved a batch of middle schoolers out of the way to zip down the hill. Trevor, on *my* tube.

Dawson gave me a nudge. "Well you found him, go tell him you want it back."

"You're not helping."

My determination evaporated watching them trudge up the hill. In my head, it had sounded good that I'd strong-arm my tube from Trevor. I just hadn't worked out logistics of how that'd happen.

Based on past experiences, the twins were useless backup since they usually morphed into cheerleaders for Trevor.

They could at least help out when Trevor kicked my ass. Instead, when he slapped me around, I'd hear comments like, "Go for his nuts. Teabag 'em."

I got it, they didn't want to become his next target—along with having a perverse pleasure of watching my ass get handed to me.

Against Trevor, I was outmatched and, even worse, I didn't have my two *friends* to rely on.

"What?" Dawson asked, adjusting his beanie. "You were the one saying you'd get it back. I'm just making sure you follow through."

"Gee, thanks."

"Look what the storm blew in," Trevor said, resting my tube on the ground. His pal set a toboggan down in front of them.

"I want my tube," I said.

Trevor smirked. "This one?"

"Duh, that one. It's not yours."

"You weren't using it. Rides good, too."

I clenched my fist.

Trevor laughed. "I'll give it back when I'm done."

When? Tonight, when everyone was home for the night? Leaving a streaky hill for tomorrow since everyone would have used it by then. Jacking up the best runs.

The hill was still pristine and in excellent sledding condition if I didn't have to wait longer.

"I want it now."

He exchanged glances with his jock friend.

"Not gonna happen. Needs broken in a little more, first. Wouldn't want you to get hurt."

So full of—

Dawson bumped my arm. "We can take turns on our discs."

"I have a perfectly good tube, right there," I said.

Trevor was jostling with his bud, a loose grip on my tube. My chance.

The snow crunched under my footsteps as I moved straight for my brother.

As I was about to reach for one of the handholds, Trevor saw me. He swung the tube away at the last moment and I stepped by.

"Hold this," he told Carter. Everyone at school loved Carter, but he'd bullied me alongside Trevor for years.

My brother gave me a solid shove, and I planted into the snow.

"Someone write you a cute note?" Trevor asked.

A paralyzing terror vise-gripped my body.

I leapt up. Trevor had my list, but hadn't unfolded it.

Yet.

I reached for it, but Trevor yanked it away.

"Now I *got* to see."

Unfolding it, he cleared his throat.

I made one more snatch for it, but Trevor evaded me again. Then, with his free arm, he put me into a headlock, my feet treading against the snow as I attempted to break his hold.

"Nolan's Snow Day List."

Trevor busted up. Carter joined in.

He read through it, line by line, every moment mortifying. I tried discerning if Dawson and Ryker were busting up over it, too. This was the reason I hadn't shared with them, either.

Without cranking my head up, it was impossible to see their faces. I heard some familiar laughs, though.

"Snuggle with Mika," Trevor cooed. He tightened his hold on me.

"Well if this isn't adorable. If you were a sixth-grade *girl*."

I felt my cheeks warm. If anyone asked, I'd blame the flushed look on the cold.

"Give it back, Trevor."

"Like your tube? So you can ride down the hill? This is pathetic."

Still holding my head, he brought the list down, blocking my vision. Trevor tore the note.

"No," I yelled.

Trevor snickered. He let the paper fragments fall like snow.

"You don't need a damn list for a snow day. But here's something you can mark off."

He dragged me toward a snowbank and threw me into it. I sunk into the lump of snow.

I brushed snow out of my eyes while Trevor yanked at my legs. Not my legs. Pants.

With another pull, they slipped off my hips and were tugged free.

Carter moved the tube in range for Trevor, who lobbed my balled-up jeans into the center.

"Trevor!" I yelled.

Receiving a nod from Trevor, Carter kicked my tube down the hill.

Dawson offered a hand while his brother slid after the tube.

My hairs stood on end. I wanted to curl in on myself as the wind struck my bare legs.

"Better cover up," Trevor said. "Wouldn't want you to get frostbite, Nolie-Poly."

He and Carter laughed as they began making their way off the hill.

I clenched my fist.

Bystanders laughed, pointing at my boxers sticking out under my hoodie.

"Not sure about your new look, Nolan," Dawson said.

I shook my head.

Rather than stand freezing without any pants, I headed down the hill, with Dawson following.

About halfway up, Ryker met me, throwing me my pants. He underthrew, and they landed in the snow. I bent down and brushed them off. Kids ripped by on the hill.

As I tugged on my snowy jeans, Ryker said, "Carter must have pulled the valve. Air's leaking out." The tube lay at his feet, looking less plump than expected.

Though my pants were frigid, they beat wearing nothing.

"Wanna take turns on our discs?" Dawson asked.

"Naw," I said.

"C'mon," Ryker said. "Trevor's just being a dick. Don't let him ruin your day."

"He already did that."

"What's next on your list?"

I huffed. "Trevor's right, it was pathetic."

Dawson bumped into me. "Now you're going to start listening to Trevor? Please. What do you want to go do?"

Whether I still had my list or not, I realized I wanted one thing very badly.

"Brinks."

———

B rink's Coffee House was packed, the normally pristine floor a wet, mucky mess.

While Dawson and I got in line, Ryker staked out a small table in the corner of the building.

Dawson pulled off his beanie and shook his long, blond hair. His cheeks were red. "Why'd you make that list?"

"I don't wanna talk about it," I muttered.

He grabbed my shoulder. "I'm not trying to make fun of you. I wanna know."

I stared at him for a moment, not believing him. "You aren't going to laugh?"

A grin broke his stoic face. "Well... I can't make any promises."

"Never mind."

"Okay, okay. I won't laugh."

I gave a quizzical look.

"Do it for Ryker. He went down the hill for your pants."

"For Ryker?"

"Telling me will be like sharing with him. We're twins, after all."

"That's the biggest load of crap I've ever heard."

Dawson peered toward the counter. "And this line isn't getting any shorter."

I sighed. "Fine."

I cringed as Dawson cracked his knuckles.

"Pretty simple, really. Living in Texas, I never got a snow day.

They're special. Providing a chance to do something you don't get to do every day."

That, plus an excuse to spend time with Mika. Although her having a cold squashed my plans.

"Huh," Dawson said. "Guess that makes sense. They tend to happen every year though, doesn't seem like anything exciting."

"Really, dude? No school should be enough excitement."

We moved up in the line.

Dawson tried pulling his hoodie off but got his arms stuck in the process. Struggling for a bit, he finally got it off and bundled under his arm. "They have their heat on too high."

"I'm still freezing."

"Yeah, cause you took your jeans off in a freakin' snowstorm, doofus."

"Not by choice."

He laughed and clapped my back. "Can't believe you let your brother do that."

I shook him off. "It's not that I let him. I kinda didn't have a choice."

"Pushover."

Easy for him to say. His brother was his best bud. Sure, they screwed around, but they had each other's backs. With mine, I had to watch my back.

"Soooo," Dawson said. "If we ever get our beverages, what's next on your list?"

"Forget about it."

"No. You want to do it. Let's do it."

Him making a big deal about it really did make it seem stupid.

"I guess go out on the lake or make a snowman."

Dawson held back a laugh, swiping his hand over his mouth to disguise it. "Okay."

"See, you think it's dumb too."

"Uhhhh... Kinda, but the lake's fun. Is it even frozen?"

"Don't tell me if it's not."

I couldn't handle any more disappointment.

In the end it wasn't worth waiting for the hot chocolate. It was watery. Normally, it slid down your throat rich, creamy, heck, a liquid version of a chocolate bar.

Snow continued to fall at a steady rate. The wind whipped, driving cold to the bone.

If Dawson hadn't been so persistent, I'd of called it and gone home. But, other than a lame snowball fight and sub-par hot chocolate, I'd done nothing else on my list. Who knew when it'd snow next that I'd get to do this again?

An opportunity, wasted.

Besides, home was bound to involve putting up with Krista and Trevor. And, if he told her about my list, I'd get bombarded with taunts and jeers. My sister was about as sentimental as a coil of barb wire.

The pathway around the lake was covered with snow, benches unusable with the accumulating powder.

Ryker blew on his hands and rubbed them together. "Freezing out here."

"You should have worn gloves," Dawson said.

"Not like you have any on."

"I'm not bitching about it."

Ryker tackled him and the two of them grappled in the snow. Flecks of grass poked up where they'd rolled. Both of their clothes were caked in white.

Dawson lay on his back, smothered by Ryker. But he wasn't benefitting. Dawson had his brother in a chokehold, legs wrapped around his gut.

Flailing, Ryker sputtered for air and, eventually, tapped. His brother obliged and let go. Ryker rolled over, coughing.

"Douche."

"Ryker, don't start again," Dawson said. "It's exhausting putting you in your place."

"Can we do whatever we were doing and get the hell out of here?"

"We can just go," I said.

"Seriously?" Ryker asked, slapping his legs with his hands. "Why'd you drag us over here, then?"

Dawson got a bundle of snow and started rolling it on the ground.

"What the frik are you doing?" Ryker asked, rubbing his arms.

"Making a snowman," Dawson said. "Sooner you help, sooner we can get going."

"Why didn't you say so?" Ryker said, jumping over next to Dawson and rolling snow.

"Should have done our snowball fight here," he added. "This packs so well."

Dawson waved me over, while he stood observing. The snow picked up again.

"Make the head," Dawson said.

Like my friends, I hadn't worn any gloves, which meant they'd gone numb.

When I put them in the snow to make a head, they burned. Ryker was right though, the snow packed well.

Once I finished the head, Dawson had made a good start on the base. I got alongside him and helped him roll it, with Ryker still working on the middle.

Looked like we were making crop circles with how many times we'd gone back over our prior pathway, crisscrossing through the grassy field.

Panting, Dawson slumped against our large bottom ball. "Perfect."

"There is no way I'm going to get the middle on there," Ryker said.

"Don't be a baby and do it."

"I can't lift this."

"Why'd you make it so big?" Dawson asked.

"Me? You're the one who made the base effing huge."

Dawson responded with a snowball that splatted in his brother's face.

Ryker stood stunned for a moment. Dawson gestured his head at Ryker as he threw another one.

Catching on, I formed a snowball, ignoring the burning sensation, and chucked it at Ryker.

It struck his chest.

"You two are both assholes."

Our barrage continued. I landed a good hit on the side of Ryker's cheek.

Ryker shook his head. "You're going down."

He sprinted after me. I started running. No destination in mind.

Next thing I knew, my legs went out from under me and my face was in snow.

A large weight landed on my back. I grunted.

"Dog pile." Dawson leapt onto Ryker.

I slapped at the snow. "Get off." I coughed.

Some of the weight left. A cold hand touched my neck and shoved my face into the snow. Wet shoes pressed down along my spine.

I pushed myself up and brushed off. I was soaked.

"Now, if you'd both stop jacking around," Dawson said. "We can finish this snowman."

It took the three of us to lift the ball. Breathing heavily, we boosted it up. Struggling, we maneuvered it to the base. Moments after setting it down, it continued moving and slipped right off, crumbling upon impact.

"Great," Ryker said.

"Let's go," I said. "I'm freezing."

"Really, dude?" Ryker asked. "We're doing this for you."

"Well, I never asked. Ok?"

"Hold up, you're getting pissed cause we're doing your stupid list?"

"Ryker," Dawson said.

"If you want to go, go," I said. "I'm not stopping you. You're right, the list was stupid."

Dawson threw me into a headlock.

"Cut the attitude. You got to do a good chunk of this."

"What? Snowball fights, barely passable hot chocolate, and getting picked on by Trevor?"

Dawson continued walking, my body in tow since he hadn't released my head. I pushed against his arm with no luck.

"Your list was a good start. Don't let that determine if today turns out shitty or not."

"When'd *you* get all philosophical?" Ryker asked.

"It's just not how I expected it'd go," I said.

Dawson tightened his grip. "So what? You got to hang with us. Be grateful for that."

"I guess," I said, unconvinced.

"Well," Dawson said, letting me go. I staggered forward. "Do something about it. We're going to go home and play video games. You can join or, hell, go see Mika if that's going to make you feel like today wasn't a waste."

"She's sick," I said. Soaking wet and continuing to stay out in this, I wasn't far behind her.

"Then be a good boyfriend and make a shit ton of soup."

A wonder he didn't have a girlfriend.

———

I took the longest shower in recent memory to thaw myself out. Dried off, I went out to the living room, snug in a hoodie and sweats. Krista, Mom, and Trevor were scattered around, lounging.

"Have you moved at all today?" I asked Krista. Her blanket lay in the exact same position as this morning.

"Who asked you, Nolie-Poly?"

I took a seat on the only vacated recliner. I wasn't about to squeeze between Trevor and Krista on the couch.

Smirking, Trevor said, "Krista, you should have seen Nolie on the hill."

Her face scrunched up. "Why should I care?"

"He forgot how to keep his pants up."

A nerf ball bounced off my head. Trevor gave me a head nod.

Mom was blind to his antics, immersed in her laptop.

Krista snorted and forced herself off the couch. She went down the hall without a word.

I wasn't sure what was playing on TV, nor was anyone else in the room. Trevor became absorbed by his phone. I preferred that to him talking to me.

The room was cozy, a fire going, the heat just now kicking on. All I needed was a blanket and I could doze off on the couch.

I checked my phone. It was about five. I still had time if I wanted to see Mika for a bit. The thought of biking over again sucked.

"Mom could you take me over to Mika's?"

She looked up from her laptop. "Now? Weren't you there earlier? It's still snowing isn't it?"

"Well...yeah."

"Trevor will take you."

My heart sank. There was no way.

"Huh?" Trevor asked.

"Can't you take him on the way over to the grocery store?"

"Grocery store?"

"Didn't you talk to your Dad about this?"

Trevor looked like a deer in the headlights. "He said he'd take me out for some snow driving."

Mom shook her head. "Yes, while you're out, running to the grocery store."

"Are they even open?"

"Yes. I called."

Trevor groaned.

He couldn't tell me 'no' since this involved Dad. Though he'd find some way that I'd owe him. Trevor never just took me somewhere. Not without a price.

Snow crunched as Trevor pulled into Mika's driveway. Headlights pierced through the snow flurries.

"I'll send you a text when we're leaving the grocery store," Dad said.

"I can't stay longer than that?"

"We're not coming back out to get you. Make the most of your time."

One reason to be grateful of how Trevor drove, I'd have a fair amount.

I shivered walking up to the door and rang the doorbell.

Mika's mom answered, Lucy peering around her legs.

"Hi, Nolan," she mumbled with her hand thrust in her mouth.

"Nolan," Mika's mom said, pulling a blanket tight around her shoulders as the wind kicked up. "That's all you're wearing? Get in."

Made all the difference these clothes were dry, unlike my drenched ones from earlier.

"Do you want to watch Frozen?" Lucy asked. "We just started."

An ironic choice. It was fitting though.

"Didn't expect to see you again, today," Mika's mom said. One light was on in the kitchen, and the sounds of Frozen traveled down the hall.

"I…" I rubbed at my neck. "Wanted to see Mika."

Her mom sighed. "You can stay for a little bit. I'm going to go up and read. Lucy. Behave."

"Yay," she said, grabbing my hand and dragging me down the hall.

"But… what about…"

Mika.

She was curled up on the couch, watching the movie.

"Mika, look who's here," Lucy said, letting go of my hand and jumping onto her sister.

"Don't do that," Mika said, shoving her aside and pulling the blanket close. "I see him."

I ambled my way over, the fire roaring and a talking snowman stealing the show onscreen. As one does.

I brushed aside a swath of haphazardly discarded used tissues.

"How are you feeling?" I asked. Unsure if I should slide up next to her.

Mika responded by blowing her nose. The tissue fell to the floor.

"Little better, but I still feel like crap."

Lucy bounced on the cushions, bounding toward us.

Grabbing another tissue, Mika said, "Lucy, can you please sit still?"

"Fine," she said, repositioning herself on the cushion next to me. In seconds, she was engrossed by the movie.

"Can I get you anything?" I asked.

"You can shut up and lay next to me," Mika said.

She snuggled up to my shoulder, the blanket conveniently falling over my leg.

I slid next to Mika and pulled her close.

Lucy giggled.

I could care less what was on the screen. Didn't care that my girl-friend was fighting a cold. Just glad I was here, wrapped up together.

"Thanks for coming over," Mika said. "I'm sure there are better ways to finish your snow day."

I kissed the top of her head. "No. There really aren't."

Which reminded me of something.

I texted Dad a quick message, asking if he could pick up some cookie dough. Asking Mom to make them was a stretch, but I could do it. Then I could check off the rest of my list.

Even if Mom said 'no' to me making cookies at nine at night, I was just fine with this moment here.

Snow still fluttered to the ground. And here I was, curled up with my girl, under a warm blanket, next to a roaring fire.

The snow would melt in a few days, but not these memories. I could start a new list for the next snow day. A chance to do it all over again.

Or, we could wing it, adding to the spontaneity of a snow day.

After all, today's best moments were the unplanned ones.

ABOUT THE AUTHOR

Josh is a writer, bookseller, and graphic designer. He graduated with an art degree from Colorado State University-Pueblo. Josh is an active member of Pikes Peak Writers, Rocky Mountain Fiction Writers, and was the former Speakers Coordinator for Pueblo West Writers. His short story, "The Galaxy Got a Whole Lot Bigger," received a Silver Honorable Mention in Q4 of the 2020 Writers of the Future Contest. He is now busy writing his next novel.

SIR GEORGE AND THE DRAGON

C. E. BARNES

Sir George went out a-dragoning
Upon one fine spring day.
He trailed the beast by spoor and sound
Until his efforts led him 'round
To where the lizard lay.

Lowered then, Sir George, his lance
To run the reptile through,
But with a screech of steel on scale,
The dragon sleepily twitched its tail
And snapped the spear in two.

Sir George was vexed, but not dismayed
For he still had his sword.
He smote his foe from every side
But couldn't scratch its scaly hide,
And still the serpent snored!

"Wake up, fell beast! 'Tis time to die,"
Sir George so bravely spoke,
And, whether caused by threats of death
Or by the leeks on George's breath,
The dragon finally woke

Its nostrils flared, its ire raised,
Its eyes were shot with blood.
The reptile raised its massive head,
Looked George in the eye, and said,
"You got a problem, bud?"

How terribly the two did fight
Is anybody's guess.
For George returned home, mad as hell,

Dumped his armor down the well.
And vowed he'd take up chess.

ABOUT THE AUTHOR

C. E. Barnes grew up in Northwest Florida but left at the age of 27 because a human can only tolerate humidity, mosquitoes, and tourists for just so long. His literary influences include Sir Arthur Conan Doyle and Herbert George Wells, which is why his sentence structure abounds with convoluted dependent clauses spliced together with an exuberance of semicolons. He is awkward in social settings and retreats behind a shield of polite formality, unless you bring up the topic of dogs, whereupon he'll talk your poor ears off. He adores his wife. He shouldn't be trusted to write his own bio.

ONE-WAY TICKET

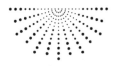

SARAH REILLY PANCOAST

29 minutes

I scrub the blood and excess hair dye off my face with the paper towels in the bathroom. I picked "Chestnut Brown number 27." Because it sounded like a normal, pretty color and because 27 is my lucky number. It's always bugged me in movies when the girl on the run dyes her hair black, or purple, or something. It seems like that would be more noticeable.

"That's a one-way ticket to Police Car Central," is what my mom would say when people in movies made a stupid mistake. People were always buying one-way tickets with my mom. "That's a one-way ticket to Extra Chore-ville" was my reminder that I was talking back. "Kaitlyn, you're buying yourself a one-way ticket to No Phone Town," is pretty obvious.

Chestnut Brown will get on a bus and blend. No Police Car Central for me. My hair was super-blond before, almost white. Of course, that was dye, too, so my eyebrows aren't blond. Yup, Chestnut Brown will blend right in. It's closer to my normal hair color. I never wanted blonde. My mom did.

The directions on the box said 30-60 minutes for color saturation. I need to move—so 30 minutes it is.

I root around in the cabinet for the box of Band-Aids.

My hands won't stop shaking. I close my eyes and take three deep breaths. That's what my PE teacher, Mrs. March, always told us to do when she taught our yoga session every year. I suck at yoga. I'm more of a cheerleader. Or, I was. But the deep breaths helped, and I went back to work on my face.

The cuts on my neck would be easy to hide behind a scarf. They had closed already. I had to pull a little to get the bloody paper towel off. One big pull, like ripping off a Band-Aid, and the towel was free. I shoved it in my back pack. I scrubbed the cuts a little to get the excess blood off so it wouldn't get all over my scarf. It's my favorite. The three cuts on my face will be harder to hide. They also won't stop bleeding.

"Hold that towel on there for a minute. If it doesn't stop bleeding you bought yourself a one-way ticket to the ER." That's what my mom would have said. Which also implied that I would die there. I never pointed that out to her. I had needed stiches on my elbow last year. That bitch Emma shoved me into a gym locker. And that other bitch, Mrs. March, didn't do anything about it.

21 minutes

"He hurt me, mom. Roy hurt me."

I told her again and again, but she didn't believe me. Not really. She broke up with him, but that was it.

"He called me fat. That's how he bought that one-way ticket to Single Town." That's what my mom said.

But she can't hurt me anymore. None of them can. Now I could buy an *actual* one-way ticket. The idea makes me laugh.

17 minutes

The cuts on my face are still bleeding. I can see red seeping through the Band-Aids.

The dye won't be permanent. Dye on dye doesn't last long, but I don't need it to. I am going to New York City. I was supposed to go there two months ago on a school trip. My mom said she couldn't afford it. Instead, her new boyfriend flew her there. She always only worried about herself. Now *I* am worried about me. That's fair.

And, I took money from them. That's fair, too.

Three more deep breaths.

I suppose I should feel guilty. But, my mom always did what she needed to do. *Who* she wanted to do. Roy, Emma's dad, my cheerleading coach. Of course, that one was for me. "This is your one-way ticket to the top of the pyramid," she told me. I didn't need her help. I got to the top on my own. Then, I quit. I don't *want* the top of the pyramid.

12 minutes

I lean against the bathroom wall, careful not to touch the tile with my hair.

The room is fairly clean. I clean it. My mom wouldn't do that. And, she used to make the biggest messes, too. I didn't clean up at the house. All I did was put the knife in my bag and clean my skin out from under my mom's nails. My fingerprints *should* be all over the house. It's where I lived, after all. And, I thought that if some of my blood was found at the scene, the police would just think I got hurt, too.

I'd be the victim.

Because I *am*.

I am restless. I check the timer, again. I won't leave the bathroom, though. It is way messier downstairs.

Normally, I would have used my phone. I owe Lucy a text. My mom, too, of course. She was always sending me really long texts. Like letters. But too many missed replies and I bought myself a "One-way ticket to Phone-Calls-Only Village". That was a miserable place I had visited before.

Lucy just wanted to know about our English homework. She isn't really my friend. But, after this she will be all over it. I can picture her in the police interrogation room. "She was my best friend but I really just wanted to help her."

I wish I could pay them all a visit. It would be so easy after mom and him. Lucy, Emma, Griffin. He pretended he loved Emma but he slept with Lucy. And he kissed me and taped it. He threatened to show Lucy or Emma or both. I didn't care about that—he wouldn't do it, they both would have known it was his idea. I just couldn't stand the idea of other people watching me kiss. I was probably doing it wrong.

Emma was my best friend before my mom banged her dad and her parents got divorced. I told Emma about Roy, but her solution to Roy was to tell her dad. Emma's dad was a police detective. That was the last thing I wanted. I'm not stupid. I would have ended up on trial. This time was different. I left a note and a video. The video was on my phone. I left that, too. And, in less than 12 minutes I will walk away. Not run. I think running would look weird. I will just walk out of the house. If I go out the back, none of the neighbors could see me through the fence and then I would be in the small woods behind our house. I was already packed. I planned to go. That's how I knew the bus schedule. That's why I had the hair dye.

9 minutes

I straighten up the bathroom a little. Trying to make it look like I didn't grab anything in particular.

I shoplifted the hair dye last week. But I did it during a regular trip to the drug store. I bought a bunch of my usual stuff. I knew I would be on the tape.

I also knew I had to wait a little. I had to have a good plan.

I knew my mom had a secret. And, I knew that secret was why she got to go to New York City. I thought Roy was back. That would be so like her. She told me he had moved back to Cleveland. Apparently, he had a kid there. But I didn't believe it.

And, anyway, it turned out to be a lot worse.

At breakfast, almost two weeks ago, my mom had told me she had news. Like big news. "I'll pick up sushi."

Oh shit.

Sushi meant moving. Sushi meant Dad's not coming back. But, sometimes, sushi meant "I'm sorry." Sorry for Emma; sorry I lost my job; sorry your dad's not really your dad.

My mom probably had sushi on dates all the time. She hadn't been home for dinner in three weeks. I ate cereal every night. But, she always acted like we had the same life. We both ate out. We both went to New York City. We both slept with Roy. We were both 17.

Most days, after school, I went home and sat in my room. But, I didn't want my mom to know that, so I went to the town library. I hadn't been there since I was little. Elementary school, or Brownies, or something like that. I should have been reading. Mark Twain was our assignment for English. I also had to finish my lab write-up and three more math problems. But, all I could do was worry. I was terrified that Roy would be back. I couldn't imagine what I would do if I opened the door and he was there, again, in my house.

I sat in the uncomfortable wooden chairs at the back cubicle and held my head in my hands. I pictured his bad comb-over. His Coke-bottle glasses getting fogged up. I could smell his cigarette-covered-by-mint-gum breath. My stomach turned and I put my head on the desk.

All I could do was worry.

Until I started to plan.

I could just leave. That was it. I didn't have to stay any more.

I wove a delicious fantasy: I could go to New York. I could start over.

Money was my only sticking point.

I had worked a part-time job during the summer, but during the school year I was supposed to focus on school, cheerleading, and "boys, don't forget boys" my mom said. She pretended like she was joking. I knew she wasn't. It was February, and that money was long gone.

But, a girl could dream.

I wandered so far into my daydream that I found the blind courage to drive home. I drive my mom's old Volkswagen Cabriolet convertible. It is pink and I hate it. It stays here.

All the lights were on in the house.

I willed myself to go to the door. I had left my book bag and my purse in the car. I felt as if I could barely walk, as it was. Plus, if I needed to, I could run faster without them.

I opened the door. But, standing inside my house, is a man who isn't Roy. There, taking up most of the entrance way, is a generically handsome, middle-aged guy. I knew the guy from somewhere. He smiled a huge, veneered smile and extended his hand.

Holy shit, it's the mayor.

"Surprise!" my mom called. She stood in the living room, holding an enormous glass of wine.

I shook the mayor's hand automatically.

"Hello, Mr. Mayor."

He laughed. "Mark, Kaitlyn, you can call me Mark."

I nodded.

My mom started talking. She walked forward, ushering me and her glass of wine to the dining room table. And she never shut up. The table was set, there were flowers, and the sushi was plated on serving platters that I didn't even know we had. We usually ate in front of the television from disposable containers.

"Here you go, baby, you can sit on this side tonight so I can sit next to Mark," my mom plopped me in a chair and danced back over to Mark.

I remember my mom putting some sushi on my plate. I remember her laughing too loud at Mark's jokes and him doing the same. Maybe they were nervous. *I* was nervous. But, mostly I just wanted to vomit.

I didn't hear much until I heard "press conference".

"What?"

Mark stopped smiling for a fraction of a beat, but my mom just plowed right along. "Of course, sweetie. Mark's divorce was finalized last month. This way is best for optics."

Optics?

This was *worse* than Roy. Okay, not worse than Roy. But, worse than *something*.

I swallowed.

"Last month, like when you went to New York City?"

It makes me smile now to think of their identical sour lemon expressions. I may not be in AP calculus, but that math I can do.

"You don't need to worry about that timing, Katie," the mayor said.

I put down my chop sticks and I left. I took the car and stayed out all night. I slept in it three streets over. They didn't look for me. Or, at least, they didn't *find* me. But, I think it is the former because I was parked in a hot pink monstrosity at the end of a cul-de-sac that was still in my development.

3 minutes

The dye is starting to burn a little, but the slices on my face have stopped bleeding.

I crack the window and turn on the fan. I don't want the dye smell to be too strong when the police come.

No one should come looking until tomorrow anyway. And the smell downstairs should be pretty consuming, I would think.

There is so much blood.

I really didn't plan to kill them. I had just planned to leave. I had my bag packed. I took three hundred dollars out of his wallet and six hundred out of my mom's purse. (You should thank me, Mark. You wouldn't have been the first man to buy a one-way ticket to Bankruptcy City courtesy of my mom.) I walked to the front door. I wasn't going to talk to them. Mark asked where I was headed. Maybe the game? No, I said, library. He laughed, looked at my mom and said you got a real nerd with Katie, huh? They both laughed.

I turned at the door and went back through the dining room to the kitchen. I slid a carving knife out of the block. When I went back in the living room Mark stood at the fireplace, trying to turn on the gas. I killed him first. I slit his throat. He made this weird, gurgling noise. Some blood sprayed, but I was surprised how much actually just poured over him. After a few seconds, he just sort of crumpled over like he was a sponge and had absorbed enough moisture.

After Mark hit the floor, I turned to my mom. She was up off the couch. I had a vague idea that she didn't want me to get blood on the fabric, and that made me laugh.

My mom was harder to kill. She fought back. That's where I got my scratches. But, in the end, I took her down with six stab wounds. I did one more for good luck. She landed on the couch. It would be ruined, after all.

The timer dings.

I rinse out my hair. I wipe down the sink. I pack the dirty towels in a plastic bag that I will dump somewhere along my route.

I don't have time to dry my hair, but I can tell it will work. Chestnut Brown will blend right in.

I walk out the back door, leaving it slightly ajar.

ABOUT THE AUTHOR

A believer that everyone has a tale to tell, Sarah Reilly Pancoast loves to spend time writing out people's stories. She used to focus on the real world, but now prefers her imaginary ones. The native upstate New Yorker spent too brief a time in Colorado, but Sarah enjoys all the traveling she does with her family. When she is not writing, Sarah is teaching, cooking, travelling and inventing backstories for people she meets along the way. Sarah's work has also been featured in the anthology *Remnants and Resolutions*.

AND ANY MORE WOULD BE INAPPROPRIATE

LIZZ BOGAARD

E veryone has a secret.
        When I was young, I had one. It was *big*. But I'd mastered the craft of keeping secrets.

Look: my family loved going down the shore, but I got "motion sickness" on boats. And I was "afraid of water." My family also loved pets, though I was also "afraid of pets." We had no pets. At restaurants I'd steal three, four, five napkins, inch up as close as possible to the table, keep them secure on my lap until I'd bunch the Bad debris up into a big ball that I'd tuck under the table while "tying my shoe." I didn't get to play in pools or play with pets or play pretend under the dining table, but oh well.

I was dedicated.

No one knew my secret.

But Mom didn't like secrets. She liked to suspect things. And I always suspected she might have a suspicion.

Mom got especially suspicious at family gatherings, where secrets were hardest to hide.

The holidays were difficult, yeah—but not *too* difficult. We all considered ourselves pretty Italian, but we weren't too strict about traditions or rules or any of that stuff. No one had that stereotypical accent that Italian-Americans supposedly have; no one had any mob ties; no one pronounced mozzarella like "moot-za-rell" or ricotta like "ra-got"; no one cared whether or not the pizza was truly "authentic"; and there was no gathering around a cake on Christmas Eve to sing happy birthday to a little plastic Baby Jesus figurine, which is something that some Italian people apparently do.

And it was fine this way. We didn't try to change. It was come and go, eat whatever, drink whatever, bring whatever, sing whatever—until one November, when a mysterious man showed up at Grandma and Grandpa's house. His name was Rob Tracey. Rob Tracey told Grandma that he was her grandfather's grandson. Grandma's grandfather moved from Sicily to Newark with Grandma's grandmother. He made friends and baked bread and did the American Dream and also apparently had an affair.

It was real and true. Rob Tracey even wrote a book about it.

Rather than get upset over ancestral infidelity, Grandma decided we would welcome Rob Tracey into the family and embrace our Italian culture "more passionately." So—as per Italian tradition—she formally decreed that, for the upcoming Christmas Eve, we would cook, serve, and consume seven different types of fish.

Seven.

Here is my secret: I do not like fish.

"Y ou're six years old." I was five. "You're not going to act like a baby today." It was Christmas Eve. "You're going to eat everything that Grandma cooks, okay?"

"Yes, Mother."

I gulped.

Mom was counting. I did one-at-a-time, separate plates from separate buffet runs. Our family kind of did it that way in general, too; there wasn't much organization involved in any holiday dinner, and no one could ever keep their seat. But whenever Mom happened to be sitting next to me, I'd fake a swallow and do a split-second-side-spit while she wasn't looking.

I flushed the flounder down the toilet, puréed the cod with my fork and mixed it into my mashed potatoes, fed some shrimp cocktail to Lady (a dog), buried the scungilli salad in Grandma's outdoor garden, cremated my mussels while pretending to play cards with my cousins by the fireplace, and the smelts (Mom said I only had to have two of them) were small enough to keep in my pocket, so I wrapped them in a sock from Grandma's hamper and sprayed them with her perfume.

I was on a roll.

Grinning proudly, I brought my smeltless plate back to Mom.

"Okay, that's six." Mom nodded at my empty plate. "Good. Now get number seven."

She handed me a plate, pointed to the linguini with clam sauce.

"Thank you, Mother."

I put my plate together, sat back down at the table, and stared at the linguine limbs strewn about the clam-filled clamshells—the final frontier. The party had thinned out a bit because most of the men were in the garage smoking cigars, so I had some leeway for sneaking around. I'd planned to put a napkin over my plate and make a run for the garbage, dump the clams, cover them with a napkin in case Mom checked, and leave a little pasta on my plate for plausibility.

I was sweating.

And just as the coast was clear, just as I was about to go for it—

"Well *hell-o* Francesca!"

I jumped. Grandma kneeled down next to me.

"How do you like the food?" She placed her empty plate next to mine.

"Grandma! Oh! Uh... hi! Yes!"

"Yes?"

"I mean, yes. Yeah. Yes, I loved it."

"Very nice!"

"I loved *everything*."

"Everything?"

"Yes oh yes oh yes... the bread, and the oil, the cheese and the..." I took a deep breath in. "The fish!"

"The fish?"

"Yes! Everything! Every fish. Amazing. All... amazing. I can't get enough. I could eat forever."

"Ah, yes. I see."

She glanced down at the clams, then further down at my pockets, then over to the fireplace, then to Lady, then I could've sworn she turned her head all the way over to the window where you could see the garden—then up at me.

She knew.

"I... uh... I'm..." I turned away; I couldn't look her in the eyes. "I'm sorry. I'm really, really, really sorry Grandma."

"No, no, that's alright." She took my chin in her hands and turned me back toward her, softly. I loosened up a little bit. "But let me teach you something here. I can tell you the best thing to say when you're too full, or when there's too much of something—too much of *anything,"* she winked. "Well, something to say to be polite," she said, "or to be *appropriate."*

"What is it?"

"My grandfather taught it to me."

"I don't know him!"

"That's okay, that's okay," she said, smiling. "But there are some big words in here, so I'm going to say it slowly." I nodded, at the ready. "Repeat after me: Excellent sufficiency, quite a denundancy, and any more would be inappropriate."

"Okay," I took a few seconds to collect myself. "Excellent sufficiency, right a—"

"No, no. Not *right,* it's *quite."*

"Kite?"

"No, no. *Quite.* Coo-white."

"What does coo-white mean?"

"Really."

"Really?"

"Really really."

"Oh," I paused, quite pleased. "Okay."

"Let's keep going," she hung her hands in the air like a conductor and started miming the syllables. "Excellent sufficiency, quite a denundancy, and any more would be inappropriate."

"Excellent sufficiency, *quite* a fun dance he—"

"No, no. Dee-nun-dan-see."

"Is that a word?"

"Likely not."

"Okay, well—"

"Oh, come *on,* Camille," Grandpa peeked in from the kitchen. "Are you teaching our sweet little granddaughter that stupid old thing?"

"Jack, get *out* of here," Grandma said.

"With that damn fake word in it?" he taunted.

"Jack…" Grandma narrowed her eyes.

"Oh, what?" he asked, playfully.

"You better shut up."

"Why? What're you gonna do?"

She marched into the kitchen and pulled a large wooden spoon out from one of the serving trays. Grandpa froze. "Shut," she held the spoon in his face, just about an inch away from his eyes. *"Up."*

And the man really did shut up. That was that.

Grandma came back to the table, spoon still in hand, laughing so hard that I thought she might cry. I didn't yet know that wooden spoons were the Italian matriarch's weapon, so I laughed, too. And we continued to continue, again and again and again and again and *again* until—

"Perfect!"

We looked down at our plates, together, and we smiled.

"Francesca!"

Mom.

"Why haven't you finished those clams?"

Oh no.

"It's almost time for dessert," she said, hovering over me. "We have to sing happy birthday to Baby Jesus, and you're gonna miss them cut the cake, and you have to stand in front of it so I can get a picture..."

"I..." I paused, stuttering, "U-uh, I, uh, w-well..."

Grandma held up my plate and started laughing, smiling big.

"Oh please, Grace—that's *mine!* You know how my stomach gets when I try to eat all this stuff. It's *much* too much. But your daughter here," Grandma put her arm around me. "She ate her whole damn plate."

Grandma took both plates, stood up, and walked away with her eyes on me until she placed a single finger to her lips, sealed our secret.

And any more would be inappropriate.

ABOUT THE AUTHOR

Lizz Bogaard is a writer and editor based in New York. She graduated from Fordham University in 2019 with a degree in Creative Writing and Psychology. At Fordham, she was Managing Editor of her creative writing concentration's student publication, *The Brink*. She also directed a feminist playwrights festival for which she co-wrote *Common Sense*, a comedy centered around an incel cult conspiring against a female writer and her lover. Since then, her short fiction has been featured in *Crooked Teeth Literary Magazine*, *The Yew Norker*, *Bewildering Stories, Internet Void*, and more. Currently, she works as a Writer's Assistant for the wonderful Otis Kidwell Burger and co-hosts a weekly reading group at Westbeth Artists' Housing. Amid the pandemic, she wrote a short (virtual) play, which was featured in Time Out New York's "Best Live Theatre to Stream Online" as part of a virtual play festival.

SPIRITUAL WALK THROUGH HAIKU

TRUST THE JOURNEY

DENISE HANSEN

Peacock Eyes
Colored eyes on us
Awakening light in soul
True colors shine.

Serendipity
Revive broken heart
Sail the summer wind at night
Serene lucid path

Travel Seekers
Travel seekers thought
Crack in the road, sprouting grass
Summer's ride, pure truth

Friend
Summertime sprouts life
Uncoil your blooming flower
Sisterhood unfolds

New Beginnings
Cockcrows, night fades
Summer dawn, pink grandeur
Silhouette of life

Birth
Red leaves fall to earth
Death rattle, gentle music
Melodic Swan Song

Red Tail Hawk
Hawk eye, discerning
Be not afraid, awakening
Glancing down on earth

ABOUT THE AUTHOR

Recently, Denise Talamantez relocated to the tranquility of the Sonoran Desert, home of the giant saguaro, hummingbirds and Javelina. She left behind the majestic views of the graphite Rockies, and her home of 25 years to travel a new path. She challenges herself to cultivate a garden of words to describe her connection to this beautiful chromatic desert. She breathes in the beauty surrounding her, creating another path for her Haikus. Her days are filled with writing, finishing her first novel *The Tyrant's Reach, WWII Germany—same horror, different perspective*, photo journaling, and experiencing life—whether minute or grand.

PERSONAL BEST

TAMI VELDURA

S am frowned out the window of his Dad's living room, slouched on the couch, as he watched the empty street outside. He'd rather be running. At least *that* would keep his body busy, if not his mind, but the pandemic had forced everyone inside for over a month, now, and if he were caught out of the house without a mask, he'd be fined.

But he couldn't run with a mask.

And it didn't feel like Friday, anyway. Sam had been out of school for almost two weeks and, just yesterday, the district had declared the rest of the school year to be canceled. It was almost the best summer ever: school canceled two months early, no finals at the end of the year, even the weather was beautiful. Cool in the mornings and perfect for runs.

Except he was stuck indoors.

He rolled away from the window onto his back and scrolled absently through his phone. Dad came into the house from the sliding door in the back, today's mail in his hand. He began sorting it on the counter and asked, "Have you thought about what you want for dinner?"

Sam sat up. "You mean we can order take out?"

Dad's expression shifted as he picked a piece of mail out of the stack, a formal letter of some kind, not a personal one. "Sure," Dad said. "Take out is fine."

"Awesome." Sam tabbed over to the delivery app and started considering sushi options.

Dad tore open his mail and, in between Sam's consideration of either unagi or yellowtail, suddenly grabbed Sam by his upper arm and dragged him toward his bedroom. Dad's face was red, creased with anger lines, and he held the letter crumpled in his other hand.

"Dad?" Sam stumbled beside him, alarmed and afraid. "Dad, what's wrong?"

"Get your shit packed. We're leaving." He shoved Sam roughly toward his bedroom, peeling off to slam open his own door.

"Dad, what on earth?" Sam followed him to the door of his bedroom and stalled at the threshold.

Dad had shoved the letter into a small spiral notebook he always carried around with him to put notes in. Sam had never thought it was odd, until now. What kind of notes did Dad need?

Then Dad pulled a duffel bag out from under the bed, and the way it landed heavily on the mattress told Sam it was already packed. A second packed bag came to rest beside the first, and Sam took a step back into the hallway.

Why did Dad have go-bags? He'd never heard of people having bags packed like this in real life.

"Dad?" His own voice was so quiet, Sam almost didn't recognize it.

Dad whirled on him, looming in a way he'd never seen before, eyes blazing with rage. "Get. Your. Bag. *Now!*"

Sam turned and ran. He scrambled mindlessly into his closet, dug out his school backpack, and dumped the contents onto the floor. He shoved two sets of clothes into the bottom of the bag, and an extra set of socks and underwear.

What was supposed to go in a bag like this? What the hell was going on?

Sweater. Jacket. What else?

Sam shoved his feet into his Toms and, in his rush, his running shoes fell off the low shelf. He froze. The Toms were comfortable, but some warning deep in his gut said the running shoes were a better choice. He swapped for the sneakers.

Just in time. Dad towered over him in the closet doorway, his face dark, since he blocked out the light from the room. "Let's go," he said quietly. Harsh. No questions, that voice said.

Sam shouldered his backpack, checked that his phone was in his pocket, and followed Dad out to the truck.

He shoved both of his bags into the small space behind the seats. Sam climbed into the passenger side of the cab and held his backpack to his chest. He buckled in, but found himself hunched away from Dad, pressed up against the door as far as he could go.

Dad revved the truck and pulled out of the driveway. He didn't drive quickly or erratically. He didn't *look* drunk, or high, or anything. Though Sam's experience with drugs of any kind was limited to his middle school D.A.R.E. program, he wasn't confident he could identify any of them.

His eyes fell on the notebook with the envelope sticking out. Something in that letter had set Dad off. Something that had scared him enough to turn into someone else, right before Sam's eyes.

Dad glanced over and Sam stared back, afraid and confused, but determined not to let it show. "Dad, you're scaring me."

The surprise on Dad's face gave Sam some hope. Dad reached over to squeeze his knee. "I'm sorry. I'm sorry, Samantha, I didn't mean to scare you. It's just... something's come up and we've got to get away for a little bit. It's urgent. Thank you for packing a bag."

Sam smiled hesitantly. The name was wrong, but with Dad the name was *always* wrong. Sam indicated his phone. "Can we still pick up sushi for dinner?"

"Sure. Sure, yeah. That sounds good."

Sam dug into his phone, but not to order dinner. If he'd been hungry at all, his appetite was gone now. Instead, he texted Mom. "Dad's being weird. He just packed me up and we're driving somewhere?"

Then he tabbed over to the food app to place an order. None of the options looked satisfying, though. Who cared if he got the fish sauce on the side?

His phone vibrated as Mom texted him back.

You're being kidnapped.

S am couldn't stop shaking. His sushi lay untouched at his feet, and he hugged his backpack tight. They'd been driving for hours now, leaving the city, and Sam's confidence, far behind. Mom's text terrified him more than anything Dad had done so far. He was being *kidnapped*? And Dad had prepared for this? *His* bags had been already packed!

He dashed his palm against his eyes, refusing to cry. Holding everything deep in his chest, where it churned and boiled and made him shake.

Mom had called the cops. Sam texted her occasional updates as Dad drove: east on Lexington, north on Valley. They were headed for the mountains. Pretty soon, Sam was going to lose his cell connection and then he'd be alone.

There had to be a way to delay Dad, at least a little bit. Until the cops could get their shit together and realize this was more than an evening out in the country.

"I—I gotta pee. Can we stop for a second?"

Dad grunted, a frustrated sound Sam had heard a thousand times in his life. But now it was directed at *him*, with layers of meaning he didn't recognize. Did Dad know he was trying to stall? Could he see right through him?

"Need gas, anyway," Dad said with a sigh. "There's a station up here."

Well, shit. Refilling on gas would let Dad drive for another six hours without having to stop. He could go through the night, like those road trips they used to take, back when they were a whole family.

Before the divorce.

Sam squeezed his eyes against a sob that threatened to break out of his chest. He'd heard Dad and Mom yelling at each other, arguing about who should get to *keep* him, like he was a pet, not a person. Then they stopped meeting at all and started screaming over the phone, instead.

A few months ago, even that had stopped. Sam thought he'd go back and forth between Mom's apartment and Dad's house every few weeks, but then the pandemic had shut down the whole freaking world, and he'd been stuck at Dad's ever since.

Sam eyed the envelope in Dad's notebook again. Was this about the divorce? He recognized some of the anger from those phone calls.

Dad pulled into a gas station and yanked the emergency brake. "Be quick," he said. "We still have a ways to go."

Sam took his backpack with him. He wasn't even sure he needed it, but he was too scared to leave it behind.

A single fluorescent bulb lit the gas station bathroom, highlighting all of its grimy flaws and none of its good side. Sam slung his backpack over his shoulder, rather than put it down on the floor, and called Mom.

The phone barely rang before Mom's voice asked, "Sam, baby, are you alright? Are you hurt?"

"No, no I'm fine." Sam said, breathless with relief and hope. "We're at the Chevron at the end of Glen and Hilldale. I asked to go pee. Is someone on the way? What's going on?"

"The police are coming," Mom said.

"Samantha." A new voice cut in, very official-sounding. "I'm Officer Florentina Tremme. Are you in immediate danger?"

"No, no I've locked myself in the gas station bathroom with my bag. Dad is getting gas."

"Good. That was smart. We have people on the way. Can you tell me about your dad? Does he have a gun or—?"

"A *gun*?" Sam sat down hard on the grimy tile of the bathroom, his legs simply giving out below him. "Why would he have a gun?" It never occurred to him that Dad might have a weapon. He'd never seen him handle a gun in his life.

"Take a deep breath, Samantha—"

"Don't call me that," Sam snapped. "Dad keeps calling me that. I'm *Sam*. My name is Sam."

"Ok, Sam. Take a breath. I need you to focus. You said Dad doesn't have a gun. Does he have a knife? Have you seen any weapon at all?"

Officer Florentina's steady voice helped calm him down. He took another breath. "No, I haven't seen anything like that. But he has two bags in the truck. They were already packed and ready. He could have something in them."

"You say his bags were ready to go?"

Sam gripped the phone against his ear. The shaking was getting worse. "Yeah, they were packed and under the bed. Who keeps bags packed under the bed? Who does that?"

"Ok, Sam, we're—"

Officer Florentina's voice cut short when a huge impact rattled the gas station bathroom door. Sam screamed and backpedaled until his head hit the sink and he couldn't shove himself any further away. It smelled like mold.

Distantly the phone said, "Sam? Are you ok?"

Another slam crashed into the door and, while Sam had thrown the deadbolt, the weak wood of the door frame cracked.

"He's coming in!" Sam shouted at his phone.

Then a third impact crushed the door in, and it slammed so hard against the wall that some of the tiles cracked. Dad stood in the doorway, a huge mountain of a man, terrifying and impossible under the flickering light of the fluorescent.

He said nothing. Just marched into the bathroom, snatched the phone out of Sam's hand, and dropped it into the unused toilet. Then he grabbed Sam's arm again, like he had back in the house, and dragged him to the truck.

Dad shoved him into the passenger side, and Sam clambered in with shaking hands, pulling the seatbelt in place on automatic. The grim look on Dad's face kept Sam quiet, despite the wild fear in his heart. *Did* Dad have a gun? Or a knife? Were they hidden in those bags he'd packed in advance?

Why did the police care that his bags were packed?

Sam risked a glance in the side view mirror as Dad pulled out of the gas station, praying he would see red and blue lights.

No lights.

Dad pointed the truck into the mountains.

They drove for hours. Sam watched the sun setting over the high peaks and wondered if Dad planned to drive through the night, like he feared. But, some distance into the pine forest, he bumped the truck off the paved road and took a broad dirt road instead. A fire road, maintained for the forest service. Fire roads were unmarked, and they crisscrossed federal lands all over the state. Sam remembered bouncing down miles of these public access roads, as a kid, when the whole family went camping for a weekend.

Those memories were full of laugher and love, not the rising terror Sam fought against as the paved road, and hope of rescue, receded behind them.

He couldn't breathe.

This truck was too small. His Dad took up too much space. There wasn't enough room to stretch out. They'd been driving for so long. Sam finally rolled the window down, even though it was nearly dark, the sky a deep blue as sunset faded away.

Fresh pine and wild air smacked Sam unexpectedly in the face. He wasn't prepared for the rush of memories that came with it: driving out into the wilderness, tying up a hammock, prepping the tent. He could almost taste the smoke of a campfire.

When Dad pulled the truck in at a trailhead, the tires cracking on pressed gravel, Sam didn't get the same rush of excitement he had remembered. There was only dread.

"Take your bag," Dad said.

As if Sam was going to leave it behind.

He slid from the truck, looping the backpack over both arms and cinching the straps tight. Dad shouldered both of his duffle bags and marched off into the woods without a glance back. Sam caught up quickly.

They marched through a forest Sam had always remembered fondly, following a barely-there track through the underbrush. Dad moved confidently through the woods and, as the final dregs of sunlight faded, he opened one of his packs and dug out a headlamp. He handed a second one to Sam.

And they marched.

Without his phone, Sam couldn't be sure how long, but they walked for at least an hour, their game trail always sloping gently upward. Woodpeckers dug into the bark of trees overhead, calling to each other across the forest, oblivious to the fate of the people below them.

Something like despair crept into the edges of Sam's heart. With the truck parked off on an unmarked fire road, Sam without his phone, and now the two of them hiking deeper into the woods, that little window of hope attached to a pair of blue and red flashing lights was starting to close. How could they find him out here?

And what if Dad really did have a gun in that bag?

Sam ducked his head and kept walking.

Eventually their gentle uphill crested onto a flat rise, and Dad kicked at a bed of pine needles there. His foot hit something solid. Then Dad yanked a large metal door up out of the ground and revealed a dark hole with a ladder.

Sam stared. "Is that... a bunker?"

"Get in," Dad said.

"You have a *bunker*?"

Dad pointed at the hole. "I'm not going to leave you here, but the door is heavy, so I'll hold it for you. Let's go."

This was not good. Off the paved road, off the fire road, hiked into the forest, and now literally hidden underground.

Sam hesitated. But, when Dad stared at him expectantly, Sam got in.

The bunker seemed to be a shipping container that had been buried in the ground. How exactly one buried a shipping container, Sam couldn't say.

He lay on a cot in a corner, the closest wall lined with stacked totes, each of them labeled and organized. Totes and storage took up half the container, sorted into two rows for easy access. The other half was divided into kitchen and cots. A full camp stove, sink, and trash setup, along with cans and cans of preserved food on the left, two cots on the right.

A fully prepped bunker buried in the woods. Dad probably thought he could live out here like some kind of mountain man. Hunting and fishing for his food. Foraging for berries or something.

Sam couldn't stay here.

Dad was snoring lightly, and had been for a while now. Time meant nothing in the dark, but when Sam got out of this he was going to buy a watch. A boring, analog one with a night light.

He sat up, freezing when the cot creaked under his weight. Dad kept snoring.

Sam had a plan. Sneak out of the bunker, make his way back to the fire road, then run like hell. He was a cross country runner. He could make it back to town on his own if he could get out of this bunker. And now was his best shot.

Sam pulled on his sneakers like he was going for another afternoon run and not a run for his life. He tied his sweater around his waist. Running would keep him warm, but if he couldn't find the fire road, it was going to be a cold night in the woods.

He spotted the keys on the counter in the little kitchen area.

Sam couldn't drive a stick shift, but he wanted to take the keys. Dad would think he took the truck, or at the very least, wouldn't be able to use the truck to chase after Sam.

Sam crept from the cot to the kitchen counter. He swiped the keys slowly, barely breathing as he listened to Dad's light snoring. He shoved the keys into his back pocket, and felt his way down the storage row until he found the ladder bolted to the container wall.

Up the ladder. Quiet, now. The door had a wheel lock, and it squeaked when Sam forced it open. He froze again. Had the sound woken Dad?

He couldn't hear anything over his own terrified breathing.

Sam shoved the door up and climbed the last two steps. The door was heavy, like Dad said, and he strained under it.

Then Dad grabbed his ankle from below.

Sam screamed, surprised and sheer terror ripping right out of his chest. He yanked his foot, but Dad held fast. The door was too heavy. It slipped out of Sam's hands and crashed onto Dad's wrist.

This time Dad screamed.

Sam ran.

He scrambled in the pine needles, slipping and coughing in the dust they raised. He pointed himself downhill and let his cross country instincts take over.

The forest looked different in the dead of night and, without a headlamp. Sam wasn't sure he was going in the right direction, but any direction was better than back with Dad, so he didn't hesitate. He dodged around trees, slipped down slopes, and scrambled through the woods with singular focus.

He couldn't tell if Dad followed, but the sound of Sam's pounding heart in his ears drove out anything else. He gasped for air, both in fear and exertion, eyes too busy picking out roots and holes to judge if he was heading deeper into the forest.

Sam crashed to hands and knees when the slope abruptly terminated in a dirt road. A dirt road! This was the fire road!

He glanced left and right, but didn't see Dad's truck. That didn't matter, he couldn't drive it anyway. Sam scrambled to his feet and let himself fly, a full sprint down the graded road, no roots or leaves to trip him up, just a small hill and beyond that, the lights of the city.

He crested the hill and gasped. A vehicle crawled forward on the road, its lights blinding, a spotlight sweeping the woods from the roof. Sam shielded his eyes as the spotlight caught him.

"Sam Waltz? Are you Sam Waltz?" A voice said through a loud-speaker. Too distorted to identify.

"Yes!" he shouted, running toward the truck. "Yes, I'm Sam!"

S am sat next to Mom at the police precinct, surprised at how busy the building was, despite the late hour. It had been almost four in the morning by the time he'd been brought out of the woods and reunited with Mom. Several desks were in open rows, each with a computer and a phone, and at least half of them with an officer at work. Lights were on in most of the closed offices along the outer perimeter, and officers kept walking in, leading people they had arrested in cuffs to somewhere in the back.

Officer Florentina Tremme had met them at the station and immediately taken Sam's statement for the record. After that, Sam had lost count of all the questions. Mom had been able to answer a few of them, and the police already had a record of his texts, so that helped. Sam had caught a few details: like Mom winning the custody case, and Dad trying to intimidate her. Something about premeditation. But it was late

—or early—and after a sustained evening of adrenaline and fear, Sam slumped against Mom's shoulder, on the verge of falling asleep.

Then Florentina put her hand on Sam's shoulder. "We found him," she said. She frowned, her short black hair shiny in the precinct light as she looked at the front door.

Sam sat up. Dad walked through the door, two officers holding his hands behind his back. One of his wrists was wrapped. Had Sam broken it when he dropped the bunker door?

He didn't feel bad.

He watched, body numb, as Dad was marched to the back and out of sight. He leaned into Mom.

She tucked his hair behind one ear and smiled down at him. Her eyes still shimmered with almost-tears. "We gotta get your hair cut, huh, Sam?"

Sam blinked.

And he smiled.

ABOUT THE AUTHOR

Tami Veldura is an enby/aro/ace author of queer fiction. Their pronouns are they/them/Mx. They write fantasy, science fiction, and paranormal stories that push genre limits. Their work has been nominated for the M/M Goodreads Reader Choice Awards and they have been nominated and placed in the Rainbow Awards.

SOMEDAY BABY

KATIE DAY

W*hat am I doing here?*
It wasn't the first time that thought had crossed Mason's mind since he left New York last night. The adrenaline still coursed through him, an overwhelming sense of relief battled with the heavy chains of guilt, eager to lock his heart back into its cage.

What have I done?

"…and the water may get a bit too hot, so you'll have to be careful and check it before you get into the tub," Mrs. Burke was saying. Mason had already forgotten her first name.

He turned from the pristine, white, silver-clawfoot tub to the woman next to him, her auburn hair in a classic bob, and gazed into her soft, welcoming eyes. The same walnut brown as Mason's mother's.

Oh, god. He had actually done it.

He had cut his family, his *mother*, out of his life.

Apart from the eyes, they didn't look at all alike. They had different bone structures, height, body types. But there was something about Mrs. Burke's eyes that made Mason wonder why his mother's had never held that same softness. Mrs. Burke's kind eyes mocked him, showed him how Mason's mother could've been.

Mason worked through the lump in his throat. Why was he still emotional? "Right. And how much is rent, again?" He hated how his question came out high-pitched.

"Two-hundred-and-seventy-five a month."

Mason turned toward Mr. Burke, who stood behind him, wearing a cozy sweater that screamed: *Typical White Middle-Class male.*

"Wow, that's, uh, really cheap," Mason muttered.

Really, what did he expect the rent to be in the middle of a small town like Belleville? It was a huge downgrade from his busy life in New York City.

Mr. Burke's lips fought to restrain a smile. "I can always raise it if you want?" He chuckled at himself. "Did you get a job in town?"

No, this was as far as Uber could get me before my credit card was declined. He probably shouldn't say that. Oh, wait. Shit. He had *no* money.

He had barely had enough cash this morning to buy a bagel and a crappy cup of tea, which did *not* taste like Earl Grey. How could he afford rent? He should've never gone into that café. Then he wouldn't have seen that stupid apartment-for-rent ad and found himself here. At first, he'd been thrown off by the fact that the apartment was in the basement of the Burke's house, and that they would have to share a kitchen. Even bed-and-breakfasts had more class than *that*. Yet when Mason saw that photo of their claw-foot tub, it brought back memories of that solo trip he took to Scotland years ago where he felt like and found himself.

Did he come here for that damn tub because he hoped he could find that feeling of wholeness once more? That certainty of who he was?

"I'm seesawing between several jobs at the moment," he said instead.

Mr. Burke shared a look with Mrs. Burke. Did they not want him here? Should he even *be* here since he couldn't even pay the ridiculously cheap rent?

What am I doing here?

"You know what? This is a really nice setup you two have here." Mason gestured with his hands across the bathroom and the bedroom down the hall. "But I think I've made a mistake. I shouldn't be here. I'll, um, show myself out."

And go where?

His cheeks burned with shame.

Mrs. Burke laid a hand on Mason's right shoulder. He held back from stiffening, as well as from easing into her touch.

"Why don't you stay here for the night and see how you feel in the morning? Let's do a trial run. Besides, I'm whipping up my famous chili, and you'll be saving my husband a week's worth of leftovers." She smiled up at him. A warm, inviting smile.

God, he'd trusted his mother's smile for so long. Like trusting the sweetness of the devil before you realized you sold bits and bits of your soul along the way.

Mason's eyes watered and he blinked the tears away. He must look like a hot mess right now. He wondered how big the bags were under his eyes. Had he remembered to pack that eye serum he brought back from Paris? He was going to need it.

"That sounds delightful." He rolled his head back to hold the tears at bay. "Um," he glanced back between the two of them. "Thanks so much."

Just for the night. He needed a place to sleep. He'd start fresh in the morning.

And then what?

Mr. Burke clasped his hand on Mason's shoulder and Mason tried not to pull away from it. Why were they both so touchy-feely? Sure, it was nice, but he didn't deserve it.

"Come. Let me help bring your bags inside," Mr. Burke said. "I saw you hiding them out earlier by the bushes."

UGH. Mason's cheeks burned even more.

L ater that night, Mason lay on top of the covers of the queen bed, his gaze tracing the cracked flaws on the slap-brush ceiling texture.

The Burkes were nice. Thankfully, not Stepford Wives nice, but genuinely nice, and it kept throwing Mason off. He wished he could find a glaring imperfection in them like his ex-boyfriend's '*I'm way too comfortable in my own skin*' attitude, or his college friend's long string of ridiculous childhood stories that couldn't be remotely true, or his old coworker's ugly sweaters that diminished her overall beauty.

Mason couldn't decide if the Burkes' kindness set his teeth on edge, or relaxed him. Or, perhaps both?

He grumbled and found his phone. He needed to distract himself by scrolling through Insta. Huh. Ed had posted an old summer picture of the family last night. One with their parents and five siblings at a picnic table. Mason and Ed had potato salad smeared on their features. *"Family is not an important thing, it's everything,"* was the caption under Ed's picture.

His father had left the family not long after that picture was taken.

The heaviness in Mason's stomach grew.

"*Your words hurt me,*" his mother had told Mason the night before. *Me, me, me.* It was always about how *he* hurt *her.* He always had to make her happy, make sure not to make her angry, please her, because if he didn't it meant...

It meant he was like his father.

Was he like his father? A coward? Was this why his father left? His thumb hovered over his mother's contact information. He should call her. He'd gotten a few texts from his siblings. He only read the one from his older sister, Jess, who proceeded to tell him that she wanted nothing to do with him.

"*I feel like I'm always walking on eggshells around you. I can never be honest with you because you always blow up when I am,*" was one of the many truths Mason had revealed to her.

"*I get angry because I feel like I'm losing you. You're everything to me,*" had been one of the many deflections his mother threw back at him.

Mason threw his head back onto the pillow.

What am I doing here?

He should take Mrs. Burke's advice. Get some sleep, and figure out the rest of his plans in the morning.

He grabbed his toiletries bag, headed into the bathroom, and eyed the clawfoot tub. He hadn't had a decent bath in a long time. He chewed his lower lip. Ah, what the hell.

He found some of his old eucalyptus and peppermint bath salts in a small jar in his bag, and tossed the contents into the running bath water. The steam beckoned him in, and as he dipped into the hot waters, it tickled his face with whispers: *You did it. You walked away. You're free.*

Am I?

Mason exhaled the weight from his chest, and slipped his body deeper into the bathtub to allow the water to cover his chest and knees.

He wouldn't have to worry about getting panic attacks if he had this piece of heaven to soak into every night. All that was missing was a nice glass of red wine. Hmmm, maybe a ruby port. Or a nice Scotch on the rocks.

As Mason leaned his head back on the edge of the bathtub, he could hear someone in the kitchen above getting some ice out of the fridge.

Guess the vents from the bathroom connected to the kitchen upstairs.

He might need to revisit his opinion on why renting a room in the basement of someone's house was a god-awful idea.

A door squeaked open upstairs. Then Mason heard an exclaimed: "Nicholas! What are you doing here? What a nice surprise!"

"Hey, Mom," a soft voice greeted.

Mason hadn't realized the Burkes had a son. He should have snooped more upstairs. He wondered how many children they had. If this was going to be a Von Trapp situation, he was booking it out of here tomorrow morning.

Ah. There was the glaring flaw.

"Is everything okay?" Mrs. Burke asked. "You and Adrian aren't fighting again, are you?"

Jess would've loved to get some gossip on *that*. Nothing pleased her more than receiving juicy tidbits to use against people.

Mason hated to admit that he used to be like that, too.

"Oh, no," Nicholas denied, a little too quickly. The door clicked shut. "Adrian's out of town and I've been craving your Friday night chilis."

"I can reheat some up for you."

The rest of the conversation was drowned out by the flowing sounds of dishes clinking, the refrigerator door opening and closing, the thump of bags, and the creaking footsteps against the wooden floor. After that, their voices became hushed whispers.

He gave up eavesdropping and focused on the warmth of heaven around his body. Oooooh. The muscles in his lower back unloosened. Oh, man. He was going to stay in Belleville for the tub itself.

"...with Dad today," Nicholas's voice carried down to the bathroom. "You found someone to rent the room downstairs?"

"Possibly. We'll see. I think the poor boy is going through something. He looks so lost. I think he's lonely."

Mason's breath hitched. He wished he hadn't heard that. How had she known? Nobody back home knew he was lonely! God, Mason didn't even want to admit that to himself.

But he *was* lonely.

"Mom, I think the purpose of renting out a room is to charge them for it." It didn't sound like Nicholas was chiding her for it. It almost sounded like he was teasing her.

Mrs. Burke tsked. "Oh, I'll charge him when he finds a job."

"He doesn't have a job?"

"He's *seesawing* between jobs opportunities at the moment."

Mason lowered his chin into the water. Oh, god.

"Seesawing?" Nicholas said. "Is that what they call unemployment now?"

"Nicholas!" Mrs. Burke laughed.

Wow. They sounded like they had a really great relationship. The honesty flowed easily between them, unlike Mason's with his own mother, which had poured out after banging against the rocky barricades for years.

"I think you'll like him," Mrs. Burke said. "He's interesting. Your father thinks he's odd because he put sour cream into his chili, but I think he's rather charming."

Nicholas gasped dramatically. "Sour cream in chili? What a monster. How can one appreciate the fine flavors you put in?"

Okay, the chili was *fucking* spicy. The sour cream was to ensure Mason didn't become a wheezing, sweating, and dying mess at their dinner table. But, hmm...He had been called charming before, but usually in a condescending tone. Mrs. Burke acted like as if she really did find him charming. As if she really wanted to know more about him.

Nope.

They were too nice.

He needed to leave this place tomorrow.

It was near noon when Mason made his way upstairs. He hadn't heard any movements in the house when he woke up, so he assumed the Burkes must be out. Good. He could leave without any awkward goodbyes. He had all his bags packed, but his rumbling stomach told him to raid their kitchen for brunch before he left and went…somewhere. Maybe his other credit card still had some room left on it.

He cracked open the door from the basement into the shared kitchen and heard a soft grumble.

"Aah! Why is this so hard?"

Mason pursed his lips and poked his head around the door.

A man with short brown hair stood at the kitchen island, brows furrowed. Mason took in the gray fitted t-shirt French-tucked inside the man's mid-denim jeans. Were those Levis? He held back a snort. A slave to mass customizations. Didn't anyone custom make their pants anymore? Mason could visibly see the man's jaw clenching through his round cheeks as he worked out something in his head. Hmmm. He was definitely aesthetically pleasing to the eye.

Was this Nicholas?

Mason scanned the kitchen, checking for any more unsuspecting family members. Clear.

The man exhaled and spoke again. "Adrian, we've known each other for a long time and we work well together." Yep. That was the voice Mason heard last night. Nicholas groaned and pinched his brows. "Gah, come on, Nicholas, are you business partners?"

Mason noticed the jewelry box on the island counter; inside it rested a silver ring with a single diamond embedded into the band. Diamonds in a male's wedding ring? Nicholas had taste. Hold a minute. Was this guy practicing his proposal?

"Adrian…" Nicholas tried again, his brows still pinched. He looked disgustingly adorable when he did that. "You're…Um." Nicholas's nose scrunched up. "Marry me?"

"Mmm, wow, that was beautifully articulated," Mason said as he fully stepped into the kitchen. He *had* to talk to this man. There was something endearing about the way Nicholas bumbled his way through his terrible, rehearsed proposal.

Nicholas jerked his head toward Mason, eyes wide. Red colored his cheeks.

"If I can add a director's note, I think you need to work on that constipated expression. In my experience, it means you're either a gold digger or knocked someone up. I think we can eliminate the latter unless he's the Virgin Adam."

A flash of anger, or panic, flashed in Nicholas's eyes. He paused, taking in Mason's demeanor, and something shifted. "No. Not the Virgin Adam. You caught me. Gold digger. Adrian has a collection of baseball cards that's worth millions if I can sell them."

"Cute that you think they have *any* value."

"Aww, you think I'm cute?"

Warning bells sounded off in Mason's head, and he knew that he should change the subject, because, yes, he did think that, but by god, he was not going to let this denim-wearing man get the last word. "Well, *now* I've realized you're the unspoken third option in this scenario which is you're very pretty, but not that smart."

"Ah, well, glad you've figured out why I'm so constipated."

"Lucky for you I'm both pretty *and* smart."

"Ooh, lucky for me."

"Then again, it could be your mother's chili."

Nicholas barked a laugh. He lowered his head a bit, rubbing a hand over a wide smile. When he glanced back up at Mason, his eyes twinkled with mirth and warmth. "You must be Mason."

"Guilty." Mason stepped further into the kitchen. Should he shake this guy's hands? What was he supposed to do? "And I'm...er, and you're Nicholas."

"Guilty."

They shook hands. Hmm. Soft hands. Mason gazed into Nicholas's inviting, warm-brown honey eyes. Was he shaking Nicholas's hand for too long? Pull yourself together, Mason!

He cleared his throat and took his hand back.

Nicholas leaned back against the counter and crossed his arms. "My parents left to run some errands, but you can help yourself to anything in the kitchen for lunch."

"It's too early for lunch," Mason said.

Nicholas stole a quick glance at the clock. "It's eleven-thirty?"

"Yes. But I decided to grace the remaining morning with my presence, which means I should be welcomed with breakfast. At least a continental one. Perhaps even a mimosa."

Nicholas's smile widened. Mason didn't know if the smile was mocking, or if Nicholas was simply enjoying their conversation.

"Mimosa?" Nicholas's tone turned teasing, almost a playful taunt. "Oh, well, if I knew you wanted that I wouldn't have finished all those off earlier this morning, you know, at the normal time people generally eat breakfast. But I'll be more than happy to whip you up a Bloody Mary."

"Only the undignified drink Bloody Marys. I'm insulted by the mere suggestion."

"I'm insulted you called me undignified."

Mason curled his lips inward. Wow. He liked this banter. Sure, his ex used to tease him back, but it was usually dry or biting. With Nicholas, he ran with whatever Mason said. Like improv. He shuddered at that thought. He dated an actor from community theater once. Improv did not translate well in the bedroom for them. He needed a different comparison.

"My mom has some sticky buns if you want those."

Mason tilted his head. Did he hear that right? Sticky buns. As in eating a man's cream off a woman's buns? Were they that kind of family? Were the small-town stereotypes correct? Had he unwittingly walked into a house of freaks? "Um. Your mom is a nice lady but I don't know if I want to eat...you know, *that* off of her. I'm not really into that kind of thing."

Nicholas widened his eyes. He grabbed the plastic-wrapped pan from next to the coffee maker. "I meant *these?*" His voice squeaked as he showcased the pan of caramelized rolls topped with pecans.

"Oh. My. God," Mason exclaimed. He pressed his fist against his mouth. The other stereotypes were true. The sexual deviants were all in New York. He winced and forced a chuckle. "Can we pretend I never said that?"

"Oh, it's already been forgotten."

"Oh, god," Mason muttered. He wanted to sink into the ground and die. He'd never been so mortified.

Nicholas cleared his throat. "I'll heat these up real quick for you. You can, ahem..." He pointed at the squared kitchen table that seated four. "Make yourself comfortable."

Mason slumped into one of the seats. His eyes swept across the newspaper, then he pulled out his phone instead and opened up Insta.

Nicholas set a cup of orange juice in front of Mason and grinned. "Here's your virgin mimosa."

Mason twisted his lips to the side to hide his smile.

A couple minutes later, Nicholas set two plates of sticky buns onto the table. He took a seat next to Mason and used his fork to cut into his own roll.

Mason inhaled the whiff of cinnamon, caramel and brown sugar. It smelled delicious. He tore off a piece, took a bite, and moaned in contentment. "This is better than soggy cereal."

"Yeah. These are one of my favorites. She does make some mean cinnamon rolls, but she only makes them around Christmas now."

"Maybe I'll charm her into making some tomorrow."

The corner of Nicholas's lips tugged. "You probably could."

They settled into an awkward silence as they ate their breakfast. Awkward, but a silence that Mason didn't feel the need to fill. God. This sticky bun was soooo good. Much better than what he thought he'd be getting.

Next to him, Nicholas wasn't enjoying his roll with the same enthusiasm as Mason. He'd only eaten half of it, his attention focused on the ring on the counter. His brows pinched again.

"When are you planning to propose?" Mason asked. *No. Don't ask that. Why? Why are you making awkward small talk?*

Nicholas startled as if he'd forgotten Mason was there. He glanced down at his roll and scrapped at the dough with his fork. "I don't know. I came home to get Adrian's parents blessing."

"Oh." Mason's voice dropped. "You don't live here then?"

"I live in Peterborough with Adrian."

A hollowness filled Mason's stomach. "So, blessing, huh? Are you asking for permission because you're scared to listen to your heart?" Mason regretted the words as they left his mouth. He sounded just like his mother. Had he left his family too late? Had he already become like her?

Nicholas threw Mason a dark glare and set his fork down. "I'm not afraid."

Mason shifted in his chair. He wasn't good with this, with genuine human emotions. He had an incredible urge to leave, but... He glanced down and inspected his cuticles. "Do they, uh, not like you or something?" Mason flicked his gaze up to Nicholas. "You seem *very* tentative about the whole thing."

"No, I'm...they're fine. I'm confident about the whole thing."

"Okay," Mason said. He didn't really believe Nicholas, but he also didn't want to press either. He'd only known this man for ten minutes.

Nicholas groaned. "How would *you* propose to someone?"

Mason blinked. "Uh, I'm the wrong person to ask that inquiry. The longest relationship I've ever had was three, four months? I'm not actually sure, because we never actually broke up." He rolled his fingers on the table. "Does that mean we're still together?"

Nicholas frowned at that. "Oh. Well. I mean, have you ever thought about it?"

Mason held his breath, then slowly lowered his guard. For once, he wanted to be seen. "I did go through a bit of a phase where I watched nothing but romantic movies and ate a pint of ice cream every night for a few months. I mean, it was mostly *Pride and Prejudice*. But yeah, I let myself fantasize it for a bit. Being proposed to, or doing the proposing."

Nicholas nodded, clearly listening to every word Mason said.

It felt weird sharing this part of himself. "In my head, I didn't really care how the proposal was done as long as it was sincere..."

Mason swallowed past a lump in his throat. "And came from the heart. I mean, this person is someone that you've *chosen* to spend the rest of your life with, and, like Harry said, when you know that, you want the rest of your life to start as soon as possible."

A softness caressed Nicholas's features, the pinch in his brows smoothing out. "You make it sound like it's so easy."

"To be fair, in my head, the other person was usually Matt Bomer or Julia Stiles, so maybe that's why."

"Ah, that makes more sense."

"Hmmm."

Nicholas stared at Mason for a while. "What brought you here, Mason?"

"Uh." Mason licked his lips. "Just passing through."

"Where're you heading?"

"I've heard Toronto is nice this time of year."

"You seem a bit tentative about that."

This time it was Mason who sent Nicholas a scathing glare.

Nicholas threw his hands up in a placating manner, lips curved in a mischievous smirk. *That little snark.* Something swelled in Mason's heart at that smirk.

"I wouldn't be disinclined if I thought to stay for a little while." Mason clasped his mouth shut as he realized what he'd said. No. He needed to leave. He didn't deserve these people's kindness. He'd already settled on that.

"You should. Stay, you know. A few of my cousins were thinking of getting together tonight for a pre-bachelor party for my cousin, Sandy."

"A pre-bachelor party? Is that a thing?"

Nicholas continued as if Mason hadn't spoken. "So, uh, if you wouldn't be so disinclined, would you like to join us?"

"Hmmm. Does it involve a strip club and an orgy?"

Nicholas quickly suppressed his incredulous look into a laughing smile. "Ah, no. It involves drinks and a karaoke bar."

Mason rolled his head back and closed his eyes as he pretended to think about it. "Mmmm. It's been a while since I've belted out Celine Dion. I accept your invitation."

"Can you even can hit Celine's vocal range?" Nicholas faked a grimace. "Could you spare us the torture?"

"Prepare to be astounded."

"Cute that you think I will be."

Mason smiled. A warm fuzzy feeling fluttered in his stomach. What was the harm in staying one more night? Maybe he could unravel the mystery of Nicholas Burke.

W hat kind of karaoke bar does not have Celine Dion?

Mason felt personally offended by this affront.

Worse, this bar didn't even know how to make Hummers. The bartender had laughed when Mason ordered it, and told him that it wasn't that kind of place. Honestly, how hard was it to blend ice cream, Kahlua, and light rum? Jerome Adams would be outraged by this very establishment.

Mason jutted his jaw and chugged the rest of his Cosmo, wincing at the excessive use of triple sec. He exhaled through his teeth as he set the drink down and glanced around at his tablemates: Nicholas and seven of his cousins. All the names blurred together, and Mason didn't care about who was who, nor about their backstories. He wanted to get drunk and sing.

He was a bit buzzed already, so he was nearing his goal. He hadn't found the perfect song to belt out yet. Most of the selections were Backstreet Boys or NSYNC. He wanted to find the karaoke bar manager and tell him that the 90s called and wanted their music back.

Mason flipped the page of the song selections book and half-listened to the conversation around the table.

"...out of town again?" the redhead next to Nicholas groaned. Ah. Right. That one was Sandy which perplexed Mason, because who named a redhead Sandy? "That's the only time we ever see you!"

"You saw me last weekend," Nicholas said. "We had lunch."

"That was a double-date. That doesn't count."

Nicholas raised his brows.

"You know what I mean."

One of the cousins who looked like Nicholas asked, "So, is he really out of town, or is that code for you guys broke up again?"

The guy next to Mason leaned in toward him and said in a loud mock-whisper: "They've broken up at least seven times since high school."

"It's serious this time," Nicholas argued.

The man leaned in further, and Mason recoiled at the stench of whiskey on his breath. "That's what he said last time."

"Don't breathe on me," Mason said in disgust.

"You know what your problem is?" the Nicholas-look-alike said. "You need to be like Beyoncé and put a ring on Adrian."

"Yeah," Sandy agreed, throwing his arm around a clearly uncomfortable Nicholas. "Maybe that will help with your commitment issues!"

"Okay!" Mason threw his hands up. He had had enough of this. The group, collectively, turned to him. "First off, you disrespected Beyoncé and you need to give her an apology. Second, these wonderful backwatered advices you're all giving makes me concerned for the people each of you are in relationships with." He grabbed the karaoke selections book and stood up. "All I want is a Hummer, but the fact that no one in here knows how to make one is a travesty."

He stormed to the bar and flagged down the bartender who was busy helping a group of women at the other end. Ah, a new bartender. Maybe this one would know. The man nodded to Mason as he continued to serve the women.

Mason thumbed the flaps of the karaoke book as he waited. Ooh. There was a song he liked.

Nicholas approached him, a sullen look in his eyes. "Sorry about them. They mean well. I think they're worried about me."

Mason huffed. "I don't expect you to apologize for your family. You should meet mine."

Nicholas leaned his back against the bar. Argh, not the pinched brows again! "Maybe they're right. Maybe I do have commitment issues."

One look at Nicholas's rosy cheeks allowed Mason to deduce that Nicholas was drunk, or at least border-line drunk to be admitting such a deep flaw.

"I mean, I've known Adrian since high school. We've been on and off for years. Maybe there's a reason we keep running back to each other."

Mason let out a bitter laugh. "You want a reason? I can give you one. Look at me. I went to college four hundred miles away because I wanted to put *a lot* of space between me and my family. At the time, I told them, and myself, that it was because I wanted to try out a new place far from home. Expand my horizons, you know, all that cliché shit." Where was Mason going with this? Huh. Maybe he too was a little drunk. "When I graduated, I found myself back home, because it was familiar. There's no uncertainty about my place there. Maybe the reason you two keep ending up back with each other is because you're both a little lonely, a little scared, and it's comfortable. You know your role, your place, how to behave, and how to react and be."

Nicholas's eyes flickered down. "Yeah. Maybe."

Time for Mason to ask the million-dollar question. "Do you love him?"

"What kind of question is that? Of course, I love him!"

Quick to the defense. Mason was quite familiar with that type of behavior. "Hey, I may not have been in romantic love before, but I do know what love is. Or is supposed to be like." Mason grimaced as he remembered his family. How had it taken Mason so long to see it? "I have been in love with the idea of someone."

"I don't want to talk about this," Nicholas snapped. "I wouldn't even have told you about Adrian if you hadn't walked in on me working up how to propose to him!"

Mason flinched. Fine. Nicholas wanted to fight with words. Mason could do that. "All I'm saying is there's a difference between loving the idea of someone, and actually loving them for who they are!"

"You don't know our relationship!"

Mason squeezed his eyes. Why did he care so much? Why did he want to get this little lesson through Nicholas's head? Was it because he wanted to remind himself so that *he* wouldn't become the one crawling back home with apologies because it was comfortable?

"Fine. You want to know why I'm passing through? Why I'm here? I just cut my family out of my life. They aren't cruel people. They didn't hit me. But, god damn it, are they toxic, energy-suckers. I left because I didn't want to become comfortable in that skin. I left so that I didn't become them." He exhaled a shaky breath. "Maybe it's too late. Maybe the metamorphosis has already happened."

Why had Mason thought he could begin anew? He was just running from his problems like he always had. He would end up back home, tail between his legs. And they would take him back, although not without punishment. They'd make sure he knew his role and place, and he'd resettle back down into their lives once again.

It was too late for him.

A hand laid upon Mason's. Whoa. He hadn't realized he was gripping the edge of the bar counter. He glanced up at Nicholas.

"Perhaps the metamorphosis is still taking place, Kafka," Nicholas said, and shrugged. "Just not in the way you're thinking. I think you just need to find it. Your role, your place, all that you mentioned, outside of them. You just need to tread longer through tentative waters a bit longer."

Mason had thought he'd found himself in Scotland, but he'd lost that feeling when he returned. Was it because he'd returned to familiarity? Is it only through uncertainty that one can find themself?

"I am uncertain about a lot of things right now," Mason confessed.

Nicholas eyed him. "I think there's one thing you're absolutely certain of."

"And what's that?"

Nicholas looked deep into Mason's eyes, unwavering and unblinking. He tightened his grip on top of Mason's hand. "You don't want to go back to them."

Mason inhaled sharply, suddenly feeling naked and bare, and aware that Nicholas saw all of that. He trembled, feeling so exposed and opened. He wanted to curl into himself and hug his chest, to hide away.

"You know you deserve more than whatever it is they gave you," Nicholas said. "If you didn't, you wouldn't be here in this crappy bar trying to talk me out of a marriage proposal."

"I'm not trying to talk you out of it!"

"Kind of sounds like it." Despite the words, Nicholas's tone was light and teasing.

Mason felt the tension he hadn't known he'd been holding in his shoulders ease out. Nicholas wasn't angry with him, he didn't hold a grudge. Who knew there were people out there who let things go? That there would be no punishment for Mason's honesty?

The bartender came over and asked for their orders.

"Can you make a Hummer?" Mason hoped he didn't sound desperate.

"I'm afraid I don't know what that is," was the bartender's response.

"Two ounces each of light rum and coffee-flavored liqueur mixed with ice cream. Do you have anything like that?" Nicholas said as he turned and rested his elbows on the bar counter. He suddenly seemed like a different person. Taking charge. Being bold. Or is that who Nicholas truly was? Damn. Mason really wanted to kiss him right now. And he wanted Nicholas's hand back on his own.

The bartender tapped his chin. "I've got heavy whipping cream. I think I can wing it."

"Make that two Hummers," Nicholas said.

Mason raised his brows, surprised.

"What? I want to see what all the fuss is about."

"You know that drink?"

"I may have Googled it. Don't act too impressed."

"Oh thank god. I can lower my standard of expectations from you back down again."

"That may be wise."

Something twirled in Mason's stomach, and he found himself wanting to surprise Nicholas in return.

"Do you want to settle the whole Adrian thing? Do you want to know whether or not he's the one you want to spend the rest of your life with?"

"I don't want to worry about that tonight, Mason. I want to drink and forget."

"Trust me."

Nicholas sighed. "Fine. What did you have in mind?"

"We drink our Hummers, then we're going to get up there and do karaoke."

"Are we?"

"Yes. You're going to pretend you're singing to Adrian."

"Am I?"

"Hmm-hmm. If you find yourself cringing while singing whatever song I picked to your imaginary-Adrian, then you know he's not the one."

"And if I find myself getting into the groove?"

"Ew. Don't say groove. If you find that you do, then you have the answers to your uncertainty."

"I don't know, Mason."

Mason rocked on his heels. "It's only a song. It's not like he's going to hear it. And I demand that you sing a song with me. You dragged me here. You're think I'm going up there alone?"

"Okay. Fine." Nicholas faced him. "What are you planning to sing anyway? *Single Ladies*?"

"Ha. Ha. Choke on your drink, Nicholas."

Nicholas laughed.

The bartender gave them their drinks, which turned out to be very, *very* close to what a Hummer should be without real ice cream. Mason was impressed. They nursed their drinks and talked a bit more as they waited for the alcohol to settle, because, as Mason told Nicholas, he refused to feel any ounce of sobriety when he did karaoke.

When he got a bit too giggly and happy, Mason went up and signed them up for the next karaoke slot while Nicholas made up with his group of cousins. Mason cringed and fake-retched at the couple singing

Don't Stop Believin'. That song had been sung to death in karaoke bars, and should be hung up and retired.

Nicholas stumbled up to Mason as the couple was wrapping up the song in a terrible, glass-breaking rendition. He needed to bleach out his ears.

"What song are we singing, Mason?" Nicholas asked, for the umpteenth time.

"You'll find out. One of my favorites."

As the couple exit the stage, Mason took Nicholas's hand and dragged him onto the stage. He grabbed one of the microphones and handed it off to Nicholas. He snatched his own and whooped into the microphone. "Get ready to have your socks rocked off."

"I don't think that's the expression," Nicholas said.

Mason scrolled through the selection on the karaoke screen before clicking the song for them to sing. He was usually not a big fan of country pop, but during his romantic-movies phase, he'd fallen in love with this song. It'd been a while since he'd heard it.

The first few beats began to play, and Nicholas raised his brows. "Is this Keith Urban?"

Mason cackled. "For your beloved, Nicholas!"

Nicholas's smile was a mixture of disbelief and amusement.

White begun to highlight the orange lyrics on the screen and Mason sang the first verse.

Nicholas shook his head, hiding a laugh behind his hand.

Mason wiggled his eyebrows suggestively as he sung. He doubled over, pouring everything he had into this, because this was Keith Urban, and for the first time, he didn't feel quite so lonely, he didn't feel invisible, and he wanted to be selfish for a change. He was going to savor it all. He trailed off and glanced over at Nicholas, who still watched him with barely concealed amusement. "Come on, Nicholas! Who are you singing this for?"

Nicholas joined in for the chorus and ugh, damn that bastard, he made *Better Life* sound so good with that buttered voice. Mason sounded like a singer from the Disney channel compared to him.

When the chorus ended, Mason decided to pass the torch and allow

Nicholas to sing the next part solo. Nicholas extended his arm toward Mason as he sang the second verse.

Mason watched Nicholas with awe. Whoever this Adrian guy was, he was lucky. The way Nicholas sang for him, with such depth and emotions that flowed out as the words exited his lips, revealed how deep their relationship went.

Love.

Mason wanted that.

The unconditional love where someone sees you for all that you are, and still chooses you. The love full of fondness and respect. The love where they appreciate all that you gave them, but didn't base their love for you on only what you did. A love where you're not an idea, you're real. Mason joined in with Nicolas, singing the chorus together once again. He sang, out of need, out of want, pleading that he would find his *someday, baby.*

A tiny part of him imagined he was singing the words to Nicholas, imagined that maybe this Nicholas could be the one. But Mason could only allow a small portion of himself to pretend that. Nicholas was in love with another, and even if he weren't, there's no way he would even fall for someone like Mason.

Yet…

He wanted to hang out a few more times with Nicholas. With someone who teased him in return, someone who laughed at his ridiculousness, someone who could look him in the eye and see his strength, and, better yet, make Mason believe in it. *"You don't want to go back to them."*

No, I don't, Mason realized. *I want to stay here with you.*

How absurd was that thought? Was that what love was?

Not something you felt like you had to give, but one that you impulsively gave freely.

Mason belted out the rest of the song with Nicholas, watching him, soaking in every sight of him, because he might never have this moment again.

He had been finally brave enough to cut off love that came with conditions.

Would he ever be brave enough to accept genuine love when it was offered?

For now, he was free.

And that feeling, that *knowing*, of himself, of who he was and all he could be, returned.

Thank you, Nicholas. For giving that part of myself back to me.

M ason groaned as he rolled over on the bed, twisted and trapped in the cotton sheets. Good god. His mouth was so dry. He smacked his lips and tried to work saliva into it. He opened his eyes, and winced at the morning light peeking through the cracks of the window blinds. His head pounded with each thrum of his heartbeat.

He untangled himself. What happened last night? They'd sung *Better Life,* ordered a ridiculous amount of appetizers, and talked the night away.

Mason didn't even remember ever talking to someone all night without trying to get sex out of it. He ran his fingers through his hair.

Didn't he and Nicholas say they were going to look around town for a job for Mason before Nicholas returned to Peterborough later today? Mason smiled. He'd get to hang out with Nicholas again. He bit his lower lip, warmth spreading through his chest.

It was a bit past ten, and Mason remembered telling Nicholas that he wouldn't be ready until after ten because he was not a morning person. Good. Mason stretched and popped a bone in his spine.

It was ten after eleven when Mason finally made it up the stairs. When he entered the kitchen, Mrs. Burke looked up from reading the newspaper at the kitchen table. She wore a floral robe, which made Mason feel better about his tardiness.

He did a quick glance around the kitchen.

No Nicholas.

"Um, good morning," Mason greeted. He looked around again. Maybe Nicholas was hiding from him.

"Nicholas left early this morning," Mrs. Burke said. "He seemed a bit frantic. I hope everything's okay. But he assured me it was. There was something he said he really needed to do."

Oh. Of course Nicholas had left.

Mason had helped Nicholas realize how much he loved Adrian, and he couldn't wait to go and propose to the love of his life.

Good. That was good.

Why did it feel like someone had punched him in the stomach?

"He said you two made plans, and he wrote down a list of job suggestions. I'd be happy to drive you around and help."

"Oh. Thanks. You don't have to do that."

"I want to. It'll give me an excuse to skip church," Mrs. Burke said with a wink. "He wanted me to give you something to convince you to stay. He said he was uncertain about this, but his faith was strong. Do you know what he's talking about? He didn't make a lot of sense this morning."

Mason searched through his drink-infested memory. Had Nicholas still been drunk when he left? Faith was strong? Wasn't that part of the lyrics of the song they'd sung last night? It must mean Nicholas was uncertain about the marriage proposal, but had faith in the decision. Well, that was romantic. And wonderful. So wonderful. He'd hoped Nicholas would stay. God, he was stupid! He shoved that thought aside. At least he'd helped Nicholas through this. He'd done something good.

That was what mattered.

Mason's eyes stung. *Be brave. Remember. Someday. You'll get genuine love someday.*

Mrs. Burke got up and grabbed a manila envelope from behind the coffee maker. She handed it to Mason. There was nothing in there that could convince Mason to stay. He'd already made up his mind last night.

"I'll go change, and then we'll head out. Sound good?"

He smiled at her. "Yeah. Thanks, Mrs. Burke."

"Help yourself to some breakfast. I was going to reheat some sticky buns for you, but Nicholas said I shouldn't be the one doing that for you. Honestly, how much did that boy drink?"

Mason's cheeks burned. That sly jerk. "Yeah, I can get that myself. Thanks."

She patted his arm. "I'll be back down shortly." And she left.

He opened the flap of the envelope and squinted inside. Did Nicholas really need that large of an envelope for something so small? What exactly was in there? Pocket change?

He poured the object out from the envelope, and it slid out onto his palm.

It was the engagement ring.

Mason drew in a sharp breath, and then chuckled softly, now understanding Nicholas's message.

"I'm uncertain about us, too, Nicholas." He wrapped his fingers around the ring. "But, fuck, yes, I'm staying."

He'd take that leap of faith.

ABOUT THE AUTHOR

Katie Day accidentally summoned a ghost, almost died in Scotland, ate chicken feet (yes, it was delicious), and pulled a sword from stone so she's the rightful ruler of Britain. She has the exceptional ability to hear the world differently than most with her unique hearing loss, or in some cases not at all. She writes primarily YA urban fantasy and romance. If you want to stalk her, she currently lives in Golden with her hubby and two hyper mutts.

I GOT YOU, BABE

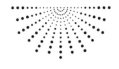

STEPHANIE AMEDEO

I f you had walked with me down the road, that day, away from campus, you would have seen my face.

I'm wearing plaid bell-bottoms, a tie-dyed shirt and loose hair, and no makeup. The year? 1971. Carrying my textbooks: psychology, sociology, economics, Spanish and English comp.

Down the road away from campus. Toward my place. An apartment. If you walked three blocks west, you would encounter the backyard fence of those apartments, two stories, in blocks of five. First you pass the high wooden fences of the backyards. Around. Then turn left. Now you're in front of the apartments. No yards here. Cement sidewalks, up four steps, up to the metal front doors, painted yellow. With strips of bare dirt or maybe tulips lining the four-foot sidewalk up to those steps.

At this point, you would have seen my place. Four doors down. And, if you were there then. You would have seen my face. As I'm walking, cradling my beloved books, I walk slower and slower. Making the turn, I'm looking to see if his car is parked in front. If it is…then he's there. I will have to go in and see him. If it's not there, he's not there. Not yet. And I've time off! Hooray!! But I will have to pay (and pay). At two or three or four a.m., beginning with the morning of the next day.

One time, a few weeks past, I turned that corner to see no car parked there. Little did I know that I would have a three-day weekend! Until the call came from the jail in Mexico. "Come and get me". But I didn't have the car. I had to go to the bank. Get money we didn't have, beg an acquaintance to give me a ride, drive down to Mexico, pay for her gas, pay to cross the border. Find the jail. Pay the jailer for release and for the car. He was filthy. And mad. He drove the car and me back to the house. Apparently, then, judging from what happened next, it was all my fault. I wished I had known I had had three days. Instead of three days not sleeping. Looking out the window constantly. Feeling rotten that I wanted him never to come back. Wondering (hoping) that he'd been in a fatal car wreck from driving while drinking.

We'd been married three weeks when I knew this was a mistake.

My father had told me, standing getting ready to walk me down the aisle, "Are you sure you want to do this?"

When I miscarried the baby, I cried. And grieved and wept. And thought, I didn't have to get married to him, after all.

The baby looked like a Barbie doll. Skinny legs. I had cramps. It was November, and we were at his family's house for Thanksgiving. I woke up in the morning with blood everywhere and pain everywhere and a little doll that I had lost.

In December, I thought I was pregnant again. I never had another period.

This was March.

Here's what happened on the Ides of March. I was doing well in my classes, but my best most fun wonderful experience on campus was being a teacher's aide for the preschool. I was majoring in Early Childhood Education. I had won the scholarship to be a teacher's aide because of my grades. I adored the campus. I loved the classes. He had dropped out the third week of the previous semester, and held one job after another, retail sales, stocking, vacuum cleaner repairs. Each time he was elated, then downtrodden, then angry, then fired. Campus was my safety zone. My safe place. And I loved the preschool. He could stand outside my other classes, but wasn't allowed on the grounds for the preschool.

I loved being the teacher's aide. My teacher was youngish, plumpish, and loved to play and sing, and read books to the kids.

After one bad night, as I was getting ready to go to the preschool, and he was snoring on the couch in the living room, with bottles stacked everywhere, I had a very difficult time covering up my black eye and the bruises on the neck. I had been wearing turtlenecks, and long sleeves to the preschool. My teacher had said, "You know, you don't have to be *that* conservative. Just have your chest covered and wear pants so you can play with them and lean over." Gently. But this particular time I couldn't cover it with three layers of makeup. I brushed my hair to flip over and cover my eye on that side. I couldn't not go. I hoped she wouldn't notice. But she did. And she sent me away. "Go to the University Medical Clinic. There's a counselor there.

She can help you. Go now." I did go to the Medical Clinic. However, I didn't see the counselor. Instead, I peed in the cup to see if the rabbit would die. Was I pregnant?

On that one particular day, I went to the Medical Clinic and it turned out positive. I held the paper in my hand that said I was pregnant, again. I'm such a fool.

The car isn't there. So, I walk along the sidewalk, up the stairs, unlock the door, and enter the place we are staying. Downstairs, there are two rooms, a front room in front, and a kitchen in back with a door out to the backyard. Directly in front of the door are the stairs to the upper floor, one bedroom and a bathroom. The bathroom is directly above the stairs, the bedroom to the left. I drop my purse, my sweater and books on the chair to my right, and my keys on the coffee table to my left. Quarters are so close I don't have to walk over to either, just pass through dropping things. He isn't there. I make and have a cup of tea in the kitchen. I look out the front window. I take a shower. I look out the window. I put on my pajamas. I look out the window. No car. No him.

I lay down on the couch, downstairs, behind the coffee table and read my textbooks. I fall asleep.

Then the car caroms up, and he stinks of drink, as usual. Walks up the stairs. Goes into the bathroom. I go up the stairs. I'm thinking, hey, now I'm pregnant, he will like me, won't hit me anymore. I have the paper in my hand to show him. I stand at the top of the stairs. I say, "hey...guess what" and don't get any farther.

He whomps me in the face with his fist, and then swipes me on the shoulder with his other arm.

I fall down the stairs.

I land on the bottom floor, looking up, pain everywhere.

He laughs.

Goes back into the bathroom to wash his hands, readying to come down to hit and hit and hit and hit some more until he's tired. This, of course, is all my fault. I said yes when I should have said no. And the matriarchs of my day said get married and don't go to college. I should have done the one and not the other. I lay there. At this particular moment in my life, lying on the floor, the first true clear thought occurs to me. This day is the last day, I'll have this day. Maybe one day. Soon, no more days at all.

I look over at the coffee table.

There are my keys.

There are my keys.

THERE are my KEYS!

I jump up. I grab the keys. I run out to the car, open the driver side and am able to lock all the doors before he runs out and bangs on the windows. "Where do you think you're going? What do you think you're doing? Open up now, or else."

I don't know what to do.

I'm just sheltering where he can't get at me.

He turns away to go back in the house, probably he's looking for something with which to break the window.

I put the key in the ignition.

He comes out from the house, slamming the door, leaves the door open, carrying (waving) the hammer we keep in the kitchen.

I turn the key.

I roar down the street, flooring it.

Where can I go?

Luck always comes in threes; charms always work in threes. The first luck charm was that I had a full tank of gas, since I have no money. I do not have my purse. I'm barefoot. I'm in my pajamas. The second luck is the best. I have somewhere to go. I head out to the highway and drive home. To my parents. My parents. They will take me in.

The third charm is the most interesting. I drive up into the driveway of my parent's house and turn off the car. I go to the door. It's locked! My parents are both at work, my little sister at High School. This is the first time I find out that they have started locking the house. I walk around. The kitchen door is locked too. I say hello to our Irish Setter in the back yard. He wags his tail. He's glad to see me. I'm glad to see him. He licks my face, wags his tail.

I get in the car. I drive to my father's office and walk in the door.

Pajamas. Barefoot. Shame-faced. The receptionist freaks out, calls him. He comes rushing out of his office. He says nothing, just puts on his hat and gets his keys, and tells the receptionist he'll be right back. He hugs me outside. "You left him."

"Yes." I can't say more without bawling.

We go to the car. He waits as I get in. It won't start. It ran out of gas in his office parking lot. "Wait." He goes in and tells the receptionist he'll be gone a bit longer. He drives me home in his car. He lets me in. I'm all alone at home. My home. It's safe. I'm home. I take a shower. I put on my old clothes from the drawers in my old room. I wallow in my old bedroom. I crawl into bed, pull up the covers, hold my old stuffed chimp named Zippy, and fall asleep.

When I wake up I hear my parents talking quietly in the kitchen and my sister yelling, "Why is she here?"

I get up. I can't tell them. We sit down to dinner. Things are very, very quiet. I'm covered in bruises from the fall. My face, my elbows, my knee. My nose is swollen. Maybe I don't have to explain much, after all. My sister comes over and raises her hand to push my hair out of my face and my reflex is to cringe. My mother cries out.

He drives up.

My father goes out. He says, "Get off my property."

I never go back.

I never go back.

I never go back.

I saved my baby. Although, she says, she saved me. Which is true. I would never have left him to save myself, alone. My baby is beautiful. I name her for my mother (her middle name), and for my family name because the divorce comes through in August and she is born in September. Although the nuns at the hospital gave me grief for giving her my last name.

She's mine.

It's you and me, kid.

To end this story,

Let me say,

It took awhile,

Before I took the keys,
And drove,
Away.
And got away.
And got us away.
But each day, like today, when I wake up, I try to say this:
Today's the last day, I'll have today.
And I have you.
My baby.

ABOUT THE AUTHOR

Stephanie Amedeo once stood, nine years old, in library stacks, an unread copy of *The Lion, The Witch, and The Wardrobe* open in her hands. Since then, she's been a reading-addicted-bookworm. Going on to read all the Narnia books, when returning the last one to the librarian, she was devastated that there were no more. Then, she had to become a writer and finish the series. However, life is what happens when you're busy planning something else. Meantime, she obtained a doctorate in sociology, married, had children, taught college. Now, here she is keeping on keeping on—writing her story.

THE SEA BEYOND

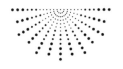

SHELLEY KITCHURA NELSON

From our back porch looking west to the foothills,
a storm moves in and fog creeps over
from the sea, far away on the other side of the
       mountains.

Hearing the foghorn sound from thousands of miles
       away,
I imagine the darkness of the storm.
Still, the fog relieves me and sits on my thirsty skin.

When the foghorn blew in the late evening hours on the
       island,
I woke and listened for the ships coming in
as they broke through the cold bay water.
Like a sleepwalker, I went to the window, cracked it
       open,
let the vapor fill the bedroom as the horn bellowed long
       and slow and even
into the space that I called home and it was good.

If I shut my eyes, I am afraid it will be gone.
I tune my ears to the sound
blowing through my body.

Bathing in the rain, then snow, shivering.
The moisture wraps around me, I inhale,
filling my lungs with water from the sea beyond.

Cool and wet it seeps in.
Chills turn into calm breathing
keeping time with the horn.

Here on the east side of the valley looking west,

there is no foghorn within a lighthouse to send
    messages
to ships and fishermen on the sea.
Still, it has found its way to me.

ABOUT THE AUTHOR

Whether observing the miles ahead of her or exploring a memory, Shelley Kitchura Nelson is forthright in bringing life's passing nuances to the page. She chooses both simple and extraordinary moments to convey the worth of noticing what happens along the way. She strives to make her writing a place readers want to return to, and remember how they felt when they first read it. Shelley currently lives on a small farm built on the rock of the Colorado foothills. Her poetry has been published in *Pilgrimage* and *New Millennium Writings*.

AFTER GRANDPA DIED

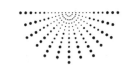

KAREN ALBRIGHT LIN

"What about your grandfather?" My husband, Wen, just couldn't let it go. Grandpa had been dead half a year and his ashes still resided in a simple grey box in our coat closet.

I blinked and sat down next to Wen on the bed. "I'll take care of it."

"How many times have you said that? He's like a stinky shoe in that closet." He flattened down the coarse waves of his crow-black hair. "You know he's going to haunt us?"

My grandfather couldn't make it to our wedding, yet, here he was, in death, very much present in our house. And Ma Yang, Wen's mother, had spotted the box only the day before. She and Wen had had a rather animated discussion about it…in Mandarin.

"What did you tell your mother was in the box?"

"Condoms." Wen had a lot of nerve staying dead-pan.

"Condoms. In our closet." I didn't even give it the dignity of a question mark. "Enough to fill a whole box." Grandpa had made quite a transformation.

"I told her it was packed very full."

"You don't think too fast on your feet do you?"

"Lying to my mother isn't something I've perfected. You want me to tell her the truth?"

"Couldn't you explain this in a way that won't upset her?"

"Your grandpa's planted in the closet."

"I suppose you blame him?"

"I don't think he had much to do with it, given his state." Wen pulled off his socks and rubbed anti-fungal cream onto his feet. The treatment was a useless move, as always.

"I didn't ask you to make up such a silly lie. And I didn't ask to have custody of Grandpa, either. And why would we keep rubbers in the coat closet?" I grabbed a towel and huffed off to take a shower.

Once done, instead of slipping off my blue silk robe and tucking myself next to Wen in the bed, I brushed my teeth twice and flossed twice, all the while brainstorming places to relocate Grandpa's ashes. If I could solve one problem tonight, I could slide into bed with one less worry.

What to do with Grandpa Randal?

His first choice, surely, would be having himself scattered over Yankee Stadium and then watered in with Budweiser. But that would never be approved.

From the moment UPS had delivered him, Wen had had the heebie-jeebies over Grandpa Randal being in our closet. Wen had groaned, "He's going to stay there? What if he's still hovering over his dusty remains, angry?"

How could I argue with that?

But Wen never forced the issue until Ma saw the box.

It would have been worse than awkward if my poor husband had decided to explain the truth of what was in the box to Ma. I began to see the benefit of the condom story. If nothing else, it offered a reprieve.

———

Though both my Grandpa Randal and Wen's father had died of leukemia, Death played favorites with destiny. The difference between their deaths: the Yang Patriarch died surrounded by family; my grandfather lived alone and cut his tether three days early, leaving him good and ripe for the maid's weekly visit. He was promptly cremated, scooped into a low-rent box, and handed over to my father. There was no pretense of ceremony. And when Dad decided to change his life, he moved away after donating most of his stuff to the Salvation Army, including Grandpa. The thrift store traced me down and called me. Did I want the ashes my father had left with them?

Okay.

A year before, I had had my hand on Father Yang's bed when he died at home, in his bed, with his mouth wide open. On the other side from me, tears flowed from Wen's sisters and Ma. They stroked his papery limbs and fine, still-living hair.

"He's hungry! He died hungry!" Ma Yang proclaimed, and ran to the kitchen.

She returned minutes later with daikon swimming in chicken broth.

After she set it on the nightstand, near Father's head, his jaw relaxed. He closed his mouth, sated.

I couldn't remember death being a hunger-making experience for any of my relatives. Maybe they'd grown tired of eating. I suppose mac-n-cheese wasn't nearly as enticing as Chinese soup.

The phone had rung as Father Yang's spirit presumably sipped on broth, his sister calling from Taiwan. She'd called because she had felt his death.

That mystical quality of passing was missing for my family.

My grandpa still hung out in the closet because I simply hadn't thought about where to sprinkle him. I preferred to believe I was contemplating a good piece of real estate for him rather than admit he was an afterthought, hidden where he rarely reminded me of my obligation.

After his father's death, Wen drove a hard bargain for a tiny piece of California ground, a place on a hill, under a newly planted tree—location, location, location.

I had joined the family in packing Father Yang's body tightly into his casket with stacks and stacks of "dead money" bought penny-on-the-dollar in Chinatown. The body could not be allowed to shake on the way to the grave. That would "shake away his descendants' good luck."

I touched Father Yang more in death than I had in life. Numbness filled the spaces between layers of my admiration and horror about the procedure.

The cemetery ritual included incense, live flowers, the cleaning of the headstone, and bows.

That night, back home, we all burned "dead money" in the fireplace, along with other items required in heaven—even clothes, including a polyester suit that must have sent the neighbors looking for shelter from toxic fumes.

Several days later, Father Yang began visiting the family in dreams, asking for more money. He was having a great time, obviously gambling the shirt off his back. As a result, my mother-in-law burned more clothes and more "dead money" without cursing her husband's addiction.

Ma Yang had burned close-mouthed, devoted. Later, she added Father's name to the dozens of Yang ancestors whose names were scrawled on the rice paper family tree. She always offered his altar the best in-season fruit; the rest of the family ate bruised remainders.

Father Yang's passing didn't so much change my view of death as it altered my view of those still living.

Finally, after half an hour, I knew where to put Grandpa's ashes. I dressed again, slipping into my shoes.

In the quiet evening, I carried Grandpa Randal down to the rough, to the ninth hole of our neighborhood golf course, and dumped the surprisingly chunky remains. He had always loved to golf and was known for creative scorekeeping, taking "free shots" out of the rough. He'd like it there, I decided, because he could golf at all hours, cheat, and nobody would know.

I promised the dusty pile that I'd visit his little mound where the grass would, no doubt, grow particularly verdant. I teased aloud, "Someday I'll put Grandma next to you." She was his long-ago, bitterly-divorced wife. After witnessing a Chinese death and all the ceremony around the burial, I could now entertain the possibility of Grandpa actually hearing me and the earth shaking over such a threat. I studied the ground for a few moments, but it never shook.

Maybe Grandpa couldn't hear me over his own snores.

ABOUT THE AUTHOR

Karen is a hopeless foodie, award-winning novelist, and produced screenwriter. Many of her stories are inspired by her experience marrying into a Chinese family. Food is often a subplot. *Mu Shu Mac & Cheese* and *American Moon* came out in 2020. When possible she, her husband, and their two boys travel as she researches recipes from around the world for a literary cookbook. She teaches for cruise lines and writers conferences in Colorado where she is part of a rich author community.

BLINDSIDED

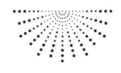

DAVID STIER

The fire raced down from the hilltop, resembling a giant dragon. The red, orange, and yellow flames rose and fell slowly, on each side, like flapping wings, and the front of the conflagration's triangle-shaped head bellowed fire toward his two-room home and small garden. Hot wind howled past, blowing off his boonie hat while slapping his long grey hair into his face. What had been a cool morning had morphed into a midday-Death-Valley kind of heat. The wind shifted and acidic smoke from the fire blew into his eyes and up his nose, blinding him momentarily. He coughed violently and his nose burned as he rubbed tears from his eyes.

Arnie stood there, jaw dropped, for about thirty seconds, watching the raging forest fire as it rolled down the slope toward his property. The tall redwoods and cedars lit up like 50-foot torches. The raging demon fire destroyed everything in its path, vacuuming up his apple, orange and other fruit trees, turning them all into flaming Roman candles. So far his three *sinsemilla* plants behind his home were untouched but that definitely wouldn't last. So much for that bit of profit.

How could the fires consume everything so fast?

Behind him, Pancake, his white female pit bull, ran around in her enclosure outside his house, barking in panic and trying to break through the hurricane fencing that rattled and shook with each lunge. Thank god he'd kept her there after getting up. Usually, he let her out to do her morning business and explore where she wanted.

He picked up his boonie hat, rushed into his house, grabbed his wallet, check book, and pickup keys. He yanked open his refrigerator and took out two bottles of water. On the way out the door he grabbed his backpack, not sure what was in it, but more than positive that it would be gone with everything else if and when he made it back.

Arnie donned his backpack. Then he bent down next to the enclosure's gate.

"Come on Pankie!" he said. "Get it together, girl! You wanna live you'll calm down—"

She jumped up and down for a moment, but finally made eye

contact, looking at Arnie with that tilted-head question she used whenever she wanted an answer. Before she could react further, he opened the gate, grabbed her up, and raced to his beat-up old Datsun. He yanked open the driver's door and threw her inside the cab, then slammed the door shut once he got behind the wheel.

He turned the key. The solenoid clicked and that was all.

Sonofabitch!

One look out the rearview mirror showed the flames just 100 feet from his home. He took a deep breath and turned the key again, praying to whatever God there was that his old Japanese beater would fire up. The engine cranked slowly, like it couldn't make up its mind, then finally caught. Arnie threw it into gear and headed for the road leading up out to Manzanita Lane and life.

He looked back once in the mirror. Flames engulfed his house, Pankie's enclosure and his pot plants as he turned the first corner. More flames raged on either side, trying to block his escape, so he floored the pedal, crashed through the wood gate and kept his truck mostly centered on the one-lane, uneven dirt road.

The race to the main road was another freak-out. Pankie kept jumping up and down on the seat, barking constantly. Arnie tried to ignore her until she bit his arm. He slapped her several times until she got the message and huddled, trembling, in the far corner of her seat.

"Dammit, Pankie!" he said, with a quick glance her way. His heart ached at the fearful look she directed at him, something he had never seen before. He thought to pet her, but didn't. Last thing he needed was to lose a finger.

"I'm sorry girl," he said. "I know this is scary shit…"

He looked back at the road leading uphill and out of the valley where his property lay. A large mature cedar had begun to topple across the road in front of the truck at the hillcrest forty feet ahead. He floored the gas and the tired old Datsun bounced up and down over the potholes he'd been meaning to fill, rear tires slipping in the loose dirt and small rocks, as it struggled to make it past the falling tree.

The cedar's trunk snapped and crackled over the raging flames on either side of the road as it slowly toppled. As they raced past, something scraped across the truck bed, sparks flying and lifting the front wheels off the ground. With a crash, the front of the truck slammed back down onto the road as they crested the hill, reaching the flats that led to the main road.

The road was better here, as the rains hadn't eroded these rills like the water that ran downslope toward his land. He slowed some but not all that much since the trees and brush on either side were burning like crazy as well. But at least there was some open space on either side of the road now—space he had cleared himself, just in case a fire like this ever happened.

After the first decent rainy season in six years, Arnie had begun to breathe easier. For the previous five years his property had avoided many horrific fires—even the Carr Fire, which burned almost 230,000 acres and destroyed over 1,000 homes.

This fire looked equally bad—at least from behind the wheel of his truck. Flames lined the road, twin raging columns heading northeast as far as he could make out, hopefully leading the way to safety.

He looked at Pankie, who still cowered in her corner. Arnie stroked the buttermilk-pancake-shaped splash of color on her coat, the reason he had named her Pancake.

"You okay, girl?" he said as he rubbed the spot behind her ear, the spot she really liked to have stroked. Her tail wagged a few times, but then the raging forest fire increased in volume. She whined, then growled, glaring at the burning vegetation.

"That's the spirit, Pankie," he said and she wagged her tail some more. "Give 'em hell, yeah?"

They turned right off Small Farms Road, onto Cloverdale, and then past the Veterans Cemetery. As they approached Redding, the fire faded and then vanished behind them, but the plumes of smoke continued to rise like weaving dark snakes. Arnie looked into the truck bed and at his tool box. He wasn't sure how many tools were still in it, but some were better than none, as his father used to say.

He pulled over and poured some water into the bowl he kept for Pankie, and she slurped it up while he took a couple of slugs himself. He remembered the backpack, which had kept him hunched over while driving, and he took it off, setting it on the middle of the seat. Then he took his wallet and check book from his back pants pocket and slipped them in the glove box. He'd worry about what cash was in the wallet once they reached Redding.

He looked back once more at the now solid black wall of smoke, flames occasionally appearing, then vanishing. He hoped something would remain of Sage Hill, but realistically he didn't think much would—especially all of the sage brush that had inspired the name.

"Okay, girl," he said as they got back on the road. "At least we made it out alive, huh?"

Traffic increased the closer he got to Redding, but it appeared that he and Pankie were some of the first folks to escape. As they approached the 7-Eleven, the empty parking lot invited him to pull in and grab some grub. He could find cheaper stuff in the Safeway downtown, but there was no telling how many survivors would be packing that place by then. As he opened the door, Pancake tried to jump over him to get out.

"I'll be back in a minute, Pankie, so chill out. You can hold it for a few minutes."

He squeezed out the door, then rushed inside to see what food they had. He was the only customer but he hurried, grabbing mixed nuts, trail mix, a six-pack of beer, and both dry and wet dog food. He got himself a giant raspberry Slurpee and grabbed a gallon of distilled water, too.

"Shit, Arn," the clerk who'd known him as a customer for years said. "Fire looks bad, man."

He set all his purchases down on the counter and shrugged.

"Me and Pankie made it out at least, but my place is toast, now. Don't know how my neighbors are doing, but it looks like a huge fire. Hope they made it out."

"Christ! Know how it started?"

Arnie shook his head as he helped load the stuff into plastic bags.

"The morning was beautiful, then, next thing I knew, the fire was racing down the hill toward my place."

"I'm really sorry, man."

"Thanks Rick. If I was you, I'd get ready for more customers as I may have been the first down the mountain."

He grabbed his stuff and hurried out so as to not have to answer any more questions. Questions would just make him think about what he'd just lost—which was about everything—didn't have any insurance neither—so he dumped the bags in the back of the truck and grabbed Pankie's leash and took her out to the field behind the 7-Eleven so she could take a leak and dump a load, or both.

Once they were back on the road, he saw more cars and trucks headed toward Redding. It looked like some had had time to pack some stuff, but most looked like they were people who, like him, had only enough time to escape with their lives.

He followed Placer to Turtle Bay Park. The place was almost empty, but he knew that would change. Lots of folks would be short of cash, and the parking lot had some freebie slots. Once they parked, he fed Pankie and himself, then called Hazel, his ex-wife, to let her know he was safe and to find out if she'd heard how the fire got started. She didn't pick up, so he left a voicemail. Then, as he started to call Luce and Greg to see if he could stay at their place for the next couple of days, he paused. They had Internet and TV and a backyard that would be a nice place to stay in this heat. Maybe he could borrow a sleeping bag or some blankets?

"Shit."

Another thing he'd lost was all his backpacking gear, some of which he'd been collecting for years. All his emergency rations, too. If he was lucky, some of the stuff he'd buried near the pond he'd made during the drought would have survived.

He decided not to call his friends and shut off his cell, then took Pankie for a walk—leash laws were strictly enforced in this redneck town so, while she didn't like it, it was what it was. As they walked, the full weight of what he'd lost finally blindsided him. He rested his arm against a nearby cedar, leaned into it so as not to collapse, and did his best to try and figure out what to do.

The Clover Fire, as it had been named, had burned for a week before the Forestry Dept. announced that it was safe for folks to return to what was left—if anything.

"Thanks Greg," Arnie said after dragging Pankie to the truck and throwing her inside the cab. "I appreciate you both putting up with us."

"No problem, Arn," Greg said. "Come on back if you need to, man," then Greg handed him a baggie of pot. "Maybe this will help once you get back to Sage Hill."

Arnie opened the baggie and took a whiff. "Smells familiar," he said, with a slight smile—as it should, since Arnie had sold it to Greg a week earlier. Now that it was legal to grow—if you kept your head down and didn't make a hassle for the cops—pot had been a decent part of his cash crop.

Greg returned the smile. "If you need more, just let me know."

And man, how *that* hurt, though Arnie knew he didn't mean it that way. Arnie had been known as a prime grower from Redding to Arcata ever since California legalized it, and here he was now taking a charity lid of his own quality *sensimilla*.

He slapped Greg on the shoulder.

"Much appreciated man. I'll pay it back with the next crop." He got in his pick up and headed out.

The next crop?

That wouldn't be for at least a year—maybe less, if he was lucky and the seeds he'd stashed were still okay.

He stopped by Safeway to pick up some food and ice for the ice chest Greg and Luce had loaned him. He also bought a 12-pack of Heineken and a half pint of Black Jack. His oldest buddy Dave used to swear by Old Number 7's *restorative qualities* when life kicked you in the ass—but that was before he'd given up booze. Arnie planned to test that theory tonight.

He put the beers in the cooler, along with the whiskey and veggies. When he looked at the lettuce, tomatoes, carrots and other stuff, his gut took the dive he'd been trying to hold off since leaving Greg's place. Until a week ago, he'd never had to buy any of the veggies that now rested in the cooler. Sage Hill's garden had been his pride and joy. He'd nursed his two apple trees and the plum and apricot tree though three freezes, too. Maybe it was a blessing he'd gotten that last look at his land as the flames had consumed it. At least he knew what he'd find in about thirty minutes. He thought about cracking a beer, but the last thing he needed was to get pulled over on a DUI. While most Redding cops and Sheriffs let him be, there were a couple who'd just love to nail his ass.

As he headed down Placer Drive, the evidence of the fire grew. Pankie looked out the window, her tail wagging, knowing where they were headed. He was glad that she was distracted and left him alone. It was hard enough just to keep his eyes on the road and not space out seeing the still smoldering ashes of the destroyed flora.

"In the latest developments of last week's Clover Fire, which destroyed over 8,000 acres," said the local newscaster which Arnie's radio managed to pick up. *"A former Redding firefighter has been arrested for arson. And, in another bit of bad news for property owners, FEMA will not distribute any disaster relief since fewer than 100 homes were involved..."*

"Bit of bad news?" he said to himself. Then he noticed Pankie giving him that tilted-head look which, at least, made him smile. "Sounds like the understatement of the year, pal."

The story continued, but Arnie heard nothing more. All he could think about were the hours spent saving his fruit trees during the past three years of freezing weather, and hauling water from the pond and pumping it from the well to keep his garden alive.

Fucking arson? By a former firefighter?

Over the past week, the scent of burned wood and ash had become something everyone in Redding had gotten used to—and not for the first time during this 5-year drought—but, as he neared his land, it got more pronounced. On either side, the remains of evergreens lined the way—the scent of burned sap making his nose itch. Charcoal-black stick figures of trees, with a few spindly branches, were all that remained. Occasional skeletal remains of Mountain and Black Oaks reached skyward, calling out to nature to heal their desiccated corpses. Charred, black remnants of wild manzanita bushes were all he saw of the greenery that had once lined the road. The combined odors, at least, helped hide the occasional stench of cooked deer and other wildlife. Luckily, Centerville, the little pissant burg he'd just passed, had survived. It looked like firefighters had contained the blaze just west of town.

Joe's Recycle yard looked mostly undamaged, too. Maybe find some stuff there to rebuild with?

They usually had discounted lumber and, with the little cash he had left, he would definitely be doing the bargain basement routine in all things, since homeowner's insurance was something he didn't have.

Better check it out soon, before it all gets picked over, but if Joe tries any price-gouging on me, he'll be missing a few teeth...

When he turned off Clear Creek onto Cloverdale and passed the VA Cemetery, his gut did another back flip. A real metaphor, that: passing a bone yard on the way back to his wasted land. Some of the trees had survived in the cemetery, but a lot of them were at least singed, along with the grass, which was now mostly brown or grey. Once fully onto Cloverdale, the only things he saw to either side of the 2-lane asphalt road was more of what he had seen earlier, with the added *spectacle* of destroyed homes and buildings with the occasional dead cow or horse in burned out corrals, bloated stomachs reminding him of a book he had—now certainly nothing but ashes—on Civil War photography.

As he neared the hillcrest leading to Sage Hill, he recalled the cedar tree that had nearly done both him and Pankie in, but it had been pulled off to the side, clearing the road. Probably the hot shot crew did that to get their equipment down into his valley.

No thanks to God for small favors, yeah?

He slowed his pickup, not wanting to see what was left of his dream, and sat atop the hillcrest for a few minutes.

"Fuck it," he finally said, and headed down into the abyss.

"Y ou stay close, Pankie," he said as he let her out of the cab. She looked around at what was left of the house and her enclosure. She seemed frightened of the twisted wreckage of the hurricane fencing and half fallen gate. She looked up at Arnie.

"I know, girl," he said with a shrug. "Welcome home."

Slowly, she circled the destruction, then her circle expanded. Arnie walked over to the faucet which, surprisingly, still worked—must still be connected to the upslope water tank—and filled her blackened metal water dish after rinsing it out. She slurped up some water, then stuck her nose to the ground and started to explore.

"Remember what I said, Pankie!" When she looked back, he made a circle of his arm. "Don't get into trouble, and stay close."

First thing was to check the upslope water supply. His solar panel towers were gone-ski—just piles of ash and charred wood, so the electric pump wouldn't operate even if it *was* still undamaged. But, maybe the emergency hand pump still worked?

He reached the water tank and, as expected the electric pump was fried. Lying on its side like a corpse, the metal burned black, and the wiring reduced to melted blobs of copper and insulation. He unlocked the hand pump. Its steel was burned black, too, and while the seals leaked some, he heard water sloshing into the tank as he operated the handle. He pumped for about ten minutes, then checked the level by slapping the tank till he heard the hollow sound of empty space, about a foot from the top.

Got water, at least.

Next, he moved to his house and pulled on a pair of heavy leather gloves—usually he used non-animal-product gloves but this was all he had left—and then started sifting through the debris with a 2x4 that was partly unburned and broken down to a point on one end. Mostly all that was left was white and gray ash and an occasional piece of charred 2x4—mostly Douglas fir, which was surprising, since that wood usually burned hot and fast. Had it been redwood, there might have been more that could be described as a building. What conduit he'd used was now twisted like aluminum pretzels and the Romex copper wire sticking out the ends was melted, looking like electrical blood veins.

Only half of the back wall still stood, and that looked ready to collapse with the next weak-ass wind. In the middle of the back room, his potbellied stove still rested where he'd set it seven years ago, but now the black iron was stained mostly grey and rust red and what black was left was pitted and runny, as though the forest fire's heat had melted the iron. One of the three legs tilted outward, giving it the look of a ship about to capsize.

That stove was over 100 years old, and he'd found it in the woods near Lassen in an old abandoned cabin, a mile off the beaten track, and down in a valley. Hauling it out had taken a lot of work. Both Greg and Dave had helped, and they cussed the whole time, Arnie remembered with a faint smile. Now, it was just a hunk of worthless crap.

He picked up a piece of conduit that was hooked on one end, thinking it would be a better tool to sift through the wreckage in what was left of the kitchen and bedroom. Something caught on the end while he fished under the sink's melted plumbing, which had fallen to one side. He yanked harder but still it wouldn't budge so he planted both legs and tried again.

"Goddamit!"

Finally the sink broke loose and he landed on his ass. Pain lanced down his leg.

"Sonofabitch!"

He stood back up and pulled up his pant leg. Last thing he needed now was a serious injury, since everything medical for him—Pankie, too, for that matter—was an out-of-pocket big-buck experience. A bent nail had stuck him, not badly though, and at least it had been burned black and not rusty.

Fuck it, man. Let it bleed...

"Maybe I should write music, yeah?"

He fished around, using the conduit for a few more minutes, then shrugged and wiped his sweating brow.

Hopeless.

He trudged out to his truck, which was another mistake, because he got his first good look at his Pop's old Ford 4x4 that his Ma had given him after the old man died suddenly from a heart attack. There were still a few patches of industrial yellow paint on it, but mostly it was nothing but a charred black ruin with melted rubber tires. The upholstery was gone, too—not that it was anything to look at before. Only the wire springs and frame were left of the bench seat. He could still make out the sprung driver's side, which drooped down, and would put his leg to sleep on longer drives to construction jobs.

His Pop had worked at the Ford Motor Plant in Milpitas and he'd picked the truck out personally, off the line, back in 1983 just before the factory closed. He'd driven it for over twenty years and, damn, how he had babied that sucker. In the 15 years Arnie had driven it, the trees around here had taken their toll on the paint, but he'd babied it mechanically. The V8 could pull a ton uphill if it had to—and it had on more than one occasion.

Arnie tried to open the driver's door, and it crashed to the ground, so he kicked the dirt, raising a cloud of ash which the wind caught and blew into his face. He sneezed and, for good measure, he kicked the ash-covered ground again, daring the wind once more, but this time it shifted and blew toward the pond.

He looked up the hill where the arsonist motherfucker's fire dragon had first appeared. Only stumps were left of the two apple trees, and the peach and apricot trees were gone completely, except for piles of ashes. He turned and looked toward the back of his ruined house at the ashes that were all that was left of his pot plants, then, in spite of better judgement, he walked up the incline. Grey leaf shapes remained around the peach tree. He stooped and picked up a handful, which turned to powder. He slapped his hands together, then washed them at the faucet.

Would have been good to grab a Granny Smith before the fire killed them all off.

He grabbed two ice cold beers and Greg's bag of pot, then clumped to the bench down by the pond and got to work rolling a joint and drinking some brew.

He took several hits, holding his breath as long as he could, and chased away the coughing with hefty slugs of Heinie.

Thirty feet away, he noted the little manzanita bush—fire hadn't reached this point anyway—that marked where his emergency stash was located. He thought about digging it up, but then remembered his single-shot 30-30—or what was left of it—was in the tool shed he hadn't looked over yet, so the extra cartridges in his stash were about as useful as a two legged stool.

Probably fortunate, that. No temptation to do something really stupid at least.

The wind picked up and funneled down the west side of the pond, rippling the green water, which still looked halfway clean. He finished off the doob and let the rippling, baby waves ease his soul. What he was going to do next, he had no idea, so he just rolled another joint and opened a second can of beer and got to work, trying to recapture some of the dream.

The sun passed behind a cloud and the temperature fell. His chin drooped to his chest and his eyes closed while he let the lapping water and gentle breeze lull him to sleep.

———————

He felt something wet brush his face and opened his eyes as Pankie's tongue woke him up. He'd fallen sideways on the bench, but the sun still hid behind the clouds. He gently pushed the dog away and wiped his face with a handkerchief. His watch said 3pm, so he'd been out for about two hours. His head hurt, too, as it usually did when he mixed beer and pot.

"You hungry girl? How about some grub?" he asked, while staggering slightly to his feet. Her tail wagged and she jumped up onto his leg, nearly pushing him into the water. He reached down and petted her between the ears, which he knew she loved. She jumped, barking in excitement.

"Okay, then," he said. "Let's go get us some food."

As they walked back up the trail to what had been their home, he noticed that the little tool shed halfway around the pond was still standing. So, maybe he still had some gardening tools to work with.

"Guess the fire didn't get everything, huh girl?"

After feeding Pankie with a can of wet food, he made himself a salad and ate some of the bulk trail mix he'd bought at Safeway. He thought about having another beer, but nixed that and settled for some water instead.

Then he faced the business of looking at what was left of his tool shed which had collapsed in on itself. He'd been proud of the tools he'd collected over the years, but what may have survived was anyone's guess. He put on the gloves and dragged the half burned T-111 siding away from the cement slab foundation and began to take stock.

The Honda generator was toast, as were all his power tools: Sawzall, Skill saw, nail gun, impact wrench and 1-inch drill driver. Some of the hand tools in the fried tool box might be salvageable and maybe some of the nails and deck screws which were now piled up, since their boxes had burned. Hopefully, the fire's heat hadn't weakened the steel.

Wait and see on that…

What was left of the 30-30 single shot rifle looked like another steel pretzel, the wood stock gone completely, except for a few bits still screwed to the receiver. Knowing, for sure, that it was useless eased his gut.

Yeah. Definitely for the best…

He unlocked the tool box on the back of his truck, something he'd not done since before the fire. He smiled at the tool belt with his favorite hammer, tape measure and pry bar, plus his second best cord-less drill and circular saw.

Pankie sauntered by, tail still wagging after a good meal.

"Not all doom and gloom, girl," he said, trying and only half failing to look at the bright side.

In the distance, he heard what sounded like a truck and some other vehicle. The engine sounds grew louder, obviously headed down to Sage Hill. He stood and waited as Greg's Dodge Ram 4x4 turned the corner, his partner Luce riding shotgun. The truck hauled a small beat up travel trailer.

Wasn't that in Joe's Recycle Yard when I passed?

Behind Greg and Luce, Hazel's FJ Cruiser brought up the rear with Arnica, his daughter, sitting by Hazel's side. There was something in the back of the FJ, but he couldn't tell what. Pankie ran around both parked vehicles and gave everyone her happy bark.

Arnie stayed where he was, not really wanting any company this first day back, but he tried to keep his face friendly-looking or, at least, not PO-ed. One of the reasons he and Hazel broke up was because he found it hard to share feelings, or so she said, and, truth be told, she was right a lot of the time. But, still, they got along and, in many ways, they got along better now than they ever had before.

"Hey, Arn," Greg said as he stepped down from his truck. "Joe'd heard of your sitrep, man, and said you could use this trailer for as long as you need—or buy it cheap if that's what you want."

"Joe said that?" Arnie asked, not quite believing it. They'd butted heads many times over the prices Joe charged for his recycled lumber. Joe didn't like pot smokers and Democrats, and Arnie was guilty on both counts. And, whether he wanted to owe Joe any favors was something else to consider. Chump was always looking for an angle.

"Yeah," Luce said. "I heard him say it so there's proof! Mwahahaha!"

Everyone laughed at Luce's evil overlord cackle, but Arnie could only force a smile which, thankfully, the others seemed not to notice—or at least pretended so.

"You didn't hold a gun to his head, did you, Luce?" Arnie asked, trying to recoup the mood with his phony straight face.

"Naw," She took out her hunting knife, something she always carried to prune fruit trees. "I just used this."

During this exchange, Hazel and Arnica had gotten out of the FJ.

"Here you go, Dad," Arnica said, handing him an envelope which he could tell held marijuana seeds. "For your next crop."

He opened the envelope and took a whiff.

A-1 prime.

"These are the Panama Reds you've been hoarding."

Arnica shrugged and copied Arnie's phony straight face.

"Well, I kept *some* back. And look what Ma brought."

Hazel walked over and gave both Arnie and her daughter a hug, then she took Arnie's hand and led him to the back of the FJ.

"Open it up," Hazel said.

The polarized glass made it hard to see what was there until Arnie popped the hatch.

Inside were two fruit trees. One apple and one apricot.

He turned away to hide the tears, which he hurriedly wiped away. Probably they thought he was grateful, and he was, some, but mostly he was still stuck down low, trying to not just give up and move on.

"If we had a spade, we could plant them now," Hazel prompted. "Is the little gardening shed down by the pond still there?"

"It's still there," he said. "I'll go get a shovel."

"You and Hazel both go," Greg said. "We'll get the trailer unhitched."

Halfway to the shed, Hazel pulled him to a stop.

"How are you *really* feeling AJ?" she asked. "That stone face of yours can't fool me, you know."

Only Hazel called him AJ. And he felt the old, unvoiced accusation. The reason they split up.

"I guess I feel as good as expected after losing what's been lost," he said. "I really appreciate the two fruit trees, though."

The wind blew Hazel's hair into her face and Arnie brushed it back, letting his hand caress her forehead.

"Those two trees need a home, so I guess I'll stick around to see that they get one. I'm sorry, lady," he said, using an endearment he'd not used in a long time, "but that's the best I can do for now."

He wanted to say more, but it wouldn't come out—at least not yet. Maybe the next time they met it would.

"That's a good answer," she said and caressed his face in turn. "Let's get the fruit trees planted while there's still light."

ABOUT THE AUTHOR

David Stier is a US Army veteran who served in Germany during the Cold War. Some of Dave's short stories have appeared in, Fiction River #18 (*Visions of the Apocalypse*) Fiction River #24 (*Pulse Pounders Adrenaline*) Fiction River #25 (*Feel the Fear*) Fiction River #30 (*Hard Choices*), Fiction River #31 (*Feel the Love*), Fiction River Special Edition #3 (*Spies*) Pulp House Issue #4, Fiction River #33 (*Doorways to Enchantment*), *Stars in the Darkness* and *The Golden Door*, and *Obsessions* by Stark Publishing. Dave was a runner up in the University of North Georgia's 2019 Military Science Fiction Symposium for "Prisoners of War." His self-published short story collection, *Final Solutions, Stories of the Holocaust* is available on Amazon and Kobo.

THE KNIGHT ERRANT

IAN NELIGH

Phillip spotted the young woman as he hurried along the street to his shoe repair shop. She was in her early twenties, wore an old leather jacket with pieces of home-made armor attached to it, and gleefully panhandled the morning commuters who moved past her on the sidewalk. Her dirty blond hair was tucked under something that looked like a chain mail hood. He pulled his gaze away, and pressed his phone to his ear to better hear the person on the other end.

"Phil, listen. It's too little too late," came the voice of his father's attorney. "Your dad would understand."

The statement made him feel sick. Phillip shook his head, determined not to lose this fight.

"Look, it's not about my—" He took a deep breath, considering his words, as he passed two women who had stopped to admire a store's window display. "Things were slow, and yeah, the pandemic sure as hell didn't help. But life is getting back on track now. And that means customers."

"Phil," the attorney said, his voice kind and patient. "It was good of you to step in and take over the business when your old man got sick. You've got a big heart. But you're still young, and now it's time to move on and close the business. It's what he'd want. Don't lose sight of what's important."

Phillip skidded to a stop on the sidewalk. *What's important?* The shop had meant everything to his father. He couldn't just let it close now. It was as much a part of his life as his father had been. He'd grown up there, done his homework in the backroom, and took over running the place when his father was in the hospital—and later, in hospice.

He took a deep breath and worked to stay calm. He opened his mouth to reply, then paused as the young woman in the armor approached him, a smile on her face. She wore a medieval-inspired cuirass, shoulder pauldrons, and even vambraces on her forearms made from what might have been soda cans. Phillip made the mistake of making eye contact, and she moved closer. Looking away, he held out his hand to keep her back, and kept walking.

"I've got nothing else," Phillip said into the phone, and meant it. Every word.

"Well, maybe you need to start looking for a job," the attorney said, now sounding distracted. "Hey, I need to go. We'll talk later, yeah?"

Phillip stared at the blank screen on his phone for a moment, then put it away and walked up to his shop. "Percival's Shoe and Boot Repair" was written in an elegant copper script on the window, and repeated on the tasteful wooden sign above the door. It was a quaint shop on a street known for its unique boutique shops and cafes—many still closed in the wake of the pandemic.

With an old key, worn so smooth it was almost unusable, Phillip unlocked the door and entered the shop. The door automatically chimed as he flicked on the lights, and he headed behind the counter. The place smelled of leather and shoe polish—scents he'd attributed to his father even as a child. Phillip wasn't going to let the store go. He couldn't. The business just needed a few good clients, something to prove it could climb out of the red. There was no need to let the business his father had run his entire life close after one bad year. It was still possible to make a profit. Everyone was saying the economy would improve, the store would just require his total commitment. He could do that.

Phillip pulled out the ledger and began to go through it. The early pages were in his father's neat handwriting. His own messy, uncoordinated penmanship was a disgrace by comparison. Just then the front doorbell chimed, and he looked up, his automatic smile tacked in place. Phillip's enthusiasm for the first customer of the day drained away as he recognized the odd panhandler he'd passed by earlier.

"Huzzah! Greetings shopkeep!" she said. As she walked through the entrance, the gray sky reflected in the metal attached to her jacket turned the deep brown of the store.

"I, um…" Phillip said, then stopped, unsure how to continue.

The young woman had the look of the road: well-worn clothing, faded jeans, and an almost imperceptible layer of dust clung to her. And then there was her bizarre jacket. It looked like she'd just come from the world's shoddiest renaissance festival.

In the last year he had learned to spot a paying customer a mile away, and it was clear she was homeless or transient. The best policy to get rid of people like her was as soon as possible. They scared away the ones with the money.

"What doth thou hither?" she asked.

"I—what?" he heard himself ask, confused by her oddly phrased question. The two women from earlier peered in the window of his shop, surveying the panhandler.

"What doth thou sell, my good man?"

Phillip looked back, meeting her bright blue eyes. He felt a sudden sinking sensation in his stomach as she came closer. He glanced over her shoulder and saw the two ladies laugh, then walk away. A single rain drop hit the display window, then another. He couldn't start the day like this. Phillip needed real customers. He had to prove that his father's business could still make a profit and the shop wouldn't just disappear with him.

He wasn't sure how, but he would have to get her to leave. He pulled his eyes away from the bits and pieces of assorted metal sewn onto her jacket and met her blue eyes.

"We—I repair shoes."

The woman shrieked in excitement, startling Phillip. Her smile broadened to a grin, and the hodgepodge of armor jangled as she hurried over to the counter.

He flinched as she reached him.

"A cobbler? Mine eyes doth taketh interest in thy wares. There are those whom call me Sir Gwen. Well met!"

"Okay," he said, doing his best to stay calm. Think of a way to get her to leave. "I'm sorry, but…"

"No need to apologize, I am but a humble knight errant and am certain you'll do fine, master cobbler," she said.

Sir Gwen bent over and reached below the counter. Phillip watched in horror as she pulled off one of her leather boots with a tremendous yank, then slammed it down with enthusiasm in front of him.

"Thou art what I seek. I am in needeth of thine own valued

s'rvices," she said. "For I am on a quest these many long years, and have boots in need of respite."

The leather on the boot was worn paper thin. It was patched, sewn, and glued, and resembled something more akin to the face of a movie monster than the high-end leather shoes he was accustomed to. On top of that, the sole of her boot was coming free, and hung down like the tongue of an enthusiastic dog.

"I haven't the coin, honorable tradesman but I swear thou shall be recompensed forthwith," she said. She leaned in, and added conspiratorially, "For I seek treasure from a goblin king."

Phillip eyed the worn boot, then looked up at the woman and her wide grin. She winked at him. It was time to take action before things got further out of hand.

"Look, I don't know what this is, or really what's even happening here," he said.

"These loyal companions have carried me to many a strange and terrible land," she said by way of explanation. "This one is in need of your craft."

Phillip nodded, his shopkeeper's reflex in place—then he shook his head.

"I'm sorry, but you need to leave. Now." He walked around the counter and escorted the woman to the front door.

"A cobbler is the key to a successful quest. Why, it certainly can't be accomplished barefooted," she protested. "And if 't be true, I'm not mistaken thee has't also the look of a squire about you. Join on my mission, and I'll make you a knight."

"Thanks. But actually, you know, I don't really have time for this— or you," he said. Phillip opened the door and gently pushed the strange girl back outside. Raindrops plinked off her armor as she stood there. She then turned back to him, her eyes tearing up.

"Wait. Please," she said.

She looked desperate—but desperate wasn't going to pay to keep his father's business open. It had begun to rain in earnest, and the streets were emptying. The day was going from bad to worse. Phillip clenched his jaw.

"Goodbye," he said. Phillip closed and locked the door, then busied himself with a display of shoe polish, waiting to make sure she left. And after a moment she did, slinking off back down the street in the rain. Exhaling with relief, he turned to go back to his ledger and the dismal numbers that awaited him, then froze.

Sir Gwen's boot still sat on the counter.

Phillip stared at the forgotten footwear. The boot, or perhaps its unusual owner, reminded him of a time when he didn't feel bitter and angry. A time when rage at the unfairness of the world wasn't threatening to drown him from within. Before his father's death, and before the pandemic took its toll, Phillip wouldn't have even considered pushing someone out of his store because they were a tad eccentric. He had focused on keeping his father's business afloat in part to keep from having to be alone with his own thoughts. And now that he was, he realized he was full of anger, frustration, and sadness.

He grabbed a tube of quick-drying sole glue and fixed the boot, then hurried through the rain to his car. He didn't have to give up on the business, no matter what the attorney thought—but he also didn't have to become a jerk in the process.

With the lone boot sitting on his passenger seat, Phillip drove through the rain, hunting for the young woman who called herself Sir Gwen. He passed a long line of the city's homeless waiting outside the soup kitchen and scanned the crowd, but didn't see the young woman's odd, metal-adorned leather jacket. He continued on, driving through unfamiliar streets near the kitchen. Trash collected along crumbling city curbs, and grocery carts filled with weather-worn possessions lined the sidewalk. A man with an unkempt beard stepped out in front of him, causing Phillip to come to a quick stop. The man flipped him off and kept walking. Having grown up in the suburbs, Phillip was vaguely aware of his sheltered existence, and wasn't comfortable in this part of town. *Come on. Where are you?*

He drove up to the light, turned the corner, and spotted Gwen rummaging through a trash bin. He slammed on his brakes, his seatbelt growing taut and cutting across his chest. The horn of the car behind him beeped. Phillip ignored it, and rolled down his window.

"Hey," he said. "Hey!"

Sir Gwen stopped digging and looked up at him. She stood on the wet ground wearing only one boot. Her other foot sported a wet, and now somewhat dirty, unicorn sock.

She grinned as she recognized him, and skipped over to his car.

"Greetings, master cobbler!"

"I'm really sorry about before," he said, feeling his face go red. The poor woman had been wandering around in the rain with only one boot, all because of him. He had never intended to become a horrible person. He handed her the boot he'd mended. "I didn't...I mean I'm... You left this."

Her eyes grew wide as she took it from him.. "Thee fixed it! What cunning workmanship."

"Well, yeah. It didn't take much, really..."

It really hadn't, but while the boot would never be as good as new, it was at least serviceable now.

"Within this wall of flesh, there is a soul that counts thee its creditor," she said. Although he couldn't place it, the line sounded familiar somehow. Maybe it was from a play.

Gwen bent down to pull on the repaired boot. As she did, her pant leg pulled up and Phillip noticed an ugly scar on her calf. What could have happened to cause that? He bit his lip, pulled his eyes away, and looked at the trash bin she was digging in moments before. Then another idea came to him.

"Say, Gwen, can I—I don't know. Can I maybe buy you a sandwich?"

Phillip sat in a booth across from Gwen at the greasy spoon he used to go to with his father. The smell of burnt bacon, and the laminated menus, brought back memories of his childhood. He stared down at the well-worn Formica table. He had come here a million times, but hadn't been back since his father first fell ill. It was irritating that the restaurant hadn't changed even one iota when so much of his own life now felt unrecognizable. With the exception of an unchecked kitchen fire, this place would likely never change. It would keep serving up runny eggs, burnt bacon, and black coffee for generations to come.

Phillip glanced at Gwen. She appeared to be only a couple years younger than him. A smattering of freckles dotted her dirty face. He watched as she attacked her second cheeseburger. After she finished, she mopped her face with a napkin, then made little round flourishes with one hand while gesturing at him with the other.

"Thank ye, good sir. For sooth your kindness is unmatched."

She tossed her napkin over her shoulder, and into the lap of the lady sitting behind her.

"You're welcome," Phillip said, trying to avoid eye contact with the angry woman in the next booth. "Afterwards, maybe I can drop you off somewhere? Is there, um, a shelter or something you're staying at?"

Gwen finished her drink, then put it down loudly on the table, trying to attract the waitress' attention.

"There is only the quest," she said, her eyes almost glowing with whatever inner fire drove her.

"The quest?"

"Indeed," she said. "I must best a witch, then save a maiden from a troll."

"A troll?"

"His name is Timothy Long Fingers," she said. "He liveth in an enchanted castle."

Growing impatient with her still empty glass, she looked around and spotted a harried waitress making her way to the kitchen.

"Wench, fill my goblet!" Gwen shouted.

Phillip tried to cover his face with one hand in embarrassment as the other patrons looked over at them. With a hard look, the waitress picked up a pitcher of soda and carried it across the crowded diner to their table. Gwen, oblivious to the older woman's skewering gaze, focused on her empty glass. Once filled, Gwen gave a content sigh, picked up the condensation-beaded mug with two hands, and drank deeply. Phillip tried to smile apologetically at the waitress. She gave him a scowl that would have curdled milk, and walked off.

"So, is there someplace else I can drop you off at?" he asked Gwen. "Other than a castle with a troll?"

"Ignorance of the Fae will avail thee not one whit," she said. "How do ye ever hope to become a knight?"

"I don't. And I'm only ignorant because they don't exist," he said. While his words sounded cold to his own ears, Phillip had begun to warm up to Gwen. In spite of her oddness, there was something he admired about her enthusiasm for her make-believe world.

"Timothy Long Fingers is real," she said. She leaned toward him across the table, her voice dropping to a whisper. "Dangerous, old, and clever. And other things fairy do creep whither the light doth not reach."

"Right. I guess—I guess I could just drop you off around here someplace..." He tried to remember if there was a shelter on Broadway.

"There's a manor," she said. "I knoweth its location well mine, valorous sir. I wilt giveth thee directions at which hour we receiveth to thy blasphemous carriage. Huzzah—let us off!"

Gwen punctuated the sentiment by pounding their table, which drew further looks from the other diners.

"You—do you mean my car?" he asked.

———

Phillip drove Gwen to the outskirts of the city. The last rays of the rain cloud-muted sun were unable to penetrate the surrounding forest. He wondered, and not for the first time, if he'd made a mistake agreeing to drive her.

He half expected to arrive at a trailer park populated by the surviving members of the Manson Family. The thought made his skin crawl; he didn't even know this woman.

Why had he agreed to this? Buying her lunch was one thing, but driving thirty minutes out of the city was something else. He wondered what his father would have done in a similar situation, and couldn't come to a conclusion.

P hillip knew sooner or later he would have to stop thinking about what his father would or wouldn't have done. He was gone now, and his decisions, for better or worse, would only affect himself—including what he decided to do with the shoe repair business.

With this line of thought making him feel even more uncomfortable, Phillip turned his attention to Gwen.

"…Those on a quest can come to ruin ere it starts without a cobbler to bless it," Gwen said. She pulled one of the knots keeping a piece of armor fastened to her jacket tight with her teeth.

"You mean—to fix their shoes?" he asked.

"Exactly so," she said.

"Wonderful," he said. He hoped this "manor" wasn't just a bonfire with a bunch of people with fingerless gloves sitting around it. If so, it would be nice if she'd let him know in advance.

"So, is this a house?" he asked, trying not to let his concern reflect in his voice.

"Nay, 'tis a glorious keep," Gwen said, her eyes set firmly on the road. "Tis just around the track's bend," she said.

The car then came in view of a mansion off to one side. It was massive, its warm yellow lights filling the night like a wayward cruise ship.

"Holy hell…is that it?" he asked. He'd rarely seen such a large house, and was now almost certain this was another part of Gwen's colorful delusion. He almost preferred the idea of the bonfire to being chased and torn apart by guard dogs.

"Thither resides Manor Du Lac—also home to a foul witch, a scampering, pus-filled she-creature of the dark abyss," Gwen said.

"Huh," Phillip said, turning his car down the long driveway. But before he could come to a complete stop, Gwen flung open her door and leapt out. Cursing, he stopped the car and hurried after her as she marched up to the house through the drizzle. The building's cross gables, rounded doors, ivy-covered walls, and pitched roof resembled a massive English cottage.

"Are you sure we're supposed to be here?" he asked, as they tromped through a flower bed and across a manicured lawn. "They might call the police on us if we're trespassing. Are we trespassing?"

"Thee whimper like a thunder-frightened maid. Onward!" Gwen shouted, increasing her speed. Phillip jogged after her.

As they reached the door it opened, revealing a woman who looked cold as rough-forged iron. She stood in the doorway and examined the two of them. Gwen and Phillip came to a stop.

"Gwen, you've come home. Thank goodness," she said.

"I scorn you, you plague-faced toad. Ugly, venomous monster. Standeth aside," Gwen said, then whispered to Phillip with a cheery smile, "My stepmother, Vivian."

Before he could respond, Gwen marched forward. Vivian stepped aside as Gwen entered the house, leaving him standing on the front stoop.

"Uhm. I'm not sure if—" he began.

"It's fine," she said, cutting him off. "You are to be commended for bringing Gwen home. Please come in out of the rain."

He followed her inside and closed the door behind them. When he turned around, Vivian was gone. The interior of the room he stood in was filled with bookshelves, stone walls, and coarsely-cut wooden beams running along the ceiling. Thick, expensive-looking throw rugs were scattered about the floor, and a collection of comfortable armchairs stood on one side of the room. It was cozy, warm, and felt oddly to Phillip like a gingerbread house made real. There was also something vaguely sweet in the air, almost like baking cookies.

Not sure what to do with himself, Phillip walked around the bottom floor of the house, hoping to find someone. He wanted to leave, but it didn't feel right to do so without telling somebody.

In his search, he came across a gigantic room with large, overstuffed leather couches and chairs, swords and axes mounted on walls, and a grand stone fireplace. The mantle held photos of Gwen as a child. In many of the pictures she was dancing ballet, or posed with an older, bearded man.

"Her father, my second husband," Vivian said from behind him. "He died five years ago."

Phillip turned and looked at her. She was a handsome woman in her late 40s, with black hair shot through with gray streaks, tied back into an uncompromising bun. She wore a black blouse which had something like faint white concentric decorations on it, reminding Phillip of the fancy doilies he sometimes saw on the tables of expensive restaurants. He found the designs unnerving. Her clothing looked expensive, and helped to highlight the thick silver jewelry she wore.

"Oh, I'm sorry," Phillip finally said, trying not to stare. She was just old enough that she could have been Gwen's biological mother, but as far as he could tell she had nothing close to anything resembling maternal empathy. He turned back around to face the photos. "If you don't mind me asking—how did it happen?"

"In a car accident," she said. "He and Gwen were returning from a performance of Richard the III. Going out to see the plays of Shakespeare was one of their little annual rituals."

Not a drop of emotion lived in her words. They were a desert, devoid of life. Vivian's eyes remained locked on his. After a moment he realized with an odd feeling that she didn't seem to blink.

"Was Gwen hurt?" he asked, looking to do or say anything to get those eyes off him.

"She was in the ICU for weeks," she said, and finally looked away. It felt to Phillip like a staged reaction. Apparently Gwen and her father weren't the only ones who liked theater. "Losing both her father and her dreams to be a dancer broke her, I suppose."

She turned back to face Phillip. "Though you've probably noticed that bit, haven't you? She needs treatment on a permanent basis. Now that she's back, I'm making arrangements."

He found the statement upsetting, which surprised him. What did he care? He didn't know the answer to that, but found he most definitely cared.

"She's harmless," he said, meaning it. Gwen was odd, make no mistake, but committing her seemed extreme.

"Harmless? And for years she's been homeless too. It's embarrassing. There's something wrong with her."

Phillip looked back at the photos on the mantel. His eyes stopped on a photo of a young Gwen and her father attending the local renaissance festival. Angry for a reason he could not explain, he clenched his fists as he turned back to the woman.

"She's not crazy," he said. "She's grieving."

Vivian opened her mouth to speak, then snapped it closed when Gwen came into the room. She had an oversized-metal helmet under one arm, and carried a backpack with odds and ends sticking out of it.

"Oh, Gwen dear, why don't you sit down and have some tea?" Vivian said in a soothing voice, the kind one used to try and coax a child from a temper tantrum. "You must be tired? Maybe a nice hot bath is in order?"

Gwen blinked, contemplating these new choices.

"It hast been a long and tiresome journey," she admitted.

Phillip hesitated, then stepped between them. He now understood the importance of Gwen's quest. She was the princess in danger, and had become her own knight errant. She was out to save herself.

"There's no time for resting," he said. Gwen looked at him, her clear blue eyes wide. "We're on a quest, after all. A troll, a castle. What are you waiting for? Lead on, sir knight."

Then her face lit up, and she nodded, "Aye. Forsooth," she said, standing taller. She ran her hands through her blonde hair, tightening her ponytail, pulled up the chainmail hood, and placed the helmet on her head. "Let us be off, squire."

Re-energized, Gwen spun around and marched toward a back door. Almost as an afterthought, she climbed an expensive-looking leather chair and pulled a decorative sword and sheath off one wall. The chair toppled over as she jumped back to the ground. Phillip watched her go, then moved to follow.

"You're making a mistake," Vivian said as Phillip stepped forward. He stopped and looked at her. She reminded him now of something like a parasite, living on bones and memories. He had a momentary thought that she was hollow on the inside, but of course that was crazy.

"Somehow I don't think so," he said, not honestly knowing if that was true or not. But he did understand Gwen and her journey now. It wasn't about disillusion, or about clinging to someone's memory. It was about taking that memory with you into the future to become something new.

Using his phone's light, Phillip followed Gwen through the woods. She hiked ahead as he struggled in the dark to keep up. He didn't know how long this game would go on for, but anything was better than standing by while Gwen's creepy stepmother locked her up. All the same, he was tired, and it was getting late.

"I didn't realize Timothy Long Fingers lived behind your house," he said.

"The enchanted castle the troll liveth in is at a new location ev'ry night," she said. "It always moves. But I knoweth a crow who shall lead us the way."

A crow? There was an uncomfortable sinking sensation in his stomach. This had been a mistake after all. What the hell had he been thinking? It didn't feel right to punish Gwen for her fantasy world, but maybe she really was mentally ill, and here he was encouraging her to run off in the dark to play some kind of game. Phillip shivered under his jacket, as he followed her into the night.

"Oh," he said then, unable to help himself, asked, "How do you see the crow in the dark?"

"Tis got a pixie with a lant'rn riding its back," she said. "Can ye not see it?"

"No, of course not," he said.

Gwen stopped and looked back at him. He moved his phone's light away, so it wouldn't blind her. In the sudden shadows that spread across her face he could see she looked concerned.

"Can thee also not seeth the elves yond walketh with us, protecting our way from the dryad spirits who suff'r no humans to ent'r their f'rest?" she asked.

Phillip looked around, seeing only the dark wood.

"No Gwen. I'm sorry. I see only a forest."

"What about the brave gnomes, with the charm candles on their tall hats to gallow hence the darkness?"

"Sounds lovely, but no. Not that either."

"I'm s'rry ye cannot see it. This is a quaint land we journey through," she said. She turned back around and continued forward.

"Did thee bringeth a sword?" she asked over her shoulder.

"No. You're the one with the sword. Is that going to be a problem, you know, that I don't have one too?"

"Not at all—ev'rything shall beest fine," she said, then added: "Unless, of course, we meeteth something yond requires m're than riddles to defeat."

Then an idea struck her, and Gwen looked over her shoulder at him, excitement on her face. "Or ye couldst mendeth its shoes!"

She continued on. Phillip took a deep breath, then hurried to catch up.

"Were you close to your father?" he asked.

"Aye. A brave king and gentle knight. And yours?"

"Also brave—in his way," Phillip said.

"Hast that gent gone from this w'rld?" she asked.

"Hm? Oh yes. Last month."

"I'm s'rry," she said.

"Me too."

She walked on a little longer in silence then said, "Liketh all true fath'rs, I'm sure that he did want thee to best be brave in his absence."

Phillip walked behind her, thinking, then nodded.

"Yeah, I think you might be right," he said.

"Mine own fath'r once toldeth me tis bett'r to visage what cometh next than what hast already did occur. Doth thee believeth yond?"

It took him a moment to translate what she was saying, but as he did, he smiled.

"Sounds like something my dad might have said—more or less."

"Me doth think he was wise."

"Yeah, me too," he said.

"Then art thee eft to turn the page?"

"I'm not sure exactly what that means, but I think so," he said.

But he did understand what she was saying. In a funny way it felt like it made him whole, like a puzzle with a missing part finally returned. An unbearable weight slid off his shoulders. Since he'd taken over his father's business during the year-long illness the weight had only grown. He didn't know that it had been crushing him until now. He was ready for what was next. It was time to let the store close. That was his father's chapter. It was time to start his own.

"Steady now," she said, interrupting his thoughts. "We approach the troll's castle. Are thee ready?"

Gwen stood at the top of a slight hill, pointing into the darkness. As he reached her side, Phillip's jaw dropped open.

A castle sat on the horizon, its giant towers bathed in the silver light of a full moon.

Phillip blinked.

It was still there.

But that wasn't all. Pixies soared past their heads on the backs of crows. Gnomes with magical candles on their hats looked up at him from the ground. An elf with coal-black eyes peered at them from behind a tree, blinked, then went back to scanning the forest for dryads.

He could see it. All of it. And it was beautiful.

The world around them was full of magic.

"I am. I am ready," he said, and smiled. "Lead on, Sir Gwen!"

ABOUT THE AUTHOR

Ian Neligh is an award-winning journalist, author and screenplay writer. He has written two nonfiction books about the wilder aspects of the West and his fiction can be found in several anthologies including *Consumed: Tales Inspired by the Wendigo*. As a journalist, Neligh has flown airplanes, ridden horses and dog sleds, run with burros, dressed up as a mascot, reenacted Civil War battles, investigated corruption and hunted for lost treasure—but generally not all at the same time. Neligh helped create the Denver Post's first podcast program and was featured on NPR's "All Things Considered" for his work.

THE WORLD IS ENDING AND MY DRYER IS BROKEN

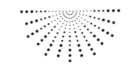

MEGAN E. FREEMAN

I hang the laundry
on the line in the garage

comfortable task
during a global pandemic
(dirty) washed (wet)
dried (clean)

when finally, stiff
and crispy
there are wrinkles
lint
creases where fabric
was pinioned to cord

(even in a national emergency
I do not iron)

I don't want
the repairman to come

I take solace in the cycle
of beginning middle end

each piece pinned into place
each taking as long as it takes

finally, a folded tower
of terry-cloth towels

I like finding clothespins
in my pockets

the wooden texture
between my lips

heaving wet heaviness
up and over the horizon

ABOUT THE AUTHOR

Megan E. Freeman writes middle-grade and young adult fiction as well as poetry for adults. Her novel-in-verse, *Alone*, is available from Simon & Schuster/Aladdin. Megan is also a Pushcart-nominated poet, and her poetry chapbook, *Lessons on Sleeping Alone*, was published by Liquid Light Press. An award-winning teacher, Megan has decades of experience teaching in the arts and humanities and is nationally recognized for presenting workshops and speaking to audiences across the country. She used to live in northeast Los Angeles, central Ohio, northern Norway, and on Caribbean cruise ships. Now she lives in northern Colorado.

LOVE IN THE TIME OF SCURVY

JERE ELLISON

After Date 1

"Clementine?"

Darcy Monroe looked up from where she sat at one of the campus bus stops.

A young man, about her age, stood there in slippers, sweatpants, and an oversized shirt holding out a tiny orange. He must have been tweaking hard to be dressed like that.

"Excuse me?" she asked. Her hand moved toward her purse.

"Clementine?"

He moved a step closer.

"Hold it!" She pulled out her mace and leapt to her feet.

"Whoa!" The orange fell to the ground, and his hands jumped for the stars. "Psycho much!?"

The streetlamp above the bus stop cast both of them in a circle of trying-to-be-yellow light.

"I don't know," Darcy said, keeping her hands steady. "*Are* you? *Are* you a psycho?"

"I don't think so." He chanced a shrug. "Just a guy with an orange."

Darcy narrowed her eyes. "Who offers people an orange at two-thirty in the morning?"

"Who pulls mace on a guy offering fruit?"

Darcy checked herself. It'd been a stressful night. "Sorry. It was an overreaction, I guess."

"You *guess*? If this is what I get for offering a clementine, I'm glad I left my grapefruit in my room."

The guy seemed nice enough. If a little weird.

"Can I...?" He pointed to the clementine.

"Oh, go ahead." She plopped back down on the bench and stuffed the mace away.

Keeping an eye on her, he picked up the orange, peeled it, and sat down on the farthest edge of the bench away from her. "Did I really seem that threatening?" He smiled a bit.

"Are you gloating over almost getting maced?"

"I just never considered myself that...intimidating." He said the last word in a low, gravelly voice.

Darcy rolled her eyes. "If you're intimidating, it's in a Norman Bates way. And that's no compliment."

He shrugged. "Anything can be a compliment, depending on who it's coming from."

She cocked an eyebrow. "Are you hitting on me?"

"No." He shook his head and crammed half the orange into his mouth. "Just eating," he mumbled.

Bugs buzzed against the streetlamp, and sprinklers *chk-chk-chk*-ed across the grass between the university's buildings.

"Why you out so late?" he asked when he was done with his orange.

"Just got back from a date." She leaned back and crossed her arms.

"Based on the mace, I take it things didn't go well."

"No. And macing someone would have been cathartic."

"Sorry?" the guy tried.

Headlights turned down the block. Darcy got to her feet as the bus pulled up.

The guy started walking away toward the center of campus.

"You not getting on the bus?" she asked.

"Nah. I'm a walker." He shoved his hands into his pockets.

The bus doors opened with a hiss.

"Keep creeping around at night, and you'll get arrested." She couldn't help but furrow her brow.

He shrugged. "Keep rejecting citrus fruit and you'll get scurvy."

"You coming, miss?" the bus driver asked.

Darcy watched the guy amble off across campus. She rolled her eyes. "Yeah," she said with a sigh. "I'm coming."

Date 2

D arcy wasn't sure what to make of this date. Couple things were going in its favor.

First, *Le Coeur Confit* was one of the city's nicer restaurants.

Second, he'd been fairly polite. He opened doors, pulled out chairs, wasn't vulgar.

There was only one problem.

"And then, *pow!*" he slammed his fist on the table, rattling the china and nearly upsetting a wine glass. "That lion's mouth snapped closed so fast that...well, if my head had still been *in* there, I wouldn't be here with you right now." He let out a hearty laugh that filled the dining room.

The Mighty Ivan was a circus performer. Up-and-coming, that is. He stuck his head places.

"Anyways, that was when we were in Arizona." He scratched his left cheek. That's important because it was, maybe not-so-ironically, the side with the lion tattooed on it.

See, the Mighty Ivan had a tattoo on his face for every animal whose mouth he'd shoved his head into. There was the lion on his left cheek, a tiger on the right, an alligator, a crocodile, two bears (they were siblings), and a pelican.

Darcy was a graduate-fellow studying biomedical engineering. And, while she was fairly-grounded in all other aspects of life, she had one area in which she felt science went out the window to make room for fate: love.

That's why she had gone to a psychic. And that love forecaster had told her the man of her dreams would be a man with a facial tattoo.

That was good enough for Darcy.

One dating profile later, in which she said her only request was that the man have a facial tattoo, and here she was. With the Mighty Ivan. The next in a string of really, *really* bad dates.

"You, uh, like to stick your head places, huh?" Darcy attempted.

"Oh, sure," Ivan said. "If you knew the smells I've smelled..." Another hearty laugh filled the dining room.

The maître d' came up to the table. "I do hope the lady and the gentleman have enjoyed their meal?"

He was ready for them to leave. Darcy had seen that face during other dates, before.

"It was *fabulous*," Ivan said. He looked down at his empty plate. "I've put so many fish in my mouth over the years, I can't wait to put myself into one of *their* mouths."

Darcy shifted in her seat. Ivan was staring a little *too* longingly at that empty plate.

"No one else could do it," he continued. "Not as well as I could. I'm the best. The world's greatest." He looked up at Darcy and the maître d'. "Not a person on this planet can put their head into animals' mouths the way I can. And when I finally do it, when I finally put my head into the mouth of a fish… do you know what I'm going to do?"

Darcy chanced a look at the maître d'. They both shook their heads.

Slowly, deliberately, Ivan raised a lone finger to the center of his forehead. "This is where I will place the tattoo. It will be the mark of my greatest achievement. I will be the master of sticking my head into things' mouths. None will meet my worth or might."

To review: Ivan was polite; Ivan was well-traveled; Ivan certainly wouldn't be boring.

He was a *little* too full of himself, though. As far as Darcy was concerned, years of sticking his head into animals' mouths had only trained him for getting it better lodged up his own rectum.

After Date 2

"Can I offer you another clementine, or are you still riding the scurvy train?"

Darcy turned to see the guy from the night before, still wearing slippers and sweats.

"You're a freak, you know that?" She scowled at him, then turned and walked away.

She headed down the sidewalk, back to the graduate dorm on campus.

"Scurvy train it is, then." He loped up next to her and matched pace.

"Are you stalking me?" she asked. "My dad's a cop. He can have you arrested."

"First, that explains the bear mace."

"It wasn't bea—"

"Second," he continued, "if I were stalking you, I would have been waiting by the bus stop on the other side of campus. Us running into each other, again, like this? *That's* serendipity."

Darcy rolled her eyes.

"So what's your name?" He jogged a bit ahead and started walking backward so he could face her.

"I learned in kindergarten not to talk to strangers."

"Strangers are just friends you haven't met yet," he quipped.

"That, or unexposed, serial, campus murderers."

"Good point." He nodded. "So how many people have you murdered?"

"What are you even doing out this late?" She ignored his comment. "It's after midnight."

"I'm a sociology graduate. That means no money. So, I'm in a drug study."

"And they keep you up all night?"

"The clinicians? No. The drugs? Yeah." He popped an orange slice into his mouth. "Right now, I get about three hours of sleep a night."

Darcy stopped. "Wait, what? For how long? Are you joking?"

He looked concerned. "I hope not. The alternative would be that it's my own body that's been messed up this past week, and the voices in my head have been *adamant* it's the pills."

She shook her head and started walking again. "Har, har…"

"Come on, I'll tell you my name if you tell me yours." He practically begged, and Darcy hated how almost-endearing it made him.

"You go first," she said.

"Reg." He stopped and held out his hand.

She almost bumped into him. "Reg? Is that short for 'Reginald' or something?"

"Or something." He gave his outstretched hand a little welcoming shake.

She groaned inwardly—it wasn't kind to encourage him—but she reached out and took his hand. "Darcy."

"Darcy? Is that short for Dar-cember... or something?"

"Your jokes are about as good as your fashion sense." She walked past him.

"I dress this way so when I *do* fall asleep," he said backward-jogging past her, "I'm dressed for it. Plus, big pockets for clementines."

"How many have you *got* in there?"

He did a weird, backward shuffle to shake his hips and make the oranges bounce around. "Feels like three."

"Bench," Darcy said.

"What'd you call me?" He looked shocked and hurt.

"No, behind y—"

The side of the bench caught his knees, and he fell backward across it, splaying out flat on the seat.

"Reg! Are you alright?" She ran up next to him.

He stared into the sky, not saying a word. "Reg?" She didn't think he'd hit his head. "Are you narcoleptic, now?"

Nothing.

Could people really sleep with their eyes open? *Had* he hit his head? She waved a hand in front of his eyes. "Reg?"

"Clementine?" He grinned and pulled one out.

Darcy practically stomped her foot. "Freak. I'm going to my dorm."

"Good night, Darcy!" he sing-songed behind her. "See you around!"

She wanted to roll her eyes, but ended up biting back a smile, instead.

Date 3

"I'm a huge fan of Aquaman, see?" Jason pointed to the gills tattooed up under his jaw bone. "I'm convinced I can breathe water with enough practice." He picked up his water glass. "It's mostly oxygen, anyways."

"Really," Darcy started, "you don't have to—"

He tilted his head back, poured it in, and took a breath.

Sometime after the (luckily already-dining-in-that-restaurant) doctor got Jason breathing and on his feet, Darcy slipped out. She left a twenty on the table for the poor waiter.

Date 4

"Then I realized," Raul assured her, "if I want my brows to be on fleek *all* the time, I need to get them *tattooed* on, you know?"

Darcy did *not* know. She wondered how far the brows would sag by the time he was fifty.

"But *then* I realized, being 'on fleek' isn't about brows. It's a way of *life*. So I got a *third* credit card in my parents' names and updated my wardrobe!"

Date 5

"Beauty marks aren't just for women!" Christopher pointed to the tattooed speck on his cheek before he 'roid raged on a nearby trashcan. Luckily, the park was mostly empty at night.

Maybe that was lucky?

"I never said—" Darcy started.

"I know *you* didn't," he said as he flung the trashcan into a tree, scattered garbage everywhere, "but *somebody somewhere* has! And when they say things like that… it just kind of…"

That's when all six foot, two-hundred pounds of bodybuilder broke down crying.

After Date 5

"Is it weird that you're the most normal guy I've spent time with all week?" Darcy asked. "Clementines and all?"

It was around one in the morning, and she and Reg strolled around campus. Somehow, they'd bumped into each other again.

"Yeah, how *do* you end up on these dates? You look like you could get better guys, easy." He started peeling another clementine.

"You're hitting on me, again," she said.

He shook his head, dropping the orange peel into a passing trash-can. "Only trying to unravel the mystery that's Darcy."

She'd already decided not to tell him about the psychic. She didn't want the ridicule.

"Well, there's a specific quality I'm looking for, and—actually—hold up."

"What?"

She'd stopped him under a streetlamp on the sidewalk. "Let me see your face."

"Why?" He dragged the word out, looking scared.

"I'm *not* going to mace you," she deadpanned.

He took a step toward her and stretched his chin out.

Gently she reached up and took his face in her hand.

"Your 'specific quality' isn't skin to bind a book with, is it?" he asked.

She turned his head this way and that, ignoring him.

No tattoo.

She sighed inwardly. "Never mind," she said. "Just checking something."

At that point, a group of guys roared down the street past them in a truck, blowing billows of black-smoke out the tailpipe that swirled into the light of the streetlamp.

"Nice ass!" one guy yelled out, as the others catcalled.

"Kiss it then!" Reg replied, not missing a beat.

He spun around and dropped his pants, mooning the truck.

Darcy felt heat rush through her cheeks as she spun away, so as to not make it look like she was staring. But not before she noticed something.

"What was that?" she asked, turning back around.

"That," he said, looking proud of himself, "was chivalry. Some say it's dead. In truth, most guys just keep it in their pants."

"Well, keep it there," Darcy said. "But I meant on the side of your..." She kind of nodded toward his butt.

"Side of my... what?"

"You know."

"Know what?"

She put her hands on her hips. "The side of your ass cheek, if you're insistent on making me speak un-ladylike."

"Oh, that." He waved it off. "A stupid tattoo I got a couple years ago with some friends. Come on. Let's get back to the dorms. Lucky you, I'm on these pills. You get a night-time escort." He made his way down the sidewalk.

"Tattoo of what?" she called after him.

"A yellow smiley face." He shrugged. "Like I said. Stupid."

Darcy watched him walk away from her, her mind running in overdrive.

The psychic had said "facial tattoo," not "tattoo on a face." A smiley face is "facial," in that it has qualities of a face, right?

Was it a stretch? Sure. But he *was* the most normal guy she'd met all week, and in a few days he'd be done with his pill study, which means the insomnia would be gone. Normal sleep was good.

"Hey, Reg!" she called out after him. "Wait up!"

He turned and looked at her. "What's up?"

"You got any more clementines?" she asked with a smile. "I hear scurvy's *horrible* this time of year."

ABOUT THE AUTHOR

A life-long storyteller, Jere Ellison has always enjoyed entertaining people with words, though he didn't actually start writing those words down until he found a good English teacher in high school. Since then, he's written six full-length manuscripts and a bunch of short stories. While the genres and flavors of these tales range from child to adult, fantasy to sci-fi, and serious to silly, they each contain one similar nugget: hope. Ellison currently is a househusband for his wildlife biologist wife, and is a CASA volunteer working with foster-care children. He also enjoys "Dungeons and Dragons" and ginger ale.

AFTER

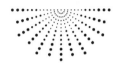

DEBBIE MAXWELL ALLEN

Journal entry: Monday ENG4, Ms. Juarez

S tupid.
       Stupid.
   Stupid.

There. I wrote something. Seven words down and ninety-three to go. What kind of English teacher makes you write for a whole week on the topic "After"? I mean, just last week we turned in eight freaking pages—eight!—on some dead guy who wrote stuff a hundred years ago.

You'll probably never read this, Ms. J. Thirty-five students times five journal entries tells me you don't have the time. Now that I think about it, you've probably got four or five other English classes where you're pulling the same stunt.

Guess what?

I'm done right now. (100 words exactly)

Journal entry: Tuesday ENG4, Ms. Juarez

O kay. Yesterday was practice. Don't worry—I'll address the topic today. My dad will kill me if I get a B.

So, the topic "After." After what? After class? That would be lunch. Haha.

After prom? Now there's a thought, not that I want to tell a teacher about it. Anyway, it's not like I'm even going—not that I couldn't get a date. Seriously, girls practically throw themselves at me in the hallway. It's kind of annoying.

They can flirt all they want. I've got other plans on prom night. Besides, I don't do relationships. Or relationships don't do me. (101 words)

Journal entry: Wednesday ENG4, Ms. Juarez

C ome on. Do we have to journal about "After" all week?
       Well, after I graduate—which dad will make freaking sure
of—I'm out of here.

I'll move out of this stupid town where everyone else knows way
too much about you and looks away when you walk by because they
remember. They glance away, but not before you see a certain expression, and it makes you wonder if they feel sorry for you or if you
repulse them.

And when I move, I won't have to see the look in Dad's eyes,
either. My friends say they can't measure up to their dads'
expectations.

Please.

Their dads will still love them even if they wreck the Escalade.

Me? I nixed the possibility of my dad's forgiveness over ten
years ago.

And though I won't visit, I'll call my little brother every week.
Phone calls are good because people don't feel like you're avoiding
them, even if you are.

Phone calls mean I won't see Caleb's hero worship when he looks
at me. Looks up to me. He shouldn't forgive me, either, but he doesn't
know it. Yet. He was way too little to remember.

Wow—I seriously went over a hundred words. I'm not even gonna
count, 'cause it smells like pizza in the cafeteria.

Journal entry: Thursday ENG4, Ms. Juarez

M an. I tried so hard to stay home today, mainly to avoid this
      lame assignment, but Dad didn't care. I swear, I could have a
ruptured appendix and he'd call the attendance office to make sure I
showed. Why do I need a lousy education anyway?

All my relatives dance around the truth. "Make something of yourself. Your mother would have wanted that for you."

How could they know what she wanted? She's not here to speak for herself. She's not here to cushion Dad's razor edges. She's not here to say, "I forgive you."

She's just. Not. Here.

I don't care what anyone says. The problem is they don't say much. And what they don't say echoes like sneakers squeaking on an empty gym floor.

It's all my fault.

Journal entry: Friday ENG4, Ms. Juarez

The last day for "After." I can't wait till Monday—is the next topic "Before"? Ha.

All right. "After" we left the house this morning, I walked Caleb to the middle school. He's usually a twelve-year-old chatterbox. Makes me wish I could afford a cell phone or something to tune him out, but I've got to remember I'm paying a penance—and the price goes up like gasoline with every year that passes without her.

Every year that drags by without her megawatt smile.

Every month without her silly made-up songs.

Every week with burned spaghetti instead of pasta a la Jen.

Ka-ching.

Ka-ching.

Ka-ching.

So, anyway, Caleb shuffles along the sidewalk, kicking stray pebbles, avoiding every crack like always because of the stupid rhyme, but—get this—totally silent. His mouth is pressed into a straight line, like he grabbed for the ChapStick and used superglue by mistake.

I bump him with my shoulder. "What's up, bro?"

He looks at me out of the corner of his eye, and then his glance skitters away.

And that's when my morning bagel hits the bottom of my stomach like a dropped barbell.

He knows.

My mind starts spinning like Caleb's stupid hamster on his stupid wheel. Going fast, but heading nowhere. Caleb is the last family member in my corner. If I lose him, what have I got?

I look at him, his head bent like he's totally obsessed with his scuffed-up Converse. He looks just like her, of course. He has no idea —no possible way of knowing—the knife in my gut every time he's flashed a grin at me for the last ten years.

Can I stack up his house of cards that's just been blown apart? I think I need some of that superglue.

I don't sling my arm around him. I don't ruffle his hair. I don't touch him at all. Just in case he shrinks away.

See, even here I'm being selfish. Protecting myself from how he'll look at me now that he knows. Now that he's figured out why no one talks about mom—especially when I'm around.

Silence. A black hole that's sucked every sound down, down deep somewhere. Someplace where the people you love go and never come back. Someplace where the people who loved you forget that they did, though they pretend they still do.

But then, there's a little squeak, like he's trying to keep from crying. His eyes stay glued to his toes, but his lips move. Just a little. "Danny showed me a newspaper article he found."

The words hit me in the gut, reminding me of the time in the gym when I looked away for a second and the weight bag swung into my middle. That bagel ricochets around like a BB in a metal box, looking for a quick way out.

I'm not sure I'm still standing, because my world has just tilted on its axis. I'm six again, and the walls of my universe have disappeared.

His eyes lock on mine, anchoring me, and I can't look away.

"So, what happened?" Caleb's words, so quiet and unnerving, sound like they come from the two-year-old he was back then. And they slice away at the scar tissue I've protected myself with for the last decade.

See, no one's ever asked me those three little words. They didn't dare, weren't sure, couldn't take the risk.

And if they had?

I would have looked away. Gone silent. But I can't take my eyes from Caleb's. He deserves an answer.

I've lain awake more than three thousand nights, planning my answer to this very question. You'd think with all that preparation, the words would slide off my tongue like butter melting across a hot ear of corn.

It was Dad's idea to practice—he's the big-time hunter. I was only six. I shouldn't have had my own .22. I wasn't paying attention to where it was pointing when I cocked it.

But, out of all the things I could say, all the excuses I could muster, all the blame I could lay, there's only one truth. And it comes to me now, for the first time. So I stop. Right on a crack. I face Caleb, rest my hands on his shoulders, lean in and peer into his clear blue eyes—Mom's eyes.

"It was an accident, Caleb. And I wish to God I could take it back."

He blinks—real slow—as he swallows my words, and it dawns on me that the words I just said for the first time in all these years are a sledgehammer, breaking apart my self-imposed prison. The prison whose bars are made of people's glances when they don't think I'm looking, whispers behind my back when they think I can't hear, and silence that suffocates the life out of me.

And no matter what Caleb thinks of me now, I just might be okay. I've taken myself off the giant hook I've been dangling from for more than half my life. It's like a flash flood washing away the giant boulders clogging a narrow canyon.

Then the miracle happens: Caleb's hands grip my arms and his eyes drill into mine. "You're right. It was an *accident*."

And though there's no whoosh, like when you break the vacuum seal on a jar of peanuts, all the sounds that were sucked into the black hole come singing back—the birds, the leaves rubbing together, the car horns honking.

And now I finally know what "after" means.

After forgiveness.

ABOUT THE AUTHOR

Debbie Maxwell Allen writes historical fiction—with a touch of the unexplainable. She explores quirky Mediterranean locations in the 18th century with moody tales of adventure and romance. She is a three-time finalist in the Pikes Peak Writers Zebulon contest. Watch for her debut series in 2021.

Debbie currently lives high in the Rockies, accompanied by her force-of-nature husband, her yin and yang cats, and plenty of visits from her children and the most adorable grandson. She travels as often as she can—preferably by train—and always with a hot cup of tea.

ABOUT THE PIKES PEAK WRITERS

Pikes Peak Writers is one of the best writers' organizations in the country. Its annual writers conference has routinely been ranked in the Top Ten of Best Conferences by Writers Digest Magazine.

The brainchild of Retired Air Force Colonel Jimmie Butler, PPW started as a conference in 1993 with just 175 story-loving writers who wanted a place to collaborate. Today, PPW is a thriving and all-volunteer 501(c)(3) nonprofit organization with more than 2,000 members.

PPW is dedicated to providing quality education for writers, year-round. Beyond the annual conference, PPW hosts free and low-cost events. From monthly writing workshops to Writers Night, there are many fun and educational opportunities for writers of all levels to find inspiration, education, and lifelong friends.

For more information on how to join, visit the PPW website at: pikespeakwriters.com

ABOUT THE EDITORS

Kathie "KJ" Scrimgeour is a graduate of the University of Colorado at Boulder. Her inspiration for blogging, flash fiction, short stories, and the long haul of novel writing comes from her many life experiences. When she's not writing you can find her somewhere in Colorado walking, hiking, or rock climbing at the local gym.

Find Kathie at kjscrim.com

Jenny Kate is the founder of Writer Nation, a podcast and Facebook group dedicated to helping writers market their work. With 19 years communications experience, she regularly writes on social media, internet marketing and face-to-face publicity.

Find Jenny at thewriternation.com

Lou J Berger started writing just shy of his 40th birthday. His short stories have appeared in Galaxy's Edge magazine, several anthologies, and recently he was awarded Finalist in the Writers of the Future contest. He lives in Centennial, Colorado with his high-school crush, three kids, and two dogs.

Find Lou at loujberger.com

Jamie Ferguson has edited over a dozen anthologies and is working on many more, including a monster-themed anthology series she's co-editing with DeAnna Knippling. In her fiction, Jamie focuses on getting into the minds and hearts of her characters, whether she's writing about a saloon girl in the Old West, a man who discovers the barista he's in love with is a naiad, or a ghost who haunts the house she was killed in—even though that house no longer exists.

Jamie lives in Colorado and spends her free time in a futile quest to wear out her two border collies, since she hasn't given in and gotten them their own herd of sheep. Yet.

Find Jamie at jamieferguson.com

Made in the USA
Middletown, DE
11 October 2022

12464635R00235